"Ah, You Truly Are a Dangerous Woman"

Ian drew back a little and scanned Addie's face. Those eyes, blue as deep water, flicked with alarming speed over her features not once, but twice. "I see that with that sharp wit of yours is also a penchant for telling the truth. A man canna trust a woman who is so inclined to face the truth without so much as flinching."

The truth? If he only knew what a bold liar she was! Guilt and her own strange reaction to Ian McTavish brought a burst of anger coursing through her. She ducked beneath his arms, escaping the prison of his hard, muscled body. He whirled with the speed of a twister, his brows raised in surprise.

"I begin to see why you have that foolish edict about no single women in your town." Addie placed her hands on her hips and glared up at him. "You don't like women very much, do you, Mr. McTavish?"

He made a sound in his throat Addie could only describe as a growl. And then he was too close, leaning over her again, close enough that she could feel his warm breath fan across the lobe of her left ear. In that velvety, rough burr, he said, "Ah, now that's where you are wrong, lassie. I like women verra, verra much."

Dear Romance Reader,

In July, we launched the Ballad line with four new series, and each month now we offer you both new and continuing stories set everywhere from medieval England to the American West—the kind of passionate, romantic stories you love best, written by the most gifted authors. At the back of each book, we'll tell you when you can find subsequent books in the series that have captured your heart.

Rising star Joy Reed continues her charming Wishing Well trilogy with *Emily's Wish* as a spirited young woman fleeing her past stumbles into a celebrated author . . . and a chance at a love story of her own. Next Candice Kohl sweeps us back to the medieval splendor of The Kinsmen as *A Knight's Passion* becomes a breathtaking romance . . . with a Welsh heiress the king intends for his brother.

New this month is veteran author Linda Lea Castle's Bogus Brides series. The Green sisters must invent "husbands" to remain in the charter town of McTavish Plain, Nebraska—and love is an unexpected complication in *Addie and the Laird.* Finally, we return to the bayous of the Louisiana Territory as Cherie Claire offers the second book of the The Acadians. *Rose* dreams of romance . . . but loses her heart to the one man her family has forbidden. Enjoy!

Kate Duffy
Editorial Director

Bogus Brides

ADDIE AND THE LAIRD

Linda Lea Castle

ZEBRA BOOKS
KENSINGTON PUBLISHING CORP.

http://www.zebrabooks.com

This book is dedicated to the Lord, who blesses me; my family, who supports me; and my fans, who sustain me. I am thankful for you all.

Chapter One

Far northern Nebraska Territory, 1862

"I am telling you both, this isn't going to work."
Adelaide Green levered the reins in her hands while she
swiveled her bottom on the hard wagon seat. Her sisters
were perched behind her, among kegs, trunks and crates.
All their belongings, and those precious mementos of
their dead parents, were wedged into the box of the big,
lumbering covered wagon that had brought them due north
from Gothenburg, Nebraska. They had journeyed through
the vast plains and grasslands and now had turned slightly
westward toward the Black Hills, where the terrain turned
more craggy and lofty peaks jutted into the blue sky.

"We are going to get caught lying about being married," Addie continued, with a frown creasing her brow.
"Then we will end up out on the prairie." She squinted
her eyes and nodded toward the yoke of oxen before
she assumed what she hoped was an appropriately frosty

expression. Perhaps that would chill her sisters into—
what?

She really didn't know.

The time to turn back was long gone. It had been left behind on the muddy, meandering banks of the Platte. The opportunity to save themselves had disappeared with summer, while Jack Frost capered a pace or two in front of the wagon train, bringing on hard frost and autumn colors with every inch the faithful oxen hauled them.

"I don't think this is exactly prairie anymore, Addie," Mattie said, without looking up from the book she was reading.

Addie pulled her faded crocheted shawl tighter around her shoulders, as if to hold back the snow she knew was only weeks, possibly days, away.

"In any case, if you two haven't noticed, winter is coming on." She shivered at the thought of being out here—unprotected—when the weather turned. How on earth could she keep her sisters safe and well when they fought her at every turn?

"Shoot-fire, we'll be lucky if *all* they do is tar and feather us," Addie said aloud, while visions of public flogging and humiliation filled her mind.

"Do you think they might try to ride us out of town on a rail, like that snake-oil salesman when we were little?" Lottie asked with a breathy throb in her voice.

Addie whirled around to stare gap-mouthed at her sister. Sure enough, the twinkle of barely suppressed excitement glittered in Lottie's eyes.

"Charlotte Marie Green!" Addie exclaimed.

"I was just wondering. You sure are a Gloomy Gus today, Addie," Lottie said, barely chastised. "You never want to do anything exciting or adventurous. I do think there is something lacking in your constitution."

Addie opened her mouth to speak, but before she could, Mattie spoke.

"Lottie, you know Addie is always like this when the sky is threatening." Matilda sighed. "The threat of a storm has bothered her since Ma and Pa died, but I think there is something kind of tragic and romantic about a gray sky. In a book this would be the kind of weather that would bring the hero, riding in front of a storm. . ."

"As usual, Matilda," Addie interrupted, "you think life is one of your silly tales." She glanced up at the clouds that bruised the vista a mauve and gray. She didn't like the melancholy of stormy weather, hadn't since the flood that had taken her parents and *him*, but Lottie and Mattie didn't know the loss Addie had suffered and so, perhaps, their view was a bit different than her own.

"Addie, I wish you would stop fretting. Nobody is going to find out, and just look how *thrilling* our adventure has been so far." Charlotte spoke as quickly as her nimble fingers whipped thread in and out of the patch of material in her wooden hoop. Deftly executed, the embroidery stitches were fine and even. It was a wonder she could sew in the rocking wagon, but she had been working steadily since they left Gothenburg, Nebraska. She had learned each and every tiny stitch while being forced to sit and contemplate her wild ways and reckless nature. The reverend's wife at the orphanage had done a proper job of trying to suppress that wildness, but Addie knew it lay just under the surface of Lottie's cool blond exterior. It waited like a slumbering giant. Now, with the scent of woods and wide-open spaces in her nostrils, Lottie was beginning to hear the lure of that siren's song again—it showed in her eyes, and in the pink in her cheeks.

And it frightened Addie to see it. She was the eldest . . . it was up to her to see that Mattie and Lottie were spared the heartbreak and loneliness that life could bring.

"Lottie, what are you stitching?" Mattie asked, turning Addie's thoughts.

"Oh, just a little something for my new home."

"I hope that piecework in your hand is a sampler with a Bible verse about truth. You can hang it over your doorway, assuming we don't get tarred and feathered before we get that far. And if all the promises that have been made are anywhere near to being the truth. Lands, maybe this old Mr. McTavish is lying to us as much as we've been lying to him. It *is* a mite much to promise that there will be a house for each one of us and a dressmaker's shop for you waiting at the end of this misbegotten journey."

"Now that would be an adventure . . . three women, alone in a strange town with nowhere to go." Lottie giggled.

"You worry too much, Addie. You always have," Matilda murmured. "We're not little girls anymore. You don't have to fret over us all the time just cause you're the oldest."

"You're still my little sisters."

"But we can take care of ourselves, and in case you haven't noticed, I've been a good bit taller than you for a long while."

Addie smiled in spite of herself. It was a point of some amusement that Mattie, the "baby" sister, had shot up beyond Addie and Lottie's height. She was built like a sapling willow, the tallest of the Green sisters, with winsome eyes and a graceful, lean build. Addie heard the rustling of book pages and knew without looking that Mattie had returned to reading her volume of poetry.

And sighing.

And dreaming of the day she would find her true love. She had some addle-brained notion of finding a softspoken, intellectual man who would appeal to her mind and her soul. She wanted none of that groping and heavy breathing—or so she said, after being courted by Felix Hottle.

Addie had her doubts about her sister knowing what

she wanted, but she kept her thoughts to herself. All she said was, "Oh, fiddlesticks, you've got your head in the clouds again. Maybe it's because you're the youngest. I just don't know." Addie moved her head from side to side and heard the grouchy pop of her own neckbones. She was tired, and Mattie was right: Addie worried about her and Charlotte all the time. And, she thought wryly, because of her vigilance they never seemed to worry at all—about anything—even when they should.

Maybe if they did have husbands she could begin to let go—but that notion brought her thoughts around full circle. Not having husbands was the reason they were in this pickle.

None of the Green sisters had husbands . . . they were single women . . . virgins, old maids, spinsters, by some accounts.

In fact, in the face of all the sympathetic and well-meaning whispers, Mattie had become a bit desperate the last year or so. She had become convinced she would never marry as long as they remained in Gothenburg, Nebraska. At least not be able to marry the kind of husband she had in mind. Mattie, as a ripe romantic, had a mind to spend her life with a pale, sensitive poet. And there weren't many among the crop of hearty, hardworking farmers of the lower Nebraska Territory.

Addie had no desire to be tied to any man who would boss and pick and treat her like a servant. And Lottie . . . well, Lottie was just plain a confusion. She had a wild streak in her a mile wide. Addie could almost pity the poor man she set her sights on. It seemed as though they would continue to share the rented house near the orphanage where they had grown up. . . .

And then that awful *handbill* had come. That twice-damned, may-it-be-sent-to-perdition handbill from the far northern reaches of the territory.

Addie silently cursed it once more for good measure.

In bold print, the accursed, infernal, had-to-be-written-by-the-devil-himself paper had promised health, wealth and happiness in the untamed northern Nebraska Territory.

There was nothing there but bears, buffalos and hostiles. Of course, the very mention of the West had gotten Charlotte's wild streak involved. Her craving for adventure and excitement had started it. Then she had come up with some ridiculous notion that men with poetry in their souls would go to such a place, and that had put Matilda firmly on her side.

For weeks the pair of them had pestered Addie until she was ready to pull her hair out. She finally had agreed to go to the meeting at the Lutheran Church to listen to what the agent had to say, just to shut them up. The whole notion sounded too good to be true, this town named McTavish Plain in the far northwest. Traveling expenses paid, a house waiting, God-fearing neighbors and plenty of elbow room, and all anyone had to do was give five years of labor and sweat to have all this.

Too perfect to be true.

Addie was skeptical as all get out, but the local sheriff had even stood up to vouch for the venture, having known someone who moved there a year or so back. With his badge winking on his chest, he had claimed McTavish Plain was near to being heaven on earth as a body was likely to find this side of the pearly gates. A place where a family could put down roots, a place where the community pitched in and erected houses for newcomers, a place where, at the end of five years' labor, a clear deed would be issued to those hearty enough to stick it out.

The agent, a pale, spectacle-wearing young man with narrow shoulders who reminded Addie of a lunger, soon had Mattie hanging on his every word. He explained the venture was all proper and legal—something known as a charter town. Mr. Ian McTavish, a man known as a "mutton baron," was gambling that folks would love the grand mountains, the sweeping vistas and this new town of McTavish Plain so much, they would be happy to come, happy to stay. Addie had to admit the lure of land bought with nothing more than sweat and toil did appeal. The lower Nebraska Territory was getting downright thick with people. There was a homestead every five miles or so now. Mr. McTavish, it was explained, wanted people to come north, and he was gambling they would be so enchanted they would not want to go on to the Oregon Territory.

Addie had a notion Mr. McTavish must be rich as a nabob and so old that he had taken leave of his senses to make such an outlandish offer. Imagine, a man giving good land away just because a body had worked it for five years. Whoever heard the like? And free passage thrown in to boot. And a house?

Maybe the old codger was just not right in the head. Maybe he had some *reason,* some deep, dark, secret desire to keep people *out* of the Oregon Territory. Or maybe he was just one stick short of a bundle.

Either way, it made Addie nervous and suspicious. But when the sheriff and the agent had told the assembled group the rest of the conditions, she got madder than a wet hen—and about a minute later relief swept over her.

There was no way her sisters were going to the northern part of the Territory, for it seemed any female who set foot in McTavish Plain had to be *married.*

While Lottie and Mattie sat with their mouths gaping open like water-starved catfish, the agent went on to explain that Mr. McTavish would take single men, if they were skilled and willing, but under no circumstances would he allow an unmarried woman to spend so much as one night in McTavish Plain. Seems the old fool had a notion that unattached women would lead to discontent in his community. The story was that old Mr. McTavish had been burned by a faithless woman in his youth, and now when he saw a single woman he saw nothing but trouble.

Mattie and Lottie had nearly burst into tears. Relief sluiced through Addie. It was over. It was done, and she hadn't even had to be a shrew. Thank God it was over.

Her glee lasted about as long as it took the three of them to walk back home. By the time they reached their front door her sisters had come up with a new plan. It was simple, really.

All they had to do was *create* husbands for themselves and join the McTavish-bound wagon train at the next town up the Platte, where nobody knew them.

It was folderol. It was the silliest thing Addie ever heard. She had been certain-sure her sisters would give up the idea in a day or two.

They hadn't.

No, sirree, they most certainly had not.

Charlotte's hunger for adventure and Matilda's romantic dreams had kept them in a fever long into the night. The next day they made Addie miserable, badgering her to think up a husband for herself. But she had no need to dream up a husband. She knew exactly what her husband had looked like. He had been young, happy and full of love for her. His wide, honest, farm-boy face had been wreathed in a pleased smile when they sneaked away to be secretly married by a minister who had been on the same train heading west. His eyes had shined brighter than the sun . . . until the flood snuffed out his life and the lives of Addie's parents on one horrific afternoon.

None of their bodies had ever been found. And she had never been the same.

For weeks Adelaide had grieved for her dead parents and her lost love, but she had kept her sorrow locked deep inside her soul, not wanting to share it or to put any more on her young sisters than they already had to bear.

After the first few years it all seemed like a long-ago, imagined dream, that secret wedding beneath the stars. That silent, solitary grief had altered Addie. She had never known the bliss of being a wife, even though she had been forced to carry a widow's sorrow. And even though she had said "I do," Adelaide was still as chaste as the day she was born.

Addie was a virgin widow. The flood had cruelly taken her young husband before they had shared a wedding night. Nobody knew; the minister had died with his flock.

Her grief had been a terrible weight. To remain strong Addie had turned inward, cherishing her secret, keeping it locked in her heart and taking her responsibility as the eldest sister even more seriously.

She had fought hard to keep her sisters safe and protected. The smallest inconvenience, the tiniest heartbreak had made her crazed to shelter them. And shelter them she had.

Now they had a dream . . . they dreamed of going north and becoming part of a town, a community.

Addie shivered at the intensity of the old and unwanted memories and brought herself back to the present. The wagon seat was hard and cold beneath her. A frosty breeze played with the strand of hair that never remained hidden beneath her bonnet.

Mattie and Lottie had talked her into the wild venture. They were nearly there . . . nearly to McTavish Plain.

It served no purpose to turn maudlin and wallow in self-pity. Her only concern was seeing her two sisters find happiness. She blinked back the hot sting of tears and focused on the rumps of the plodding, faithful oxen.

In the end it had not been their pleading or cajoling that had made her agree. The real reason she went along with them was that in her heart of hearts she hoped they were right. Maybe in a new, burgeoning country her sisters would find the love she had been denied.

She prayed they might. She prayed Matilda and Charlotte would find husbands who were flesh and blood and not creatures of lie and imagination.

If only this reckless scheme didn't blow up in all their faces. Addie must've said as much out loud, because Lottie had put aside her embroidery and was staring at her like she had sprouted horns.

"Can't you enjoy this just a little?" Charlotte asked while she looped a soft blond curl behind her ear. "I swear, Addie, you are too cautious. You have to take a chance on life or it is going to pass you right by. Just think of all the unexplored places out—*there.*" She gestured expansively.

"Too cautious? Don't you mean foolhardy?" Addie asked defensively. "I'm not like you, Lottie. I don't want adventure or danger. Lord knows I've had all of that I can stand just keeping body and soul together after Ma and Pa died." She shook her head from side to side. "I can't believe I let you two talk me into this . . . this . . . madness."

"It's her red hair," Mattie whispered knowingly to Lottie behind Addie's back. "It makes her headstrong and high-strung—Papa always said so."

"This has nothing to do with my coloring," Addie said sharply, glad she had the thick leather reins to cling to. "And you were too little to remember anything Papa said." She felt as if she were coming apart at the seams today, all nerves and tears searing the backs of her eyes.

"And besides, my hair isn't red, it's auburn. And don't try to change the subject. It is a miracle we have made it this far without getting caught in the tangle of lies we've left behind us." She pursed her lips and focused on the lead wagon.

"As soon as we reach McTavish Plain and you see the newness and the space . . . it will make you feel better," Charlotte said sympathetically.

Addie stared in misery at the wagon in front of them. A chicken coop full of Rhode Island red hens strained against the ropes lashing them against the wagon's side. They were her chickens . . . her responsibility, just like her feather-brained sisters.

The comparison nearly made her laugh out loud.

"The letter will be waiting for you when we get to McTavish Plain," Charlotte was saying, unaware that Addie had pictured her in russet feathers. "All you have to do is read the letter and act like a widow. Once that is done you'll feel better about all of this. And then our new lives can begin."

"I doubt it," Addie whispered, again assaulted by memories of her secret wedding and how that had ended in tragedy. "How can I feel better knowing more people will hear these lies we have created?"

"Oh, never mind that now," Mattie said, dismissing Addie's concern with a wave of her hand. "You should cry and wring your hands like this." She shoved her hands forward so Addie could see while she demonstrated with great enthusiasm. "I mean, when you get the letter . . . lean on our shoulders and act like you are going to swoon. We will do the rest."

Charlotte leaned forward on Addie's opposite side, peering up into her face. "Don't say too much or you'll make a mistake. Let us do all the talking."

"Yes, we will do *all* the explaining. It will be more believable that way," Matilda agreed. "Nobody with an ounce of compassion would start questioning a woman who has just lost her husband."

"You make it all sound so simple," Addie said with a weary sigh, suddenly feeling much more than six years Matilda's senior. She hoped that tragedy never took away any of her sisters' enthusiasm and faith in life. She hoped they would never learn what sorrow could do to a body.

"It *is* simple. The letter will be there for you, and

Mattie and I have our stories straight,'' Charlotte told her with a wink.

In a sudden burst of temper Addie harrumphed. ''And what happens when *your* husbands don't show up in a respectable length of time? Don't you think people are going to wonder? Even some doddering old fool like Mr. McTavish is bound to notice the lack of *three* husbands.''

Addie's mind had created an image of Ian McTavish based on what she had learned and heard about him. In her mind's eye she could picture ''crazy old Mr. McTavish''; white-haired and mad as a hatter, most of his teeth missing and a bleary, unfocused look in his eyes, wandering the streets of a tent city making sure all the women were wearing wedding rings.

A stifled giggle nearly escaped her lips. Mattie and Lottie exchanged exasperated looks.

''Everyone on the train has been told—and believes, might I add—that my husband is a sea captain,'' Matilda said with a tone of extreme impatience bleeding into her voice. ''After a proper mourning time has elapsed after you receive word of *your* loss, I will receive a letter informing me that Samuel Smith perished in a terrible storm—body never recovered, of course. Then I can find the man I'm looking for.'' She set her chin in a way that told Addie there was no room for doubt.

''Matilda Green—excuse me, I mean, *Mrs. Smith*—if all you want to do is get hitched to the first available man, then why didn't you accept Jacob Stolt's proposal?'' Addie asked in a frustrated squeak.

''He had four daughters. And . . . and he wanted a *son!*'' Mattie said wistfully, holding her book against her bosom like a shield. ''I want a husband who is a deep thinker. I want a man who will read poetry to me and be content to . . . to hold my hand.''

''Lord have mercy,'' Addie muttered under her breath. Her sister was in for a rude awakening if she really thought that was what went on in the marriage bed. But she didn't intend to be the one to tell her. No, let her find out how ridiculous all those notions were when she met a man who sent her pulse racing like a runaway team.

"If you find this perfect man of yours, Mattie, you may change your mind about . . . well, physical things," Addie advised gently.

"No. I will not. I will find a man who reads Lord Byron and Elizabeth Browning." Mattie stuck out her bottom lip in a girlish pout. "And if I don't, then I will be an old maid. I want some sparking and pretty words. I want *romance.*"

"Lord help us all. . . ." Addie said under her breath. "And how about you, Charlotte Green? Have you come to your senses yet? Have you heard enough of this nonsense to know we are all headed for perdition in a wicker basket?"

"And what exactly does that mean, Addie?" Charlotte demanded.

"It means, how on earth do you plan on keeping *your* husband from showing up? Don't you think people in this magical kingdom of McTavish Plain can think? Or do you think all this fresh air and adventure is going to make them thick as a rock?"

"You know perfectly well I have thought about that. I wish you would stop acting like we haven't been over all of this a dozen times." Charlotte pricked her finger on her needle—something she *never* did. Glaring at Addie in silent accusation, she stuck the wounded appendage in her mouth.

"Tell me one more time," Addie demanded. "It's all buzzing in my head like a hive of bees—I am having trouble keeping all the lies and new names straight in my mind."

Charlotte took her finger from her mouth and sighed meaningfully. "My husband, Shayne Rosswarne, is off on a cattle drive, taking a herd up to market. So don't be slipping up and calling me Green anymore. I am Mrs. Rosswarne now."

"Shayne Rosswarne." Addie let the name roll off her tongue. "Your husband sounds like a good, hardworking man. Funny, though, Lottie, I can't seem to recall his face," she teased with a crooked smile.

"Oh, don't be flippant, Addie. It *is* a good story. There are risks aplenty on a cattle drive: flood, lightning and Indians. Certainly enough reasons for him to be delayed in coming to McTavish Plain. Then later . . ." Charlotte waggled her brows suggestively. "My husband is going to go out in a blaze of glory."

Addie shivered in spite of the fact that the sun was beginning to peek out from behind the gray veil of low-hanging clouds.

"Has it occurred to either one of you that there might be something seriously wrong with women who spend so much time thinking of ways to murder, kill, maim and generally misplace their husbands?"

Matilda giggled and grabbed the back of the seat for support when the wagon hit a rough patch. "There is nothing wrong with us! And you say *I* have an imagination! Why, the very thought that anything could be wrong with us—it is too funny. Besides, George Eliot often has such things in his books. Although, now you mention it, there is a rumor that George Eliot is really a woman."

"Oh, saints above. We are all doomed!"

Charlotte clucked her tongue. "Goodness, Addie, the way you take on. We haven't hurt a soul making up these stories. After all, the husbands we are talking about are not *real*. It's not like we are really going to hurt anybody."

Addie rolled her eyes heavenward. "I am getting an ache in my head. Let's not talk any more about it."

There was no point talking to them. Every logical argument she pointed out was quickly twisted into a circle until it came back to where they started. Her foolish, charming sisters had made up their minds. And now because of it, the Green sisters were all headed for disaster.

"Adelaide, we aren't doing anybody any harm. Besides, McTavish Plain needs us," Mattie said as she rocked back and forth with the sway of the wagon.

Addie whirled around, accidentally pulling the lines of the traces with her. She almost sent the poor oxen veering off toward the western horizon in her haste. "And how, may I ask, did you arrive at that deduction?"

"Your baking and creamery was the pride of Gothenburg. No man with a pulse could pass up your cobbler or baked goods. I am an excellent schoolteacher. Have you forgotten my graduating class was the largest in the county? I inspired those children. Charlotte's reputation as a seamstress is not unearned and—"

"And your lack of modesty is shocking," Addie interrupted dryly. "What would Mama say?"

"She would say this is no time for false humility, Addie Green—excuse me, Mrs. Brown. We have skills that will be an asset to a growing community. McTavish Plain does need us—all of us." Matilda hugged her book closer and a soft, dreamy look came into her eyes.

"Yes, it does. Besides, it will be a grand adventure," Lottie piped in.

"You think everything is an adventure, Lottie." Addie exhaled a heavy breath. "But sometimes it is not. Sometimes life is hard and cruel and dirty and disappointing, and it rarely, if ever, has a happy ending like one of Mattie's books. And I pray daily that you will never find that out the hard way."

Chapter Two

"The old Indians say the mountain is haunted by the spirit of a Salish maiden." Buck Hendrix, the wagon master, spit a mouthful of tobacco juice on the ground near his boot. Addie was repulsed by the action, but to her horror she saw a glitter in Lottie's eye. The man was brown . . . one muckle-dun shade of brown, from his battered hat and hair to his weathered face and tobacco-stained teeth . . . right on down to his dusty boots.

"Haunted? By ghosts?"

"Well, kinda, Mrs. Rosswarne. The Indians believe when a spirit stays in a place it becomes holy. The story goes that the girl was some sort of princess who was forced to marry the most butt-ugly . . ."

Addie stifled a gasp, but the wagon master heard her and shuffled his feet.

"Beggin' your pardon, ma'am." He inclined his head in her direction but never missed a beat in the story. "She was forced to marry the most cantankerous old chief of the Lakota tribe."

"And then what happened?" Lottie asked.

"Story goes, she ran to the mountain and threw herself off a cliff to keep her virtue."

"That's a terrible story," Addie said, frowning. She was anxious to see them on their way, fearful of the stormy sky. Yet Buck Hendrix dawdled, eager to tell Lottie and Mattie his story.

"To the Indians it ain't. You see, Mrs. Brown, they believe at the last minute the old ones took pity on the girl and turned her into a bright red bird. The Salish believe if they see the bird, they have been given the promise of happiness in love forever."

"Oh, how romantic," Mattie gushed. "Thank you, Mr. Hendrix. That is a lovely story."

"A bunch of folderol, if you ask me," Addie snorted. "And those clouds are growing darker by the minute. Do you think we might get started?"

"Yes, ma'am, Mrs. Brown. As you say, we are burning daylight." Buck Hendrix chuckled as he walked away.

"Men . . . useless to their very bones," Addie chided as she gathered her skirt and climbed into the wagon seat. "I wish I had never left Gothenburg."

The gloom of the past days had been burned away, and along with the rays of weak autumn sunshine had come a feeling of excitement that had rippled through the small train with the knowledge that they would soon reach McTavish Plain.

Even though the snap of fall was in the air, the stream of sunshine was quite warm. Addie felt both hopeful and nervous.

The ruin of the foolish Green sisters was fast approaching.

"Stop it," she muttered to herself. "Mattie and Lottie have thought of everything. Maybe, just maybe, it will work."

She forced herself to focus only on positive thoughts

while the oxen plodded along, following the wagon in front of them. If she did exactly what her sisters said, and picked up her letter right away, it might be all right.

Yes. If she quickly picked up the letter informing her that her nonexistent husband had died and she was now a widow, things might be manageable. She wouldn't be forced to lie about where her husband was or what he was doing or when he would join her.

"And if I don't have to lie, I might be all right."

Suddenly the other wagons lumbered to a stop. Addie blinked herself back to the present, sawing back and forth on the leather leads until the oxen slowed and finally ambled to a stop.

Adelaide stood up in the wagon box and squinted her eyes beneath her sugar scoop bonnet. The wagons had come to rest on a grassy, treeless knoll that overlooked a valley and a meandering stream. She scanned the area looking for the reason they had stopped.

Was it Indians? They had been mercifully lacking on this journey, but now a knot of fear joined the winged fluttering in her middle. People all along the trail had warned her of hostiles. Buck Hendrix had been all too eager to use his own style of graphic description in telling what could happen to three lone women. Another reason, he had said, why those "husbands" shouldn't be allowing their wives to travel alone.

"Charlotte, get the rifle," Addie said over her shoulder, searching in vain for what had caused the delay.

The valley below was a dusky green, but the thin grove of trees that lined the riverbank were gold, red and yellow. Beyond, the landscape turned mountainous. Evergreens and pines towered high, climbing up the side of the craggy landscape, thickening until the incline was dappled with deep forested shadows.

Then she saw it—the reason the wagons had halted. Addie blinked and rubbed her eyes.

In the long hollow of shadow cast by two tall jagged peaks, like a pearl nestled in sage-tinged velvet, it was like the watercolors done by fanciful young ladies at overpriced finishing schools.

Addie forced herself to look again—calmly, critically, but the vision remained unchanged.

Neat, whitewashed clapboard houses gleamed like polished ivory. A dark brown velvety ribbon of road wound through the scene and culminated at the doors of a steepled church, pearly white and winking in the sunshine.

Addie had more than half-expected McTavish Plain to be a ramshackle collection of cabins and tents in spite of the reassurance of the sheriff and the agent. This town had solid-looking houses and a school, and she could see shingles swinging in the breeze at various businesses along the main streets.

Curling tendrils of silvery gray smoke climbed into the periwinkle sky from some of the little houses. Real windows shimmered like fish scales and below them there were bright bits of color.

"Fall flowers. . . . Imagine that," Addie mused to herself.

"What?" The sound of Mattie's voice and the clunk and thunk of her sister climbing over crates drew Addie's eyes to the back of the crowded wagon.

"What's wrong?" Lottie held the rifle in her hand. Like her careful stitching, she always hit what she aimed at.

"Why did we stop, Addie? And why did you want the rifle?" Charlotte hiked her skirts and crawled over a humpback trunk toward the seat, her eyes narrowed as she looked for the source of trouble. "Has something happened?"

Words crowded the back of Adelaide's throat but refused to be spoken. She stared at the town below while the thrumming of her own pulse fluttered in the hollow of her throat.

The church had a real bell. Who would've thought it? Way out here in the far north—a bell to call the town to worship.

Her stomach fell to the level of her cracked and trail-worn shoe tops. This town, this *McTavish Plain* was like rubbing salt in an open wound. Just the sight of it brought a hungry pain to her middle.

When they were found out . . . when their lies caught up with them and they were forced to leave this lovely town, Mattie and Lottie would be bereft. And so, Addie admitted silently, grudgingly to herself, would she.

When the wagons started moving again, Addie picked up the lines and urged the oxen forward mechanically. A part of her mind had gone numb the moment she saw the town. It would've been so much easier if it had been a collection of tumbledown shacks and tents.

But now it was real . . . substantial and worth trying for. Now there was truly something to lose if the three sisters were caught in their little white lie.

Addie's heart was lodged somewhere between her throat and her stomach as she followed Buck's sharp and rather colorful directions to a meadow where the other wagons had stopped. She maneuvered the oxen to the meadow—the common, she heard someone call it. Several strapping youths were busy helping to unhitch the cattle and water the livestock. It appeared to be a place where all the town stock was looked after together.

Another wonderful idea, she grudgingly admitted to herself. Phrases like *safety in numbers* and *many hands make work easier* flashed through her mind.

She allowed her bonnet to shield her eyes as she looked at well-tended vegetable gardens, neat lines of wash and taut fences. McTavish Plain was no slackard's haven, that was plain.

Good old Mr. McTavish had not made pie-crust promises. It annoyed Addie a bit when she realized that somewhere between the top of the knoll and the town her benefactor had subtly changed from crazy old Mr. McTavish to Good old crazy Mr. McTavish. Addie didn't want to examine her reasons for that switch too closely . . . not now, not when she was still taking it all in, still finding bits of wonder and civilization here so very far from Gothenburg.

After a moment she swallowed hard and allowed the thought that had been buzzing at the edge of her mind to emerge. Good old Mr. McTavish had not lied. . . . The only lies that had been told were the ones that came from Addie and her sisters. Guilt and her own sense of right and wrong battered at her conscience.

"Oh, look!" Mattie squealed. She raised her skirt high as she strode across the meadow. Several of the men who were helping to unleash barrels of molasses and crates of housegoods stared. But Mattie was careless of the long expanse of ankle and bit of calf she was showing.

"That must be the mountain Mr. Hendrix told us about. . . . Red Bird Mountain, I think he called it. It is . . . glorious," Lottie said. "Oh, smell it, Addie. Fill your lungs with it." She closed her eyes, inhaled and spun in a great circle.

Addie did take a deep breath. The pungent attar of high mountain air, the snap of coming winter and the tang of pine settled on the back of her tongue.

Suddenly Lottie was there, her cheeks pink with excitement. She pointed to the northwest. "One of the men on the train told me that no more than fifty miles in that direction is a great rock tower the Indians call Bad God's Tower. They have a legend that the rock grew to save seven maidens from a bear."

"Lands, you are starting to sound as fanciful as Mattie, with all that 'Bride of the Red Bird' nonsense," Addie said, and though she didn't want to look, she found her gaze sliding to the craggy peak with a halo of clouds.

"And see that peak, Addie? That one where the shadows are deepest? That is the very one the Salish maiden jumped off of; Mr. Hendrix told me himself. She ran from that ugly Lakota man and jumped from that cliff and turned into a bright red bird."

"Foolishness."

Mattie continued to stare at the mountain peak as if she hadn't heard Addie's remark. "And the Salish believe if a woman who has a pure love for her man sees the bird, then the couple will be under a mystical protection blessing and will be happy forever."

"Now I know you have gone completely soft in the head. You are starting to sound like a loon."

"Oh, Addie, stop being such an old killjoy. Mattie is just telling you the stories that she has heard."

Addie stared at her sister in shock. It was not like Lottie to defend Mattie's lovesick ramblings.

"We are finally out of Gothenburg . . . and now maybe I am going to have some excitement in my life. I know one thing for certain-sure. The first chance I get, I'm going to see that tower and those peaks where the Red Bird maiden is said to live. You just see if I don't."

A wave of sadness folded over Addie. She had not been prepared to see such a change in her sisters. "I swear you two and your imaginations will be the ruin of all of us."

Addie wasn't sure why a ball of prickly emotion had taken up residence in her belly. Perhaps it was the little town, or maybe it was the way Charlotte's eyes had teared up when she vowed to go to the black mountain tower where the Indians thought the devil dwelled. Whatever the reason, she found herself choking back a hard lump as she tugged her shawl tighter around her shoulders and walked beside her sisters.

"Look, Mattie, it *is* a castle," Charlotte said, pointing. "Just like the picture books you read to the children back home."

"Lottie, don't you start teasing me—"

"I am not teasing. Look. It really is a castle—well, almost a castle," Lottie said with a laugh.

Adelaide turned and allowed her eyes to climb, following Lottie and Mattie's gaze upward beyond the town. Beyond the last buildings, where a silvery blue river twined down from the majestic peak where the Indian maiden's spirit lived in the form of a red bird.

A huge stone structure, gray and solid as the crag it sat upon, jutted up from the gray-green prairie. It was a brooding pile of stone with twin towers planted squarely in the teeth of the wind. Addie swallowed and blinked, but the apparition remained. She shivered involuntarily and fancied she could almost hear the mournful sound of it soughing around the stones. Just as she loathed gray, gloomy skies, she did not envy anyone who would live in a house that sat squarely in the path of winter storms and high mountain gusts.

"Who in their right mind would have built such a thing?" she heard herself whisper. "It must be cold as ice inside those stone walls."

"Good old Mr. McTavish, of course," Mattie said with some authority.

"How do you know?" Charlotte challenged.

Mattie shrugged. "The agent told me all about it. He said Mr. McTavish built it for his sweetheart to remind her of home. Isn't that the most romantic thing you ever heard? He wanted her to be his princess in this new land." Mattie sighed.

"Now I know the old fool is crazy as a loon. Any woman who lived in that pile of stone would shiver 'round the clock," Adelaide said as she turned her back on the monstrous building.

"Maybe that was the plan," Lottie said with a wink. "Maybe in his youth old Mr. McTavish had a hankering to keep his sweetheart warm."

Addie felt the heat of a blush climbing to her hairline.

"So, what happened to his sweetheart?" she heard herself asking.

"Oh, it is a sad story." Mattie shook her head in sympathy. "While he was here, working to build her a grand home, she fell in love with his cousin and married him. They say Mr. McTavish has never been the same."

"Hmmmph. That is probably why he is so determined to see all the women in town married," Addie said with a frown, but a part of her felt a stab of pity for the man who had been jilted. She knew how loneliness could hurt.

She cleared her throat and put on the armor of authority that had stood her in good stead for years while she shoved the memories of her own ill-fated love to the back of her mind.

"Well, sisters, I suppose we should be about our business. That wagon isn't going to unload itself."

But it practically did. For the people of McTavish Plain were exactly as the pale, bespectacled agent had said they would be. They came by the dozens with smiles and welcomes and willing hands.

"Darling, I just heard that you made the whole long trip without your man." Addie was pulled into a bone crushing embrace. Her face was engulfed by a soft bosom and the scent of starch. Waves of sensation and the memory of being safe and loved washed over her, and for the first time in years she was near to weeping as she thought of her own mother.

"I am Gert Thompson. My husband, Miley, is the

teamster here in McTavish. We also run the livery, if you ever need a mount. What is that man of yours thinking, to let such a pretty little thing travel all alone?'' Her questions came fast and loud.

Adelaide swallowed hard. She had not rehearsed for such contingencies. What should she say?

"It was a matter of need, not choice," she mumbled.

Gert eyed her up and down for a moment and then she smiled. "Well, of course it wouldn't be choice, not if that man of yours has eyes in his head and anything but ice in his veins. If you need anything at all, you come to me."

Adelaide watched her go, her gait long and purposeful, the full gingham skirt fluttering with each step. The first hurdle was over and it hadn't been too bad. Perhaps she could manage until she got the letter.

"Ladies, if you will follow me, I will show you to your houses," a slat-thin man with hollow cheeks announced. His face seemed to be wreathed in a perpetual smile of sympathy, which made sense to Addie when Lottie whispered that he was McTavish Plain's mortician and coffin builder.

Addie nodded, and they fell into step behind him, walking silently down the street. For a moment she almost felt as if she were attending a funeral . . . her own.

It wasn't long before all three sisters had been ushered off, escorted by the somber man in the frock coat, to the houses that waited to become their new homes. First they saw Mattie's, and she was left with a handful of women to help her settle in, then Lottie. Finally Adelaide found herself alone. For the first time since her parents' deaths she was without her sisters. She politely but firmly refused the help of the women.

"It's long overdue for three grown women to live

apart,'' Addie chided herself sternly as she leaned against the solid front door of her new home—her eerily silent new home.

She walked into the front parlor and looked out the window—a window with real glass in it. The view was true north, toward the mountains and old Mr. McTavish's crazy castle up on the knoll.

"Dotty old fool," she pronounced, glad to have someone upon whom to vent the sudden wave of unhappiness. "This is all your fault, filling my sisters' heads with piecrust dreams."

She did not add *and my own head as well,* though she thought it.

Warmth bled into her bones as the black potbellied parlor stove sent blasts of heat through the room. She flung her shawl on the back of a tall oaken rocker that was exactly like the rockers in Mattie and Lottie's houses. A gift from Mr. McTavish, one brawny man had explained as he helped them carry their trunks inside. All the furnishings were built right here in town by the cabinetmaker, a man who had once been a ship's carpenter.

He knew the difference between an adz and a saw. Addie ran her finger over the back, admiring the simple, clean lines, the delicate scroll of vines carved deep and true. She had never seen so fine a rocker.

A log popped and sent a shower of sparks through the vent hole in the top of the stove. Addie watched the crimson glow at the door seam until her eyes burned. She blinked rapidly, telling herself it was staring at the flames that made her tear up so, but inside she knew the truth.

It was the silence—and being alone—and wanting this so bad she was more than willing to go along with the lie.

She jerked her hand abruptly from the back of the rocker and set it swaying. The new rungs creaked against the smooth wooden floor, making the silent house seem more empty.

She had to get out. With determined steps she left her new house and pointed herself in the direction of town—and people.

Chapter Three

McTavish Plain was the kind of town most women dreamed of raising their children in. However, Adelaide Green—Mrs. Brown—was not most women. Having lost her first love so young had carved a deep and abiding wound in her heart.

Addie wanted no man in her life, no man to care for and worry over and ultimately lose. And therefore she had lost any chance to have children of her own. It was a situation she accepted, or so she told herself as she walked.

She couldn't help but look at the homes . . . homes with families in them. Clean laundry fluttered on a taut line at the back of a white clapboard house. Cloth snapped in the breeze, tiny dresses and pinafores popped, their ruffles looking like the wings of birds. And a little farther down the line were the long white cloths used for diapering an infant.

Addie tore her eyes away. It was silly of her to long for things that could not be. To have children she needed a man in her life . . . but she was being maudlin and silly. Her sisters were enough family. Lord knew they caused her so much worry she didn't have any *need* for children.

With a deep intake of breath Addie drew herself up and stiffened her spine. She would unpack her trunks and wash everything in strong lye soap. She would get her new house in order and she would cleanse herself of the past and start life anew.

Just as soon as she picked up the letter.

Addie had made the decision to rush up the plan a bit and get the letter as soon as possible. Maybe if she could stop being pressured into pretending she was a happily married woman she wouldn't feel so *discontented,* or be so fretful that her sisters and she would be found out. After all, Addie really was a widow, even if her sisters didn't know it . . . and even if her marriage had been in name only . . . she was a widow all the same. Or so she consoled herself as she continued to walk through McTavish Plain.

She turned and walked west up the wide, well-leveled main street. Gothenburg's primary thoroughfare had become a sea of mud in the winter time, rutted and jagged from the iron-rimmed wheels of wagons. Would this road do the same? Right now it was hard packed and smooth. Everything about her was orderly and showed the pride of a town.

The paint on the buildings was fresh and the stoops in front of each door swept clean and welcoming. One business in particular caught Addie's eye. Tucked between the apothecary and the blacksmith's shop was a narrow building with a wide, empty picture window. Above the door painted in flowing script was a sign that said CHARLOTTE ROSSWARNE — LADIES'S DRESSMAKER AND SEAMSTRESS. Directly across the street, with the wind ruffling her blond curls, was Lottie. Addie smiled at the picture her sister made. There was such a look of wonder and fulfillment on her face as she stared at her storefront, it made Addie's heart ache with love for her. Her wide eyes were aglitter with satisfaction and anticipation.

Addie had never seen her look more beautiful . . . or more vulnerable. She could not bear it if they were found out and her sister lost that innocent glow.

She would do whatever was necessary to see that Lottie and Mattie were able to keep their dreams.

"Mama and Papa, I will keep them safe. I promise," Addie whispered as she crossed the street. She looped her arm around Lottie's shoulders and felt her sister's body trembling.

"Lottie, are you ailing?"

"It is nice, isn't it?" Her voice was husky and thick with emotion. "I mean . . . look at it, Addie. That sign means a whole new life in a new place—what we did is not so terrible, is it?"

"I suppose not. Not if it means this much to you. It is what you wanted and what Mama and Papa wanted for you." Addie gave her a little squeeze and tried to tell herself that all that was true. They weren't hurting anybody by telling the lies. After all, if crazy old Mr. McTavish wasn't nursing a broken heart and an old grudge, he wouldn't have made up such a silly rule anyway.

The more Addie thought about it, the more she decided it was crazy old Mr. McTavish's fault that she and her sisters had been *forced* to lie. Addie was feeling much better about the whole mess when Lottie turned to face her. She sniffed and straightened the bottom of her weskit.

"I think you're right. Mama and Papa would be happy to see we've taken steps to ensure our place here. Now, what are you doing out here in the evening air? I would've thought you'd be elbow deep in dough by now."

"I decided to go get the letter—now."

Lottie's eyes widened. "Now?"

"Yes, right now." Addie straightened her back, preparing for the onslaught of disapproval.

"Don't you think you should wait a day or two?" Lottie frowned. "I mean . . . it seems a little soon to start asking for mail."

"I don't think I should wait—I don't *want* to wait. Besides, Lottie, we had an agreement. You and Mattie knew my terms." Addie raised a brow and silently dared Lottie to disagree. "The sooner I don't have to go around playacting that I am some man's happy little wife, the happier I will be."

Lottie frowned, her golden brows knitting together. Then she shrugged, causing her shawl to bunch around her delicate neck. "Fine. If your mind is made up, then I'll go with you."

Addie nodded. "If you wish. I'd be happy of the company. Soon enough I won't hardly see you and Mattie."

"Are you missing me already?" Lottie said with a crooked smile.

"I was, but I am wondering why."

They both giggled and then fell into step side by side. Addie's thoughts were racing ahead now, eager to have done with her part of their charade. Once she opened the letter and played out the lie through the grief-stricken shock to mourning and then finally as a widow resigned to her solitary fate, she could concentrate on Mattie and Lottie. Perhaps she could spend a few days helping Lottie set the shop to rights. That would take her mind off her empty house.

With a feeling of purpose urging her on, Addie walked past the blacksmith's shop. The clang of hammer on anvil was loud and steady. She did not so much as slow her step as she read the sign overhead: TRESH — BLACK AND TIN SMITH. She marched resolutely past the mercantile and the cabinet shop. Did not even blink as the sign for the butcher shop squeaked over her head. She kept her eyes focused on the neat block lettering that proclaimed STATIONER and, in smaller letters, MAIL.

The metallic tinkle of a tiny bell over the door announced their arrival. Addie looked around but saw no one. Lottie cleared her throat loudly a couple of times.

Nobody appeared. The shop remained silent. Just when they were about to turn and leave, a man popped up from behind the counter and scared the life out of them.

"Afternoon, ladies." He smiled, revealing a wide space between his two front teeth. His arms were overly long— or perhaps they just seemed so, since the sleeves of his simple homespun shirt were held far above his bony wrists by back silk garters. "May I help you, Mrs. . . . Mrs.?"

Addie wondered how he was so sure she and Lottie were married, and then she remembered McTavish's rule.

No unmarried women in McTavish Plain.

Therefore, any woman he met in town had to be a Mrs. Somebody.

Addie was both annoyed and curious about the way the little community functioned. She wondered how the single men fared. Did they go to neighboring towns to look for wives? *Were* there any neighboring towns? Or had old Mr. McTavish brought these people so far from civilization that the men had no hope of getting married unless they used a service from the East, or went traveling in the hope they might find a willing woman?

Lottie poked Addie in the back, effectively halting her thoughts about the single men and how far they had come from Gothenburg.

"Ma'am?" he asked again.

"Yes." Addie stepped forward, her legs feeling about as strong as a newborn colt's. "I am . . . I am Mrs. Adelaide Brown." She managed to choke out the lie. "This is my sister, Charlotte Rosswarne." Addie grabbed a bit of fabric on Lottie's sleeve and pulled her forward. "I think—that is to say, I wonder if I—if *we*—might have any mail?'' Addie stammered, unable to find the right words. But if the young man noticed her discomfiture, he did not react.

"Well, let me take a look here. . . .'' The man disappeared behind the counter again. While he was gone, Lottie rolled her eyes toward the ceiling. When he popped back up he was shuffling through a pile of envelopes, muttering names as he discarded them one by one.

"You must be some of the new arrivals,'' he said as he peered up from under wispy brows.

"Yes,'' Addie said, watching the pile of missives shrink with each passing moment. "Just today.''

"I am John Holcomb.'' He glanced up from reading. "It's a real pleasure to meet you both. I usually don't get to meet new folks 'til after Sunday services. Most generally, folks get settled in 'afore they think about mail.''

Lottie pinched her—hard. A tendril of panic slipped through Addie. Maybe she had been too impatient. Maybe she should've waited a few days . . . perhaps a week.

She twisted the slender gold band, identical to the one on Lottie and Mattie's fingers—and prayed he would not become suspicious.

John's fingers moved with deft practice until he had run through the pile of letters. He looked up and frowned. "Nope, not a thing here for Mrs. Adelaide Brown. Sorry.''

"What?'' Addie gulped. She actually swayed a little on her feet, lurching unsteadily toward the half counter. She had posted the letter herself. The man at the stop along the way was sure it would reach McTavish Plain in a few weeks, certainly long before the train's slow-moving oxen could make the trip. She cast a surreptitious glance at Lottie, who had lost all the color from her pretty cheeks.

Adelaide swallowed hard. "If it is not too much bother, could you look again? Just to be sure?'' She heard the panic in her quivering voice and forced herself to smile. "I—well, to be honest, I am expecting a letter from my husband. You understand."

John smiled sympathetically. "Sure, ma'am. It'd be no bother a'tall." Once again his long, bony fingers sifted through the papers while his eyes skimmed over the lettering. Once again he shook his head. "Sorry, ma'am, but it isn't here—yet." He smiled brightly. "Now, don't you go worrying none; we get a delivery of mail next week down from Belle Fourche when Miley goes and picks up supplies. I bet'cha it will be in that batch."

Adelaide turned away. Lottie said something polite to John Holcomb, but language had lost its meaning to Addie. She put her hand on the knob and opened the door, stumbling outside. Her heart had wedged itself tight in her throat.

"It will be here next week, Addie . . . ," Lottie began. "Don't start worrying—"

"Don't. Don't say another single word." Addie glared at her sister. "I have heard all I want to hear."

"But—"

"No. I am going home now to unpack. I suggest you do the same. Since there is no letter, there is no reason in the world that we three should be anything but thrilled to be here. After all, we haven't received any tragic news. Nothing like the death of a loved one or anything."

"Now, Addie—" Lottie was trotting along, trying to match her sister's determined, angry stride. Her curls were bouncing like springs with each step.

"I don't want to talk to you right now, Charlotte *Rosswarne,* for if I do, I shall surely say things I will regret," Addie snapped. From the corner of her eye she saw Lottie lurch to a standstill, her eyes round as saucers at the tone of Addie's voice.

"Good afternoon to you, Lottie. I hope this arrival is everything you wished it would be."

* * *

"Dear Lord, are you punishing me for all my transgressions?" Addie muttered as she marched down the street. Her feet moved of their own accord, plotting a course toward her new house. With each footfall questions repeated themselves inside her head.

What had happened to the letter? What did it mean? Why wasn't it here? What could have happened? Could somebody have found it—intercepted it?

Does anybody know the *truth?*

She paused and looked back, half expecting to see the face of some stranger—someone who knew her for the liar she was—but nobody was there. She stared down at the dusty, frayed hem of her dress and the shoes peeking out from under her everyday petticoat. The black leather was cracking across the toes and they were in need of a good oiling.

Addie picked up a handful of her skirt and glared at the tattered, travel-stained hem in disgust. She had grown right tired of her worn calico, her droopy, sun-faded, sugar-scoop bonnet and down-at-the-heel shoes. The thought of the two good black dresses Lottie had sewn up for her before they left Gothenburg made her bottom lip tremble. Addie had been planning on wearing those mourning dresses along with Mama's good cameo brooch.

She had been planning to cut a fine, fashionable figure while she was in mourning for her dead husband. In fact, every dust-laden mile they had traveled she had thought about it, dreamed about it. The truth of the matter was, she had been looking forward to being a widow. In a strange, disjointed way, it was as if she was finally getting the opportunity to grieve openly for her secret husband, to show a little respect for the boy she had married so long ago. Yep, she had been planning and scheming, but now she had a new secret to add to the old one she carried close to her heart.

Now she'd have to stay in her calico until the double damned letter came, informing her of the death of the fictitious Mr. Brown.

If it came.

Oh, Lord. What if it never came?

"Tarnation," she said aloud as images of doom washed over her. If the letter never arrived, she would be locked in a hell of her own making. She wouldn't be married, but she wouldn't be free. Each day would crawl like a year as she was forced to swallow the poison of her own lies.

She knew her sister well enough to know that Lottie had made a beeline to Mattie's house to tell her about the lack of the letter. Like as not they had their heads together right now. By morning Addie would be in deeper than a toad in a butter churn.

"It would be just like Lottie and Mattie to come up with another foolish plan." But in the back of her mind there was a little voice that refused to be fooled.

Addie had gone along with the plan. . . . She couldn't deny that. . . . She had let herself be talked into it. And no matter how much she would like to believe she was blameless, a part of her knew that was not true. Addie pulled her shawl tight around her shoulders. She was going home to unpack and then she was going to go milk the cow and start the churning. It was time to quit woolgathering and get settled in to this new life of hers as a married woman, awaiting her husband.

Addie rose before dawn to soak dried apples and make crusts. By the time the rooster crowed she had milked and skimmed off the cream. Now she was putting two apple pies on her kitchen windowsill to cool. But even after all the emotional cleansing of good hard work, she was still furious with herself.

"I knew something was going to go wrong," she told herself as she punched the lightbread dough down and set it to rise once more. "I should've held my ground—not gone along with their foolishness."

She was about the put her fist into the soft, springy dough once again when a knock on her back door sent her whirling around. Her calico skirt swirled at her ankles and her breath caught in her throat. The last thing she wanted was company. If it was Lottie or Mattie she would . . .

Chapter Four

"Mrs. Brown?" a gravelly voice asked from the other side of the solidly bolted door. "Mrs. Brown, are you to home?"

"Yes?" Addie wiped her hands on her apron. "Who is there?"

"It is Horace Miller. I am the minister of McTavish Plain's church."

Addie felt color rise to her cheeks. The minister! Her hair was pinned wildly up on her head and she was quite certain she had flour on her nose. Her appearance and her mood were not fit for company, and still, she couldn't very well leave the parson cooling his heels on her doorstep. She ran her palm over her hair, trying to smooth the worst of the unruly strands. Then she went and opened the door.

A middle-aged man with cheeks scrubbed rosy by the cold air stood smiling on her stoop. "Good morning, Mrs. Brown, and welcome to McTavish Plain."

"Good morning," Addie said, feeling awkward and ill at ease.

"I know it's a bit early, but I saw your light and . . . I try to keep up with the families as they arrive. I wanted to welcome you . . . Is that apple pie I smell? My, my, your kitchen is toasty warm." He rubbed his hands together. "A bit nippy this morning, isn't it? While I was walking by I thought I smelled apple pie in the air, but . . ."

"Yes, it is apple pie. I was doing a little baking," Addie explained, gesturing to the bowl of dough and the pies on the sill.

The minister hiked himself up on his toes, put his nose in the air and sniffed loudly. Addie was put in mind of a red-bone coon hound on the trail of his quarry.

"A little baking? My, my, Mrs. Brown, I haven't smelled pie like that since my sainted mother passed on." He paused for a moment to shut his eyes and tilt his head heavenward.

Addie found herself following his gaze to the sky, half expecting to see Horace Miller's mother looking down upon her. When she looked back at the minister he was staring at her with an expectant look on his face.

"Yes, that is some mighty fine-smelling pie. . . ."

She smiled, and the silence stretched between them for longer than was polite. Though it was the last thing she wanted, she heard herself offer, "Would you like to come in?"

"Oh, yes, indeed I would. Nothing better than a nice, warm cook stove on a cold autumn day."

A smile bigger than the Powder River Valley flashed across his face. He came in, and Addie could swear she saw him drool. His sharp eyes fastened first on the bread dough and then on the pies.

"Would you like one . . . to take home with you?" Now why in thunder had she said that?

"Oh, I couldn't . . . I *shouldn't,* but, well, I would be pleased as a pig in mud. My Harriet is a good woman and plays the sweetest tunes this side of heaven on the organ Mr. McTavish brought up from St. Louis, but she is not much of a cook," he confided to Addie in the most conspiratorial of stage whispers, touching his index finger to the side of his nose.

"Then it would be my pleasure to send one home for you and your wife." Addie doubled an old flour sack and tested the side of the pan for heat. "It's cool enough so you won't burn your fingers. Just drop the pan by when you are finished."

"That I will, Mrs. Brown, that I will, and thank you. I believe we are lucky to have you among us here in McTavish Plain," the Reverend Miller said with a twinkle in his eye as he bent over the golden-brown crust and filled his lungs one last time. He smacked his lips, and Addie wondered if the pie would last until he reached his house, or if he would dig right in and indulge before his wife ever caught sight of it.

"Yessiree, we are most fortunate to have such a skillful cook among us here." He gave her a wink and a nod, along with the compliment. As he left, she wondered what he had meant by that strange gesture.

By noontime she knew.

A line of men, tall, short, bald and full-haired, some clean-shaven, some sporting beards, but all *hungry,* lined up at Addie's kitchen door. She had wondered about the men's opportunity to court, when she should've been wondering about their opportunity to *eat.* For they acted as if they hadn't had an adequate meal since arriving in McTavish Plain.

The first one or two had been shy and awkward about getting down to the business of requesting her services.

But after a half dozen had knocked, stammered and finally spit out what they wanted, the rest must've heard, because they came fast and furious like shot from a cannon.

Addie had time to do little but open her back door and answer questions about her cooking and what she would charge for breakfasts, box lunches and suppers to wrap up and take away. She suspected the good Reverend Miller had stopped at every unattached man's house on his way home and put a flea in their ear, but she couldn't prove it.

And so she listened and tried not to laugh aloud as they blushed and dug the toes of the boots into the dirt, as if they were asking for some lewd favor instead of a loaf of bread or a haunch of roasted venison.

Orders for pies, bread, butter, cobblers and even fresh eggs had grown, so that Addie had finally brought out the ledger she had used in Gothenburg to keep track of her egg money.

Now she stared at the list of men's names in stunned silence. She would be up past midnight just to fill what was due tomorrow, not to mention the rest of the week and beyond.

She sagged into a kitchen chair. One thing was certain, at this rate she would be rich as Croesus before good old Mr. McTavish had a chance to throw her out of town for being a liar and a single woman.

Addie tore a piece of paper from the ledger. If she was going to fill all these orders for baked goods, she was going to have to go into the mercantile and get supplies.

She scrawled out what she would need to have food for the men: flour, sugar, cinnamon. Lard for crusts, maybe some more dried fruits. The men who had wanted full meals had agreed to provide the game for her, which was a blessing, since she didn't have a smokehouse or a well-stocked larder.

Addie grabbed her shawl and the little basket she used to carry her small parcels and set off for town. She was glad of the diversion . . . at least it kept her mind off the missing letter.

Mr. Gruberman was bald and had a few missing teeth, but it was impossible for Addie to judge his age because he had the energy of a yearling colt and eyes that twinkled with ageless mischief. He held the list at arm's length when he read, but then, he didn't seem to need to read the labels on tins or bags as he scurried through the crowded and well-stocked mercantile, gathering her supplies with a speed and agility that made her feel downright feeble. Addie watched in amazement as her purchases piled up on the counter.

"I'll need to send my boy 'round with the wagon to deliver the barrel of dried apples, peaches and the hundredweight of flour," he said while wrapping the cinnamon sticks in brown paper and tying the bundle with string.

"Thank you, that will be fine, Mr. Gruberman," Addie said. "I'll take the cinnamon and the sugar cone with me now."

He leaned across the counter and whispered, "You know, ma'am, it is a lucky thing Mr. McTavish sticks to his rule about no single women in town." Mr. Gruberman winked lasciviously at her and chuckled with glee when she gasped in shock and drew back.

"Whatever do you mean, Mr. Gruberman?" Addie tucked a lock of stray hair under her sagging, faded scoop bonnet and tried to pretend her cheeks were not burning from mortification. Had he really been trying to take liberties?

Or did he *know* something?

"If you weren't already leg-shackled, every unmarried

man in McTavish Plain would be lined up at your back door to come a'courtin'. Including me.'' He waggled his brows.

He *had* been taking liberties. Well, the nerve!

''A woman who can cook like you would be beating suitors off with a stick.'' He chuckled again, and his eyes twinkled merrily. ''If'n she wasn't already hitched, that is.''

Addie swallowed and forced herself to meet his amused gaze. ''And how do you know whether or not my cooking is any good?'' Addie asked with one brow arched, hoping to divert the conversation from her marital status.

''Preacher said so.'' He tucked his chin and grinned widely. '' 'Tain't likely a man of the cloth would up and lie about it—now would he?'' Gruff laughter brought heat rising to the roots of her hair.

''Well, I—no, I guess he wouldn't,'' Addie said quickly.

''Just the same, little lady, if'n you weren't already married off . . .''

''I am married!'' Addie said too fast, too forcefully. ''Old Mr. McTavish hasn't got anything to worry about.''

''Old Mr. . . . ?'' Mr. Gruberman slapped his skinny thigh and laughed. ''Old Mr. McTavish! Tarnation, Mrs. Brown, you are a caution.'' He turned his back and snagged a tin of Arbuckle's coffee from the top shelf. ''I near forgot to put this in your order.''

''I'll carry it.'' Addie took the can and tucked it into her basket.

'' 'Tain't often I meet a women who can cook and enjoy a good laugh to boot. Aye, you are a huckleberry. If that don't beat all . . . *old* Mr. McTavish. A caution— a pure, ring-tailed caution. Your man is a lucky galloot to have a fine cook and a woman who knows how to josh as well.''

He went on muttering while Addie wondered what was wrong with him and if it was safe to be alone with him. It would be rude to leave while he was talking, so she stood there, gasping and blushing in turn as he teased her.

Ian McTavish nibbled on a pickle fresh from the brine barrel while he listened unashamedly to the palaver between Gus and the tall, thin woman at the counter. He rubbed his fingers through his thick beard and watched the woman over a stack of gingham dress goods.

Upon his return from Belle Fourche, Ian had discovered another party had arrived in town. How could he not have heard about it? Every man jack he spoke to was in a twitter about the cooking of Mrs. Brown, but he had sure expected something different . . . something more than that scrawny, leggy female who was listening to Gus.

Ian watched her, trying to decide whether she was as plain and homely as he first thought. Her hair was a wild thatch of rusty-looking curls that kept creeping from under the saddest excuse for a bonnet he'd seen in many a year.

Aye . . . and her cheeks . . . they kept turning a blotchy, mottled red each time old Gus gee-gawed at her about how lucky her husband was to have caught her. And those eyes. Were they slate gray or mossy green?

She was no bonny lass, to be sure.

Lucky? Gus just kept saying how lucky her man was.

If her husband was lucky, then the poor creature must look like the south end of a northbound bear. Ian shuddered and took another pickle from the barrel. He narrowed his eyes and took a bite of the sour pickle.

She had just called him *old* again. Her remark about his age stung, but not as much as Gus having the granite-carved ballocks to laugh when Ian was standing no more than two ax handles from him.

Wait until I am alone with him . . .

When Mrs. Brown left Ian was going to give *old* Gus a piece of his mind. Then he would see if he felt quite so canny as he was acting in front of the plain bit o' muslin that he kept teasing and complimenting.

Ian looked the woman up and down once more and replayed the *old* remark in his head again. Hell, she didn't look more than half a dozen years shy of forty herself. Just who in blue blazes was she to call him *old?*

Uppity bit of baggage, this Mrs. Brown, uppity and sharp-tongued and not to his liking a'tall.

Ian turned his attention back to Gus, who was still leering at her like a fox in a henhouse. The old fool!

"Now you run along, Mrs. Brown. I'll send my boy 'round with the wagon soon and he'll be more'n happy to unload these supplies for you," Gus said.

"Thank you, Mr. Gruberman." Mrs. Brown paid him, smoothed her unruly hair under the edge of her bonnet once more and hurried outside. As soon as she was gone, Ian eased himself from behind the stack of dress goods. He sauntered to the counter.

Gus was bent over double, laughing.

"Damn it, Gus, you're a blatherskite and a rogue," Ian growled.

"Old . . . old Mr. McTavish. She called you *old.*" Gus chortled and made snorting sounds through his nose. "Did you hear her? Said it plain as day, she did. Not onc't but twice. Old Mr. McTavish."

"I heard her. Now stop your laughing. You sound like a Missouri mule braying at the moon. I have no patience with the likes of you."

Gus drew himself up straight and wiped at the moisture dewing the corners of his eyes. "Sorry, Ian, it was just so funny. She is a hoot, that one."

"I must have missed the part o' the conversation you find so amusing," Ian said with a frown, his burr growing more pronounced as he grew more agitated. "Did Horace really say she knew the difference between a bucket and a frying pan, or was that more of your nonsense?"

"Sure as shootin'." Gus lounged on the edge of the counter. "He came by here with an apple pie that would make a man's mouth water. Wouldn't even share when I offered to get a knife . . . a man of God shouldn't ought to be so stingy, it ain't Christian, and I told him so, I did."

Ian grinned and leaned an elbow on the counter. The position put him nearly nose-to-nose with Gus. "Imagine that, nary a bit passed your lips, eh? Her cooking is bonny?"

"That good." Gus sighed. "And more . . . from what Horace said, though I wouldn't have a personal knowledge 'cause he was so stingy."

"I ken your meaning, Gus. You think the reverend is a mite tight-fisted."

"Yep, though not as tight-fisted as a Scot." Gus chortled as Ian glowered at him. "Tell me, Ian, have you made Angus and Fergus into a pair of gloves yet?"

"Not yet, but the thought is mighty tempting." Ian fought the temptation to smile.

"Well, I can't sit around here discussing your bad temper and thrifty nature all day. I best give Toby a holler so's he can get these supplies to Mrs. Brown."

"No need, Gus. Toby won't be doing any delivering today, at least not to Mrs. Brown," Ian said, drawing himself up.

"And why is that, Ian?" Gus asked with a wary frown. "She said she needed the supplies right away—now, you ain't going to be holding it against her that she said you were old—are you? 'T'weren't her fault—she's new in town. You got no call to take your high Scots temper out on a newcomer—and a woman to boot— 'sides, all those hungry men are countin' on that food."

"Dinna get ruffled wi' me, Gus." Ian glared at Gus, astonished by the man's protective attitude. "I am not going to hold it against her. I'll take the supplies to Mrs. Brown's house myself. I think it is high time she met *old* Mr. McTavish."

Chapter Five

An hour later Addie had churned the butter and made a pan of scones. She had a bowl of dried peaches soaking and another of apples resting in a bed of cinnamon and sugar. If she didn't stop for dinner and hurried through the evening milking, she just might be able to fill the orders she had promised by tomorrow's breakfast.

If she only slept a couple of hours and had no interruptions.

The clang of a harness drew her eyes to the kitchen window. A wagon was pulling up to her back door. She wiped her hands on her apron and opened the door, glad to see the badly needed supplies being delivered so promptly.

A man whose height and breadth was shocking, since Gus had called him a boy, stood on the threshold. His hair was long, his auburn beard unkempt. His dress was a careless marriage of buckskins and well-worn woolens that might have been tartan plaid when new but now were simply faded pastel lines of color. For a moment Addie thought he might be an Indian, but eyes the color of a cloudless blue sky peered from under brows both sun bronzed and wind weathered.

This was a man . . . all man, lean, hard, tall and a bit threatening. If Addie had been blind, she would never have made the mistake of labeling this brute *boy*.

But Gus Gruberman had said he would send 'round his "boy." A sobriquet that was completely absurd, since this strapping fellow would make two of Gus Gruberman on his best day.

"Ma'am." The *boy*'s accent sent shivers up Addie's spine. It was an unusual blend, part trilling Scots burr with a soft Southern drawl that was both deep and melodious. She rubbed her hands along the exposed flesh of her arms where she had rolled her sleeves back, but the raised chill bumps remained.

"Are you from the mercantile?"

The man raised thick brows and let his glance slide to the wagon loaded with supplies and the lettering on the sideboards proclaiming it the property of Gruberman's Mercantile.

"So it would seem, lass."

Addie felt heat creep up her cheeks. Of course he was from the mercantile. What a foolish question . . . and what a churl he was to go out of his way to make her know just how foolish.

"Where do you want the supplies?" he asked in that voice that both grated and caressed. She had a moment of unease, but when she glanced up she found the *boy* looking not at her but at the baked goods lining her table.

He swallowed hard, his Adam's apple working in his throat above the split leather shirt stretched across his wide shoulders.

Was he going to salivate like a hungry hound?

"Anyplace you can find room is fine." The hiss of a pot boiling over drew Addie's attention. She dashed to the stove. A mixture of molasses and spices was nudging

up the lid and dribbling down the side of the pan. It landed
on the hot iron, sizzling and filling the kitchen with its
aroma. Addie grabbed up her folded sacking and moved
the heavy pot to a cool spot.

Then she turned around.

And nearly bumped her nose against the giant *boy's*
chest.

"Are those . . . scones?" His blue eyes were wide, but
the heavy brows were furrowed. He extended a long arm
and one enormous finger in the direction of her table.

Addie frowned and ducked under his leather-clad arm.
"Yes. I made them this afternoon. I've always been partial
to scones and fresh milk at bedtime. Tomorrow I'll churn
and have fresh butter—nothing like a scone with fresh
sweet butter." She was talking too much, but this man—
this *man,* not a *boy* but a man—affected her.

He was big, powerful and seemed to dominate the entire
expanse of her new kitchen. Each time she looked at him
she felt small and feminine—and those were two things
Addie had rarely ever felt.

"Scones . . ." His voice was little more than a rumbling
whisper as he stepped by her. His moccasin-covered feet
made no sound at all. The giant—for that was what he
was—moved like smoke. He was agile and graceful like
a mountain cat. He stared down at the pan of fluffy yellow
things with single-minded intent.

Addie sighed. Another poorly fed man on her doorstep.
Was this all that old Mr. McTavish was attracting to his
town? Could he not see that his hardworking, eager citizens were in need of a good feed?

"As soon as the wagon is unloaded you can have one,"
she promised, hoping to bribe him into unloading her
supplies before dark.

The giant's head came up with a snap. A grin spread
across his face and slashed the heavy beard in half. Even

white teeth glimmered. A tracery of fine lines appeared at the corners of his eyes.

"As you wish, lass."

With the same catlike grace, he sprinted to the wagon and hefted two fifty-pound bags in one heave. With one balanced on each wide shoulder, he brought them in and placed them against the wall.

In only a few minutes the wagon was empty and the size of Addie's cozy kitchen had been shrunk by the mound of supplies—and the presence of the man himself. He seemed to require more room—more air—more of Addie's regard than any man she had ever encountered.

"Now then, Mrs. Brown, I'll take you up on that offer of a scone," he stated with a triumphant twinkle in his eye.

"Shall I toss it to you or would you like to sit and have it with a dipper of milk—fresh from this morning." She smiled sweetly back at the twinkle in his blue eyes.

"Fresh milk? Aye, a dipper of fresh milk would be a bonny thing, if you have some to spare." He cocked his head and studied her as if her claim was too outlandish to be true.

Addie walked to the dry sink and wiped out the dipper with the corner of her apron. Then she extended it into the big crock she kept her fresh milk in. By the time she turned around the giant had already removed a scone from the pan.

He winked and smiled. And then the scone disappeared into his maw in one bite. Crumbs lay in the tangle of his beard. She had to stifle the urge to laugh.

"Would you like another?" This poor man was obviously starving. Given his size, it undoubtedly took a lot to keep him going.

"Aye, I would." He helped himself to the scone and simultaneously folded himself into one of her kitchen chairs. He took the dipper from her hands and drank with his head tilted back, his eyes closed. His Adam's apple worked steadily. When the second scone disappeared into his mouth he sighed in pure, unabashed satisfaction.

This was a man who took pleasure from eating . . . and other things too, Addie suspected.

"Not in years have I tasted such as that. You are a fine cook, Mrs. Brown."

Addie grinned, feeling a burst of pride. There was a certain satisfaction in having a hungry man appreciate her cooking. Mattie and Lottie's praise lacked the heartfelt enthusiasm that these hungry men of McTavish Plain conveyed with a smile or a boyish sniff of spices and warm cooking smells. It was foolish, Addie knew, but she felt a rush of warmth and pleasure at seeing this stranger enjoy something she had made with her own two hands.

"Thank you, Mr. . . . uh . . . Mr. . . . ." She lifted her brow, waiting for him to speak.

He grinned wolfishly. "I think you may have heard of me, lass. I am *old* Mr. Ian McTavish. And I am pleased to welcome you to McTavish Plain."

"You—you are *old* Mr. McTavish? I mean . . . uh, that is, Mr. *Ian* McTavish."

"Aye." His grin grew more feral. Without seeming to move he was suddenly there, bending over Addie, crowding her, taking more space out of the small kitchen.

"Not his son . . . but Mr. Ian McTavish himself?"

"Aye, one in the same, lass."

She could feel his breath, had the impression he was sucking all the air . . . all the energy from the room.

No, that wasn't true. The nearer he came, the more the air around her crackled with energy . . . with life. He was like no man she had ever met. He was big, dangerous and compelling. There was a strength about him, and the way he looked at her seemed to taunt and tease in equal measures.

"I am pleased to make your acquaintance," he said in a husky whisper. And though she was sure he could not manage it, he actually got a little closer.

Addie fought to control her heartbeat and the urge to shrink from him. In a moment he would be *touching* her person. Who did he think he was? She had thought him old and dotty and weak-minded—

"I was wrong. Very, very, wrong," she said, more to herself than to him. He was big, strong, *virile*, though Addie could not remember thinking of any man and that word together in her life.

"Aye, you were that, lass." He placed a wide hand on either side of her body—trapping her between leather-clad arms as big as trees. "And tell me, now, why did you think I was an old man?"

"Well, what was I to think?" She forced herself not to turn away from his gaze, though his eyes fairly sparked with mischief and his nose was no more than an inch from her own. With each halting intake of breath she smelled pine trees, the scent of leather and a wild attar that reminded her of wind blowing across cornfields.

"I dinna know, lass. You tell me. What were you to think?" His voice was low and sultry . . . almost suggestive. The rush of chill bumps across her neck and shoulders made her shiver.

"Well, I thought you were old because of this town. . . . I mean, to give away land and houses . . . It is a crazy notion."

"Old and crazy, am I?" His eyes were no longer twinkling. Now the blue was hard and cold as shards of mountain ice. And still Addie felt hot and cold and all too vulnerable beneath his steely gaze.

"I see you are a lass who takes a deal of pride in speaking her mind—whether 'tis wise to do so or not."

Addie bit her tongue to keep from telling *not old* Mr. McTavish that as the eldest of three orphan girls she had learned early to be assertive. Many was the time she had wished for someone else to make the decisions . . . someone else to speak up for them. Instead she smiled stiffly and said, "Thank you for the compliment."

Those cold blue eyes narrowed. "I dinna mean it as such." His lips twitched beneath the full russet mustache. "In fact, I have no envy for your husband at all, Mrs. Brown. You have a sharp tongue, and you are no great beauty." His burr was thick as molasses as he said the last.

"I made no claim to being such," Adelaide said evenly. "But I take pride in my skills, pitifully small though they may be."

"Ah, you truly are a dangerous woman. For now I see that with that sharp wit of yours is also a penchant for telling the truth." He drew back a little and scanned her face. Those eyes, blue as deep water, flicked with alarming speed over her features, not once but twice.

"A man canna trust a woman who is so inclined to face the truth without so much as flinching."

The truth?

If he only knew what a bold liar she was! Guilt and her own strange reaction to Ian McTavish brought a burst of anger coursing through her. She ducked beneath his arms, escaping the prison of his hard, muscled body. He whirled with the speed of a twister, his brows raised in surprise.

"I begin to see why you have that foolish edict about no single women in your town." She placed her hands on her hips and glared up at him. "You don't like women very much . . . do you, Mr. McTavish?"

He made a sound in his throat that Addie could only describe as a growl. And then he was too close, leaning over her again, close enough that she could feel his warm breath fan across the lobe of her left ear. In that velvety rough burr he said, "Ah, now that's where you are wrong again, lassie. I like women. I like women verra, verra much.'' Then he leaned away and let his eyes roam over her from the top of her unruly hair to the cracked toes of the shoes peeking from beneath her skirts.

And she felt every inch of his scrutiny. That gaze, so raw, so male, left no doubt about what he meant—what he implied about liking women and what he liked them for.

Addie's face was hot with humiliation, her breasts strangely itchy and full feeling in an odd way she had never experienced before.

Ian McTavish made a low, satisfied sound in his throat. ''Ah, I ken you take my meaning plain enough, Mrs. Brown.''

He turned, and in one swift, silent stride he was out the door. The soft thud of it closing behind him left Addie trembling. Perhaps there were good and valid reasons why there were no unmarried women in McTavish Plain.

Chapter Six

Addie worked all through the night just to finish the orders by sunrise. When she had scrubbed her face and hands, twisted her unruly hair into a knot and put on her bonnet, she brought the first of the orders to Gus Gruberman. She knew she must look a fright. Her eyes felt as if sand had been rubbed into them and her back ached from bending over the table.

The last thing she wanted to do was run into Ian McTavish, and so of course, in the perverse way of fate, his was the first face she saw.

" 'Mornin', Mrs. Brown," he said with a crooked grin and a narrowing of those startling blue yes. He was leaning, with his ankles crossed, against one of the tall posts that supported the roof hip over Gruberman's Mercantile. She couldn't look at his face without blushing furiously, so she lowered her eyes.

At his side was a monstrously huge dog, the color of creamy oatmeal with eyes that were a curious blend of gold and brown and almost as arresting as the man's beside him. His gaze followed her every movement, but he never even so much as twitched a muscle.

"Ah, let me introduce you to Darroch," Ian McTavish said, lightly resting his palm on the tall dog's head.

" 'Morning, Mr. McTavish," she said stiffly, scooting carefully by, pulling in her skirt so no part of her even brushed against him or his hound. "Darroch. Excuse me, please. I have business with Mr. Gruberman."

"O' course, we wouldna want to keep you, Mrs. Brown," Ian McTavish said with a wink, and then he laughed.

He laughed, and though Addie tried to block out the resonant rumble, it seeped into her body and the soles of her feet like warm sunshine. The sound was both annoying and enchanting. Against all reason Addie wondered what it would be like to hear that laughter often.

She mentally pulled herself up short. It was dangerous to even entertain such thoughts in passing. Anybody could see Ian McTavish was a rooster on the prowl. And he was a threat to her—in more ways than one.

Why couldn't he have been old or dotty or both? Why did he have to be rough, rugged with a quick, sly mind?

He watched her with an unreadable expression in those bottomless blue eyes and she knew . . . just knew if she made one mistake it would cost her sisters their happiness and security.

She hurried on into the mercantile and forced herself to smile when Mr. Gruberman appeared. The sooner she learned to ignore Mr. Ian McTavish, the better off she and her sisters would be.

After she had emptied her basket of breads, biscuits, pies and fritters and one roasted chicken the reverend had dropped by after sundown, Addie was lingering in the store, stalling until Ian left. She half expected him to appear in Gruberman's, sneak up behind her and whisper in her ear that he knew she was a liar—that was how probing those eyes of his were.

But thankfully he left, ambling away with the huge hound at his side, stopping to say a word to several women in the street. Addie noticed their reaction to him was much like her own . . . giggling, awkward and embarrassed.

"But that is silly. He is only a man," Addie muttered when she was outside. She slung the empty basket over her arm. "What I need is a visit with Lottie." And with one more glance over her shoulder to make sure Ian McTavish was nowhere about, she set off for the dress shop.

Lottie was ankle deep in ruffles of a beautiful, soft woolen plaid when Addie arrived. She knocked on the door and then opened it. From the corner of her eye she thought that she saw a flash of dun-colored buckskins and plaid woolen.

Addie turned and peered up the street, but there was no sign of Ian McTavish or his dog. Still . . .

Shaking her head and calling herself a nervous ninny, Addie walked into her sister's dress shop. Lottie, it appeared, had been as inundated with orders for piece goods as Addie had been for foodstuffs.

"See, they do need us here," Lottie said around a mouthful of pins as she carefully cut around a pattern of heavy brown paper. "They have all the wool in the world and a loomsman who turns it into wonderful piece goods, but nobody here is skilled beyond the ordinary stitchery. I have orders for a dozen good winter dresses and five coats in the latest fashion."

"Then I 'spect they will be awed by your skill with needle and thread, Lottie." Addie sighed, sinking into a kitchen chair beside the table. "Are you eating, or working 'round the clock on frocks and coats?" She glanced at the cold stove.

"Oh, yes. The ladies usually bring me a little something when they come to be fitted." Lottie smiled and winked. "All I have to do is put on the pot for tea. In fact, I may never have to cook again." She stared at Addie for half a minute, then she stood up, took the pins from her mouth, placed her hands at the small of her back and stretched.

"What's wrong? You have a face longer than the trail from Gothenburg."

Addie frowned and chewed her bottom lip. "I—that is, I believe . . . oh, it is too foolish to say aloud."

"Tell me what has you wound up tighter than Papa's old pocket watch."

"I think Ian McTavish is following me," Addie said in a rush. Now that the words were out and she saw the incredulous look on Lottie's face, the whole notion seemed completely mad. But she had seen . . . or she thought she had seen . . .

"Oh, Addie." Lottie shook her head and laughed. "I swear, I thought something was really wrong." Lottie picked up the scissors and concentrated on her pattern. "Why on earth would Ian McTavish be following you?"

"I don't know . . . maybe he knows."

Lottie's head snapped up. "No. He doesn't know anything and he won't unless you start acting crazy and slip up. Besides, Ian McTavish is not the kind of man to follow any woman around."

Addie fiddled with the strings on her tired old bonnet. "And how do you know so much about him?"

Lottie shrugged. "The ladies. They gossip. I know most everything there is to know about everybody here. I know that Nate Pearson is a runaway slave and so is his wife. I know that Gert Thompson drove a team long before she married her husband, Miley. And I know that Ian McTavish loved a girl from Scotland who jilted him and married his cousin. He is the kind of man who women follow around, not the other way 'round." Lottie smiled.

"He doesn't have a wife, and the story is he doesn't want one. In fact, Chloe Pearson says Ian's favorite saying is 'Why make one woman miserable when he can make many happy?' "

"Of all the silly gossip," Addie said, looking out the window. "Sounds like the man is stuck on himself."

"Maybe, but I also hear there is an Indian princess from the Salish tribe who has been trying to get him to scratch her itch—or so I hear."

"Charlotte Green!" Addie said in unabashed shock, whirling away from the window. "Where on earth did you learn language like that?"

Lottie shrugged again and pinned another piece of paper on a newly folded piece of wool. "The ladies. They say that and more. Women here aren't like they were back in Gothenburg. They speak plain and speak their minds. You'd be surprised what I know about what goes on—"

"No. I don't want to know anymore about our neighbors or anything else you have learned. I think I will go now and see how Matilda is doing." Addie realized that there were depths to Lottie that had never been plumbed—depths that she didn't want to think about.

Addie stepped outside and adjusted her bonnet against the glare of the sun. She felt a little better. And if Lottie was right, then Ian McTavish would sooner walk over hot sand than be near her. Yes, she was feeling much better until she looked up and saw him standing across the street in front of the butcher shop. His blue eyes were trained upon her. He didn't even make an effort to disguise his interest.

"Mrs. Brown." His hand was idly stroking the head of the dog beside him. There was something unconsciously sensuous about the way his fingers lightly curled into the fur, swirled, lingered.

He is following me!

A tight, drawing sensation tugged at Addie's middle.

And a strange hollow spot grew right beneath her breast-bone as she watched him. She swallowed hard and tore her gaze away from his weathered hand. "Mr. McTavish."

"Out for a little air?" he said mildly.

"Yes. I—I had deliveries to make and thought I would stop by and see my sister."

"Yes, the deliveries. I saw you earlier . . . remember?"

"Oh, so you did." Addie was stammering, finding it hard to think beneath the gaze of those blue eyes. And why did she feel beholden to explain anything to him anyway?

"Tomorrow I will make sure you have a buggy to use so you don't have to make several trips to town with your basket."

"How do you know I will need to make several trips?"

He grinned. It was slow, deliberate and full of wicked intent. "There is not much that goes on in McTavish Plain I miss, Mrs. Brown."

She felt the heat rising in her cheeks. How could a man use the most ordinary of addresses and make it sound so "come-hither"? she wondered.

"I appreciate your offer, but that won't be necess—" she began, but he had somehow moved away from the butcher shop and mounted his horse while she was blushing and stammering.

He rode across the street, Darroch, the huge hound, walking beside the horse, an animal of bigger than normal proportions with wild eyes that snorted when Ian reined it near her.

"I insist, Mrs. Brown. I have brought you here to live, lass, and you are now my responsibility." He narrowed his eyes and studied her for a moment, then he added, "As are all the citizens of McTavish Plain."

She nodded silently, mesmerized by the size of the horse . . . and the man.

"This is my town and I do my best to see everyone

in it has exactly what they need—including you, Mrs. Brown." Beneath the thatch of hair upon his upper lip she could have sworn his mouth quirked in a suggestive smile. And then with a throaty chuckle he wheeled the horse around.

"Good day to you, Mrs. Brown."

Ian rode only as far as Gus Gruberman's Mercantile before his thoughts made him wonder what he was about. There was something about Adelaide Brown—something unusual and compelling he could not name but was helpless to ignore. He tied Dow to the hitching post and told Darroch to stay.

Then, scratching his beard in bewilderment, he went inside and found Gus.

"Did Mrs. Brown happen to mention when her husband would be arriving?" Ian asked as he picked up a bottle of liniment. He pretended to read the label, hoping Gus would simply take it all as gossip and answer without noticing Ian's agitation.

He didn't.

Gus turned and leaned on a shelf, looking Ian up and down, as if he had just crawled out from under something wet and covered with moss.

"You are giving a lot of thought to Mrs. Brown." Gus pulled up the tall stool he kept behind the counter and pulled a folding knife from his pocket. He brought out a heel of cheddar wrapped in cheesecloth. "I mean for a married woman. I ain't seen you quite this *curious* since that wagon train headed on to Oregon stopped for a few days last spring. And whatever happened to that yellar-haired girl that took such a fancy to you?"

"She went on with her family and you know it." Ian averted his eyes, still reading the liniment label. "I should be curious about new people, but you are wrong, Gus. I am curious about her husband. Did she happen to say what skill he was bringing to town?''

Gus cut a piece of cheddar and handed it and a salt cracker from a painted tin to Ian. Ian bit down on the cheddar and waited for Gus to answer.

''Ah, I guess I was confused, but if you are asking about her man . . .''

''I am.''

''Well, I don't think she said what he turned his hand at.''

Ian frowned. ''She is a strange woman, that Mrs. Brown. I find her to be all nerves and bite. What kind of man would be married to a woman like her?''

''Ha! I knew it wasn't her man you were curious about; it is her!''

''Not a bit of it. I only wondered what kind of a man he will be.''

''You mean what kind of man would she pick, since she doesn't pay you any mind?'' Gus chuckled and cut himself a generous chunk of cheese.

Ian was none too happy that Gus had skewered him with the truth. He *had* wondered what kind of a man Mrs. Brown would be drawn to, since she seemed to be most determined to avoid him. But he could not very well admit that he was spending his time thinking about a married woman. He was known to be a randy son of a buck who chased everything in skirts, but he had never even given a second thought to a married woman . . . until now.

''As if I would be wanting attention from her. She is plain as pudding, with her hair the color of the setting sun and eyes that put me in mind of a frightened doe.''

''Plain?'' Gus's brows shot upward and nearly touched the deep, grooved wrinkles in his forehead. ''Funny words for a man to use when talking about a plain woman. I think you need to think about getting yourself a wife,

Ian, instead of spending so much time thinking about somebody else's missus.''

Ian glowered, but heat crept up from his beard. Gus had only given voice to what he had been thinking himself.

"You know I have vowed to live alone. I wilna be sharing my hoose with any woman. They are nagging creatures and not for the like o' me.''

"Uh-huh. Still angry at Fiona for taking up with your cousin, so you'll paint all women with the same black brush, won't you?''

"Fiona made her choice. And I am better off for it. She would never have warmed to such a savage land. I am happy living alone, just me and Darroch and Angus and Fergus. We do right well,'' Ian said forcefully.

"Ah, I see,'' Gus said softly.

"I hope you do see. I have no interest in any woman beyond the obvious. I was only wondering what kind of a man Mr. Brown was, that's all.''

"Whatever you say, Ian McTavish, whatever you say. I would not presume to suggest you are lonely.''

"I do not need nor want a wife. If I ever find myself so lonely I canna stand it, then I will go visit Grass Singing.''

"Ha! She has been after you to come share her blankets for more than a year since her husband died. If you haven't done it yet, then I doubt you are going to,'' Gus said in disgust as he wrapped the gauze around the cheese and put it into the pierced tin pie safe. The aroma from the three loaves of bread and apple pie Mrs. Brown had delivered made his mouth water. He wanted to eat now, but he was annoyed with Ian and determined he would not share a single bite of his larder with a man who didn't have the sense to know he should have a wife.

Gus turned and glowered at Ian. "I know one thing— if Mrs. Brown weren't a married woman, I'd be slicking back my hair and picking posies real quick.'' Gus stuck his jaw out, daring Ian to disagree.

Ian narrowed his eyes and watched Gus for a long moment. ''But she *is* a married woman, Gus.'' What he did not say aloud, though he thought it, was that it might be better if they both remembered that fact.

Against Ian's better judgment he turned Dow south . . . toward Mrs. Brown's house. Even before he got there, he knew her house was silent and empty. No thread of smoke came from the chimney, no light burned in the window.

A strange sort of melancholy gripped Ian, the likes of which he had not felt since boarding a ship and leaving Scotland as a stripling youth. He told himself he had simply been hoping for another pan of hot scones or more information about her mysterious husband.

He hoped her husband would hurry and join her soon. Mrs. Brown was not the kind of woman who should be left alone.

''Especially around the likes of me,'' Ian muttered as he reined Dow and headed toward his empty stone house. And every mile he rode he wondered if Gus was right.

Was it time he quit flirting like a tomcat and found himself a wife?

''And what on earth did that child do to deserve such punishment?'' Addie asked Matilda. The skinny boy swung the ax and splintered another log into kindling. His whole body was a study in sullen, silent rebellion.

''This time he tipped over the outhouse.''

Addie giggled. Matilda gave her a don't-you-dare-let-him-hear-you-laughing-at-his-antics look, but she couldn't help it—the notion was funny.

"It might interest you to know there was someone in it at the time," Matilda said through clenched teeth.

"Oh." Addie tried to school her features, but the child had the face of angel—and the demeanor of an imp, if Mattie's stories were to be believed. "Not you?"

"I'd rather not talk about it," Matilda snapped. Then she sighed "Scout is going to devil me into gray hair. I have got to find some way to harness his energy. If he is not dipping the girls' braids into the inkwells, he is carving his initials in the walls. It is a wonder I get any teaching done at all."

"Well, I am sure you will bring him to heel. You have a knack with ornery boys."

"And you have a knack with single men. I understand you have all the single ones in McTavish Plain eating out of your hand—literally."

Addie shrugged. "I am busier than I ever expected. And since I stopped by Lottie's, I have learned she is too. For the first time in our lives money won't be a problem." Then Addie thought of Mattie and pulled herself up short. "Are you doing all right? I mean, how much of a stipend do you get?"

"I am fine. The money more than covers my needs. And the reverend and his wife have started a fund to purchase more books. I will be able to get the latest editions of poetry next spring." Mattie's attention was suddenly back on Scout. She took a step toward the boy, who had stopped chopping wood and was leaning on the ax handle. "Scout—I said a full cord of kindling!" She turned back to Addie. "So, if Lottie is fine and you are fine, what is bothering you?"

Addie thought about how Lottie had reacted to her fears that Ian McTavish was following her. She had felt foolish and silly and somewhat hurt that her younger sister had dismissed her concerns so easily. But Lottie was right: It was nonsense. Addie was ready to reject her nervousness as guilt until she happen to glance up at the western horizon.

There, silhouetted against the lowering sun was a horse and a rider. The wind blew the stallion's mane, the hound's fur and the long scarf of plaid wrapped around McTavish's neck.

The tableau was a strange combination of movement and inert power. All three were big, muscled, spirited—and alone. There was a compelling dignity about the solitary nature of the trio that watched—and a stark loneliness that sent a wrenching pain through Addie's soul. That empty hollow beneath her breastbone grew larger as she watched.

"Ian McTavish," Addie whispered weakly.

"What on earth did you say?" Mattie asked with a frown.

Across the green meadow, Addie felt his probing blue eyes upon her. "Ian McTavish is bothering me."

Chapter Seven

Saturday afternoon Addie was footsore and jumpy as a frog on a hot griddle. Everywhere she went, Ian McTavish was either there or appeared within moments. If she looked up, it was his craggy, bearded face and suspicious blue eyes she saw. If her arms were full of parcels, it was he suddenly taking the weight from her hands. When her basket was almost overflowing with food orders it was Ian who was snatching it off her arm to carry.

She had decided to get a horse and buggy, thinking maybe if she didn't walk she wouldn't be so easy to catch.

Gert Thompson was a strange combination of motherly concern and gruff ability rolled into a well-upholstered frame. She hugged Addie often and well as they discussed the buggy and horse rental.

"You know, little lady, if you spoke to Ian, I am sure he would arrange a buggy for your use," Gert said with a easy grin.

"No," Addie snapped, realizing too late that Gert had

seen her reaction, hardly one that a settled married woman would have.

"Ah, so Ian has been flitting and flirting, has he?" Gert leaned on a stack of grain. "Too much tomcat in that one. You mustn't let him bother you none, missy. What he needs is a wife."

"Why isn't he married?" Addie heard herself ask. She wanted to bite off her tongue. She didn't care why he wasn't married. She didn't care anything about him except that he had the power to wreck her sisters' dreams.

"He got close . . . once. But the girl he wanted was back in Scotland, and while he was here taming a country and making his mark she settled her sights on his cousin. Took it real hard in the beginning. Then he turned into the biggest flirt a body ever seen. Now he just leaves a trail of blushing faces or broken hearts." Gert laughed, and Addie could see she liked Ian.

"Let me tell you, Mrs. Brown, if I were twenty years younger and single, I'd be doing anything I could to get that man. Miley has a saying that applies right well to Ian . . . the wilder the colt, the better the horse. And I reckon he's gonna make some woman a right fine stallion!"

"Mrs. Thompson!" Addie exclaimed as images she didn't want to examine popped into her mind.

"Oh, now, don't get all hot and bothered. After all, you and me is married women. We know which side of the bed a man sleeps on, now don't we?"

Addie swallowed hard. Finally she managed to nod. This was a predicament she had not anticipated. It never occurred to her that other women would be so plain-speaking, and that she would be expected to know what they were talking about.

How could a virgin know such things?

* * *

Addie flicked the reins, and the nimble-footed mare increased her speed. She was now clopping toward Lottie's house to pick her and Mattie up for Sunday services.

It had been a long week. She was tired of baking, tired of the heat of her kitchen, tired of seeing Ian McTavish everywhere she went. But most of all she was tired of her dragged-out appearance. This morning she had actually felt the sting of tears behind her eyes as she looked in her trunk for something to wear to church.

She had washed and dried her hair in front of the stove, piling the wavy mass on her head and using Mama's good tortoiseshell combs to hold it.

Feeling as if she were a naughty child, Addie had taken out one of her mourning dresses. "What would it hurt if I wore one? Maybe folks will think I am a solemn, church-going woman."

Addie had finished off her appearance by applying a thin film of lard to the outside of her scuffed shoes.

Addie clicked her tongue and the sleek bay mare moved out smoothly. The wheels on the buggy were painted bright yellow and they sang a trill song as the conveyance sailed over the roads. The fall air was sharp with the coming of winter. Higher up on the mountain the color of pale yellow and russet added a splash of fire to the rocks. The trip to Lottie's house was quick.

She called out and the door opened. Lottie was in a confection of cream and pink that made her golden curls shine like new-minted coins, and right behind her was Matilda, wearing navy and white stripes, looking cool and pretty.

"Oh, Addie, you are wearing black," Lottie said in disapproval before the door was even closed behind her.

It grated on Addie's raw nerves. She found herself growing angry and resentful that she had no pretty frocks and that her best clothing was stark black. After all, her sisters and their crazy scheme were the reason she was in this pickle.

"You may have forgotten, Charlotte, but I don't have any good dresses of pale color. I wasn't *planning* on being a wife."

Her sister's face fell. Unshed tears glistened in two pair of wounded eyes. Addie felt a stab of guilt.

"I'm sorry. I didn't mean to snap. Besides, what does it matter if I wear black or not, nobody is going to notice me with the two of you around looking pretty as sunshine. Mr. McTavish pointed out I am no great beauty."

"He did what?" Matilda said as she settled herself in between Lottie and the seat rail. "What kind of a conversation were you two having when he said that?"

"Yes, Addie, just what were you and Mr. McTavish talking about?" Lottie said. "I met him the other day when I went to buy thread at the mercantile. He is a handsome son of a gun."

"There you go with that plain speaking again, Lottie," Addie admonished. "Lands, I don't know what to make of you, but I hope you aren't going to pick up some of the habits of Gert Thompson."

"Gert is a strong, forthright woman. Besides, Addie, this is a new place; we have to learn a new way of doing things. Women in McTavish Plain don't stand around and let men make all their decisions. There is a sense of adventure here."

"Adventure my aunt Sadie. Hurry up or we'll be late for services."

It took only minutes before Addie was tying the reins to the hitching post at the side of the neat, white-washed building. The bell on top was pealing, echoing in the valley.

"I hope the preacher does a good job," Mattie was saying to Charlotte. Addie made sure the little mare was properly tethered; she would hate for her to get free and return to the livery. Absently she made a mental note of the other horses tied at the railing. Thankfully there was no wild-eyed stallion tethered with the rest. For the first time in days she relaxed a little.

They entered the church as the first strains of "Rock of Ages" was being sung. The church was divided more or less evenly, with families on one side and all the single men of McTavish Plain on the other. Every pew on the "married side" was full. A single pew on the "single side" was empty.

"We'll have to go sit on the unmarried side," Lottie whispered to Addie.

"So it would seem. Next week we'll have to get here earlier." She didn't even want to think about the significance of this.

Was God telling her something?

Until that accursed letter arrived she would be seeing portents and warnings in everything that happened.

They walked quickly down the aisle and slid in. First Mattie, then Charlotte, with Addie on the outside. Matilda grabbed a hymn book and shared it with Charlotte. Addie picked up one of her own and quickly thumbed to the correct page. She was singing at the top of her lungs when she felt the hair on the back of her neck prickle with unconscious awareness. A hollow pit opened in her middle.

She didn't even have to look to know that Ian McTavish was coming down the aisle. Every nerve in her body came alive with awareness. Her skin was hot . . . and cold . . . and too sensitive. She felt the seams of her dress. The hard bones of her corset, the garters above her knees. Every whisper of sound, every nuance of movement seemed a hundred times more vivid as Ian McTavish walked up the aisle of the church.

And then, in spite of her fervent prayers to heaven above, he stopped beside her.

The congregation broke into song, unaware and uncaring of the condition of Adelaide Green, or rather "Mrs. Brown." She moved her lips, but she was not sure any sound came from her or even what hymn was being sung.

"Mrs. Brown." His husky whisper abraded skin already alive with awareness. She could not answer, could not move . . . in fact, she was barely able to drag air into her lungs.

"Mrs. Brown?" His burr rubbed over her flesh like a caress.

"Mr. McTavish," she whispered.

Oh please . . . I cannot look at him.

But he filled the edge of her vision all the same.

He was dressed in a buckskin shirt that was intricately worked. Beads, porcupine quills, bright designs of exquisite handiwork ran up the arms and across the laced front. Tiny russet-colored chest hairs peeked from between the lacings at the cleft where the shirt didn't quite meet across his wide, hard-muscled chest.

Addie swallowed . . . hard. She was light-headed, dizzy, her stomach alive with butterflies.

"The church appears to be full to bursting. If you give your permission, I think I can squeeze in with you and your sisters, Mrs. Brown."

If I give permission. Ha! He will do what he wishes.

The refusal was on her lips. She wanted to turn to him and tell him to find another place—any place but beside her. She wanted to bolt from the church, to put as much distance as possible between herself and this confusing giant of a man.

She wanted to do all that and more. But she didn't. Instead she nodded, stiffly—only once—and shuffled nearer her sister. Unfortunately, Lottie did not do the same, and so Adelaide was wedged between Ian McTavish on the one side and Lottie's mass of curls on the other.

It promised to be a long, long service for Addie.

Ian felt Adelaide Brown stiffen the moment he stepped up beside her. It amused and annoyed him. Did the woman think she was in peril? Plain as pudding and a feather brain to boot!

There were no more hymnals, so he was forced to lean over her shoulder to share hers. He started to sing and she grew more brittle—rigid as a block of ice.

But beneath that veneer of frosty reserve there was something else . . . something potent and primal that called to him. Though he tried to deny it, there was something appealing about Adelaide Brown. Each time he inhaled he caught a whiff of her scent.

Ian had lived wild and rough in the mountains. He knew every person and animal had a distinctive attar, and Mrs. Brown was no different. Her scent was fresh-scrubbed, clean and faintly reminiscent of the spices she used in her baking.

For a moment Ian closed his eyes. He could almost identify ginger, cinnamon and allspice—perhaps even honey on the back of his tongue with each breath—almost but not quite.

The fragrance was subtle and enchanting. It was, simply, Adelaide Brown. For the first time in many years Ian felt a taut drawing of his insides. It wasn't lust—no—he was a man who did not deny himself physical pleasure or the company of a willing woman. No, this sensation was deeper, more profound and a hundred times more frightening.

He had vowed that no woman would ever control his heart or his mind and yet . . .

Ian was jarred to awareness as the sounds of shuffling feet and rustling fabric intruded upon his thoughts. With a jolt he realized the congregation was sitting down—heads bent in prayer while he stood, awkward and embarrassed.

He quickly folded himself beside Adelaide Brown and

bent his head. But once again he found himself noticing things . . . like the way her hands lay easy and relaxed in the hollow of her lap.

The lass had very nice hands. Capable, not frail, but he found nothing about them masculine either. Her skin was creamy, even on the knuckles, and he could see the tracery of veins across the back.

She had small wrists—he could easily have spanned them with his thumb and index finger—and her fingers were long and well shaped, the nails short but not too short.

They were the hands of a strong, forthright woman. They suited her.

Ian frowned and looked up, forcing himself to concentrate on what the Reverend Horace Miller was saying. The sermon was about coveting things that were not one's own.

Like another man's wife.

Ian saw the irony that Reverend Miller had chosen that particular vice to preach on, or perhaps God was trying to tell Ian something. He shifted uncomfortably and forced himself to ignore Adelaide Brown . . . but it wasn't easy.

The sermon was longer than some and shorter than others, Addie thought. Horace Miller had a way of slamming his open palm on the pulpit at regular intervals. She suspected it was more to keep the congregation from dozing than for a special emphasis on his words. Though she certainly would not have dozed—not today—not with Ian McTavish sitting beside her.

A million meadow butterflies had been in her middle since the moment his shoulder brushed against hers. And why did he have to lean over her like that? Couldn't he have remembered the words to the hymns? Surely he was doing *things,* just to be contrary.

And why did he have to *smell* like that? A fresh, woodsy

fragrance wafted to her nose each time he shifted slightly beside her. And he seemed to be shifting quite a lot.

Taking care not to turn her head, she looked at him from the corner of her eye.

He was a big man, and his mode of dress made him look all the better—she meant *bigger*. The leather trousers he wore were also decorated with an intricate beading pattern that ran down the leg. His feet were in soft-soled moccasins . . . like an Indian. Then she remembered what Lottie had said about the Indian princess, and that Gert had mentioned a Salish Indian woman as well. A strange, hot tide flowed through Addie. There was an odd, prickly emotion that lay inside that rising river.

It was . . . no, it could not be! She didn't even *like* Ian McTavish, so how in blue blazes could she be jealous?

He was awful. He was rude and bold and too forward. He told her she was plain, he watched her like a hawk. If he had half a notion what was going on, he wouldn't have even a moment of remorse as he packed up Mattie, Lottie and Addie and sent them out of his town.

He was a mean man.

But he was also the most compelling man, rugged and sensual, she had ever met. He had a way of looking at her that seared her soul. And when he spoke her entire being nearly purred in response to the sound of his voice.

He was temptation on the hoof! But it was more than his sensual presence that had Addie upset and flustered.

Ian McTavish was powerful and lethal as a snake. If she made one misstep . . . acted in any way that might make him question her marital state.

Lottie and Mattie would be heartbroken! Their dreams and hopes and wonderful innocence would be gone.

If only the letter would come, so Addie could begin her mourning. But then, in a shuddering flash of clarity, Addie realized that when the letter arrived, she wouldn't have the barrier of a make-believe husband between her and Ian McTavish. Right now she was Mrs. Brown, a married woman, a woman with the protection of another man's name.

When the letter arrived she would be a single woman. She would have no defense against him, against the lure of his voice and the probing of his eyes.

Addie turned the wedding band she and her sisters had purchased from a traveling tinker on the Platte 'round and 'round on her finger. The ring had meant nothing—until now. She wore the slender golden band like armor.

But what would she do when the magic of it was gone?

Ian was only vaguely aware of Horace Miller's sermon, but he was acutely conscious of Adelaide Brown's sharp intake of breath. It was as if she had some horrible thought that squeezed her chest, forced the air from her. For one impossibly dunderheaded moment, Ian had the urge to put his arm around her, to pull her close, to offer her the strength and comfort of his body to use as she willed.

He nearly choked on the thought. Never in his thirty-odd years had he dallied with a married woman. Never had he wanted to.

Until now.

What was wrong with him? Had he taken leave of his senses? Or was Gus right? Was his lonely life catching up with him?

Ian was blessedly saved from having to answer his own question when Horace Miller ended his sermon with a thwacking slap to the pulpit. As everyone sat up ramrod straight, he smiled beatifically and moved smoothly to a new topic.

"We here in McTavish Plain are doubly blessed. Not only do we have a wonderful town full of promise, but Ian's *unique* relationship with the Indian tribes has enabled us to live in peace. It is time to once again share our bounty and goodwill with the tribe."

Addie's imagination hung on the reverend's telling

phrase when he spoke of Ian's *unique* relationship with the tribe. What did that mean? Addie had heard of white men taking Indian wives whom they never brought among their own folks. Could Ian be that kind of man?

While she was puzzling over that, the preacher began to call upon the new people one by one. He introduced the new arrivals to the congregation and added a little about them for all to hear. Addie tried to concentrate on her neighbors, memorizing faces and names, listening to their stories and how they came to be here, but at the edge of her mind was her continued curiosity about Ian McTavish.

"And our last arrivals are Charlotte Rosswarne, Matilda Smith and Adelaide Brown, whose husbands will be joining them shortly. We are very pleased to welcome such fine, upstanding families to McTavish Plain."

Though his words made her think once again of what a liar she was, Addie was grateful for the chance to stand, to be away from the hard, muscled length of Ian beside her. Because of her nervousness and the weakness in her knees she accidently tread on Ian's foot as she stood.

"Oh, pardon me, Mr. McTavish," she said quickly, turning to look at him, feeling the heat of embarrassment climb her neck and fill her cheeks. Because he was sitting down and she was rising they were more or less on eye level. It was the first time she had seen him from this aspect.

His eyes were not just blue—they were a bottomless blue. His hair was thick and wildly curly. The beard was not plain brown but alive with russet strands, and his lashes were so long that at the corners they seemed to battle for which direction they would sweep.

He was the most masculinely beautiful creature she had ever beheld. There was a sensuality about him that made her heartbeat do a strange, awkward dance, feeling for all the world like fish flip-flopping.

He stared at her unblinking while her temperature rose. She couldn't breathe . . . nor think . . . nor look away. It was as if he absorbed her will, kept her unwilling eyes focused only on him. Adelaide caught herself wondering what it would feel like to stroke his jaw. Would his beard be soft or coarse? If she touched his chest, would he allow it? Would he touch her in return?

"For goodness sake, Addie, stand up!" Lottie whispered harshly and jabbed Adelaide in the ribs. The pain snapped her from the strange paralysis.

"What?" She blinked, and sure enough she was sort of crouching, staring into Ian McTavish's face.

She stood and looked around. The congregation was watching her. Lottie had a half-smile on her lips, but Matilda looked horrified and embarrassed near to death.

"Oh, just sit down!" Mattie hissed. "You are acting like a ninny. Everyone is watching."

Addie slid into the seat. It wasn't difficult; her bones felt quite watery. There didn't seem to be any strength left in her at all, just a strange sort of humming sensation.

She touched her forehead. Was she coming down with the ague? Could she have contracted a fever?—the grippe?

Beside her, Ian McTavish cleared his throat. Was he laughing at her? Furious with herself and him, she turned her head to the side and looked at him again—full on.

But he wasn't laughing. In fact, his expression was odd, slightly confused, and there was a faint stain of color in his cheeks.

Reverend Miller was still talking, droning on in a way that was somehow comforting. Addie turned around and forced herself to look at him, the pulpit, the big Bible beneath his hand.

"And so since Miley Thompson will be in Belle Fourche picking up the mail, Gert will drive one of the wagons," he was saying. "Is there anyone else who would like to volunteer? Don't hold back, this is an excellent opportunity to spread God's blessing and see for yourself that our red-skinned neighbors are friendly.''

Lottie jabbed Addie in the ribs again—hard. "I'm going to do it, Addie," she whispered.

"Do what?" Addie asked weakly. She had paid so little attention, she couldn't say for sure what was being discussed. There had been some mention of letters and Belle Fourche. She supposed that Miley Thompson would now fetch her letter from Belle Fourche. Was she happy or sad about that?

"I am going to drive a team to the Indian village," Lottie said in a rush. Addie looked at her—saw the gleam in her eye and understood her sister's intent.

"Oh, no you are not," Adelaide said in horror. "Have you lost your mind?"

"It will be *exciting,*" Lottie whispered while she glared at her older sister. "I'm going to do it. I can drive a team almost as well as you can."

Lottie's hand flinched. She was going to raise her hand—to volunteer to go into the wilds—to meet Indians—to have some stupid adventure regardless of the danger. Addie thrust her hand toward the ceiling.

"I'll go. I can drive a wagon. I drove all the way from Gothenburg, Nebraska," she said too loudly.

Every head swiveled to stare at her.

"Well—fine," the preacher said with a beaming smile. "Gert will be happy for the company, I am sure. And Mrs. Brown, if you will stay after services and speak to Mr. McTavish, he will give you all the particulars."

Addie swallowed and felt herself losing starch. "Mr. McTavish?" she repeated weakly.

"Aye, lass." The velvety, rough voice nibbled at her ear. "Dinna you know that every year I trail a half dozen

cattle and woollies to the tribe?'' he said with a half grin
and one brow arched. ''I wilna be lonely now that you
have decided to come. At this time of year the weather
can turn bad, and if we canna get back to town, we could
be together for several weeks.''

Chapter Eight

"I am so angry with you, Addie." Lottie looked like a furious kitten, spitting and hissing as they walked to the buggy. "You knew I wanted to go. You knew, and you snatched the opportunity right away from me."

"You had no business even considering such a trip, Charlotte Gre—I mean, *Mrs.* Rosswarne," Addie snapped.

"Oh, but *you* could, Mrs. Brown?" Lottie countered.

"Don't even start up, Lottie. I would never have said a word if it hadn't been for you! The last thing I want is to be in the company of *that man* day in and day out."

"When will you stop trying to rescue me, Addie?" Lottie said in a voice that was brittle with emotion. "How long is it going to take for you to realize I am a grown woman? I am capable of making my own decisions."

"This is a fine mess. I put myself out to keep you from harm and now you are angry with me?" Addie said, ducking her head to hide the tears in her eyes. People were filing out of the church, some walking toward home while others collected their buggies and horses. Gus Gruberman came out, and right behind him was Ian McTavish. Addie turned away, but not before she and Ian locked gazes.

Did he see her crying?

"Kind of tempting the fates, ain't you, Ian?" Gus drawled.

"You would do well to keep your troon out o' my business," Ian said in a low voice. For a moment there Adelaide Brown looked as if she was about to weep.

But why? The question clawed at Ian's insides like a cat in a bag.

"Look, friend, it ain't no skin off'n my nose if you want to go a'chasing after a married woman."

Ian tore his gaze from the three women. He stood up a little straighter and glared at Gus, the truth hammering at his conscience. Was that what he was doing? No, she was just a new woman in town . . . and from the look of her, one who had problems.

"Are you daft? I am not chasing her. She volunteered to go, or were you blind to that?" Ian said, refusing to acknowledge what he secretly feared. There *was* something about Adelaide Brown that beckoned him. Something unique and strong, something he did not want to face. "She is a member of the community now, Gus."

"Ah, so you are just making sure she is settled in, like?"

"Of course." Ian smiled awkwardly. "You canna go jumping to conclusions like that, Gus."

"I ain't a'going to argue with you, but for once in your bull-headed, stubborn life, take some friendly advice. Find yourself a wife—your own wife—not some other man's, before it is too late . . . for you both."

Ian glared at Gus once more, and then he turned toward the three sisters. He had known Gus a long time, since they both were trapping beaver in the high streams. It was just nonsense, what Gus was saying . . . nonsense.

"Oh, Addie, here he comes," Mattie said in a harsh whisper. "And I think it is time that Lottie and I went home."

Addie swiped at her eyes. She didn't have to look to know that *he* was Ian. It was small comfort to see that he made Matilda as nervous as a cat in a room full of rockers.

Addie drew in a long, shuddering breath and straightened her bodice. She forced herself to look at the tall, muscular man walking toward her. His thick brows were drawn together in a slash above eyes that were stormy and threatening as a lightning-filled sky. Addie drew herself up to her full height, resisting the temptation—just barely— to stand on her tiptoes.

"I'm not afraid of him," she whispered to herself.

"Well, I am," Matilda admitted.

"Cowards, the both of you," Lottie pronounced.

"You bet I am, and not ashamed to admit it. Now come on." Matilda grabbed Lottie and urged her toward the buggy. As she passed by Ian, she said, "I am sure, Mr. McTavish, that you and Addie have things to discuss. Would you mind seeing that she gets home safely?" And before he could even answer . . . "Thank you. Come by later for dinner, Addie."

Ian McTavish arched one brow, and his blustery expression altered slightly as he watched Lottie and Mattie scamper into the buggy.

Addie was alone.

"I will consider it my honor and duty to protect her since you asked so nicely. I promise to see her right to her door." Then he turned his intense gaze full upon Addie. Now he looked *wolfish*. "Perhaps I can even see her tucked up safe and sound in front of a warm fire," he whispered low, so only she would hear.

Then he winked.

She wanted to sink into the earth and disappear, but unfortunately the ground beneath her feet remained solid and immovable as the man before her.

Addie turned and began walking. She told herself she was not running from him ... *she wasn't!*

We have much to discuss, you and I, Mrs. Brown,'' Ian said in that velvety rough burr as he fell into step beside her. He had to shorten his stride a bit so he did not outpace her.

Addie couldn't speak. All she could do was stare at the toes of her shoes as she put one foot doggedly in front of the other. *Her sisters had left her alone with Ian*—with the man who had the power to ruin them all.

She was stunned and hurt by their abandonment.

Ian saw fear in Adelaide's wide eyes. And he realized they were both gray and green, a strange, muted blending of colors like light filtered through mossy water.

They were pretty eyes, gentle, thoughtful eyes ... eyes that reflected fear. And though Ian reveled in baiting and teasing her, seeing her blush and stammer, he did not wish for any woman to truly *fear* him.

Especially this woman.

Once again he found himself curious about her husband ... about the kind of man he was, though Gus would likely not believe that. Ian felt sorry for Adelaide Brown, who suddenly seemed so alone and frail that he wanted— no, he needed to do something to make her feel at ease with him.

"Will you talk with me over a plate of your scones, Mrs. Brown?"

She looked up—way up—into his face, disarmed by his boldness. There was an almost childlike expectation in his expression. It was a mystery how he could be both fearsome and boyish at once. Against her better judgment, her common sense, and everything she feared about Ian

McTavish, she heard herself say, "I think I might be able to find a crumb or two for you, Mr. McTavish."

"And a dipper of sweet milk?" He waggled his brows playfully.

"You, Mr. McTavish, never know when to stop." Addie ducked her head so he wouldn't see the grin plucking at her lips.

"Aye, you have the right of it, lass. I have been known to push and prod and beard the lion in his den."

"So am I to be the lioness, Mr. McTavish?"

He gave a bark of laughter and tilted his head to the side. "I canna deny you seem to guard your sisters like a lioness guards her cubs."

"They are young . . . my ma and pa would want me to look after them." She inclined her head toward the sharp hills above them, wanting to change the subject, wanting his attention on something besides her and Mattie and Lottie. "I have heard those mountains are haunted."

His eyes narrowed, looking the color of a deep mountain lake as he turned and scanned the horizon. "Those peaks are said to be the home of the Red Bird maiden. Do you believe in ghosts, Mrs. Brown?"

"I never thought about it, but no, I suppose I don't."

"Sometimes when the wind blows it sounds like the voice of a woman, but when I try to hear what she is saying, I canna," he said softly.

"Why did you build your house in the teeth of the wind?" Addie shivered as she thought about the wind whistling and howling. It would come soon with the snow and the cold. She had to see Mattie and Lottie safely settled before the winter set in.

"It reminded me of Scotland, that craggy stone—" Ian said softly. He stared at the great rock mansion for a moment. Then he appeared to shake himself, throwing off whatever dark mood had threatened to grip him. He was once more grinning at Addie.

"Darroch and Dow are at Gert's livery. Do you think you might have a morsel for them as well?" Ian asked blandly, switching the subject back to food.

It was all too much for Addie, the service—having Ian sitting so close that she had felt the heat of his thigh, seeing his strength in every sinew and muscle—up close—*too close*. Then being forced to volunteer in order to save Lottie from herself. Now he was using his dubious charm to wheedle food not only for himself but for his horse and his sad-eyed dog.

"Is there anything *male* in this town that isn't in need of feeding?" Addie's nerves were stretched to the breaking point. "From what I can see anything that runs solitary in this place, be it two-legged or four and male is half-starved. Maybe you should change that consarned rule about no unmarried women." She glared up at Ian, silently daring him to challenge her . . . but he didn't.

He laughed. The skin around his blue eyes crinkled handsomely and his smile split the heavy beard in two. The sound rumbled like water over stones. It was deep, melodious and brought a warm burst of satisfaction to the deep hollow of Addie's soul.

But why? Why should Ian's laughter make her feel *complete*?

"Ah, I knew you were a dangerous woman, Mrs. Brown. I have reasons for my rules. Discontent leads to broken homes and towns. I want McTavish Plain strong and sound. Families let their roots run deep and true. I have no quarrel with a man having a nip of whiskey for his health, but single women in town soon mean whores and grifters . . . then there would be tent saloons and *other things*. You may be right about empty bellies, Mrs. Brown, but I dinna think of men's stomachs when I made the rule. 'Twas other parts of their anatomy that concerned me, and the trouble that *rises* from those parts . . . if you take my meaning."

She got his meaning loud and clear. This conversation was more humiliating than the one she had had with Gert. Did no one in this town observe proprieties? Heat crept up her neck toward her cheeks.

He laughed again. "Aye, lass, I see you do understand what I am about. Now, come, Mrs. Brown, let's go fetch my hungry animals and go to your home. After you have fed three of the starving males in town we can begin to make plans for our trip. And you may want to do a little extra baking so all the unattached men in McTavish Plain wilna starve whilst you are away."

She was still speechless. No suitable retort would come, so she obediently fell into step beside him, wishing she had never gotten out of bed this morning and that she had never agreed to this mad plan.

Darroch, the oatmeal-colored hound, was quiet, steady and polite. The stallion Dow, whose name meant *dark* in the ancient Scots tongue, Ian explained, was as mean-tempered and rude as his master. The animal tried several times to bite Addie on the walk to her house.

She kept a pace away, making sure to watch him from the corner of her eye. "Is Darroch the only dog you own?" Addie heard herself say when they reached her house and Dow was put into the corral next to her milk cow's bier.

"He is now. I had his mother and father, but time and the cold winters wore hard on them. They died last winter within a fortnight of each other." Sadness tinged his words.

Addie's heart was pierced by the restrained emotion. She turned away from Ian and looked instead at Darroch's soulful eyes, but they were also heart-rending. There was a sad dignity about the dog—and the man, though he worked hard to hide it.

She didn't want to know that about him. Addie didn't want to hear that he had broken dreams and old scars. It was dangerous to let herself get too close. . . .

Addie frowned at her foolish, soft thoughts and shoved them aside. She opened the front door and the dog walked in, as if he knew the place. Like the gentleman he was, he went to the fireplace in her tidy parlor and stretched out his lanky frame. She could almost hear his sigh of contentment as his pale lashes swept downward.

"You'll be spoiling him," Ian quipped as he walked past Addie and into the kitchen. He busied himself looking at the array of baked goods on Addie's long plank table. He didn't touch, but he leaned over them, inhaling deeply, lingering over a deep-dish cobbler made from peaches and a strudel that had him frowning as if he was not sure what ingredients it contained—or perhaps he was debating with himself about sampling it. Addie wasn't sure what was going through his mind, but she could not ignore the strange thrumming delight she felt while watching him.

"He needs a mate," she heard herself say.

"Who needs a mate?" Ian asked absently.

"Darroch," she said quickly. But the truth was, she had been thinking about Ian. He looked up at her, and she felt her cheeks burning. She struggled to find something to say and blurted out, "It isn't natural for creatures to be alone—the only one of their kind. It is cruel and it is lonely."

Ian tilted his head and frowned. "And would you be speaking of the dog, Mrs. Brown, or of me?"

Had he known what she was thinking?

"I assure you, Mr. McTavish, your marital status is no concern of mine."

Liar! a voice inside her head screamed. She had started with one little white lie and now it seemed they spilled from her lips on a regular basis.

He raised one brow. "Now wasna you saying all the male critters in McTavish Plain were nearly starved?"

"Yes, but—" Addie shuddered when Ian started walking, slowly, silently, toward her. She backed up a step.

"And wasna you suggesting my rule about no unmarried women was foolish?" His eyes glittered with predatory delight.

"Yes, well, but—"

He was close now, so close she could see the tiny spikes of midnight around the dark middle in his eye. She took another step backward and found herself up against the dry sink.

"Then I dinna think I am too far from the mark when I question your meaning, Mrs. Brown. You, like most females, seem to have an uncommon wish to see all menfolk leg-shackled."

"Well, I never!" Addie was thunderstruck by his remark. "How on earth can you say such a thing? *You* are the one who demands marriage of all women—not me. I am un—" Her lips slammed shut at the last possible moment.

"You are . . . what?" Ian was so quick, his motions so smooth, she was unaware of what he was going to do until he reached out and grasped her shoulders. "What were you going to say, Mrs. Brown? Are *what?*"

She swallowed hard and tried not to notice the masculine, outdoorsy scent of him. She didn't want to be aware of those blue eyes, clear and sharp as a summer sky, or the canny intelligence in them.

"I was going . . . well, I was going to say that I miss my own dear husband so much . . . that I am so very unhappy when we are apart. I wish that kind of contentment for everyone." She was repulsed by the quickness of another lie. And that one built upon another like a wall.

"And are you really so happy with your man?" Ian purred, his voice low and rough.

"Yes ... of course."

"I wonder, Mrs. Brown ... I wonder. What kind of husband leaves a woman like you alone? What kind of man have you bound yourself to?"

He bent his head to kiss her. Addie's first impulse was to break away and slap his face ... but as Ian's lips, firm and cool and insistent, made contact with her own, something happened to her mind and her body.

She didn't want him to stop. She didn't want to slap him.

For the first time in her memory Addie could not resist temptation. And that was what Ian McTavish was, *temptation*. His hold on her shoulders was gentle yet firm. His tongue ran along the outer edge of her bottom lip. . .teasing, persuading her to part her lips.

She opened her mouth with a soft sigh of shuddering contentment.

As quick as summer lightning, his tongue invaded her mouth. Once again she thought—no, she *knew* that she should protest.

She was supposed to be a proper wedded woman ... a woman of virtue. But she didn't protest. Lord, she *couldn't*. It was as if Ian McTavish had taken her will and replaced it with raw, hungry sensation and a need for him alone.

Addie found her body arching toward him. She hungered to mold herself to the contours of his hard body. Between her legs there was a strange, taut sensation. She had never felt the kind of bone-melting, blood-heating excitement that thrummed through her entire body ... her soul.

Ian's exploration of her mouth was gentle, stunning and thoroughly unexpected. He never moved his hands, never made any attempt to switch his light grip from her shoulders to any other part of her person, but she felt as if she was being enfolded into an all-consuming embrace, into strength, into protection, into *him.*

There was such heat, such maleness emanating from his tall, hard form, her skin nearly seared with it. It was as if she belonged here—as if she had been created for him and he for her.

Never in her life had Addie known such a total and complete sense of *rightness.*

Too soon he stopped kissing her and raised his head. He looked into her eyes, his own now slightly smoky, like a sky before a thunderstorm.

"As I said, Mrs. Brown, I canna help wondering if you are as happy with your marriage as you say. Is there anything you would like to tell me . . . about your husband?"

As if dashed by icy water, Addie broke free of the strange, seductive spell. She slid around Ian and marched, somewhat shakily, to the kitchen door and flung it open.

"It is time for you to leave, Mr. McTavish. You have sorely tried your welcome."

His eyes fastened on her mouth. She could feel his gaze there, almost taste his kiss again . . . for one smoldering instant she thought about returning to his arms, but then he grinned—wickedly . . . boyishly . . . unrepentantly.

"But . . . I thought . . . that is, the scones." He wore that boyish expression that was so unnerving. "I wouldna want them to go to waste."

It took all her willpower, but Addie fought off the urge to give him whatever he wanted—whatever he asked of her.

"Oh, how very considerate of you, Mr. McTavish. Well, allow me to make sure they do not go to waste." Addie snatched up the pan and a clean dishcloth.

"Ah, you have a generous spirit, lass," Ian said, beaming.

"You think so?" Addie turned the pan out into the cloth. Then she turned, stuck two fingers in her mouth and whistled.

"Ach, you dinna mean to—" Ian took one halting step toward her before Darroch streaked by, headed for the door Addie held open.

Flipping the edge of the dishcloth, she tossed the entire batch of scones outside. The happy hound was on them in a second, gulping them down almost before they hit the dirt. Ian stumbled outside, aghast at the sight.

"Ah, what a waste."

"Good-bye, Mr. McTavish," Addie said before she slammed the door.

Darroch finished the scones and looked up at Ian, his flews lifted in contentment. Then he licked his chops. Ian heard the lock click in the kitchen door behind him.

"You are a fickle beasty, Darroch, and that"—Ian jerked his head toward the door—"is a cruel, heartless woman."

Ian stalked to the corral, mumbling curses as he went. She had no call to get all twitchy—after all, she *had* returned his kiss. And to give the scones to Darroch—it was too much.

"Ah, now I understand. Her husband was happy to let her travel here alone because he couldna endure her cruelty anymore."

Chapter Nine

Addie didn't sleep that night. Each time she closed her eyes the memory of Ian McTavish's face, voice and hands took control of her mind. She could smell him . . . taste his kisses, feel the flutter of her own heart each time she thought about him.

She tried to summon the picture of her long-dead husband—her first, sweet love—but she couldn't remember what he looked like.

Johnny had pale hair and eyes—that was a solid fact she knew, even if she could not recall his face. He was as opposite Ian McTavish as hot from cold, but try as she might she couldn't remember his features, the set of his mouth or the shape of his nose.

She turned over and gave her goosedown pillow a mighty slap, all the while wishing that it was his face she saw each time she drifted toward slumber. But it wasn't. It was Ian's face.

Addie tried to wipe the feel and taste of Ian McTavish

from her mind by remembering Johnny's kisses. But time had evidently dulled those tender memories completely.

Deep inside, Addie wondered if Johnny had ever made her feel the dangerous desire Ian McTavish had conjured within her. Had she ever felt as though she were tumbling through space and time, out of control and not caring if she was?

Had any man ever thrilled her that way?

Could any man ever again?

"I have to stop this," she said, flinging back her counterpane. She padded into the kitchen and ladled herself a dipper of milk from the crock she kept cooling in a tub of water.

Surely that would bring sleep.

She sipped the milk and stared out the window. There was a fingernail moon, enough light to limn the lush grassland with a frosty blue veneer. Against her will Addie's eyes sought out the pile of stones Ian McTavish called home.

There was a single light flickering on the hilltop. It was no more than a golden winking, fluttering. There one moment, gone the next.

"I hope he can't sleep either, damn him. . . ."

But then, on the heels of that thought, she hoped he was sleeping like a baby. She hoped the kiss had meant nothing . . . less than nothing.

His comment about her marriage had shaken her almost as much as the kiss. The man was arrogant and bold as a prize-winning rooster, but he was certainly not stupid. His intuition about her not being happily married was uncannily accurate.

If things kept going on as they were, he was soon going to figure out she had lied about her husband, or at least about being happily married to a make-believe husband. It would not be long before he was on the scent of her sisters and their fake marriages as well.

"And then what will happen to Lottie and Mattie?" She shivered in fear. Ian McTavish might act as house-gentle as his hound when it suited him, but Addie had looked into his eyes. He had a soul as wild and fierce as his unruly stallion. He would have no qualms about seeing three lying women removed from his perfect little town.

Ian couldn't sleep. He had prowled the house like a wraith with faithful Darroch and the otter pups at his heels. He had poured himself a healthy portion of good Scots whiskey and still he could not rest. He had given a smoked fish to Angus and Fergus and watched the otters spit, scratch and do mock battle until it was gone.

And still he could not sleep.

He had made plans to move the flocks of sheep, to cull the bull calves, to increase the tillable acreage for the town.

And still he could not sleep . . . because he could not get the image of Adelaide Brown from his mind.

"And the lass believes my house is cold and drafty, does she?" he muttered as he built a roaring great fire in the hearth, filling the room with light. Within moments he was shedding clothes because the house was too hot. The otters were at the door, wanting to go prowl in the cool night.

Ian's thoughts were also hot and cold. Two faces swam in his mind: Fiona, his long-ago fickle sweetheart and Adelaide Brown—someone else's wife.

Fiona had been sweet and mild, and biddable as a summer's day. "And the moment my back was turned she was off to wed Doogal." Her eyes had been pale blue—her hair the color of flax—a tiny thing who needed a man to care for her. "Or at least wanted a man to dance attendance upon her."

Adelaide Brown was tall, rangy, with a spine of steel, a will of iron . . . ''And a tongue that cuts like a knife.''

She had flame-colored hair that was wild and refused to be tamed. There was nothing about Adelaide Brown that could hold a candle to Fiona as far as feminine beauty, and yet . . .

When Ian had looked into Adelaide's eyes, that strange blending of gray and green, like pond water in strong sunlight, he felt dizzy, as if he was falling down a long, steep hill. And when he kissed her—

''Ach, such a woman. Cold and prickly on the outside, but her soul is like a banked fire waiting and wantin' someone to stoke her to life.''

Darroch whined and rested his heavy head in Ian's lap. Absently he stroked the dog. ''It would take only a whisper to fan those embers into an inferno, Darroch. And she is a woman that could fair singe a man with her passion.''

And the hell of it all was that Ian *wanted* to be singed. He wanted to go up in one great ball of fire . . . he wanted to be seared and branded by the glow of her desire.

He wanted another man's wife like he never wanted anything in his life.

Adelaide had touched something in him that he had sworn was dead and buried. He tossed back his second whiskey and stared through the darkness to the town he knew was below. It was his town, his creation—it was going to be the testament to his life's work and sacrifice.

''It is more important than wives and husbands and my own lust-filled thoughts, Darroch. I will do anything to see this town grow and flourish. To leave somethin' of substance when I am but dust.''

But how would he stop his blood from heating and his heart from pounding every time he was near Adelaide Brown?

How could he deny the attraction he felt?

* * *

The next few days passed uneventfully for Addie. There were times when she saw Ian, riding Dow across the plains, the scowl on his bearded face almost as dark as that of his steed. But he never stopped, never made any attempt to speak to her.

Thank God. And because of his distance she had begun to relax a little. She even began to look forward to the trip to the Salish village . . . a little.

Addie spent her days baking, cooking and getting ahead on all her food orders so her time gone would be no hardship on the men who had come to depend upon her. The small tin box where she kept her money was overflowing. Lottie and Mattie appeared to be settling in well. Mattie even recruited her pint-sized nemesis, Scout, to do the milking, feeding and egg gathering at Addie's house while she was away.

On the day before she was to leave, Addie decided it was time to make another show of expecting a letter from her *husband*. Though it galled her to do so, she pretended to be the attentive wife. She delivered her weekly order to John Holcomb, the man who handled the mail, and smiled when he greeted her warmly, pulled out a pocket knife and cut himself a generous piece of the mince pie she had delivered right there on the spot.

"I hope when Miley gets back from Belle Fourche I'll have a letter from my man," Addie said sweetly.

John Holcomb licked his fingers clean and smiled. "For your sake I hope you're right. You know, Mrs. Brown, Ian has been almost as anxious as you have to hear from your husband. He will be right glad when you get word from him."

"What do you mean?" A tingle climbed up her spine.

"Ian is real eager to meet your husband. Several times

he has stopped in to pick up his own mail, and it seems like he always asks about you and your letter.''

"What sort of things does Mr. McTavish want to know?" Now Addie's belly was knotted with fear.

"Common things . . . what he did in Nebraska—have you received any mail from anyone—you know, the kind of things a body asks when he is worried about a friend. Mr. McTavish takes a real personal interest in the people of McTavish Plain.''

"I see," Addie said weakly. And she did see—she saw that Ian McTavish's personal interest was rife with suspicion. She saw that she was standing in quicksand and could sink at any minute.

Addie shifted the lines in her gloved hand and adjusted her bonnet for more shade. She and Gert, each driving a wagon, traveled side by side. Ian was herding the cattle and the sheep behind them so they would not choke on the dust churned up by many hooves. Since daybreak Gert had been asking questions about Addie's husband. It was getting harder and harder for her to paint a picture of the nonexistent man. And the main reason was that every time she tried to conjure up a picture of Mr. Brown, she found herself seeing Mr. McTavish.

"Tell me, Addie, is your husband one of those slat-thin galoots?" Gert's voice carried easily over the distance from wagon to wagon.

Addie sighed. She had hoped she would not be forced to describe him again. Her lies were beginning to stick in her craw and she was getting confused about what she had said so far. "Why do you ask, Gert?"

"Your cooking is becoming a legend in McTavish Plain. I figger your husband has to be fat as a potentate or thin as a rail. I have heard it said that some men do have a hollow leg." Gert laughed. "All the menfolk are just green with envy and the womenfolk . . . well, you know how it is. We're all curious about your husband. And of course your sisters' husbands as well.''

"Yes, Mrs. Brown.'' Ian's velvety voice washed over her. "We are all curious.''

She didn't know when he had ridden up beside the wagons. "Aren't you worried about the cattle straying, Mr. McTavish?''

"Ah, now, Mrs. Brown, would you begrudge me the fine company of yourself and Gert?''

"No, it isn't that . . . exactly.''

"Well, don't fash yourself. Darroch will keep them moving through the draw. When *do* you think your husband will be arriving?'' he asked, keeping to the subject with the same tenacity a hound keeps gnawing on a bone.

"He'll be here soon,'' Addie said with little conviction, regretting once again the necessity of taking this trip.

If only Lottie was not determined to have some grand adventure.

"You don't sound too anxious, honey,'' Gert said with a frown. "Is there anything wrong? Any problem . . . You can talk to me about anythin', you know.''

"No, no, of course not. He will be here soon . . . I am sure of it. Lottie's and Mattie's husbands too. They all will.''

Ian rode back to the cattle while his mind turned over everything Adelaide had said and what Gert had said. A kernel of suspicion had been planted when he kissed Adelaide, and now with each question she answered that seed grew and flourished.

And now Gert had given him something else to think about. Perhaps Adelaide's husband was a worthless drunkard. Maybe she was trying to hide the truth from Ian for as long as possible in order to secure her place in McTavish Plain.

Or maybe her husband was a skirt-chaser. Maybe the lowdown, worthless son of a buck had run off with another woman. Maybe Adelaide did not even know where he was. Her stiff-necked pride would keep her from telling Ian the truth if it was something like that.

"That would be just like her," he muttered. "She would carry the load alone, not wanting anyone to show her pity or kindness."

Especially the likes of me, Ian thought.

Or maybe the bastard mistreated her.

That thought sent a shaft of cold, bitter hatred coursing through Ian.

"If he lays a hand on her . . ." Ian was stunned by the degree of fury he experienced.

There was something strange going on between him and Adelaide Brown, something strange, powerful and growing daily.

She was always there, just at the edge of his consciousness. It was like a banjo tune that refused to be forgotten, or the smell of some long-ago sweet memory that lingered in the mind. She was Adelaide—she was uncommon—and the damning part of it all was that she was not free. She was bound by the laws of man and God to another man.

A man Ian was beginning to hate without ever knowing him.

Ian McTavish clamped his hands tight around Dow's reins and forced himself to concentrate on moving the cattle. Adelaide was not free.

He could do nothing but watch and listen and learn. But when Adelaide's husband arrived, if he did indeed turn out to be a ne'er-do-well, then Ian would deal with him.

"And most harshly, by God, if he is not the kind of man she deserves. I will deal with him most harshly."

* * *

All through the day Gert's good-natured curiosity kept Adelaide's mind busy. She had answered questions about her husband's height, weight, coloring, religion, personal habits and even his boot size. Now, as the sun was waning and night was not far away, Adelaide was weary to the bone, not so much from driving the team, but from trying to keep one step ahead of Gert and remember what she had said.

Suddenly Ian shot by the slow, lumbering wagons and galloped up a hill. "There it is. Just over the rise."

Addie turned to look at the moment a din of whoops and the sound of many pony's hooves filled the shadowy twilight.

"What is that?" Adelaide asked, pulling her team to a halt, the hair on her arms and nape standing on end. She reached for the rifle beside her.

"No need for that. It's the Salish tribe. They have seen Ian. Most of them think the ornery cuss hung the moon . . . 'course, most of us in the town think so too, though we'd not want him to know it." Gert winked and clucked her tongue at the team.

Addie gulped down her terror. A small band of warriors, looking fierce and forbidding as anything Addie might have imagined, rode over the rise. They circled the cattle and, with all the finesse and organization of excited children, finally drove them into a pen formed of living trees and scrub brush lashed together with strips of rawhide. Women and children came pouring from the trees in a living wave, pointing and laughing. They brought empty baskets to the wagons and began to inspect the goods that had been sent by the townsfolk. Bolts of cloth, blankets and Addie's golden loaves and all the things she had baked were soon being split up into various baskets.

And behind the gabbling group, sitting regal as a princess on an ox-blood pinto mare, was a young woman with silken hair and snapping black eyes. Suddenly she kicked her pony and flew beyond the warriors. When the Indian maiden was abreast of Ian she launched herself into his arms, her mare veering off at the last minute.

Addie's mouth dropped open. She had never witnessed such wild abandon or such open sensuality. Ian had no choice but to catch the woman or be knocked from his saddle.

Dow, the fractious stallion, took the rough use with a snort and halfhearted rear, which only served to settle the maiden more firmly into Ian's arms. She nuzzled his bearded face and kissed his neck, dipping her head low to the V of his laced-up buckskin shirt.

"Easy, now, lass," he said with a throaty chuckle. "You'll have us both unseated if you keep that up."

A cold, hollow pain lodged itself beneath Addie's breast. She didn't like Ian. She wanted him to leave her alone . . . but at the same time she wanted to yank the woman from his lap. It wasn't right that she should be there, in his arms, making him smile. . . . It wasn't right.

"Come along, Addie," Gert said. "Let's leave Grass Singing to deal with Ian while we see to the rest of these supplies."

"Yes, of course," Addie agreed with a rusty catch in her voice.

"Dinna go, Mrs. Brown, Gert," Ian yelled. "I'll be helping with the unloading." Ian brought Dow alongside the wagon. Grass Singing looked at Addie with pure hatred in her dark eyes.

"McTavish . . . stay me," she said with a pouty pursing of her full bottom lip.

"You seem to have your hands quite full as it is, Mr. McTavish. Gert and I can manage, I am sure." Addie snapped the lines smartly on the team's rumps and headed into the expanse of tepees, while a thick, hot lump formed in the back of her throat.

She wasn't jealous . . . she wasn't.

Night was full upon the village by the time the supplies were unloaded. Addie was hesitant and apprehensive around the savages, not knowing what to expect and causing a spate of unintelligible chatter when they saw her hair.

They crowded around her, touching the fiery locks until her heart was beating hard and fast. Gert laughed.

"Addie, you'll have no peace until you divert their attention. Give some of 'em what you have stashed under your wagon seat."

Addie reached under the buckboard seat and brought out the cloth. She peeled back the corners and unveiled a pile of piecrust sticks. Long the favorite of Lottie and Mattie, she had made up a batch, baked golden brown, slathered with sugar and cinnamon and packed them beneath the wagon seat, thinking to give them to the children of the tribe. But the crispy strips were quickly disappearing, snatched by young and old alike.

Addie was surrounded by laughing, chattering children and smiling warriors with bare chests and shrewd eyes.

"What they say is true, I reckon." Gert laughed.

"What do you mean, Gert?" Addie asked, barely keeping her feet under her as she was jostled while one hand after another shot forward for a stick.

"You've heard the old saw: The way to the heart is through the stomach."

Several times a dark hand went not for the pastry but for Addie's hair, her coloring almost as fascinating as the treats.

"You'd best be careful, Addie girl. That red hair of

yours is causing a stir. I think it's time to find Ian and
see what can be done for our sleeping arrangements—
before you get carried off and some brave starts offering
Ian ponies for your hand in marriage,'' Gert said, shaking
the dust from her ruffled calico skirts.

Addie smiled weakly, but she couldn't find the same
humor in the situation that Gert did. ''Do we have to
bother Mr. McTavish?''

''He would be plumb offended if we didn't let him
take charge of us! You know how men are . . . they got
to feel like we need them or they turn plumb cantankerous.'' Gert was already striding away, toward a large
tepee painted with hunting scenes on the outside. The door
flap was open. Addie could see figures inside, silhouetted
against a central fire.

Ian sat cross-legged just like several other men with
dark, weathered faces. When he saw Gert he rose in one
smooth, fluid motion and stepped outside.

The moment he cleared the tepee the beautiful Indian
maiden appeared like smoke on the wind. She touched
Ian's arm and gazed up at him.

Addie couldn't stand to think of Ian—or the beautiful
black-eyed woman who had flown into his lap with complete abandon. She stood back while Gert spoke with Ian.

''We have a tepee all to ourselves, it seems. Come on,
let's me and you get some shut-eye,'' Gert said when she
returned, but Addie only half heard her. She watched as
the Indian girl took hold of Ian's wrist and tugged at him.

''Who knows, maybe tonight Grass Singing will convince Ian to share her tepee. Lord knows she's been trying
long enough,'' Gert added with a shake of her head.
''Maybe she has finally worn him down.''

Addie turned away. She could not allow herself to think
of Ian . . . or of where he might be going . . . or of where
he might be sleeping tonight.

                               *   *   *

Gert went to the tepee after giving Addie directions on which one it was. Addie went to the stream that ran beside the village and washed her face and hands in the icy water.

Still her eyes burned with unshed tears.

"Silly . . . just plain silly. The man is a rogue. He has probably got half a dozen women in this village and others," Addie told herself harshly . . . but it didn't lessen the tight pain in her heart or shrink the lump in her throat.

She heeded the call of nature and stood staring at the shimmering water for a while. Finally, when she had regained some control of her emotions, she headed back to the village. But the landscape seemed strange, unrecognizable.

It took Addie a moment to realize that the fires had all gone out. Now only glowing embers sparked in the night. She turned in a circle, trying to decide which tepee Gert had pointed out.

But they all looked the same.

She was bewildered, unable to decided which way to go, when a trio of young girls appeared. The girls looked at Addie and then spoke to her in a spate of Salish language.

Addie gestured, making a pillow of her hands. "I don't understand." She laughed nervously when they frowned and shook their heads. Thinking that she could gesture in a way they would understand, she put her palms together and leaned her cheek against her hand, closing her eyes.

The girls shook their heads.

"Sleep?" Addie repeated the gesture. "Where can I sleep?"

The tallest of the three girls, who couldn't have been much over seven, suddenly smiled. She grabbed Addie's hand and pulled her toward a tepee.

Was it the one Gert had indicated?

"Is this my sleeping place?" Addie asked.

The girl gestured for Addie to go inside.

Addie glanced around at the other tepees. They all looked the same . . . except for the one where she had seen Ian with the other men. She could go ask, but what if Ian was not there. . . . What if he was with Grass Singing? A sharp pain cut through her heart at that thought. And she didn't understand why—didn't want to think about why she felt as she did.

Addie raised the door flap and ducked inside. The area was awash in shadow from a very small fire, but the tepee was warm.

"Are you here to help me warm my blankets?" A rich, masculine voice asked from the shadows.

Addie whirled around. For a moment she thought she imagined the voice . . . but she saw movement, and then she saw *him*.

He was tall, wide shouldered and naked as the day God made him. And she realized with a little catch of breath that she had hoped it was Ian McTavish . . . but it was not Ian who looked her up and down in surprise.

Chapter Ten

"I must thank Chief Broken Ax for his hospitality," the naked man said. "He told me I would have something special, but I never expected . . ."

"Who are you?" Addie croaked, stumbling backward over a pile of furs. She found herself on her backside, looking up at her first view of an unclothed man.

The angle and the fact that he made no move to hide himself only seemed to draw her eyes to his . . . parts.

He laughed, a throaty sound of male arrogance that made her cheeks burn more than they already did. "I am Aleck—Aleck Bowen, and who are you?"

The man was freshly shaved—freshly bathed, from the look of him. Water still dripped from the ends of hair that appeared to be the color of darkening corn silk.

"I . . . my name is Addie," she squeaked, wishing he would move back so she could get up. If she attempted to now, she would end up nose to . . . well, she couldn't move until he did.

"How long have you been with the Salish?" he asked

in a comfortable, easy manner that indicated he felt no discomfort whatsoever in their circumstance.

"Been with the Salish?" He had a long, red scar that ran from collarbone to pelvic bone, right near his . . .

She jerked her eyes upward, but not before she saw his *parts* had begun to grow and thicken.

Did they all do that? Or was it some malady peculiar only to him?

"I haven't been down to winter with them for a while, not since old Broken Ax quit going to the coast for the cold months. He has made a lot of changes—but you gotta be the best one of 'em. Have you been sold off to a buck, or were you captured?"

His questions made no sense to Addie. She couldn't think, couldn't speak with him looking at her and with her sprawled back on the pile of furs.

The man—Aleck—smiled, displaying even white teeth and a single dimple. Then suddenly he was bending down on one knee. He reached out and stroked her cheek with his index finger. She shrank back, wondering if she should scream or make a dash for the opening. Of course her dash would have to consist of a most unladylike crawl out the flap.

"I think there is some misunderstanding. You see, I was looking for a tepee—" Addie stammered.

"Well, you found the right one, sugar." Quick as a snake striking, he reached out. His hand cupped behind her head. His bare arms were like iron as he drew her forward. She braced herself for the kiss she knew was coming.

"Let the lass go, unless you wish to draw back a bloody stub where your hand used to be."

Ian's voice was the most wonderful sound Addie had ever heard. She couldn't see him from her position on the furs, but she felt his presence, his strength—*him*.

"Ian," Aleck said without releasing his hold on Addie.

"Broken Ax has just one surprise after another. Look what he sent to warm my blankets."

"He dinna send her, you fool. Like as not she is lost." Ian glowered down at Addie, and she felt her cheeks burning again. "Get up, woman. Have you no shame?"

"Well, I can't very well get up with this . . . this *man* leaning over me!" She was humiliated and confused and too tired to be subjected to a dose of Ian McTavish's blustery tongue right now.

"You two know each other?" Aleck asked, leaning back on his haunches.

"Aye, we know one another. Now get back, and for pity sake, cover yourself. We could use your er . . . *twig* for a lodgepole if it continues to grow," Ian said in disgust.

Aleck chuckled proudly. Addie fought the urge to look at the part of Aleck's anatomy she knew Ian was referring to. But as if an imp had taken possession of her soul, her disobedient eyes did slide in that direction. She had never imagined that a man could be so big . . . so hard . . . so like a stallion.

Was Ian's body like that? Were his private parts so alive, so *threatening?* And even though it was wrong and improper, she thought of Ian naked and like *that.* She tried to remove the image of Ian from her mind, but it would not be banished. Though it was this stranger who had cupped his hand behind her head, it had been Ian McTavish's touch Addie yearned for.

Unbidden pictures of him holding Grass Singing once more flitted into her mind.

She *was* jealous. She was jealous of Ian McTavish, the arrogant, opinionated, *dangerous* Ian. The sickening realization cut her deep—left her raw inside.

"Let her up, Aleck," Ian said once more. "I dinna want you to make more of an ass of yourself than you already have. She is a married woman."

Aleck snorted. "I don't believe it. You are just saying that to have her for yourself."

"She lives in my town." Ian's eyes were bright and hard. His hands flexed at his sides. Addie had the impression that he wanted very much to crush something with those callused hands.

She shivered.

"You are frightening the lass, Aleck. Now do as I say." Ian's voice dropped to a low, threatening timbre.

"Tsk. If anyone is frightening this beautiful woman, 'tis you, with your gloomy words and hairy face." Aleck finally rose to his feet and took a step away from Addie. "Do you never scrape it? I've seen grizes with less fur on their face."

Ian cocked a brow. "You always were a talker, Aleck."

Ian took two long strides and hit Aleck in the face with a doubled fist. As the tall, naked man slid to a pile of buffalo robes, Ian looked down at Addie and shrugged.

"The man has a jaw fragile as glass . . . always had." He leaned near, very near, to help her to her feet. His warm, moist breathe was soothing—and disturbing. He had one hand around her waist. Then, as if it was the most natural thing in the world, Ian bent his head and kissed her—hard.

She grabbed his shoulders, clung to him, trying in vain to fight the dizzying effects of his kiss. His beard was soft against her face. She felt his chest, warm and hard against her breasts. Her nipples hardened. She arched against him.

And then it was over.

He raised his head, dragging in long draughts of air. Slowly, sensuously, he rubbed the pad of his wide thumb over Addie's bottom lip.

"I canna keep doing this, lass. You are a proper married woman, but you have a naked man at your feet and another stealing your kisses. This is why I dinna allow unmarried women in my town. Can you imagine what would happen if you were *not* wed? Likely Aleck and I both would be tossing up your skirts—or killing each other for the privilege.''

Addie slapped him. She slapped him so hard that her elbow hurt from the impact. Fury powered her tongue as she glared at Ian.

''No man could *toss up my skirts* unless I wanted it. And the last two men on earth I would ever want are you and him. Don't ever lay hands on me again, Ian McTavish.'' And then, with all the dignity she could muster, she gingerly picked up her skirts, stepped over Aleck's naked body and went into the crisp night air to find the right tepee.

''I'm sorry, Grass Singing, I canna do it,'' Ian said softly, rubbing his hand over the Indian woman's back.

''But you have no wife . . . no woman,'' she purred, rubbing her body sinuously over his.

But he simply wasn't interested. It amazed him—it confused him—it even disgusted him, but the fact was, he didn't have any desire to bed Grass Singing. All he could think of was Adelaide Brown, *Mrs. Brown,* with her flashing eyes and stiff neck. She was most beautiful when she was in a raging temper, and Ian seemed to be able to put her there with no effort at all. She was an unlikely siren, but his body and his mind had succumbed to her song.

He was falling in love with a married woman.

Ian paced back and forth in front of the small fire at the edge of the village. He was aware of Grass Singing's eyes, roaming over his body. Unfortunately, it did nothing to make him randy.

Hell, it would be for the best if he just accepted her invitation. Lord knew she had been after him long enough.

But he wasn't interested. She was beautiful, no denying that . . . but the only woman to capture more than his passing fancy since Fiona had broken his heart was Adelaide Brown.

"I will sleep in the unmarried men's tepee," he said as he turned to face her. "There can be nothing between us, lass. I am not the man for you."

"It is the white woman with the hair of fire that freezes your body and heart tonight," Grass Singing accused.

"No, Grass Singing, it is not." But Ian was lying.

It was Adelaide Brown, morning, noon and most of all at night. His body reacted only to her . . . his eyes sought her out . . . his hands itched to touch her.

He strode toward the bachelors' tent feeling the pinch of his buckskin breeches, cursing himself as a blatherskite and worse.

"I am bound to hell for coveting another man's wife," Ian snarled in disgust as he flipped open the door flap and stepped over a sleeping man.

"Addie, you look like you been rode hard and put up wet. I swan, you tossed and turned like you had chiggers in your bed last night," Gert said with a yawn.

Addie pulled her bonnet tight and tied the limp strings beneath her chin. She had spent most of the night thinking about what had happened. "Did I keep you awake?"

"I've slept better." Gert yawned again.

The night had been long. One unanswerable question had run through Addie's head like a meandering stream.

What would have happened if it had been Ian waiting naked in that tepee?

Though she would have preferred to deny it, Addie had the uncomfortable fear that if it had been Ian, she might not have left.

And that frightened her to the marrow of her bones.

She was falling under some sort of spell when it came to Ian McTavish. Even when he was crude and insulting and talked about someone tossing up her skirts, there was a trilling excitement that flashed through her.

Addie hoped to avoid both Ian and Aleck for as long as possible, while she sorted out her feelings and came to grips with this peculiar weakness where he was concerned. But fate seemed to be conspiring against her, because when she turned around she saw they were both walking straight toward her.

"Mornin', ma'am," Aleck said cheerfully. There didn't appear to be so much as an ounce of remorse or embarrassment in him.

"Likely she doesna recognize you with your truis on," Ian snapped.

"And I am surprised anybody can recognize you with all that brush on your face," Aleck said with a smile, striding past Ian and coming to stand directly in front of Addie.

"How is your jaw?" Ian quipped. "I could give it another adjustment if you'd like."

Aleck never bothered to look at Ian, but his face colored slightly. "We never had a proper introduction last night."

He picked up Addie's hand and brought it near his lips. She had only heard of men doing such foolish things in Mattie's books.

"Now dinna start with your fine airs and graces," Ian growled as he straightened. "And dinna start regaling her with tales of your gentle life in Tennessee before you came west. Half of what you say is lies anyway."

"Ian, if you aren't nice to me, I swear I will take you up on that offer you made years ago," Aleck threatened.

"And just what offer would that be?" Ian narrowed his eyes and met Aleck's teasing gaze.

"To come share your home in McTavish Plain. You said there would always be a room for me."

"You blatherskite! I dinna make any such offer," Ian denied.

"Ah, but you did. Right after I sewed up that wound you got from that bear."

Ian's face was a mask of emotion. Addie knew the moment he remembered.

"So I did, but since you havna taken me up on the offer, I doubt you'll be doin' so now."

"Now that you have such lovely neighbors, I may just do it." Aleck grinned wider.

"In a pig's eye! Aleck Bowen, dinna be trifling with me or the women in my town."

Addie glared at him, but he shrugged and then began busying himself with hitching the horses and checking their traces. Ian and Aleck were like two dogs snarling over a bone. And if that was true, then she was the bone! The thought was sobering, to say the least.

"Can you stop arguing? I want to get back home." Addie jerked her hand free of Aleck's light grip.

"As you say, lass." Ian narrowed his eyes and watched her for a minute. She could almost feel the speculation in his gaze.

Addie was relieved the letter had not come. In fact, she offered up a fervent prayer to the heavens that it would never come. Suddenly her faceless, pretend husband seemed to be all that stood between her and a life of ruin.

Aleck and Ian moved away, saying their farewells to the chief. As Addie prepared to climb into the wagon, Grass Singing appeared silently. She leveled a gaze at Addie that was pure loathing, and then she said, "You go."

"Yes, I am going," Addie said uneasily. There was something almost threatening about the way the woman stared at her.

"No . . . you go from McTavish town. He no want you.

He no like you. He say to me that he make you go. You go now. He want you to leave his town.''

Addie stiffened. Someone had put words to her own worst fears. Ian McTavish *was* determined to drive her out. He had been watching her. And, she realized with a jolt, he had been taking liberties with her in order to shame her into leaving. And when she was gone . . . what would happen to Mattie and Lottie?

Grass Singing moved away, but not before she repeated one more time, ''McTavish no want you in his town.''

The trip back to McTavish Plain was twice as quick and twice as silent. Gert seemed to sense that Addie was in no mood to chatter, or perhaps she was simply too tired to talk. Ian rode between the two wagons, with Darroch at his side since there were no cattle to drive. Several times Addie glanced at him to find him scowling darkly. And each time he did, Grass Singing's words echoed in her brain.

What was she going to do?

Maybe the letter was lost.

Maybe she and her sisters could secretly post another letter and somehow get it to Belle Fourche without anyone knowing. Addie's pretend husband could write that he'd been ill . . . taken a fever and was not able to travel . . . maybe not until spring . . . or even longer than that. Addie had to find a way to remain in McTavish Plain . . . for her sisters' sakes.

When near to sundown they pulled into town, they were greeted as if they had been gone for weeks instead of days. Her sisters were at the head of the crowd.

''Oh, Addie, it is so good to see you. How was it?

Were the Indians fierce?'' Lottie's face was alive with enthusiastic curiosity.

"Addie, will you come visit my classroom tomorrow and relate your tales to my students?'' Mattie asked.

"I just want to go home and sleep in my own bed,'' Addie whispered miserably. Miley Thompson took the team from her as soon as she jumped down from the wagon.

"You look all tuckered out, Mrs. Brown. I'll do the unhitching for you.'' He smiled in understanding. ''Me and my old woman are used to such.'' He grinned affectionately at Gert as he spoke. Addie saw a real bond of love between them. A bone-deep loneliness settled over her.

How did one find a love like that?

"Mrs. Brown, I am right glad to see you,'' John Holcomb said, separating himself from the crowd. ''You've got mail and I know how itchy you been to get word from your husband.''

Addie's belly dropped to the level of her boots. But when Ian reined in Dow and dismounted nearby, her heart followed it right to the dusty street.

"Mail?'' Addie said weakly. She felt Ian's eyes upon her.

"Uh-huh. Miley brought it from Belle Fourche. I know how you've been waiting to get a letter. Got it right here in my vest pocket.'' And with that he drew out an envelope and placed it in Addie's trembling hands. ''I'll bet it is a letter from your husband—don'cha think?''

But Addie knew what it was. It was the announcement of her ruin. For when she opened the letter and declared herself a widow, Ian McTavish would pounce on her like a cat on a mouse. He would throw her out of McTavish Plain . . . just as Grass Singing had said.

Chapter Eleven

"Open it, Addie," Lottie encouraged. "Open it now so we can all hear what it says." She punctuated her last sentence with an elbow to Addie's ribs.

Addie looked at her sister, wishing for all the world she would lose her voice. Didn't she understand? But, no, how could she? All Addie had talked about was this damnable letter . . . how she wanted it to come . . . how she wouldn't be happy until she had it in her hands. Well, now here it was.

An old saw about being careful what you wished for suddenly popped into her head. Well, Addie had sure gotten her wish!

"Why dinna you read it now, Mrs. Brown? We all have been waiting to hear word of your man." Ian's words drew Addie's gaze to his face. His blue eyes were as deep and unreadable as a high mountain lake, his bearded jaw set in such a way that she knew to argue would be pointless.

She swallowed hard and ripped open the envelope while

Mattie and Lottie crowded closer. They had no way of knowing it would only be a matter of minutes now before Addie would be packing her things and leaving McTavish Plain for good—and if they were lucky, it would only be her! The way Ian McTavish was staring at her, she couldn't imagine him waiting too much longer before he sent Mattie and Lottie on their way, as well.

Addie knew the words inside the folded paper; she had them memorized by heart. She could feel the tension in her sisters as they waited in front of her.

"What does it say, Addie?" Lottie asked with an innocent smile.

"Yes, Addie. What news of your husband?" Mattie managed complete sincerity. "Is he hale and hearty?"

Addie swallowed hard. She never would've believed her sisters had such a deep capacity for deceit. Of course, her own ability to spin a yarn had been a bit of a shock as well.

If only there were some way to let her sisters know the dread she felt now that the letter had arrived. But with half the town crowded round her, she had no opportunity to let them know of her change of heart—or that Ian McTavish was laying for her . . . just waiting for an excuse to boot her out of town.

Addie looked up. Ian was standing right behind her siblings. A head and a half taller than her sisters, his view was unobstructed . . . his eyes unblinking as he waited and watched.

"Will he be arriving soon, Mrs. Brown?" Ian inquired in that rough purr that made her stomach flip-flop, though she told herself it was *just* a *voice* and he was only a man.

Addie couldn't delay the inevitable any longer. With trembling fingers she unfolded the sheet of paper . . . the sheet on which she had composed the terse explanation of her pretend husband's death.

She glanced up.

Ian was studying her with narrowed eyes. Grass Singing's words ran through Addie's head like a curse. Would Ian order her packed and gone by sundown? He was not a cruel man, she knew, but he was stubborn and he lived by his own rules. His thrice damned rules that had put her in this mess.

"Read it, Addie," Lottie urged again.

Lowering her head, Addie stared at the paper and pretended to read. "It . . . it is not from my husband." Her voice was barely a whisper. She did not have to fake sadness and regret because the thought of leaving McTavish Plain . . . of leaving her *sisters* in McTavish Plain, filled her with sorrow.

"My husband has had an accident."

"Is he bad hurt?" Gert asked, her concern sending an arrow of guilt through Addie's heart. True, faithful, motherly Gert, another person Addie had deceived . . . was about to deceive even more.

"He . . . he . . . is dead."

"Dead?" A dozen voices repeated in chorus.

In a wash of unshed tears, she saw the townspeople coming close to her like a living tide of humanity. She saw their round eyes, faces pinched with concern. The crushing weight of her own guilt bore down heavy when she looked at those kind faces.

Why had she ever lied? Why had she come here to this perfect little town to live among perfect people who cared?

"Oh, ma'am, I'd like to offer my deepest sympathy," John Holcomb said, wringing his long-fingered hands together.

"That's right, Mrs. Brown. We're awful sorry," echoed several men.

Addie nodded in the direction of their voices, but she couldn't really see them through the tears in her eyes. Real tears for all the wrong reasons.

It was as if her heart were being ripped from her breast with anguish—not over the passing of a pretend husband but because of the generosity of these people and her own sins.

"Well, now, if this doesn't just paint the barn red," Gus Gruberman said.

Addie had seen him earlier, his bald pate shining as if he had waxed it.

"What do you mean, Gus?" Miley Thompson asked in a husky whisper.

"This puts a real knot in the milk-cow's tail—don't it, Ian?" Gus rubbed his pointed chin thoughtfully.

Addie sniffed and listened.

"I dinna ken what you mean, Gus." Ian hadn't been able to think, had barely been able to drag breath into his body since Adelaide had read her letter.

She was a widow . . . she wasn't anybody's wife anymore. God . . . or perhaps all the demons of Hades had read his darkest thoughts. He had wanted Adelaide free.

Now she was. *Now she was free.*

"Well, if she ain't no married woman, she cain't stay," Gus said simply.

Ian's gut contracted painfully when he registered Gus's voice. All his secret hopes plummeted to earth. His skin felt too small for his bones. "What?"

"It's your own rule, Ian," Gus reminded him smugly. "You never have had a single woman in McTavish Plain. Can't start changing the rules now, much as I like Mrs. Brown."

The whole town quieted. A strange, taut silence made Ian's belly twist.

"Before the first wagons arrived in McTavish Plain, you said no single women. Now Mrs. Brown is mighty single. Free as a bird, you might say."

"That she is," Ian agreed softly. His world was turning topsy-turvy. How could it be that the very obstacle he had wanted removed was going to be the cause of his losing his Adelaide? He couldn't let her leave town.

It was too much. He wanted to shout that he had changed his mind . . . that the rule was foolish. But all he could do was stand there with his heart in his throat while Gus rattled on and on, repeating every stupid thing Ian had ever said.

"Ian McTavish, you cannot mean to turn her out," Gert said, her hands on her hips and fire in her eyes. "I've known you to be a mule-headed, cantankerous galoot, but you can't be so cruel."

"Mr. McTavish would never do such a thing . . . ," the Reverend Horace Miller challenged, but it was obvious by his pale face and wide eyes, he truly had no confidence that Addie would not be riding out of town soon.

"Of course he wouldn't," Nate Pearson agreed.

"Mr. McTavish, you can't." Mattie's eyes were wide and awash with tears. "Addie . . . do something."

"What would you like me to do, Matilda?" Addie asked numbly. There was no use in fighting and she sure as shooting wasn't going to beg Ian McTavish, not after what Grass Singing had told her. She thought of the times he had kissed her. Were those kisses meant to shame and humiliate? Did he get even more satisfaction by her response to him?

"I know what we can do so's Ian's consarn rule will stand *and* we can keep Mrs. Brown," Miley Thompson bellowed. "We have more'n enuff single men here in town . . . heck, she's been feeding most of 'em already. Mrs. Brown can find herself a new husband from the men here. There are a few who are half good-looking when they get cleaned up proper and shave and whatnot. She wouldn't *stay* single, least ways not for long."

"Oh, yes, Mr. McTavish, give Addie a chance to find a new husband soon," Lottie piped up.

"Now hold on . . . ," Addie choked out. "What about

a respectable time of mourning? After all, we are talking about my *husband* dying.'' Her impulsive sisters had once again put the cart before the horse and Addie was going to be left to drag along behind unless she did something—and fast.

Ian looked down on Addie with such intensity that the rest of what she was going to stay stuck in the back of her throat. When he was near like this she had trouble breathing . . . thinking. She found herself mesmerized by his eyes and the force of his personality.

''And what length of time would you consider a respectable mourning period, Mrs. Brown?'' he asked bluntly.

''A year . . . at least,'' she stammered, wishing she did not feel the heat and strength of his body. How easy it would be to lean into him—to take some of that latent strength for her own—to allow him to support her—to make the hard decisions.

But that was about as likely as hell freezing over. Grass Singing had told her how he felt. Addie straightened her spine and planted her feet.

''And during that time you would be here in McTavish Plain?'' Ian's eyes roamed over her face.

''Well, of course—'' She tried not to notice how blue they were today . . . how bottomless and unreadable.

''You would be a single woman.''

''Yes, Mr. McTavish, that would be the case,'' Addie snapped, hating herself for wishing he would kiss her again . . . for caring what Grass Singing had said. For feeling this terrible draw for a man who didn't even *like* her.

''There is merit in what Miley says, Mrs. Brown. The canny man has found the solution for both our . . . problems.''

The way he lingered on that word made her belly contract. Was she no more than a problem to be solved or eliminated?

"I'll allow you to pick a husband from the men in McTavish Plain."

Addie didn't know whether to laugh or scream. On the one hand, she resented Ian's arrogance in *allowing* her anything, but a year's mourning would give her a year in which to settle in. Surely by the end of that year Ian would have changed his mind or found someone he disliked more than her.

"If you canna or wilna pick a man, then you must repay all the money spent to bring you here and you must leave."

"What?" Addie asked, jerked back to harsh reality by his thrifty Scots nature. The people around her mumbled, shuffled their feet and whispered among themselves.

Ian glowered them into silence and continued. "Or you must agree to let *me* pick a man to be your husband."

"You?" Addie nearly choked. Ian was willing to pick her a husband? And what kind of a man would he choose? Grass Singing's words chimed once again through her memory. "*You want to pick a husband for me?*"

He stepped nearer. He was so close, she could see the tiny flecks of gold in the blue of his eyes and the glint of satisfaction. The scent of fresh air and maleness clung to him. She was overwhelmed by him ... by his size, his strength ... by *him*. And she did not *want* to be.

"You have the right of it," Ian said.

"I think in a year's time I can—"

He shook his head back and forth, the long hair whispering on the collar of his buckskin shirt. "I canna let you stay here for a year as a single woman," Ian interrupted. "It would be against my rule. You have one month, Mrs. Brown."

His words raised chills upon her spine. In one month

the winter would be hard upon McTavish Plain. Addie felt dizzy, light-headed.

"In one month pick a new husband, or I'll do it for you."

Ian watched Adelaide's eyes roll up in her head and knew she was going to pass out. He bent and caught her in his arms before she hit the ground.

"Mercy! The shock of her husband's death and all this blather about leaving was just too much for the little thing!" Gert scowled and hit Ian on the shoulder with her open hand. "Ian, I am plumb shamed by you putting Addie through all this marrying nonsense at a time like this. When she should have the peace to mourn for her dead husband you are talking about picking a replacement. The man ain't hardly cold in his grave—wherever that may be."

"It ain't decent," Miley added as he put an arm around Gert's shoulder. "Ain't decent a'tall."

"Oh, poor, poor, Addie," her sister, Matilda Smith, said. Ian saw her flick a glance at her sister, Mrs. Rosswarne. There was something in her eyes . . . something that made Ian slightly uneasy as he stood there holding Adelaide.

"I canna change what has happened or bring back her husband. We have rules in McTavish Plain and they must be abided by. But right now I am taking the lass home."

The crowd was glaring at him, the look in the townspeople's eyes accusing and judgmental. They could not know how much Ian hated himself at this moment.

He cared for Adelaide and he had hurt her. But it had been the only way he could think of to keep her in town—and he couldn't agree to a year. He would go mad if he had to sit and watch her . . . wait for her for a year. Hell, he had barely managed to keep his hands off her when she *was* married. It didn't sit well with him, but that was the truth of the matter.

"Do you need any help?" Gus asked, a wide smile wreathing his face. Ian glanced around. Gus was not the only one grinning. John, Hank and a few other single men were smiling like skunks in a henhouse.

Single men? Smiling?

The realization hit Ian like a fist to the jaw. The fools intended to court Adelaide—*his Adelaide*. What if she did take a liking to one of them? What if she decided to marry one of *them* before Ian could persuade her that *he* was the right man for her?

He wouldn't have it! She was his. She had been his since the first kiss—only he hadn't known it then . . . and she didn't know it now. But that was a small matter. With a little time he could set things to rights with her.

Ian could win her . . . if he had the time and the privacy.

He was going to win her! He had to.

"I am taking her home," he repeated, hoping that the townspeople would go to their homes, to talk about him over their fires, to condemn him, but at least to leave him alone with Adelaide.

They didn't.

They fell into step behind him. Their voices were like an indicting chant. What a fine woman Adelaide was, and how she deserved better.

As if he dinna know it!

"I can manage the lass fine," he said over his shoulder. "There is no need for you to come along. I can care for her . . . alone."

"Oh, we know you can, Ian, but we'd kind of like to be around . . . you know, when she wakes," Gus Gruberman said with a wink. "Might give one of us the inside track. Are you sure you don't want me to take her?"

"No, you old fool, I dinna want you to *take* her," Ian grumbled. He shifted Adelaide in his arms. Her sisters were right behind him, practically walking up on his heels.

He wanted them to go away. He wished that half his

town weren't already making plans to court Adelaide Brown. But most of all he wished that Adelaide liked him a little better.

Addie came awake with a start. She had been caught in the most terrible nightmare. . . . She dreamed she had gotten the letter and the whole town—

"Are you with us again, lass?" Ian was standing beside her bed along with most of the town. Crowded into her bedroom, they stared at her with sympathy in their faces.

"It wasn't a nightmare," Addie moaned. "The letter . . ."

"Aye, lass, you got a letter. You are a widow," Ian said bluntly.

Gus, Miley, Gert and Mrs. Miller were standing around the bed. Addie wanted to crawl under it and hide.

She could perish from shame. She was a liar, she was a cheat. And when she looked into Ian McTavish's cool blue eyes, she was afraid he knew her for what she was.

"Have a sip of whiskey, lass. It will steady your nerves." He thrust a cup into her hands, watching her with those unnerving eyes of his, harder and bluer than a wintry sky.

"I think, Mr. McTavish, it will take more than a little whiskey to steady my nerves."

Chapter Twelve

"Ian! How could you?" Gert said, her face grim. "Only a man with a cold, hard heart would do such a thing to a woman in mourning. One month . . . why, it is positively un-Christian!"

Gert had managed to get Ian alone in the corner of Adelaide's bedroom. She was spitting at him like a wild cat, and for one moment he thought he might reach out and grab his ear like she would a wayward child.

"I have my reasons, Gert," Ian finally said in his own defense.

"Reasons! Reasons, indeed. You hurt her, Ian, you cut her deep."

And as Ian studied Adelaide's face, he knew it was true. Could he mend that much hurt in a month?

"Miss Addie, will you go to the Sunday social with me?"

"Miss Addie, could you sit by me at the Cromarties' anniversary dinner?"

"Miss Addie, the harvest dance and social is in three weeks. Will you save a dance for me?"

Ian was sick of it. Morning, noon and night it was all he heard. Miss Addie this . . . Miss Addie that . . . and he was no nearer to charming the lass into marrying him than he had been a week ago, when that damnable letter came.

One week gone, three left. Three short weeks to change a woman's mind.

Could it be done? Was it even possible?

How did a man who had lived rough carving out a place for people to live woo a woman as fine as Adelaide? Especially when most of the town, including Adelaide herself, glared at him like he had sprouted horns and grown one cloven hoof.

"I should've given her more time," he mumbled miserably. "But I canna risk some other man winning her."

He had let his wild Scots nature take control of his tongue. And now he was stuck with the consequences of his actions. But he had managed to keep Adelaide in town, in spite of his own rules about unmarried women, though the way he had managed it also forced Adelaide to allow every man jack who didn't have a wife pay her court. They were sparking her with all the frenzy of a swarm of bees after a new queen.

"Damn. For every foot I go forward, I get knocked back two."

It was a damned sorry position to be in.

Ian went from fits of furious jealousy to blue melancholia, but he couldn't find a way out of the maze he had created.

"Adelaide had little reason to like me and even less, now that I acted like a mule-headed fool with no compassion for her loss."

It seemed Ian could only follow like a lovesick pup and feel the bitter sweep of jealousy each time she smiled at one of her suitors. Something drastic was going to have to be done. But he didn't know how to mend the rift between them.

And so it was one morning that Ian was sitting in front of Gus Gruberman's mercantile watching Joe Christian carrying Addie's basket up the street, admiring the way the sun brought out the freckles on her nose, and at the same time his gut was burning with jealousy because he was not beside her.

Ian managed to keep his temper in check and his chair tipped back on two legs, acting calm as a summer's eve while he scratched Darroch's head.

But inside he was a raging tempest.

Adelaide was smiling at Joe. *Smiling.* Hell, it seemed as if she smiled at every bachelor in town—except him. In his haste to find a way around his damnable rule, he had tarred himself with a black brush.

" 'Morning, Ian," Joe greeted him with the same frosty reserve all the townspeople had displayed since the day the letter arrived.

" 'Morning, Joe. Mrs. Brown, you are looking verra well today." Ian's gaze only flicked over Adelaide, but he saw enough to cause his breath to lodge in his chest. She had blossomed during her mourning. Today her hair was caught up in a black ribbon, the rusty curls hanging down her delicate nape in soft ringlets.

Was it because he had forced her to think of other men as husbands? Was that what had brought about this change in her? It took all his willpower to keep from pulling her into his arms.

Ian swallowed hard. He wanted to touch her neck, he wanted to sip her skin and feather kisses over her throat and down her shoulders.

"Fine clear autumn weather we're having," Joe said awkwardly. There was a taut suspense between the trio.

Ian grunted. "Looks like snow to me."

Adelaide's black dress was plain, proper and the most seductive attire Ian had ever seen. She was buttoned up tight from the curve of her jaw to the toes of her shoes. It seemed her necklines got higher and her sleeves longer, but Ian had seen the fire in her eyes—knew it burned there now, just waiting to be fanned into a flame. He wanted to be the man that ignited that simmering burn.

He wanted Joe to go away.

"Is the sawmill running itself?" Ian narrowed his eyes at Joe. He let his chair tip forward until the front legs hit the wooden stoop with a thud.

Adelaide jumped. It fueled his frustration and loosened his tongue to know *he* made her so jumpy. The only person he could vent his wrath upon was Joe.

"Are there no folks needing any boards cut today?" Ian nailed Joe with his eyes, silently damning him for being so near to Adelaide—where he wanted to be.

Joe frowned. "No . . . yes. I thought I would just walk Miss Addie as far as the mercantile."

"And now you have done," Ian said in a low, rumbling voice.

"If you will excuse me, Miss Addie? And thank you for the hot bun."

"You're welcome to come again tomorrow if you find you have a hankering for another," Addie said sweetly . . . too sweetly, in Ian's estimation.

"Thank you, Miss Addie," Joe said as he walked away.

Addie turned and watched him, wishing that Ian did not make her knees feel like water each time he glanced her way. While Joe had been here Addie had felt as if she had a confederate. Now she was alone with Ian, and no matter what the occasion, whenever she saw him lately his brows were knitted together in a deep frown of disapproval.

She had done everything she could think of to soothe his apprehension about having her in town. She had Lottie add more lace and material to the necks of her dresses. She had her hems lowered until they dragged in the dust. Even with a troop of men at her door from morning till night, she had kept herself aloof, showing little interest in any of them.

But no matter how much she tightened her corsets or knotted her laces or buttoned herself in, Ian McTavish glared at her.

He didn't like her. He thought she was a scarlet woman who would bring his perfect town down in ruins. Why that mattered to her she couldn't say—she didn't want it to matter. She couldn't *let* it matter.

But it did.

She supposed he was furious about not being able to eject her the moment she received the letter. But one month . . . until she picked another man! Of course, the sly, hard-hearted devil knew she wasn't going to do that. She knew his game.

Ian *knew* Addie would not pick a man, and she wouldn't accept one he picked for her. The villain did think fast on his feet, she'd give him that.

He had figured her out in a heartbeat.

She would not pick a husband. She would be forced to leave.

He would win.

"At least you havna forgotten how to smile." Ian's husky burr did things to her insides—things she didn't understand or want to examine too closely.

She realized she had been smiling . . . dreaming about how she could put a knot in Ian's tail. Addie pulled herself up to her full height, glad he was in the chair. For once they were of a size.

"I hope the way you treated Joe makes you a happy man," Addie snapped. "He was being kind, but I suppose that is difficult for you to understand."

Ian stood up with his easy animal grace and took a step

toward her. She swallowed hard, but she did not back up an inch. He was big ... so tall and wide through the shoulders. What did his face look like beneath that heavy beard?

"Tell me, Mrs. Brown, have you made up your mind as to whom you will marry?" Ian's voice was harder than he intended, but damn it all, it took every bit of control he possessed to keep from stealing another kiss. She smelled of soap and sunshine and that elusive combination of spices that he found so seductive. His groin tightened and his head spun with desire. He fought it, tamped it down, but just barely.

He wanted her. She hated him.

"No, I have not, and frankly, Mr. McTavish, if you keep snapping at anyone who speaks to me, I will be hard-pressed to make a decision in only a month."

"Joe had work; I simply reminded him of it."

"And isn't it fortunate, Mr. McTavish, that you have no work to occupy you?" Addie gathered her skirts and slipped past him. He watched her walk away, feeling as if the sun had gone behind thick, gray clouds.

"Ah, but that is where you are wrong, lass," he whispered. "I do have work to do, but I canna stop thinking about you long enough to do it. I should be moving sheep and cattle before the snow falls, but I canna leave." He wandered into the mercantile, staring like a fool at her ramrod stiff back as she busied herself looking at bolts of bright-colored cloth.

Bright calicos ... not black.

She didn't act like a woman in mourning. Her eyes were not red-rimmed from weeping. Her face was not pinched with sorrow. Adelaide was carrying her loss well.

The old doubts and questions about her husband returned to his mind. If the man had been a wastrel or a gambler, then maybe she *wasn't* as sad about his passing as folks thought.

It was an intriguing notion, and one that made Ian's blood thrum through his veins. Maybe she hadn't loved him.

But did that mean she could grow to love Ian—and in only three weeks?

"It ain't going to change by just wishing," Gus said from behind Ian.

Ian hadn't heard Gus approach. Of course it was just another indication that Ian's brain had turned to mush over Adelaide.

"I canna understand when you talk in riddles, Gus," Ian said dryly, tearing his gaze from Adelaide.

"I mean, if you want her, you are going to have to get her, Ian," Gus snarled. "And that means being nice to her. Tell her she looks purty . . . and quit growling like an old bear every time you see her with another man."

Ian spun around. If Gus could see how he felt, then did Adelaide know? He was about to ask when the clop of hooves coming into town drew his and Gus's attention.

"And just when you thought it couldn't get any worse . . ." Gus chuckled. "Ain't it amazing how the Lord always slaps down the arrogant and the stubborn? I'm an old man, but I do declare, this is promising to be the most entertaining autumn I've seen in a donkey's age."

"Ain't it just damned amazing," Ian agreed as he scowled up the street.

There, silhouetted against the morning sun with the snow-dusted peaks of Red Bird Mountain in the background, was Grass Singing and Aleck Bowen.

"Good to see you, Ian." Aleck dismounted and tied up his horse in front of Gus's store.

"I canna say the same," Ian grumbled.

He went to Grass Singing's horse and looked up at her. "I dinna expect to see either of you until spring. What are you doing here, lass?"

Grass Singing's dark eyes narrowed at his greeting, but Ian had no time to smooth her ruffled feathers. His mind was on Adelaide . . . and Aleck Bowen.

"We come town," Grass Singing said. She threw her leg over the pony's back and jumped toward Ian. Instinctively he put his arms out to catch her. She slid sensuously down his body, her breasts dragging across his chest, leaving no doubt as to her meaning.

"Grass Singing . . ." Ian was determined to let her know that he was not interested . . . and would never be, not since he was in love with Adelaide.

"Well, Mr. Bowen. Grass Singing." Adelaide's voice had the effect of a blue norther, freezing Ian's blood in his veins. Just short of dumping Grass Singing into the street, he settled her feet onto the ground. But he was not as quick as Aleck, who had hopped up the two steps of the mercantile's stoop. Now he was leering down at Adelaide.

"Mrs. Brown, you are prettier than a summer sunrise." Aleck swept the basket on her arm from her in one smooth motion. "Let me carry that for you. Yessiree, you are looking fresh as a buttercup, but I declare black ain't your color. You should be in somethin' bright to match your eyes and hair."

"She is in mourning," Ian said sharply. "Her husband died in an accident." And though Ian was speaking to Aleck, he was watching Adelaide, trying to gauge her feelings. He had not noticed so much as a flinch, or even a tightening of her lips when he mentioned her husband.

Hope once again flickered inside Ian's chest. If she had not loved her husband . . .

"You mean you are no longer a married woman?" Aleck said with all the finesse of a bull elk going into the rut. He must've caught his blunder, for he quickly added, "I mean, I'm awful sorry for your loss, Mrs. Brown."

Ian wanted to flatten him again. In fact, he did take a step toward Aleck, but Grass Singing took hold of his arm and stopped his forward momentum.

"I talk you," she said.

"Later," Ian said.

"Now. Chief Broken Ax sends warning. You must listen. Snow come early and deep."

Ian turned to look at Grass Singing. She would not be above lying if it would suit her purpose, and yet he had felt the morning breeze sweeping down from Canada. There was ice behind that wind . . . ice and death if he did not bring the flocks in.

"Broken Ax says this?"

"Yep. I was there too. All the signs say early snow and plenty of it. Now, why don't you run along and bring your woolies to safety, Ian? I'll be happy to keep an eye on Mrs. Brown while you're gone."

Ian glowered at his old companion. Aleck laughed and slipped his arm around Adelaide's waist.

"May I walk you home, Mrs. Brown?"

Adelaide's gaze lingered for a moment on Grass Singing. Then she turned and slipped her arm into the crook of Aleck's elbow. Ian nearly choked on his jealousy.

"Thank you, Mr. Bowen, I would be pleased to have your company. And why don't you call me Addie?"

"I would be honored to, Addie." Aleck turned back and winked at Ian, and then they walked off, the evergreen boughs whispering and soughing with each breeze.

Ian was biting his lip and part of his mustache to keep from bellowing in jealous fury. They were only a few feet away from the mercantile when Adelaide suddenly stopped, tilted her face toward Aleck and said, "Tell me, Mr. Bowen, do you have a wife somewhere? Or are you a *single* man?"

* * *

Addie didn't know what had come over her, but sometime between Joe's leaving and now, she realized that Ian didn't like Aleck being around her.

She didn't know why. . . . It might be that Aleck was not one of Ian's productive, married townsmen, or maybe he didn't want Aleck being friendly with her since Ian disliked her so much. Whatever the reason, she took deep satisfaction in deviling Ian.

Addie had never learned how to sashay around and bat her eyes like other women did, but now she tried, feeling Ian's gaze on her back as she and Aleck walked away.

"Aleck, how do you feel about peach cobbler with fresh cream?" Addie was almost shocked by her boldness. It was all Ian's fault. He had a way of making her do crazy, reckless things.

Aleck's smile rivaled the sunshine. "Addie, I just might propose marriage for cooking like that."

"Oh, no, Aleck, don't do that," Addie said, flicking a glance at Ian as she and Aleck walked away.

"And why not?" Aleck said with a good-natured snort. "Am I too rough and barky to make a husband? Or was it 'cause you saw me in my altogether and I don't measure up . . . so to speak."

Addie felt her face flaming. She looked back to assure herself that Ian was not within earshot, and then she said, "No, Mr. Bowen. I don't want to get married at all. But Ian McTavish is making me."

"Making you?" His brows rose to his cap made of badger hide. "Now, why would he be making you?"

They had reached her house, and when she opened the kitchen door the smell of yeast and the warmth from her stove invited them in.

"Because he is a bully, I suspect." Addie tied on her

apron and started dishing up the cobbler for Aleck. It felt good to be honest with someone. It was strange that she felt she could confide in Aleck Bowen, but as he said, maybe it had something to do with her seeing him in the "altogether."

"Well, now, that is mighty peculiar doings." Aleck took a bite of the cobbler, slathered in cream. For a moment he sat with his eyes closed. Then he opened them and said, "Melts in the mouth, Addie. Are you sure you don't want to marry me? I promise I wouldn't expect nothin' from you but your fine cooking."

"Be careful, Aleck, I might just take you up on that offer!" Addie laughed nervously. Right now she had Aleck occupied with a plate of cobbler, but she didn't know how long that would hold him. When he looked at her there was a decided twinkle in his eye.

"You know, Addie, I was surprised as a possum in sunlight when you said I could walk you. We got off to kind of a rough start with that first meetin'."

"It was Ian."

"What was that?" Aleck asked around a mouthful of peaches.

"I said, it looks like the weather is going to change soon."

"Yep, it is. That was why Chief Broken Ax sent Grass Singing to warn Ian. He has sheep in the deep draws at the foot of Red Bird Mountain. If Ian doesn't get them out soon, they will be stuck when a big storm hits. They won't have a chance."

"Surely he has lived here long enough to know that," Addie said, trying to wipe the picture of Grass Singing slithering down Ian's body from her mind. She turned out a bowl of dough that had been rising.

"Yep, that's true, but he seems to be muddle-headed lately, as if he's got somethun' on his mind. It ain't like him a'tall. And o'course Grass Singing jumped at the chance to see him.''

"How long will you be in town, Aleck?" Addie asked, anxious to change the subject. Each time she thought of Ian and that Indian girl . . .

"I ain't made up my mind, but if I can eat like this, I might just stay a long, long time.''

Addie doubled her fist and pummeled the center of the dough. But it didn't erase the image of Ian's arms around Grass Singing.

She was angry and confused. What did she care if Ian McTavish made a spectacle of himself in the middle of town? He could do as he pleased. After all, he was not married.

He was not married.

Addie swallowed hard and refused to let her thoughts wander in that direction. She didn't like Ian—*she didn't.* And *if* she was thinking about him as a possible marriage prospect, it was only to spite him for his bone-deep mean streak, and not because she cared about him.

Chapter Thirteen

The snow started as nothing more than a few tiny flakes swirling down on a northerly breeze. By noon it covered the earth, making the road a brown grosgrain ribbon against the white. By late afternoon snow was beginning to pile up against the cowshed.

By dusk it was obvious that this was one of the big snows everyone talked about. A snow that did not stop . . . a snow that could kill anything left out in it.

Addie looked out at Red Bird Mountain. The peaks were pearly white in the distance, the treeline shimmering like an emerald necklace, meandering through canyons and cliffs. As much as she didn't want to do it, she wondered and worried about Ian McTavish.

It had been three days . . . three days since he rode by with Darroch loping at Dow's side. Three days since he had frowned at her and said something nasty to Aleck Bowen about lounging on Addie's porch and returning to Broken Ax's camp before he got snowed in at McTavish Plain.

Aleck had only laughed and said maybe he wanted to be snowed in, in town.

Nobody had seen Ian since.

Three days of cold ... three days of silence ... of peace for Addie.

So why didn't she feel happy about that?

"He is too ornery for anything bad to happen to him," Addie said, but she didn't really believe her own words. A million deaths waited in winter, and twice that many on a mountain like Red Bird.

Addie rubbed her hands up and down her arms, but she was chilled bone deep while she stared out the window of her snug little house at the Red Bird peaks.

Aleck had assured her that Ian would return in a few days—joked that she should enjoy a little peace and his company while the cantankerous Ian was gone.

Aleck was right. She should be enjoying it.

But she wasn't. She spent her days casting glances at the mountain and her nights tossing and turning like a child's top.

It should've made Addie happy that Ian was occupied elsewhere ... that she would have a few days respite from his probing eyes and disapproving attitude and his glee that she would soon be gone because she would *never* pick a husband from the single men of McTavish Plain or accept anyone of his choosing.

It should've, but it didn't.

Addie told herself she didn't care about Ian. No, it had to be something else that was making her so edgy. It couldn't be worry. To be concerned about the safety of that bearded bully she would have to have tender feelings for him.

"And I would be a fool to allow myself to care for a man who doesn't even *like* me."

* * *

Between the snow and the shortening of the days, it was nearing dark by late afternoon each day. Addie had fallen into the habit of doing her outside chores early, seeing her animals snug and safe and then putting yeast on to soften for tomorrow's bread. Then she would fix herself a cup of coffee that she laced with sugar and heavy cream, her one true vice.

But this afternoon she kept rising from the table to gaze again and again at the mountain summit beyond her window. Once she thought she saw the flicker of a fire, but it was far off and indistinct.

"Probably my imagination. Or some sort of reflection on the snow," Addie muttered and returned to her coffee, but it had grown cold.

When it was full dark, and she had reheated her coffee twice in a pan on the stove, she was sure it was a fire on the apex of the mountain.

"Where Ian is." And the terrible hollow feeling that Addie was sure could not be worry intensified.

Ian fed more sticks into the flames. Darroch snuggled closer and Ian rubbed his head. "Poor hound . . . you should be stretched out in front of a proper fire with a rug beneath your bones, instead of here in the cold and weary from keeping the wolves at bay."

He thought of Adelaide's house, warm and snug, redolent with the scent of baking bread, filled with her own special aura. He thought of her capable, slim hands, kneading dough, making scones.

His mouth watered so much he had to swallow.

And then he thought of Adelaide herself. She acted proper and stern, but Ian knew that deep inside a great hidden passion was waiting to be awakened. Maybe she had never been truly wanted by a man . . .

Maybe she had never *wanted* a man.

Maybe she had been hurt and now sought to keep her heart safe. In any case, Ian was determined to be the man to melt her frosty exterior and awaken the warmth beneath the surface of proper, straitlaced Adelaide Brown.

He shifted his position. Cold seeped into his bones from the icy stone he sat upon; the wind whistled and howled around the sparse trees, nudging beneath his buckskins and the woolen scarf wrapped around his neck. Even the shearling coat he wore did not prevent frosty fingers of wind from finding a way inside.

He concentrated on the image of Adelaide's mysterious eyes, letting that fill his mind and heat his blood. It almost worked, until he remembered his old *friend*.

"No doubt that blatherskite Aleck is doing his best to keep Adelaide busy while I am gone. Aleck with his hard, clean-shaven jaw, twinkling eyes and dandified Tennessee boy manners."

Unconsciously Ian scratched his own bearded jaw, his nails scraping against the hair that covered his chin.

Did women prefer men without a beard?

"Perhaps . . . but 'tis a high price to pay." He sat for a moment contemplating that and then said aloud, when Darroch raised his head, "But Adelaide is a rare woman . . . a woman worth peeling a beard off for."

Darroch whined and sniffed the icy air. The hound was aware of something beyond Ian's perception. Ian stared into the darkness below but saw nothing. He returned his attention to thoughts of Adelaide and how he might win her. Ian pondered that as the snow fell, silent and steady on him and the flock that nestled into the narrow box canyon.

"Perhaps I should wash off the scent of wool and horse and scrape my face clean. Do you think she might see me in a new light?"

And then he heard what Darroch had already sensed . . . the low, plaintive howl of a solitary wolf.

The hair on Ian's nape rose when that call was answered by another . . . and another. . . .

Then, like quicksilver they came from the trees. Shadowy shapes that meant death.

Aleck was playing checkers with Gus at the back of the mercantile when Addie walked in, stamping her feet on the gunnysack at the door. Her breath left a little cloud as she unwrapped the scarf from her neck and peeled off her coat.

She had heard through her other suitors that Aleck had taken to sleeping in Gus's back storeroom since Ian left town. Joe had speculated openly that Aleck was working up the nerve to court Addie. Now he and Gus were sitting on kegs of molasses, their game board resting between them on the top of a huge barrel of corn meal. They were arguing more than they were moving the black and red pieces, but they seemed to be enjoying it. They didn't seem to know she was there. Addie stood quietly, just watching them—listening to their masculine banter.

"Ian has roamed these mountains for nigh to ten years, Gus. If he is late it is because he chooses to be—he probably went to Broken Ax's camp."

Addie stiffened to know that Gus was concerned. She had almost managed to convince herself that her worry was just a womanly affliction.

"Just 'cause he is wise in the ways of the mountain doesn't make him bullet proof," Gus snapped. He raked his fingers through his thinning hair. "Aleck, I am telling you, I saw a fire up on the side of Red Bird Mountain last night."

"You're eyes are playing tricks on you," Aleck jibed.

"Not hardly. Ian is up there. That was his fire. And we should go look."

"There wasn't any fire," Aleck said stubbornly.

"I saw it, too," Addie said, drawing their attention for the first time. "What does it mean, Gus . . . a fire?"

"If there was a fire, it means he has settled himself in nice and cozy," Aleck said, in a way that made Addie's teeth set on edge. Aleck doubted Gus and he doubted her—and he didn't seem to give a fig if his friend was in trouble.

"Listen, Addie, if Ian *wanted* to get back, then he would have. Maybe Grass Singing lit off to join him up there." Aleck's grin was sly and satisfied.

Addie looked away. The mere mention of Grass Singing made her heart contract painfully, and a little voice in her head told her that was exactly why Aleck had mentioned it.

"Nonsense," Gus roared. "He has no reason to stay on the mountain and more than a few to return to town." Gus slid a glance at Addie.

"Such as?" Aleck asked with narrowed eyes.

"Never you mind. I just know Ian ain't of a mind to sit in the snow—lessen he had to."

"Oh, quit running on and take your move, Gus."

"I did see a fire last night," Addie insisted again. "From my kitchen window I could see it plain."

Gus looked over Aleck's head at her. He studied her face for a long moment; then he smiled sympathetically. "If Ian isn't back by sundown, Aleck and I will go out in the morning and look for him."

"I ain't his mama, Gus," Aleck whined. "But if it will get your mind on the game and I won't have to listen to you fret like an old woman, then fine. I'll go."

Gus smiled at Addie again, and to her utter amazement he winked! She made herself a promise that when Ian came back she was going to kill him herself for making her look like a fool in front of Aleck and Gus . . . and to herself.

The day dragged on for Addie. She didn't remember to eat lunch, but not an hour went by that she didn't glance out her window, and if she was in town delivering baked goods, she found her gaze going to the mountain.

Then in the afternoon, when she could not count any more hours, Addie flung her basket over her arm and walked out her front door. Gus had promised he would make Aleck go look for Ian in the morning . . . just one more night to wait and to worry.

But as Addie rounded the house where McTavish Plain's weaver lived, she saw a flock of ewes and yearling lambs, with crusts of hard ice and new snow frozen to their woolly backs gambol into town.

She ran closer to the street and was ready to plant her feet and read to Ian from the book when she saw him, riding behind the herd. Darroch was slung across the front of Ian's saddle. Blood dripped down the hound's shoulder and over Ian's leg.

"Oh, Lord."

Adelaide dropped her shopping basket and ran across the crust of snow. Ian halted Dow, and without hesitation she laid her hand upon Ian's leg. The leather of his buckskins was soft and cold beneath her hand. Unconsciously she rubbed her fingers along his leg above his knee.

"Oh, you're back," she said in a breathy whisper.

Ian's heart near exploded from his chest. Adelaide . . . *his Adelaide,* was staring up at him with concern in her eyes. Today they were the purest gray, soft and caring. Her nimble fingers danced along his leg, setting his aching body on fire. He wanted to yank her up and take her home. Just to look down into her lovely face was enough to make him forget every ache and wound. He reached down and impulsively cupped her face in his hand.

"What happened to Darroch?" she asked.

"Wolves," Ian said. "They came upon us in the night. Darroch fought them long and well." Ian swallowed hard. "He saved the flock except for one old ewe."

"He's not . . . oh, tell me he is not dead," Addie said

with a rusty catch in her throat. "I couldn't bear it if he died."

Addie held her breath while she waited for Ian to answer. There was so much blood . . . and Darroch was as limp-jointed as a ragdoll. In a short time she had developed a warm spot in her heart for the lonely hound.

"He lives—for now." He smiled down at her. "I dinna know if either one of us would ever see the town again."

Something warm, liquid and potent trickled through her body. Ian had smiled at her—actually smiled. In that moment she let her guard down and dared consider what she had been afraid to face.

She didn't hate Ian McTavish—she didn't even dislike him. With his hard ways and his brusk manner, he had managed to nudge his way into her heart.

It didn't bring her any joy, but it did not distress her either. It was simply a fact of life; she had developed deep feelings for Ian McTavish.

"Bring Darroch to my house. I can bandage him and see to his wounds. And you look as if you could use a cup of hot coffee."

"Aye, that I could, lass. But I must see to the sheep."

"Roamer Tresh has left his anvil, and Miley and Gert are coming from the livery."

They were busy herding the sheep through town and would soon have the flock penned and safe.

"Bring him now so we may tend him. Please . . . *Ian.*"

His head swiveled around at the sound of her voice. *Ian.* She had used his given name—not Mr. McTavish.

"As you say, Adelaide," he answered, his throat closing with emotion as he dared give life to the name that haunted him day in and day out.

"Nobody has called me Adelaide since my pa died."

"Then it is high time someone did."

Chapter Fourteen

Addie brought a sheet from the linen trunk in her bedroom and spread it upon the kitchen table.

Ian tenderly laid Darroch on it. The hound did not move or even whimper, though he was awake and his pain-filled eyes followed Addie about the room as she set water to boil.

"A pack of wolves came on the tail of the storm," Ian said softly. Addie glanced at him and realized he needed to talk. So she went about laying out things she might need and listened quietly.

"I dinna think they were really hungry . . . not like a wolf can get. It is too early in the season for that. They were more likely schooling their young ones, teaching them how to find the weak and the old." Ian stroked Darroch's head while he spoke.

Addie separated Darroch's bloody fur and washed it with the water. The pan she wrung the cloth into soon ran pink with blood. She found three deep slashes in Darroch's shoulder and one up on his neck, near his throat.

And one ear was bit all the way through, a small flap of skin hanging at the edge. Mercifully the bites were mostly in hide, sparing his muscle for the most part.

"He is weak and exhausted from no rest and loss of blood," she told Ian.

"The wolves deviled us all night and into the dawn." Ian petted the dog, speaking in a low, rough, soothing voice that made Addie quiver.

She glanced at Ian from under her lowered lashes. There were sooty smudges of fatigue beneath his eyes that made her heart contract with sympathy. She had an overpowering urge to touch his face, to cradle his jaw the way he had done hers. She wanted to hold him . . . to comfort him. It would have given her great pleasure to hold him until he slept in her arms. Instead she cleared her throat and said, "You look tired, Ian. Have you eaten?"

"Darroch needed care."

She smiled at his pithy answer and returned to the task of cleaning Darroch's wounds. Ian's affection for his dog touched her deeply.

"I have a couple of old roosters stewing on the back of the stove."

"Aye, the smell is making my belly draw up and near touch my backbone."

His smile was tired and, oh, too winning. Adelaide's heart skipped a beat each time she looked at him. She tried hard to sound normal as she said, "A little broth in the both of you after I stitch up these bites and you'll be right as rain."

"And perhaps could you scratch up a dumpling or two as well, Adelaide?" Ian said with a boyish grin and a lift of his brows.

Addie couldn't resist his teasing. "Still daring to tread where wiser men would not go, Ian?" she asked, willing her knees to stop wobbling.

"It would seem so, Adelaide; it would seem so."

He reached out and lightly gave her hand a squeeze. She looked at them—her smaller one encased within his darker, calloused hand, and something blossomed inside her heart.

An invisible connection formed between them. Born of humor and concern for Darroch, it was strong—almost tangible. Addie never imagined she could have such a bond with a man—especially not with Ian.

"I'll get my sewing kit from the bedroom," she said nervously. She couldn't let Ian see how she was trembling. "Once he is sewn up, it will just be a matter of feeding him until he gets his strength back."

She turned away before Ian could see the unshed tears in her eyes. Once in her bedroom Addie took a few extra minutes to compose herself before she brought her sewing kit. But the moment she was in the same room with Ian, her hand began to shake. It took three tries before she threaded the big needle with silk thread. Finally she managed it and looked up to find Ian watching her with a solemn, intense expression.

"Thank you, Adelaide," he said softly.

She ducked her head to hide her trembling bottom lip from him. She was grateful to have Darroch to focus on. Gently as she could manage, Addie pushed the needle through Darroch's hide. He whimpered weakly and watched her with his soulful eyes.

"Oh, poor, poor, Darroch. I am sorry to hurt you," she whispered.

"He knows you are trying to help him. You've fine hands, Adelaide." Ian's fingers stroked through the tangled fur, swirling—almost hypnotic as he tried to comfort the animal.

"You mean strong hands?" Addie frowned. There was a tightness in her chest and a strange fluttering heat lower in her body . . . like a hunger.

"No, I mean you have fine hands. They are slender

and well formed. The hands of a good and caring woman, Adelaide."

Addie looked up and tried to laugh off the spell that was capturing her. Suddenly her little kitchen seemed hot and small. "I said I would feed you, Ian. There is no need for you to make up folderol to win your supper from me."

"No folderol. You do have nice hands. You have a nice name. Adelaide suits you. It is uncommon . . . and a wee bit elegant. Addie is not enough name for a woman of your character."

Addie swallowed and focused on Darroch again. Oh, if Ian kept saying nice things to her, she would weep. She had to find a way of keeping her frayed emotions in check.

"And by that do you mean 'character' is just another word for *shrew?*"

"No, Adelaide, I dinna think you are a shrew."

She risked looking up at him again. They held each other's gaze while a hot tide of emotion flooded through Addie. She had never felt such an intense reaction to anyone in her life. Never felt the burning need to win someone's regard, respect . . . *love?*

Without meaning to, she actually swayed toward Ian. He was like a lodestone. She had no more will than a fragment of iron in the dust.

She wanted him to kiss her again—to put his lips on hers and wrap his arms around her because he was a man and she was a woman . . . not because he wanted to shame her into leaving town.

She wanted him to say nice things and she wanted him to mean them.

Darroch whimpered. The small sound was enough to pull Addie from the enchantment of Ian's eyes. Grateful for the hound's distraction, and sorry for his pain, she lowered her head and began to sew the next tear in Darroch's skin.

Ian had told Adelaide she had fine hands—what he had really meant was that he wanted her hands on him. He could almost feel them now, strong and smooth, coursing over his body.

He wanted to unfasten each and every one of the dozen tiny pearl buttons that marched down the front of her dress, starting with the one done up tight under her chin.

Her back was so rigid, he was sure she was wearing a whalebone corset. His fingers twitched when he imagined undoing the laces—one by one—and setting her luscious bosom free. Then he would taste each breast slowly, thoroughly. And he would cup his hands around her, savoring the weight of each wondrous globe until she cried out in ecstasy.

Adelaide kept herself under tight restraint with that tight-laced corset and all those layers of clothes. Maybe she was afraid of what would happen if she let herself go, but Ian yearned to make her lose her grip on that mastery.

He could envision her, hair down about her creamy shoulders, the heat of desire simmering in her eyes. Her beautiful mouth half open, inviting his kiss. . . .

Ian shifted in the straight-backed chair to accommodate his stiffening member. Never had just thinking about any woman had such an effect on him. He didn't need to even touch Adelaide and he was hard as a post.

Ian was somewhat splayed over the end of the table in order to reach Darroch. She had seen something—an expression of pain or intense concentration flash across his face.

"Are you in an uncomfortable position?" Addie asked innocently.

"Aye, most uncomfortable," Ian admitted wryly. "And you, Adelaide, are you *comfortable?*

"I have a little kink in my neck is all."

She finished the stitch and stood up straight. She put her hands in the small of her back and stretched. With her head thrown back and her eyes closed, she was as seductive as a woman could get. Her breasts were thrust out, just inviting his hands to cup them, to hold their weight, to taste their nectar.

Ian nearly groaned in agony. She had no idea what she was doing to him—but how could a widow be so innocent? Once again questions about her husband swirled through his mind.

He made a little sound in the back of his throat. She looked at him as if she could read his mind and . . . blushed.

"I'm going to get some bandages." Addie gathered her sewing basket and left the room. She didn't want to believe she was running from Ian, but she was. She needed to put some distance between them before she lost her head completely and made unseemly advances toward him.

How could he make her feel all weak and itchy inside? She had never encountered anyone or anything like Ian McTavish. And why him?

Roamer Tresh, the blacksmith, was certainly everything a woman could want in looks and form. Joe was pleasant to look upon, with a nice, even disposition. Even Gus, with his wicked sense of humor and forward ways, was a better choice than Ian.

Why him? Why Ian McTavish?

She had no answer except that her heart and mind were contrary and illogical. She was foolish and seemed to like causing herself pain.

Addie rolled the strips of material into neat little cylinders before she finally gathered enough courage to return to her own kitchen. But she needn't have worried, for instead of pinning Addie with his blue eyes, Ian's head was resting beside Darroch's strong neck.

Both man and beast were snoring.

A tight catch beneath her breast halted her steps. She was frozen, staring at Ian and Darroch. Then she smiled.

Emboldened by the fact that Ian was asleep, she closed the distance between them. Then she reached out—and abruptly snatched her hand back.

Touch him!

Taking a deep breath for courage, she reached out once more, this time laying her palm lightly on his shoulder. The heat from his body seeped into her hand.

She sighed in contentment. Touching him felt so . . . *proper.* But how could the merest touch make her feel as if she had found a missing part of herself? How could stroking that wide, muscled shoulder make her heart flutter like a bird with broken wings? And how could combing her fingers through his thick, soft hair make every nerve in her body sing with excitement?

She allowed her eyes to roam over his face, his hands, his body, and all the while she was touching him, lightly, tentatively, here and there. Feeling the softness of his beard . . . the corded muscles of his arms.

There was nothing about him that she could find fault with. Her curiosity and need to touch him—feel him— left her breathless with excitement.

"What do you look like beneath that beard?" she whispered softly. Were his cheeks lean and chiseled? Did he have a dimple?—a cleft? Was his jaw round or was it square and rough-hewn?

She wondered . . . oh, Lord, she wondered!

And she puzzled about his body as well. Were the same dark strands of hair, shot through with rusty hues, duplicated on his chest? Was he browned from working without a shirt, or was he pale from being covered by his buckskins?

She remembered her embarrassing meeting with Aleck, but her mind was not on Aleck's body—it was focused on Ian. And though seeing Aleck without clothes had been her first and only glimpse of a naked man, her mind was busy trying to construct an image of the big, hard, muscled man before her.

Did Ian's hair darken and thin out as it shot downward toward his manhood? Was his staff hard and thick? Was the end red and angry-looking, as Aleck's had been?

"No," she whispered softly, breathlessly. "Ian will be well made, fine and strong. Ian will be *beautiful*."

Addie sighed, feeling her pulse thrumming in her throat. Her hand now rested on the nape of Ian's neck. The muscles were taut, even in sleep. He was a strong man. A man formed and tempered by the land he had claimed.

"What brought you here, Ian McTavish? And why are you so hell bent on seeing me married off to some other man?"

Addie pulled her hand back in shock. She had finally given voice to the question that had nagged at her— deviled her morning, noon and night.

Why did Ian want to see her wed someone else?

"Oh, stop, you ninny. Grass Singing told you why. He doesn't like you." She stood staring at him while the truth of those words ripped a raw hold in her heart. She wrapped her hands around her waist, hugging herself as if she could stave off the pain of that fact.

She cared . . . oh, she cared for a man who held her in contempt!

While he slept, Ian's mind conjured wonderful images of Adelaide in his home. The place was no longer cold and harsh. It was warm and redolent with the scent of spice and *her*. In his dream Adelaide did not dislike him.

She was his, willingly, without threat of being sent away. She wanted to be with him, actually cared about him.

He felt her hands upon him, warm, tender and possessive. It was the best feeling he could've imagined. She touched his shoulder, his neck . . . exploring him, claiming his body as she had already claimed his soul.

In the cottony realm of his mind, he could almost hear her voice . . . asking what he looked like beneath the beard . . . asking why he wanted her to marry someone else.

Ian came awake with a start, knocking the chair backward with his knees. He leaped to his feet, ready for battle, when he realized the hammering he heard was not his heart but someone banging on Adelaide's back door.

The knock came again, louder, more insistent. Ian wondered if he should open the door, or would Adelaide take offense? It wasn't his house, after all.

"Just a minute." Her voice floated from the front parlor.

How long had he been asleep? He looked at Darroch— his great chest and neck encased in pristine white bandages.

"Adelaide." Even her name was like a song.

She had tended his dog while he slept, and he had dreamed of her. A warm, liquid feeling coursed through his chest when he thought of Adelaide doing womanly things while he slept in her kitchen.

As if he belonged.

She came from the front parlor and nearly collided with him. His hands came up, instinctively curling around her shoulders to steady her.

She gave a little sigh—was it from fear or satisfaction?

"You're awake." She looked up at him. Something as fiery and intoxicating as Scots whiskey swirled through his gut.

"Adelaide, I need to tell . . ."

"Addie? Addie, are you in there?" Aleck's voice had

the effect of an avalanche. "Are you all right? Open this door!"

Adelaide jumped back from Ian as if she had been scalded. She shook herself, as if to remove some unwanted thought before she smoothed her skirts and went to the door.

"Aleck, I'm sorry. I was bringing in wood for the front fire. I didn't hear you."

Aleck stepped inside, giving Ian an inquisitive look. "I heard from Gus you was back and that your dog was poorly. I brought the wagon to take Darroch home."

"That was very thoughtful of you, Aleck," Addie said.

"Ah, but wasna it?" Ian said dryly. He moved away from the table feeling foolish. He had allowed his wonderful dream to cloud his mind . . . to make him think that Adelaide cared.

"Have you no manners, Ian?" Aleck said with a frown. "You are bleeding all over Addie's clean kitchen floor."

Addie whirled around, her eyes sliding to the pine boards beneath Ian's feet. There was a drying pool of rusty brown beside the upset chair leg. A new spot was forming beside his moccasin-covered foot.

"Ian, you are hurt." Addie's eyes roamed his face, as if she expected to find some answer hidden just beneath the surface. "Are you in pain?"

" 'Tis no more than a scratch," Ian began, and then suddenly Adelaide was beside him. With a strength that surprised him, she righted the chair and pushed him down into it. She kneeled beside him. Her hands were hot coals as she touched his thigh, probing and examining the rent in his flesh. It was his dream, only this was better. . . . It was real.

A smile tickled the corners of Ian's mouth. He wanted to kiss every hairy maw of that wolf pack. Hell, if he had known a little scratch would get him this kind of attention, he would've let them gnaw off his left hand at the very least . . . maybe a foot even.

"McTavish." Grass Singing's voice brought three pairs of eyes to the still open door. She stood there, wrapped in a dark fur robe. "I come you . . ."

Adelaide looked at Ian and her eyes seemed to change, to become hard and shuttered. He saw it—no more than a flicker in her extraordinary eyes, but it was real. He witnessed a brief glimpse of hurt. Then she drew in a breath and rose, as graceful as breaking dawn.

"It would seem, Mr. McTavish, that you have a more than capable nurse quite willing to tend you." She stepped away from him.

The tenuous bond that had connected them snapped like a frozen branch under a blanket of snow. He felt the icy cold wall form between them again.

Aleck and Grass Singing had done this. And the hell of it was, Ian wasn't too damned sure it was not intentional.

"I think you'd better go," Adelaide said flatly.

Ian wanted to explain. He had to tell her what was in his mind and his heart. "Adelaide, I—"

"Now," Adelaide said, stepping away and turned her back to him.

Ian stood up stiffly. He gathered Darroch in his arms and walked out into the frosty twilight. The door slammed shut behind him.

"Grass Singing, I would speak with you—now," Ian said over his shoulder.

He had had enough.

Chapter Fifteen

The trip to Ian's house was made in silence. Ian was angry and frustrated, Aleck seemed preoccupied and Grass Singing—well, who knew what went on in her head?

There had been a moment when he and Adelaide had seemed almost friendly toward each other. He had found a scrap of his courage and was on the verge of telling her that he had great regard for her as a woman.

Then Grass Singing appeared, and as suddenly as a clap of thunder from a clear blue sky, everything had changed.

The wagon wheels made soft slushing sounds through the fresh snow as it climbed the hill toward Ian's house. A long gray shadow cast from the peaks of Red Bird Mountain sliced across the landscape.

Ian looked at his home dispassionately, trying to see it through Adelaide's eyes. It was cold and gray and forbidding. And though he had cut the stones from living rock and built it to stand for generations, it did sit in the teeth of the wind and the shadow of the great, haunted mountain.

Unconsciously, Ian pulled his tartan scarf tighter around his neck, as if to ward off an icy gust.

"McTavish?" Grass Singing said, reminding him that she sat beside him on the wagon seat. He had momentarily forgotten her. Thinking of Adelaide had a way of doing that to him. All he need do was remember the way she moved, or the way her voice felt when she spoke, and all rational thought fled.

"McTavish!" She elbowed him roughly in the ribs, making his leg throb with pain. They had reached his house and he climbed stiffly from the wagon, noticing that the movement started fresh bleeding. If Grass Singing saw or cared about his wound, she said nothing.

"Come inside, the both of you. 'Tis time we spoke. This canna and wilna go on any longer, Grass Singing."

As quick as he could manage it, Ian made sure Darroch was settled on a pallet near the fire. Mercifully, Angus and Fergus, Ian's other pets, were out foraging in the icy stream that tumbled behind the house. At least Darroch would be spared their nonsense while he was so weak.

"I'll fetch in some more wood for the fires," Aleck said diplomatically. Ian nodded stiffly. What he had to say did not need a witness.

As soon as he was gone, Grass Singing strode boldly toward Ian. "McTavish—" She shrugged off her buffalo robe and wrapped her arms around Ian's neck. On tiptoe, she ground her pelvis against him.

"Stop." He took her hands and removed them, holding them in front of her. Her eyes were stormy black pools.

"The winter Black Elk died I felt sorry for you. Your

father has always treated me fair, so I have been patient wi' you, allowing you liberties I wouldna have given anyone else. I thought I had made it clear last spring that we couldna have anythin' between us. You must find another husband, Grass Singing—from your tribe. I havna a thing to offer you.''

"It is the woman with the hair of flames. She has poisoned you against me.'' She wrung her hands, trying to free them from Ian's grip. "I can make you want me.''

Ian shook his head. "No. Not tonight or any other night.''

"You *do* want me,'' Grass Singing said forcefully. "McTavish love Grass Singing.''

"No. I never said words of love to you in act or deed, lass. You have created a fantasy. This must end—now. I want you to go and I want you to stay with your tribe and find a husband.''

Grass Singing jerked free. She narrowed her eyes and snatched up the robe from the floor. "The flame-haired woman has taken your manhood.''

"Maybe. She has taken my heart. I dinna want to hurt you, Grass Singing, but you shall not come to me again. You shall not come and make cozy in my home as if I have given you leave to do so.''

Her face was a mask of fury. Grass Singing was spoiled and used to getting her own way. Black Elk had been rich in ponies, and being Broken Ax's daughter had given her privileges within the tribe.

"You be sorry,'' she spat, her eyes blazing with fury.

Aleck walked back into the room, kicking the door shut behind him. He peered over the stack of wood, glancing from Ian to Grass Singing and back again.

"Aleck, take the wagon and see Grass Singing gets to her village safely,'' Ian said.

"She's not stayin'?''

"No," Ian said bluntly. "Grass Singing wilna be staying in McTavish Plain any longer." Ian glanced down at the blood pooling by his foot. "And neither will you."

Aleck's brows rose to his hairline. "You are as techy as a bear in his den, Ian."

"Since my company is so hard to bear, you won't miss me." Ian glowered. "In fact, Aleck, why don't you winter with Broken Ax and the tribe?"

Days passed in a flurry of snowstorms and work. Addie had orders for baked goods that kept her in the kitchen late into the night. And though her hands were busy, her mind was always up on the hillside in the bleak stone house Ian called home.

One moment she was cursing Ian McTavish and the race that bred him . . . the next she was in fervent prayer for his recovery.

How badly had he been hurt? Was the wolf rabid? Did he need help up there all alone?

She was ridden with guilt over the way she had sent him from her home. She was still stinging from the pain of seeing that Grass Singing felt comfortable enough to come fetch him, as if they had an *understanding*.

Maybe they did . . .

But even that did nothing to quell Addie's thoughts. She worried and fretted and imagined all manner of calamity. Nobody had seen hide nor hair of Ian or Darroch. But nobody seemed concerned either. Only Addie watched and worried and wondered. And in the midst of her confusion was still the ridiculous courtship she had to endure as the one and only acknowledged single woman in town.

There were moments when Addie mightily resented her sisters' good fortune in being undiscovered. And then she would have bouts of gloomy remorse at her uncharitable thoughts as she fended off the good-natured attentions of one bachelor or another.

Joe Christian made a habit to be at her door every morning to pick up his order of sticky buns. And more often than not he took the opportunity to present her with some small token.

One morning it was a small wooden shelf to hang on her wall to hold her spices. Another dawn it was a small set of haircombs done in polished pine.

"I made them from the scraps at the mill," he explained, like a shy boy slipping them into her hands.

Another day it was a tiny three-legged stool. "So you can be comfortable when you milk."

And he was not the only man who found the time to seek her out and give her gifts. Gus Gruberman would always have a little bundle wrapped in brown paper and tied with string under the counter when she brought his two loaves of bread to the mercantile.

Once she had found a length of ivory-colored ribbon.

"That'll bring out the roses in your cheeks, Addie," he had said with a wink that made the blood rush to her face.

Another time it had been a whole bundle of cinnamon sticks.

"Spicy as you, Addie girl."

There had been gifts of writing paper from John Holcomb at the post office. Baskets of dried garden goods from several of the single men who farmed on the common at the edge of town.

Not a day went by without some handsome, hungry man showing up on Addie's doorstep with a shy grin and a gift to cement their courtship. But not once had there been so much as a glimpse of Ian McTavish.

"Oh, why does it matter?" Addie sighed as she fluted the edge of a pie crust. Tomorrow it would all be over, at the harvest dinner and dance.

She would miss her sisters, and her house, and Gert and Miley and . . .

Tears stung the backs of her eyes as she took inventory of the life she had made. Neighbors, friends and the untamed surroundings of McTavish Plain had laid claim to her heart.

She would miss it all. Because Addie had made up her mind good and proper. She would not choose any of the good-looking, willing men in McTavish Plain to wed.

"Oh, Addie, you look just fine." Mattie clapped her hands together as she surveyed her handiwork.

"See, I told you that you could still be fetching as a posy in spite of wearing black," Lottie added smugly. She had rummaged through Addie's presents from Gus and had created little roses made of silk and ribbon. Mattie wove them through curls in Addie's hair and fastened them with the haircombs made of pine.

"Look—just look how pretty you are." Mattie thrust a small looking glass into her hands. "And the gentlemen will be so pleased you are wearing some of their gifts."

Addie looked in the mirror and assessed herself critically. She had a plain, squarish face with average features. She was certainly not what anybody would call a great beauty, just as Ian had pointed out.

Like as not, none of the men in town would want her if there were anybody else to choose from.

Her gaze dropped a little lower to examine the dress. Lottie had insisted on adding cream panniers trimmed in black lace to the overskirt of Addie's best mourning dress. Though the neck was quite high, the bodice plain and form fitting, the light-colored panniers did lessen the severity of her frock.

"Well, Addie, what do you think?" Lottie asked eagerly.

"Thank you," was all Addie managed to say to both her sisters. She was no longer angry at them for getting her in this fix. At least they were happy. If Ian had any suspicions about either of them or their husbands, he had kept those thoughts well hidden.

Unlike his opinions about me, Addie thought.

"Addie, stop being so contrary. When are you going to tell us your decision?" Lottie gathered up snippets of fabric and bits of lace from the braided rug in Addie's bedroom.

Addie looked at her sisters, and a current of pride rushed through her. They were great beauties—both of them. Lottie's hair rivaled the sun and Mattie's eyes were thick-lashed and mysterious. Addie would miss her sisters when she was gone—but at least she could leave knowing they had gotten their hearts' desires by being able to remain in McTavish Plain.

"I can't believe you have kept your choice a secret from us," Lottie said over her shoulder as she tidied up Addie's bureau.

"I want everyone to be surprised." Addie picked up her heavy black fringed shawl. It had been a gift from Aleck, who had returned to her house the morning after she had patched up Darroch.

"I don't want word getting out and having all my beaux brokenhearted—and I know how you gossip, both of you," Addie managed to say with a smile, though her heart was breaking.

Lottie harrumphed and Mattie widened her eyes as if they had never indulged in idle chatter.

"Well, I never! How could—" Mattie began.

"Now don't start up." Addie held up one hand in her defense. "Help me load the pies and the blueberry cobblers into the buggy. It would be nice to arrive on time for once." Though she really had no desire to go, Addie played her part well, rushing her sisters and fretting that they would be late. And in spite of her big show, as usual, they arrived late.

Dozens of horses stood tethered outside the barn. Buggies and wagons and buckboards lined the road outside. Addie knew the barn would contain every child, woman and single man that called McTavish Plain home.

This was a momentous occasion. Everyone expected the only single woman in McTavish Plain to pick a husband.

Addie screwed up her courage and walked through the door. Single men were lined up along the wall, their eyes finding her immediately, following her every move, as if she had a big target painted on the front of her frock. Darned if she didn't feel like a tethered turkey at a shooting match.

"Oh, look, Addie." Mattie sighed. "They are all waiting for you. How romantic." But her dreamy smile faded quickly to be replaced by a frown. "And there is that scamp Scout! Land's sake! Look what he is doing!"

Before Addie could see what offense the mischief-maker was up to, her sister had bustled off toward a table laden with pies, tarts and fancy cookies. The boy saw Mattie coming and tried to flee, but Mattie's hand snaked out, and she latched onto his ear. Amid howls of pain she marched him toward an unoccupied corner, issuing orders and admonishments with every step. It was a good thing the band was tuning up, making discordant notes on fife, fiddle and banjo, or else someone might have come to see why the boy was yelping like a hurt pup. But soon Mattie was smiling and Scout's head was hanging in shame, a tiny grin curving his lips.

Addie would miss all this.

By unspoken accord the band finally played the same tune. A familiar waltz filled the air. Couples paired off, their heels swirling little piles of sawdust into random design as they performed the graceful steps in the center of the big, lantern-lit barn.

"Addie, you having to pick a man is just about the most excitement I've had since we got here," Lottie said with a long-suffering sigh. "I thought McTavish Plain was going to be different. Even with the Indians living so close, it is still boring. I hoped I would have an adventure of my own by now."

"I'm so glad I was able to brighten your life with my difficulty, Lottie." Addie arranged her baked goods on the table, trying hard to swallow the lump that was forming in her throat. But it would not be banished. She turned back to her, wishing she could tell her what was really going to happen and at the same time wishing she didn't have to leave.

"Doesn't it give you one moment's pause that I don't want a man—a *husband?* From the beginning I said I didn't want to be married."

Lottie shrugged. "But I never knew why, Addie. You should be married. You are a marrying kind of woman. You need a man and a family to look after. Besides, there is something kind of exhilarating in knowing you have to do it—that time is running out. It adds a bit of spice. In a way I envy you, Addie. I get shivers just thinking about it."

"What I get when I think about being forced to pick a man—a stranger for a husband, like he was so many yards of piece goods—is not the shivers."

"Well, you had better brace yourself, because here all those 'piece goods' come."

Addie glanced up to see a wall of men heading her way. Joe was grinning at her in that open, friendly way of his. Gus had a wicked gleam in his eye. He gave her a wink, as if they shared some naughty secret. John Holcomb gave her a shy smile that assured all and sundry that he was as steadfast and honest as a summer's day.

Why couldn't she simply pick one? Life with Joe or Gus or John wouldn't be unpleasant. They would rub along well enough together. She liked each one of them for different reasons.

But that was it: She liked them. She didn't want to marry a man she only *liked*. She wanted to marry a man she loved to distraction. Addie wanted a grand passion almost as much as Lottie wanted a grand adventure. Addie wanted . . .

The barn doors opened and a gust of wintry wind swirled a pattern of snow inside. Everyone, including Addie, turned to see the man silhouetted in the setting sun. The latecomer was standing in the doorway as if he was hesitant to step over the threshold—to take that last, tentative step required to join them. One booted foot was poised, not quite in the air, but neither was it planted firmly upon the barn floor.

Whoever the man was, he was tall—his long legs thick and corded with muscle within straight-cut black trousers. The superfine frock coat, also dark as a winter's night, was snug through the width of his shoulders.

The winter moon reflected on the snow behind him to create mauve and blue lights upon the hard crust. His hair, still damp and dark as a beaver's sleek pelt, was combed severely back from his wide forehead.

He took a deep breath and put his boot over the threshold.

Addie had the impression that the small step had some strong significance for him. She scanned his face, trying to find some clue to his motives.

His cheekbones were high and prominent, his nose a haughty blade. The clean-shaven jaws were lean and square enough to have been chiseled from the craggy summit of Red Bird Mountain.

It was not a handsome face, not in the classic sense. It was too hard . . . too strong . . . too manly.

There was a stubborn set to the clefted chin. It was a

face with character—definite opinions and determination. It was a man's face.

"Who is that? And where has he been hiding?" Lottie whispered to Addie.

Her gaze roamed over his features. There was a severity to the slant of his dark brows as he met her gaze. . . .

"That," Addie said, frozen to the floor while she stared into his crystalline blue eyes, "is Ian McTavish."

Their gazes locked and held across the huge expanse of the barn. For a moment it seemed as if there were nobody else there, no Lottie or Mattie, no eager suitors, only Ian and Addie and the white-hot current that flowed between them.

He took another step.

He was no longer a bearded mountain man in faded tartan cloth and buckskins. Ian was dressed like a proper gentleman from head to booted toe.

She noticed he wasn't limping, at least not much. His wound must've healed. But thoughts of his leg brought thoughts of how that hard, muscled leg must look when not covered by an ell of black cloth.

Addie's heart fluttered; her hands shook. Her knees began to go liquid. His eyes held her own like a flame holds a moth, even though the risk of burning is only a heartbeat away.

She felt . . . *something*. The blood pumping through her veins grew warm under his gaze. The excitement she felt was hot, untamed and powerful.

Her corset was too tight.

Her shawl too heavy . . . the folds of cloth too thick.

She wanted to tear at the buttons holding the collar tight around her neck. The black tulle Lottie had fastened to her jaunty bonnet seemed about to strangle her.

Addie wanted to rip her gaze from Ian, to run into the cool night's darkness before it was too late.

But too late for what?

The tension was too much. It was unbearable and yet she could not move.

"Addie, girl, I believe this is my dance." Gus looped an arm around her waist and twirled her away, rescuing her from herself. It was the only way she would've broken eye contact with Ian. But in the next spin Ian's face flashed by.

His eyes followed her around the dance floor.

His expression of blatant disapproval was even more severe and noticeable than before. Now that Addie could see the downturned corners of his full mouth, undisguised by a beard, she nearly wept. Was that what his lush beard had been hiding? Had he shaved to let her see the full measure of his ire?

But then she looked into his eyes, colder and harder than the stones of the mountain behind his home, and she knew the truth.

Ian McTavish had spruced himself up, shaved and shed his buckskins for the happy occasion of her downfall. He was standing there glaring at her, his eyes following her every move, and she realized that he knew what her decision would be.

He *knew!* He was smart and shrewd and he had figured out she would refuse to take any of McTavish Plain's men for a husband.

Ian was slicked up and already gloating that she would be packed and leaving his town in just a few more hours.

How smug he looked . . . how handsome. Now that she realized, it all made sense.

Ian, handsome, slick, shaven Ian, would look the perfect innocent when she refused all the men and he was *forced* to ask her to leave.

Addie shook that wayward thought from her head. But in this moment when her heart was vulnerable and raw and aching with feelings she dared not consider, Addie realized that she wanted more than anything to prevent Ian from winning this battle of wills.

There had to be a way! Oh, how she longed to set arrogant Ian McTavish back on his long, muscled haunches!

Chapter Sixteen

Adelaide was so graceful she seemed to float across the sawdust-covered floor as Ian watched, his mouth dry, his pulse thrumming in his own ears.

Gus was holding her too damned close! In fact, what was Gus doing holding her at all? Didn't the man himself point out that Ian wanted Adelaide? Didn't he tell Ian to speak pretty words and be nice to her in order to win her? And now there he was, big as life, laughing and *waltzing* with Adelaide.

"My Adelaide!" a voice inside Ian's head bellowed.

"Gus is the veriest scoundrel for taking advantage," Ian snarled beneath his breath.

He had half a mind to call that silver-haired fox outside and beat him to a bloody pulp. But while Ian was momentarily distracted, plotting Gus's imminent demise, Joe Christian tapped Gus on the shoulder. With a smile of regret, Gus relinquished his too-tight hold on Adelaide.

Quick as a wink, Joe became the rival who stared into Adelaide's sweet, pale face. Now it was Joe's hand at her tiny waist—a waist nipped in so tight by that rigid whalebone corset, Ian was certain he could span it with his two hands.

If he had the chance! If those other bounders would back off and give the lass some room to breath! Why were they lining up? Did they mean to dance the lass's feet right off?

Didn't she notice how Ian had shaved and scraped? Didn't she see how the black coat fit . . . how he had worked for hours to put a shine on the boot leather?

Didn't she see him or the heart on his sleeve?

"For her."

Joe said something and Adelaide laughed. A clear, sweet sound that caused a hot bead of sweat to break out on the back of Ian's neck.

Ian growled—actually growled. "I should put the cur through his own sawmill blade; that will cut him down to size." But once again while red-hot notions of murder and mayhem sprouted in Ian's mind, another man stepped forward and swept Adelaide into his arms.

John Holcomb didn't hold her so close, Ian noticed with prickly relief, but the way he looked into her face . . . his lusty yearning was evident in every line of his body, every stiff step and shallow breath he took.

Ian could see it; could Adelaide? Did she return his feelings?

A red wash shimmered before Ian's eyes. He managed to keep himself from throttling the lot of them—but just barely.

How was he going to woo the lass when there was a wall of men around her?

How?

Addie clung to her partner while her heartbeat thumped and fluttered an irregular cadence. Ian's eyes were still hard and cold as shards of ice. She remembered that one time he had smiled at her and his eyes had danced and twinkled.

Would he ever smile again? Would her leaving make him happy enough to smile? Or did he save his smiles for Grass Singing?

While Addie was puzzling over that question, Gert's voice rang out. "Ian McTavish, you are a good-looking son of a buck with all that fur cleaned off your face. Come here and let me have a proper look at you."

The dancing halted. Everyone watched Ian.

Addie wished she could have the freedom to yell out her feelings, her wants, her intentions as easily as Gert did. But Gert was married; only a married—a happily married—woman could say such outrageous things and get away with it.

But by her own machinations Addie was not married. She alone lived under the stigma of being a single woman in Ian's town of married women only.

Gert put her hands on her hips and waited for Ian to comply. At first he looked puzzled, then troubled, but he put one foot in front of the other until he was standing before Gert like an obedient child waiting for inspection.

And inspect him Gert did. First she spun him around, and then when his back was to her, while the whole of the town looked on, Gert splayed her palms across Ian's wide shoulders and rubbed, like a tailor admiring the fit of a garment or the breadth of the body beneath it. Miley laughed while his wife checked girth and shank, as if Ian were a horse she might bid on at a sale barn.

"Those big arms of yours look right nice in a good-cut coat. You been hiding under all that hair and buckskin— haven't you?"

"I dinna do no such thing," Ian replied gruffly. A faint stain of pink rose in his neck and clean shaven cheeks.

"Ha! What were you afraid of, Ian? That some pretty filly might want to see you broke and hobbled?"

"I am afraid of nothing, Gert," Ian said defensively.

The youngest of McTavish Plain's married women began to work their way nearer to Ian. Carolina Martin, the woman who sat side by side with her husband at a loom and turned McTavish wool into McTavish woolen goods, had a decided sparkle in her eye. As did Susan Reed, Dorothea Pollock, Mary Hubbard and a half dozen others.

Suddenly Ian looked a lot less *un*comfortable and a whole lot more like a preening peacock. He was enjoying the attention and the compliments and the less-than-chaste gazes from the flock of women gathered round him. Addie felt a mixture of annoyance and another emotion that she did not want to examine too closely. She told herself it could not be jealousy. . . .

"Mmm-mmm-mmm." Gert shook her head from side to side. "A fine looking son of a buck. And me married and old enough to be your . . . auntie."

A burst of laughter followed Gert's remark. Some of the married women whispered and giggled behind their hands. Husbands soon appeared from nowhere to take their places at their wives' sides. Now that Ian had shed his buckskins and tartan cloth, he was less a man's man and more of the kind that women gave a second glance to.

"I'd never have believed you could be such a handsome hunk of flesh," Gert fairly cooed at him. "If I wasn't so danged happy with my old Miley, I'd be setting my cap for you, Mr. McTavish!"

The men roared with hoots, catcalls and laughter, while both Ian and Miley's complexions took on a ruddy hue. Then the crowd turned and Miley became the brunt of a little ribbing. The tension of Ian's arrival evaporated into good-natured horseplay, but Addie felt a strange, cold knot in her belly. Ian McTavish had indeed told her that "he liked women verra, verra much," and now she was seeing the proof of it. Not only did Grass Singing have a tender spot for him, even married women were not immune to Ian's charms.

And he welcomes the attention from all but me!

Slowly the kernel of a plan began to sprout in Addie's mind. If Ian was a man who valued his freedom *and* liked the ladies, then maybe all was not lost. His tomcatting nature and the attention he was receiving had given her one slim chance to save herself, one new idea that might save her. If it worked, she could stay in McTavish Plain and not have to marry anyone.

A tap on her shoulder brought Addie turning round. She stared up into the slate gray eyes of Gus Gruberman. She had been so lost in thought, plotting a way to escape Ian McTavish's carefully laid trap, that she had not heard him approach.

"The band is playing again, Addie girl. Would you risk another turn around the floor with an old fool who has two left feet?"

"I would be honored," Addie said truthfully.

As they began to dance, Gus cleared his throat. Then he looked down into Addie's face. "You know, Addie girl, I am a mite older than you, but I still got a little life left in me. If you find your back against the wall . . . I'm here. I mean, if you can't see your way clear to pick another galoot from this town, I'd be proud to call you wife." His usual wink was missing. His Adam's apple bobbed when he swallowed and added, "I just wanted you to know."

"Thank you, Gus," Addie choked out. "It is good to know I have a friend, but I couldn't do that to you." Neither would she pick Joe nor Roamer nor John nor Pete nor Michael Jones, the new printer, a man so pale and thin, he looked as if he needed a wife and about a month in the sunshine.

"But Addie, if you don't marry, you'll have to be leaving," Gus said softly.

"So it would seem, Gus." Addie did not tell Gus she was sure Ian had planned it this way all along. She watched him laughing and joking with Harriet Miller and Gert. Every now and again, when there was a lull in all the praise he was getting from his adoring flock of hens, he would cast a sly, speculative glance her way.

It made her blood boil with anger, but it also made her weak in the knees. She just didn't understand it. In some ways she and Ian were like a tomcat and a female cat. They circled, they spit, they flashed their claws. . .

She didn't trust him—most of the time she didn't much like him—but she couldn't deny that he was a man who made her breath catch and her heart skip a beat.

He was like a splinter in her hide. She couldn't ignore him, but it would mean the world to her if she could find a way to keep him from succeeding in his quest to get rid of her.

An hour had passed and Ian had yet to work up the courage to ask Adelaide to dance. He had watched every son of a buck in town twirl her through the thin layer of sawdust on the floor, the bile rising in his gorge with each step, and yet he couldn't muster the sand to do it himself.

Him. A man who had hand-fought grizzlies, taken down an elk with little more than a bow and a knife . . . had battled Indians, mountain lions, cut trails through thigh deep snow and lived rough in a cave all winter to trap the beaver to make the money to see McTavish Plain be born from nothing.

He was terrified of a slender woman with flame red hair—terrified to his boot heels of asking Adelaide to dance.

The fear was not of being turned down, or even being laughed at by the townsfolk, or of stumbling on his still aching leg. It was the terror of laying his soul bare—of letting her see how much he cared for her. Ian was afraid if he said one civil word to Adelaide on this night when she was so beautiful she must've been touched by angels, that the dam of his control would burst.

He was afraid he would fall to his knees in supplication, vowing his life, his heart, his benighted *soul* if she would let him love her.

Ian couldn't do it. He couldn't take such a risk. He couldn't let Adelaide see how she unmanned him.

And so he watched and he bled and he died a little inside, feeling a raw ache of longing so sharp it sliced his heart to ribbons with love and need and fear. He stood on his stiff leg, feeling his own uneven stitches pinch and pull, and then around midnight, when the men playing the instruments took a cider break, Gus Gruberman walked to the middle of the barn. In a deep baritone voice he gazed at Adelaide and said, ''The time has come for Addie Brown to tell us her decision. Who will you pick, Addie girl? Which man jack among us will have the privilege of wedding you tomorrow morn'?''

Chapter Seventeen

Adelaide's eyes widened like a deer trapped by a hunter. She swallowed so hard, Ian could swear he heard her throat working convulsively.

She was afraid. He couldn't stand it, her being stiff with fright. His impulse was to protect her.

He strode to the center of the barn, angry at Gus for making her do this ... more angry at himself for ever starting the damned mad foolishness in the first place. When he made the rule about no unmarried women, he had in mind to keep unscrupulous men from bringing in whiskey and gambling and soiled doves that would taint his town and make it little more than a watering hole on the way to the Oregon Territory.

He never meant his rule to cause a moment's worry to someone as fine and good as Adelaide Brown.

"Ah, Ian, I have a notion you are as anxious as the rest of us to hear which man will be her husband," Gus said gruffly.

Ian narrowed his eyes at Gus, mumbling half-meant

threats of violence under his breath until he heard Gus chuckling. He glared at the silver-haired fox.

"Have a care, old friend; don't poke fun too hard or I may clout you on the chin."

Then, suddenly Adelaide was there, glowering up at Ian as if he were the devil himself. And if the weight of his guilt was any kind of measure at all, maybe he was old Scratch. . . .

"Mr. McTavish, *you* were the one who bade me choose. You were the one who gave me a month to mourn my husband's passing before taking another man to stand before the preacher—so don't be taking Gus to task."

Ian blinked at the outrage in her wonderful eyes. She hated him—and the lass had good reason to do so, for everything she said was true.

How could he have been so stupid as to think he could win her affection after committing so many sins against her?

"You have been all-fired certain of me from the first, haven't you?" she fumed.

Ian opened his mouth to answer, but Adelaide kept shouting at him, pointing her finger at his breastbone, jabbing at the third button on his shirt until he took a step backward . . . and another . . . and another, until he was retreating before the furious female. If his heart hadn't been in his throat, he would have laughed at the absurdity of a man of his size trembling before a lass who barely reached his chin.

"You, Ian McTavish, with your smug attitudes and your disapproving gazes. You with your town and your rules and your cock-sure notions about what makes a town strong and what makes a town weak. Well, I've got news for you, Mr. McTavish, you aren't going to win."

"Win?" he croaked. Lord, but the lass was beautiful when she was in a high temper. He wanted to grab her hand, to suck that lovely, dainty finger she was using like a weapon. He wanted to kiss her until she was mad with passion and need.

"I am going to call your bluff, Mr. McTavish. You were certain I wouldn't do it, weren't you? You were sure I would be too humiliated to pick. Well, I'm not! I'll pick a new husband to satisfy your high-and-mighty rules."

"You will?" Ian's heart was pounding like a war drum. Would she pick Gus? Joe? Pete? Roamer?

He had backed her against a wall and now she would fight like a wildcat. He would lose his last chance to win her love when she became another man's wife.

It was unthinkable. And it was his own fault.

"That's right. I'll pick." Addie turned to face the crowd, her skirts swishing with the motion. The long black veil on her hat fluttered. Her spine was stiff as a ramrod, her temper hot as gunpowder. Ian felt his loins stir, twitch and harden. Adelaide was one hell of a woman. She was strong, proud. She would raise up fine, lusty sons and beautiful daughters.

"I pick . . .

No! No! a voice inside his head yelled.

"Ian McTavish to be my new husband!"

She had just picked *him?*

Adelaide turned back to Ian, her chin jutting out defiantly. Confusion swirled in his mind while he tried to sort his emotions, to separate longings from reality. He could not trust himself to believe he had truly heard her right.

"Me?"

"That's right, Mr. McTavish. *You.*" She put her hands on her hips and leaned toward him. "After all, any man who is so fond of the married state—or at least of seeing women in the married state—should be that way himself. Don't you think?"

Addie's heart was beating so hard, she was sure that

Ian could hear it, but she couldn't back down now. If her plan worked, she would not have to leave.

If she was right, Ian would refuse her, and then she would appeal to the townsfolk. Ian would have no choice but to let her stay . . . *unmarried!*

Any minute now. Any little minute now, he would refuse to take her as his wife.

Ian swallowed hard and swallowed once again. Was it possible that his dream could be coming true? She was picking him?

Yes, she was, but he looked into her eyes, all lightning and anger, and realized she was not doing it because of any affection. She had picked him in a fit of rage.

Why?

His brows knitted together as the full impact of all she'd said settled in his lust-fevered brain. She had told him he couldn't win.

Win what?

Ian searched Adelaide's face. There was the slightest twitch of her lips. It wasn't a smile, but it was the flickering expression of victory. His hunter's instinct brought prickles along his spine.

It hit him.

The sly vixen had bearded the lion in his den! She thought Ian would refuse to wed her. She thought by grandstanding in front of everyone, she could force him into taking back his demand that she marry.

But then another aspect of her decision came upon him like an icy dousing of cold water. She was going to marry him—to punish him! She had starch in her, starch and grit and a fine, high temper. If Adelaide was of a mind, she could certainly make a man's life hell. But she also had passion and a soft heart and alluring curves and eyes that made Ian's head swim.

It could be one or the other. She could be hoping he would let her remain an unmarried widow, or she could

be planning to marry him and make him regret it with
every shrewish deed she could imagine.

But it didn't really matter. Either way Ian was willing
to have her and consider himself lucky in the bargain.

"Yes . . . by thunder, yes!" Ian beamed at Adelaide.
"Agreed, lass. I'll take you as my wife."

It only took two heartbeats before Ian yanked her to
him, feeling her tremble slightly beneath his grip upon
her shoulders.

"And now let's have a kiss to seal the bargain."

He bent his head and did what he had wanted to do all
night long. He covered her mouth with his and made
himself a promise to win Adelaide's heart.

Addie was off balance when Ian grabbed her, as she
was in the process of taking a step backward to avoid his
advance and tripping on her own hem at the same time.
The long black tulle veil Lottie had added to her dress
was tangled around one ankle. She had no choice but to
cling to Ian's wide shoulders.

Clinging to Ian?

When she realized that she was *holding* him, grasping
him as if he were her only shelter in a storm, she clenched
her hands into fists and placed them between their bodies,
pushing ineffectually against his muscled bulk.

What had gone wrong with her plan? Ian didn't want
to be married in general. That was evident in the pleasure
he took from the crowd of women around him and his
association with Grass Singing.

And he really didn't want to be married to her in particular. He proved day after day when he gave her nothing
but icy stares and had worked so hard to get her to leave
his town.

But if that was the case, then why was he kissing her
with all the passion and tenderness of a lovestruck suitor?
Why were his hands tender in the way they clamped her

body to his? Why was her heart pounding like Roamer's hammer at the anvil?

Addie had never been kissed like this. Not even when Ian himself had stolen kisses before. This kiss was hot, wild and all-consuming. Ian filled her senses with his manly presence. He smelled of strong soap . . . and starch and *him*.

He held her so close, she could feel the imprint of his shirt buttons through her bodice. She could feel the bulge of his chest muscles beneath her fists, only her hands weren't clenched into fists anymore. They had opened of their own accord and were rubbing over the taut, hard planes of his body, up to the point of his shoulder, round to the nape of his neck.

Somehow her traitorous hands were actually caressing the curls above his shirt collar, tangling in the strands with complete abandon. His hair was soft, she noticed, as her fingers buried themselves into it. Soft strands of hair and rock-hard muscle to touch and caress and wonder at . . . His lips were firm—neither soft nor hard—just *nice*. His bare face, without the beard, felt right and a little strange.

Addie sighed. Like her fists, her lips were suddenly open.

Quick as a flash of lightning, Ian was doing things with his mouth . . . his tongue!

Oh, the heat. Spiraling waves of sensation sizzled through Addie. She nearly whimpered from the surprise of each onslaught of feeling. And yet he did more, promised more, and her heart cried out with the sheer beauty of his touch.

Oh my. Oh . . . the sensations . . . dark, sweet, seductive. Was this what it was like to have a man make to love you? Was this the special, secret bond that grew and flourished and strengthened a man and a woman through years, seasons, through a lifetime of work?

Addie moaned softly and yielded herself to his embrace.

Muscles contracted ... others relaxed. Her body molded itself to the contour of his form, seeking a better fit, finding a way to be closer.

Closer ... nearer ... a part of him. Dear God ... she wanted to be part of him. How could this be? How could *any* of this be real?

His hand slid up and cradled the back of her head.

She felt whole. She felt boneless.

His other palm, hot as a sadiron even through frock, petticoat and corset, caressed the small of her back.

She moaned again with unexpected pleasure.

She wanted to feel his hot hands on her bare flesh. She wanted to know how his skin felt. She wanted—no, *needed*—in a way she had never dreamed was possible. This was more than need, or hunger—this was madness, and fulfillment and all manner of things she could not put a name to.

Addie had no word to describe this incredible dizziness or the throbbing heat that kept curling inside her.

''Ian, there'll be time enough for that after the weddin' service in the mornin'.'' Gus's voice penetrated Addie's lust, but only a little, as if even Gus was part of this erotic dream.

''I think maybe it would be a good idea if they didn't wait,'' Gert said with a strangled cough. ''They seem to be in a bit of a rush for the honeymoon.''

There was a moment of silence and then a spat of nervous laughter, but it was far away and unimportant. Addie could pay it no mind, not with Ian holding her.

Ian pulled away, his eyes smoky with passion. He grinned down at her and she saw for the first time the dimple that had been hidden beneath his beard. Then he winked at her and she realized that Gus knew nothing about looking naughty when he winked, for Ian was the picture of deviltry and the promise of earthly pleasures to come.

"Good idea, Gert," Ian said loudly. "Let's get the marrying done right now. Reverend Miller, pull out your book."

And Addie must have been drunk with Ian's kisses because she never managed to utter a word of protest as Ian slipped his arm around her waist and positioned them before Horace Miller.

As if in a dream, the blushing minister mumbled the words that would bind them together as man and wife. Addie murmured her agreement after Ian and then glanced up at her new husband.

Ian McTavish was smiling. Really smiling.

It seemed only moments later that Ian was accepting slaps on the back, as if he had won some great contest. Addie tried not to let her thoughts run in that direction, but from the way everyone was acting and congratulating Ian on his good luck, she did feel like the prize at a shooting contest.

Like that turkey everybody wanted to win.

"That dinna take long," Ian said cheerfully. "Much quicker than I had imagined."

"Hm . . . like a mercy killing," Addie mumbled, still stunned with what had happened, still trying to understand when her plan had become a piecrust dream—easily made—easily broken.

Ian looked down at her with amusement in his eyes. " 'Tis the groom who is supposed to look upon marriage like death itself, Adelaide. Not the bride." Then he laughed again.

The sound came from deep within his chest. It rumbled up like thunder across the prairie. Addie tried to ignore it . . . and him . . . and the intoxicating aftereffects of his touch, but how could she when her body craved his like a drunkard craves pear wine?

She looked away, seeing her sisters dipping punch and smiling happily. Of course they could be happy. They still had make-believe husbands making a pretend journey to join them here.

Addie blinked back hot tears that suddenly came from nowhere.

Sometime between her proposal to Ian and their hasty wedding ceremony, hard cider and whiskey had appeared. Now a cup of something was thrust into her hand. With a dazed sense of being outside herself, Addie smiled weakly as toast after toast was raised to the newly married couple—the first and only couple to be wed in McTavish Plain.

She and Ian had become celebrated oddities by saying "I do." At least now she had company in being unique . . . if she considered Ian McTavish company. The old saw about misery ran through her head.

How could he have done this to her? She had been so sure, so all fired sure . . . she had *known* Ian would refuse her.

The jug was passed and passed again. Tom and Michael and Gus and Roamer drank deeply, slapping Ian on the back, giving him winks and congratulations.

How quickly her suitors had deserted her. How quickly they got over their sorrow at losing her. It appeared the men had never wanted Addie at all—in fact, it seemed everyone was pleased with her choice . . . everyone, that is, but her.

Addie took a degree of perverse pleasure, knowing most of her erstwhile suitors would be muzzy in the head tomorrow. Too bad, she thought, that tonight was Friday and not Saturday eve. She would like to sit in her pew and watch them suffer as Horace Miller delivered a rousing sermon on the evils of drink.

But she sighed and told herself it wasn't Saturday night, but Friday. Tomorrow morning the men could all sleep till noon if their swollen heads dictated. This was just one more evening to them. To Addie it was the beginning of disaster.

She was wedded, good and proper. But good Lord, how was she going to share bed and board with Ian McTavish day after day?

Addie felt a pinch on her finger. She looked down to find she was twisting her new wedding ring on her finger, turning and turning the golden band with the dark reddish stone. She had been wearing her false wedding ring since she arrived in McTavish Plain and had only removed it after getting the letter. But that make-believe wedding ring had never felt like this.

This was Ian's ring. Placed there with his own hand. It felt foreign, heavy. . . . It was the mark of Ian's possession of her.

"The ring looks bonny on your dainty hand, Adelaide." Ian's voice rubbed over her skin.

She glanced up to find he was watching her, that unreadable expression on his face—in his eyes.

"And it fits as if made for you, wife."

"As snug as a noose," she snapped.

"Once again you speak as if you have been condemned." Ian tilted one brow upward. "I ken you are not entirely happy about the way things have turned out, Adelaide. But I canna understand why. 'Twas *you* who asked *me* to marry you. If you dinna want me, then why did you not pick another man?"

She was momentarily stunned by his words. Addie had been so busy nursing her wounded pride, she had not truly thought of that. She was the one who proposed, loudly and in front of witnesses. She could never claim he forced the issue. And she could not mope around acting like the injured maiden either, for Ian was sharp and watchful and would soon become suspicious. If she told him that she had planned for him to refuse her, it would put him on her trail as surely as a hound after a buck.

Addie raised her chin and stared up at Ian, once again feeling that odd, disconcerted, out-of-joint sensation at his new appearance. Only Ian's eyes were the same, and yet with the shaggy hair cut above his collar and full beard gone, he looked even more *dangerous.* Yes, and *ruthless,* and though she was loath to admit it . . . *handsome.*

The man was handsome as sin.

She mentally shook herself, shedding that thought, and made herself a promise; Ian would not best her in this struggle again. He might have won this battle, but he had not won the war. Not by a long shot!

And she was just about ready to fire the first shot.

Chapter Eighteen

"Come on you two, it's time for the first dance," Lottie said cheerfully, grabbing Addie and Ian's wrists and towing them to the center of the barn.

"We must now dance for our supper," Ian purred as he pulled Addie into his arms. He took the hostile wind from her sails when he looked down at her with feigned concern in his eyes and said, "What troubles you, lass? You have gone quiet as a mouse, Adelaide. Quite different than the woman who was bruising my breastbone a few hours ago."

She opened her mouth. She *wanted* to sear the hide off him with her tongue, but suddenly she could think of nothing to say to her new husband. For once again her body—traitor that it was—had reacted to him in a most shocking way. And though her rebellious spirit, still stinging from Ian's having outwitted her—outmaneuvered her wanting to be a shrew, her body had other ideas entirely.

Her nipples went hard, her thighs tingled and the places

on her person where Ian put his hands felt scorched beneath the layers of clothing.

It was too much. . . . It was frightening and powerful and more than Addie could stand. She unconsciously squirmed in his arms, but all she succeeded in doing was fitting herself more firmly against his lean, muscled form.

She fought the invisible touch of his eyes, trying instead to focus on the crowd that watched them so intently.

Addie heard bits and pieces of conversation as Ian waltzed her around in the circle made by her neighbors. Between the slurred words and the spinning turns, she heard only scraps of sentences and disjointed murmurings.

"—wedding night" reached her ears on one turn.

And then "—lucky Ian . . ." on the next.

"—married a *widow.*"

And so it went. With each sweeping turn, she heard a different voice here, a different phrase there.

"—no shy virgin . . . knows what married life is all about."

"—won't need to break her in . . ."

"—big, wide bed . . ."

The last bit was followed by lewd laughter that brought heat to Addie's cheeks and understanding to her numb brain.

Ian had married her . . . believing she was a widow . . . and he would be expecting a wedding night.

A wedding night with a widow of some considerable experience!

She was a virgin. She had no more idea of what went on between a man and a woman than she had years ago when she had kissed her poor, doomed husband and said, "I do."

She couldn't let Ian McTavish into her bed! No matter how expertly he kissed her, no matter how her body burned to learn what mysteries the marriage bed held.

He would know in an instant that she had lied . . . and

then he would start putting two and two together and he would come up with three lying sisters!

"Careful, lass," Ian warned in his husky burr, and for a moment she thought he could read her mind, but then she realized he was referring to her misstep.

She sagged against him when her legs became no more substantial than water. He took her weight, but she felt him wobble . . . only a tiny shake, but it made Addie's belly flip-flop when she remembered his recent injury.

"Well, lass, I think we have done the pretty and our duty. Let's borrow a buggy and head for home. My aching leg is telling me that it promises to be a cold night," Ian said with a seductive smile.

"You have no idea how cold," Addie said beneath her breath, feeling a mixture of concern for his well-being and her own instinct for self-preservation clashing like water against stone. "No idea at all."

Within moments the good-byes and well wishes were being said. Addie managed to snag a bottle of whiskey from Gus. He gave her a puzzled look, but she was spared trying to explain, since the crowd had begun to grow so exuberant that Ian had grabbed her hand and nearly dragged her to the waiting buggy.

She saw him limping and knew he had not been teasing her about the pains in his leg, but Addie had to check herself; thoughts of Ian's wounded body brought carnal images that nearly scalded her soul.

The harness bells jingled merrily as the horses plowed through the snow on the path Ian had created with Dow a few hours earlier. A plaid lap robe and a hot potato had been provided for Addie's hands. Warmed bricks rested beneath her feet.

If she weren't so miserable, she would've been enjoying the moonlit ride.

"Who did all this?" Addie said as Ian shifted himself on the seat beside her.

"Your sisters thought of everything, lass." Ian's rough velvet voice skipped over her skin. He grinned broadly, the picture of an anxious bridegroom.

"My sisters?" she squeaked, while she turtled deeper into her scarf and pulled the lap robe tighter around her legs. "They did all this?"

"I saw them flitting 'round like a couple of wood sprites. They even packed you a bag." Ian nodded toward Addie's old moth-eaten carpetbag in the back.

"I wonder what they selected for your wedding night?" he said softly and scooted a little nearer to her. She caught the masculine scent of starch and fresh air mingling with the smoky attar of the whiskey used for their wedding toasts. Addie unconsciously inhaled, drawing his scent in, causing a spiral of sensation to telegraph through her middle.

Addie gulped—hard—and flattened herself against the railing on the seat. She was going to have to keep her guard up. It was obvious Ian thought he was going to find out just what she wore at night, but as far as she was concerned, she intended to keep her corset laces knotted. She stared straight ahead, the glow of the moonlight shimmering on falling snow. Surely there was a way to divert his attention from their wedding night.

Maybe it would continue to snow—a lot—too much for them to get home.

No.

Then she would be forced to snuggle beneath the lap robe with him, and that would lead to ruin.

But surely that pile of rocks Ian called home would be drafty, damp and cold. She could sleep in her heavy coat . . . her boots on . . . under a pile of buffalo robes . . . in front of a roaring fire . . . as far from a bed as she could get.

She drew the woolen scarf closer around her neck.

"Are you chilled, lass?"

"No. I am fine." Addie made herself as small as possible and huddled against the cold black iron rim of the seat.

"Well, you are shivering like an aspen leaf in the wind." Ian slanted a glance at her, but as usual his dark blue eyes were unreadable, no more than blue-black shadows within the paleness of his face. After a moment he said, "Ah, 'tis beginning to snow harder now."

Addie tilted her face up, peering out of the folds of her scarf. Fat flakes landed on her nose, eyelashes and lips. God had answered her prayer for snow . . . now if only . . .

Ian watched Adelaide with her face raised toward heaven and thought he would surely die from pleasure at the sight of her.

She was beautiful. Her glowing skin and flaming hair looked luminescent beneath the frosty moonlight. Her profile was feminine yet strong. Hers was an image that would make a proper Scotsman spout poetry.

Ian cleared his throat and tried to compose a verse worthy of his bride, but nothing came to mind. He cursed himself for a clumsy dolt, but still no pretty words made themselves available. He caught Adelaide watching him, but she quickly turned away.

"Adelaide, is there something you wish to say?" he finally asked.

"No."

"Something is causing you to fret. Is it the weather? We'll be home soon."

"It's not the weather . . . it's—"

"It is, what?" he pressed, wanting an answer, wanting nothing to mar the perfection of this night.

"You look . . ." Addie straightened her spine and looked away.

"Am I so homely you canna look upon me anymore?" Ian asked. "Without my beard am I too coarse and ugly?"

She wanted to curl up against him just to listen to the rough-soft voice purr from within him.

"No. Not at all ... it is just so *different* with your beard gone and your hair shorter."

How could she tell him that she was a bundle of nerves because she never expected this to happen—that she was a virgin?

"Then if 'tis not me, why are you so ill at ease?"

"Your voice is the same, of course." She made the mistake of turning toward him. Even by the shimmering moonlight his eyes were vast, unfathomable. "Your voice and your eyes are unchanged."

"Perhaps I should keep talking to you all the way home or staring at you as if you were some magical creature that might'na be here if I blink or look away."

"Perhaps." She caught herself grinning at his foolishness. It was so easy to become entwined in the web of temptation Ian spun around her. "Well, at least you don't have a weak chin," she said with a grin.

His bark of laughter startled her. "Is that what you thought? That I grew my beard to hide the flaws of my face and my character?"

"Of course not. A man like you would have no weakness of character," Addie blurted out, wishing she could call the words back. She felt the burn of her heat in her cheeks—so noticeable in the frosty night air.

"Ah, lass, it gives me a warm feeling to know you hold me in such high regard. Tell me ... is that why you chose me?" Ian's voice was ripe with amusement, but when Addie snapped her head around he was watching her with a sober expression on his very handsome, very clean-shaven face.

A man had no right to be so handsome.

"I . . . that is . . . I—" She could think of no suitable lie, and she wasn't about to tell him the truth.

"Ah, well, a little mystery between a man and a woman is a good thing," he said with a chuckle. "But tonight we will begin to know each other better. Won't we, Adelaide?"

Addie swallowed hard. Ian's words frightened her, but they also thrilled and excited her. Desperate to distract him and herself, she reached for the bottle beneath the lap robe. The snow had begun to fall harder. Now it was not so much a romantic sprinkling, fogging her judgment where Ian was concerned, it was downright prickly as wind drove it into her face.

"Would you like a drink to warm you?"

He blinked in surprise, and then a slow, sensual grin spread across his face. "Ah, lass, you are the kind of woman ever' man dreams of marrying."

Ian's eyes were sparkling as he took the bottle and tipped it to his mouth. "No shrewish maiden to nag if a man has a nip, no blushing virgin to cry and shrink from a man's touch. I am a lucky man."

He tipped up the bottle and took a drink. When he was finished, Addie took one herself, feeling the liquid burn all the way to her belly—and lower. And yet, even with the unaccustomed whiskey in her veins, all she was aware of was Ian.

Ian beside her, the breadth of his shoulders in the sheepskin coat. Ian's rugged good looks, each breath he took made her hold her own unconsciously, as if she was waiting, anticipating some unknown event. Each beat of her heart it was Ian who held her attention and made her want to risk everything.

"Have another," Addie suggested quickly. She could not let him get her into the marriage bed! Her sisters' happiness depended upon it.

Maybe if he was skunked she could fend him off or . . .

let him believe they'd had a wedding night. Didn't men often drink until they had no memory of events?

"In fact, Ian, why don't you have two. It is nippy out here." Addie urged hopefully, holding the bottle aloft. She was chagrined to see only a small amount was gone from the long-necked bottle.

"You are an angel, Adelaide, but I canna think it would be good for me to drink more. I dinna want you to think you chose a drunkard for a husband." Ian clucked his tongue at the horses. "The house is over that last rise. And then we shall see what may be done to get you out of that snow-covered coat and scarf."

"So soon?" Addie choked. Her heart had been beating in time to the soft swish of the horses' hooves through the snow. Now it quickened to a frantic pace. She had to find some way of avoiding Ian.

But how?

"It is such a beautiful night, Ian."

"That it is." He agreed. "A proper night for a wedding."

"Oh, yes, but it seems a shame to waste the rest of it." Panic was rising in Addie's middle. Her nerves were tighter than a fiddle string with anticipation. And with each clop the buggy drew nearer to the house . . . and her ruin.

"Waste the rest of it, you say?" Ian turned and looked at Addie, his brows pinching together in the middle.

"Mmmm. We could drive round for a little while."

"Are you not cold, lass?"

"No. Not a bit," she lied. Her toes were near to frozen and her backside had gone numb. "It would be so romantic—the moon, the snow and all." She tried to adopt the dreamy look that Mattie often wore when speaking of things romantic.

"Are you ill, Adelaide?" Ian asked in alarm, his brows furrowing in concern.

"No. Why?"

"For a moment there . . . it looked like your eyes were rolling back in your head. If you are going to swoon, I would rather you did it at home. Too much excitement for your delicate constitution, I'd guess. A warm fire and a warm bed will turn the trick. I canna risk you falling ill from the cold, Adelaide."

And so once again it seemed Ian easily outmaneuvered her. Addie's best efforts to delay her wedding night and the disaster that lay in her marriage bed came to nothing more than her own frosty breath and shattered hopes. Ian quickened the horses' pace and by the silver moonlight she soon had her first real look at his house—her house.

It was big, gray and imposing. Addie stared up at the lonely structure and realized it did look like a castle. Built of rough-hewn stone, it rose from the snow covered rocks as if by magic. Wind shrieked and moaned around the steep upper stories. It was a mournful, unholy sound that made her shiver and pulled her shredded nerves more taut.

She jumped a foot when Ian gently touched her.

"Come, lass, I'll soon have you warm and snug in our marriage bed."

Chapter Nineteen

Ian's shoulders and head were covered with a thin crust of snow, his lashes tipped with white flakes when he gently handed her down from the buggy. Addie was so stiff and cold that she stumbled, falling against him.

"Ah, lass, you warm my blood," he said huskily when her bosom came into contact with his chest.

Suddenly Addie was warm . . . at least her cheeks were, as blood rushed to her hairline. Then her body began to thaw from the middle outward. First her breasts got sensitive and heavy. Her nipples grew so tender, the soft muslin of her corset cover rasped against them. The next moment she was wrapping her arms around Ian's neck, twining her fingers in his cold, snow-dampened hair.

"Adelaide." His husky voice started a coil of sensation spiraling from her naval outward. "I never dared hope you would choose me." His breath fanned over her cheek. He nipped at her bottom lip.

And she was kissing him again!

In spite of all her fears, in spite of her better sense and the danger she courted, she was kissing him *again!*

A voice inside Addie's head branded her fool, a reckless idiot and worse, but she could not pull away from Ian. His mouth was hungry and tempting. She threw all caution to the wind that howled around his stone castle in the lee of the Red Bird Mountain's peaks.

"Ah, Adelaide, I never thought to say so, but I am beholden to your dead husband. His passing, God rest his soul, has given me a woman of great passion and experience. I canna ask for more on my wedding night."

His words sobered her. Once again she was confronted with the dilemma created by her own lies. Ian expected to spend his honeymoon with a widow of passion and experience, not a blushing virgin with a guilty conscience and secrets to keep.

"The bedroom is on the second floor at the end of the corridor," he whispered in her ear, nipping the lobe in a way that made hot shivers skip down her spine. "I'll see to the horses and be right up."

Addie swallowed hard and managed a weak smile. "Don't hurry on my account."

Ian laughed and chucked her chin. "A passionate bride with a sense of humor. I think I am in heaven, lass—but I promise you, in a short while we will be in Paradise together."

He raked her face and body with such a look as Addie never thought possible. In that one glance her flesh seared, her nipples ached and her belly flip-flopped.

Oh, what was she going to do?

Ian had unhitched the buggy and was leading the horses into the dark barn. He missed Dow's welcoming whicker but knew his ornery stallion would be well cared for by

Gert and Miley until he could return their team and bring Dow home.

The small hairs on the back of Ian's neck prickled.

He was being watched.

He spun around, peering through the door into the veil of grayish white. The snow was heavy and wet and had rounded the edges of every outbuilding and rock until they looked some frosty confection created by Addie's own beautiful hands.

"Ian? Where are you, man?" Aleck Bowen's voice was muffled and hollow through the storm. Then Aleck appeared like a wraith. The pale moonlight was just enough to see by—barely. He was leading a horse whose saddle was almost covered with snow. The animal's head hung in fatigue.

"It's a mercy you have a big barn, Ian. My mount has plumb give out."

"What are you doing out on a night like this?" Ian said, feeling more annoyed by Aleck's sudden appearance than concerned for his health. He turned his back to his old companion and lifted the heavy padded collars from the horses's necks. He walked them into their stalls in the dim confines of the barn. Immediately the sound of hay being chewed filled the air.

"Broken Ax's young warriors are becoming restless. I thought it was a good idea if I left the village before I had to kill one of them."

Ian snorted at the notion. Though he and Aleck were hard, seasoned frontiersmen, the skill of a Salish youth was not to be matched. Ian felt his way to the lantern hanging from a beam and struck a match. When the wick caught, filling the barn with a pale golden glow, he turned it down and lowered the chimney into place.

"Lawdy! What happened to your face?" Aleck exclaimed. "You haven't been that naked since we came west together."

"I had my reasons," Ian said dryly. He pitched a little more dried prairie grass into the horses's stalls to give them warm bedding, while Aleck removed the now dripping saddle from his mount.

"Varmints? I onc't knew a man who got varmints in his beard, and by spring they had traveled south and were in his—"

"No, I dinna shave my face because I have varmints!" Ian snapped.

"I have a feeling there's a story behind this," Aleck chuckled.

"Why are you here, Aleck?" Ian's patience was wearing thinner with each passing second. The last thing he wanted was Aleck Bowen along on his wedding night.

"Remember the day I saved your hide from that sow griz?" Aleck said with a conniving grin.

"I remember."

"You told me that if I ever needed a place to lay my head, I could always come to you."

Ian shifted uncomfortably. He had made that promise, but the fact that Aleck was bringing it up now was not a good sign.

"What about Gus?" Ian suggested.

Aleck shook his head in only half-believable sorrow. "I'd surely like to get to town, Ian, but in case you ain't noticed, the snow is running hock deep out there. 'Sides, Gus wears a body out with all his palavering and chess playing. I need peace and quiet. I figure it is high time I accepted your hospitality."

Ian blew out a frustrated breath. He wondered if Aleck had done this on purpose—but how did he hear about the wedding when he wasn't in town?

"You may as well come up to the house. I have a bottle of whiskey. We need to talk."

* * *

Addie stood in the doorway of the room, swamped by her own disbelief. She had been so certain that Ian's house would be a cold pile of stones; instead she found it solid, snug, a safe haven from the storm that promised to be long and fierce.

Oh, it was definitely a bachelor's house, bare and untidy with dust covering every surface, but it was not harsh or cold.

A fire had been laid in the huge fieldstone hearth. She found an empty tin full of long straws on the mantel, a solid piece of pine, and lit one. She soon had a pair of pierced tin lanterns burning as brightly as the logs in the hearth that were seasoned so they caught fast. Sooner than she would've believed possible, the room was warm and cozy, the leaping orange flames soothing. She allowed herself a slow, assessing look at the entire room while she warmed her toes and hands before the blaze.

The floor was plain wood. The empty space before the hearth was dominated by a bearskin. Like the bear rug, the bed was enormous.

Made from hand-hewn pine, the headboard was at least eight feet high. The mattress lay so high from the floor, Addie was sure she would need a stool to climb into it. She crept toward it and curiously pressed down on the surface. The top rebounded pleasantly, the frame creaking slightly at the pressure she exerted. It appeared to be stuffed with cotton, or maybe straw, for it was firmer than goosedown would've been.

"Oh, my," Addie said aloud, suddenly consumed with imagining the sound it would make when—

"That's enough of that, my girl," she told herself sharply, turning away from the bed and all the pictures it brought to mind.

"I cannot lay in that bed with Ian. I cannot," she said fiercely, hugging herself as if to find some comfort.

But the taunting question rang through her mind.

How could she not? She was his wife. She had picked him from all the men in McTavish Plain.

"I don't have a prayer of avoiding what surely must come." And in a moment of pure honesty, Addie admitted, she didn't really wish to.

Ian had ignited the dry, lonely tinder of her soul just as easily as she had lit the fire.

"You look half frozen," Ian admitted grudgingly to Aleck. He uncorked the bottle Adelaide had brought from town, feeling his pulse quicken at the thought of her upstairs . . . waiting, for him. He glared at Aleck, willing him to go straight to Perdition.

Aleck folded himself into the big pine chair in front of the fireplace, unaware of Ian's murderous thoughts. A few coals still glowed and sparked from the fire he laid before he rode to town. Ian added three more logs, and a flame sprouted among the coals.

"Planning on staying long?" Ian asked sharply.

"Only till the spring thaw," Aleck joked. "I feel froze all the way through. Snow started falling when I was only a little nearer to your house than I was to Broken Ax's village. I had to keep going." Aleck's Adam's apple worked while he swallowed the whiskey. "Ah, that is fine, smooth and has a moreish taste."

"Are matters with Broken Ax so dire?" Ian frowned, wondering if this was some foolery on Aleck's part. But then, he still hadn't told Aleck that he was now a married man . . . or that his lovely bride was waiting anxiously upstairs. . . .

"Oh, there are the usual rumblings of uprising. The Cree and Lakota nearby seem to be working themselves up, but the Salish have been peaceable so far."

Aleck leaned forward and offered the bottle back to Ian. "Grass Singing is moping around like a lovestruck calf."

"She is no concern of mine." Ian took a drink, hardly feeling the burn down his throat. He was a long way from being skunked, but he had drunk more than usual.

"Funny, Grass Singing doesn't seem to agree," Aleck said, retrieving the whiskey and tipping the bottle to his lips.

Ian stoked the fire. His gaze drifted toward the stairs. Would Adelaide have lit the fire he had laid before he went to town? Was she now brushing out her long hair . . . was it curling over her slender throat? Or would she be waiting for him to help her undress? He had planned to undo each tight little button on her dress . . . then remove that strange hat with the flimsy black veil hanging down the back.

Where had she gotten such an ugly thing? Ian wondered fleetingly before his mind went back to building fantasies of lust.

He had waited and wanted to see Adelaide naked, her hair trailing down her back. He had planned on drinking in every inch of her form, wanted to touch every inch—

"In fact, the way Grass Singing tells it, you two were just about to start sharing the same tepee—permanently." Aleck's voice ripped through his thoughts like cold lightning.

Ian swung around and stared at Aleck in disbelief. "Dinna be daft. Nothing of the sort ever was between us."

"She tells it different. 'Course, she is a widow. I reckon

she is mightily lonely,'' Aleck said with a suggestive wink. "Yep, nothing like a widow woman, is there, Ian?''

The sound of Ian's low baritone voice had brought Addie down the hall, curious to see whom he was talking to. She had thought it must be Darroch. The last thing she expected to see was Aleck Bowen making himself cozy. Now she stood at the top of the stairs in the dark, clutching her night rail to her chest, not able to see either of them below, but she could hear clearly.

"I dinna know what you are gettin' at, Aleck. If you canna talk about somethin' else, then—''

"Ian, why did you skin your face? I been waiting to hear the story, but you are taking your sweet time in the telling.''

"Since you wilna be content until you have poked your troon into all of my business, I may as well tell you. I have taken a wife.'' Ian's voice was hard and flinty.

"A wife?''

Addie heard a sound that could be nothing but Aleck slapping his own knee in amusement. A part of her felt guilty for eavesdropping—but it was a small part.

"Seein' as how Grass Singing is still in Broken Ax's village and you claim you had no intention of marrying her, who *did* you marry?''

"Adelaide Brown.''

"Ha, the Widow Brown took you for her husband? I don't believe it. She has more sense than to get tied up with an ornery cuss like you.''

"It might put a kink in your tail to know *she* asked *me* to wed her.''

"She asked *you?*''

"It was a shock to me as well,'' Ian said softly. A cold, hard fist squeezed Addie's heart.

Was he not as happy as he pretended? Could it be she was not the only one feeling confused with the twists and turns of their marriage?

"You do have a way with widows," Aleck said with a chuckle that ripped Addie's attention back to the conversation below. "First Grass Singing, and now the Widow Brown. You are a sly fox, Ian McTavish."

"She is no longer the Widow Brown, and I dinna like your tone, Aleck. You flap your tongue against your teeth too much."

Addie crept a little farther down the stairs, straining to get a glimpse of the man she married.

"Grass Singing is an Indian—beautiful as sunrise, but a savage. She would never have been accepted by your upstanding townsfolk. But Addie Brown ... not only respectable, but a great cook."

"She has fine talents, I agree."

"Talents? Is that what you call it now, Ian? *Talents?* She is a *widow.*" Aleck's words were slurred and muzzy from the whiskey he was drinking.

Addie moved away from the wall and stood in the triangle of light that filtered up the stairs from the lamps and the fireplace below. Her bare feet made no sound as she knelt down to peer between the spindles of the pine stair railing.

"Everyone knows about widows. Once they've had a man in their bed regular—"

Ian was quick as a striking rattler. Aleck's shirt was bunched in his fist and Ian was lifting him from the chair.

" 'Tis the whiskey talking, I know, 'cause if I dinna think that was the case, Aleck, old friend, I'd have to clout you in the mouth for even thinking of Adelaide in such a manner."

Addie swallowed hard, shocked by the barely leashed violence in Ian, but if Aleck was bothered at all he hid it well. With the crooked grin of a man well on the road to being drunk, he chuckled and said, "Whiskey, hell, the moment I saw her I knew she would be the kind of woman to give a man a good ride. First it was Grass

Singing who warmed your blankets, and now you have another willing widow to warm your bed and cook your meals. You are to be congratulated—''

Ian hit him.

It was just one quick jab to the nose. Not hard enough to break cartilage, but hard enough to start a slow trickle of blood.

''Do shut up, Aleck,'' Ian growled.

Addie could stand no more. She had been discussed like the lowliest trollop in a saloon. So much for Ian's lofty ideas about keeping men's notions on an elevated plane by not allowing unmarried women in McTavish Plain. She was married now and her reputation was in tatters, and the disgusting exchange had taken place in her own new home.

It was the lowest degradation she could imagine . . . speculated upon . . . her morals and her *passions* discussed over a whiskey bottle.

Her parents would have died of shame to think it.

Addie suddenly found herself moving briskly down the stairs, her night rail whispering along the flooring as she went.

Ian turned, his eyes widening at the sight of her. And Aleck, still wearing the idiot's grin, with blood dripping off his chin, followed her progress with bleary eyes. If she hadn't been fuming mad, she might have been embarrassed by being in her gown, but she was mad. Mad enough to chew nails and hide and whoever got in her way.

''Adelaide—'' Ian began.

''Don't you 'Adelaide' me, you snake.''

Ian blinked and slowly released Aleck, who settled back into the chair with a thud. He took a step toward her. His hands were flexing open and shut in a convulsive gesture.

Did he want to touch her?

"But Adelaide, lass, why are you mad at me?"

"Why, indeed, Mr. McTavish? How very shrewd of you to gain a cook, housekeeper and bedmate with a simple ceremony."

"Adelaide—" He narrowed his eyes.

"No, let me finish. You have been strutting around prouder than a whitewashed pig. I wondered why . . . why you accepted me . . . why a man who loved the ladies would be so willing to get married. Now I know. But you may have congratulated yourself a bit too soon, my fine sir."

"What do you mean, Adelaide?" His voice was a throaty growl.

"I mean, I have no intention of sharing a bed with you . . . not tonight . . . not ever." Whether she was afraid of his reaction or if she feared the loss of her own courage she wasn't sure, but she turned on her heel and ran back up the stairs before Ian had a chance to respond.

"Miss Addie sounds a bit peevish," Aleck said with a hiccup.

"She is not Miss Addie; she is my wife," Ian roared as he ran after her. Lovely, slender ankles and calves were exposed to his view with every step. The curve of her back and buttocks through the sheer fabric was as sensual as anything he could've imagined. He wanted her with a white-hot hunger that quickened his step.

He heard the bolt of the lock shoved home only an instant after the bedroom door slammed shut in his face.

"Adelaide, you have locked the door," Ian said from the other side. Surely she did not *mean* to bar him from his own bedroom. Not Adelaide . . . not *his bride*.

Addie shivered and backed up a pace, staring at the closed door. "I know I locked it. I *meant* to lock it. And it shall remain locked."

She was so angry with Ian—but she was also angry with herself. There had been moments—not many to be sure, but a few moments—when she had felt warm and protected by the looks he gave her. She had felt a current of passion arcing between them.

Those feelings had frightened and confused her, but now she knew them for what they were.

They had been Ian's crafty attempts to manipulate her. He had thought himself the husband of a woman who would tumble happily into his bed. He had thought himself married to a fine cook and a playful bedmate. He thought himself getting the better of the bargain.

Well, he was wrong.

"Open it, Adelaide."

"No."

Lust and frustration flowed in equal measure with the whiskey in Ian's blood. In a burst of unbridled emotion, he raised the flat of his hand and brought it down against the door—hard.

"Adelaide—let me in!"

The sound made Addie jump, but she lifted her chin and glared at the sturdy cross-barred pine door. "Go ahead, bellow and bluster like the great bully you are, Ian."

Shaking from head to toe, Ian sucked in a breath. It was not anger or even sexual frustration that had him on the ragged edge. It was the pain in his heart. He had wanted things to be perfect for his Adelaide, and now a barrier of wood and misunderstanding lay between them.

Adelaide wrung her hands and waited. But after a few minutes she still heard nothing from the other side of the door.

He must finally have gone away.

In a quiet, trembling voice she said, "I'm not afraid of you, Ian McTavish."

There was a long, audible sigh, and then the voice that still had the power to make her heart trill replied, "You may not be afraid of me, lass, but I am surely afraid of myself."

Chapter Twenty

Adelaide was kissing him . . . great, wet, sloppy kisses. Her hair tickled his nose.

Ian grinned and rolled over, wanting to pull her to his body, to hold her closer. He nuzzled into her. . . . Her whiskers poked his cheeks. . . .

Her whiskers? Poked his cheeks?

Ian's eyes snapped open. He was eyeball to eyeball with a shimmering trout that was lying next to him on the floor. Two matching sets of bloody puncture marks were evident behind its gills.

"Angus! Fergus!" Ian gained his feet and found his voice. With the fish clutched in his fist, he bellowed again. "Where are you two imps of Satan?"

His belly was roiling and there was a loud banging in his head, and the scent of the trout was not helping matters one bit. Something nearby groaned and moved. It took a moment for Ian to realize the sound of misery had not come from him.

He frowned and peered at the shapes beside the cold hearth.

Aleck and Darroch were curled together, covered with a buffalo robe, snoring loud enough to bring down the stones of the house.

Ian's pained gaze returned to the fish. "Come out, you two devils!" Ian said, scanning the nooks and crannies of the room. "I know you're here." Grasping just above the tail, Ian shook the fish like a limp weapon.

Two pairs of glittering black eyes appeared. Sleek heads, whiskers aquiver, poked from behind a stack of wood. The otter pups made deep, throaty sounds as they tumbled out. Needle-sharp teeth flashed in greeting when they stared up at their master.

"You two dolts should be skinned and made into gloves, and I swear, the mood I am in . . . ," Ian said sourly, flinging the trout between them. The otters looked at the fish, a treasured offering for Ian, in some confusion.

"I dinna want the damn raw fish. Angus and Fergus, go. Take it into the kitchen and leave me and my pounding head in peace." Ian put his very fishy smelling palms on his temples and squeezed. It didn't help; his head felt as if it was about to fly away.

It was at that moment, when Ian was swaying on his feet, his bladder so full it felt as if it would burst, Darroch and Aleck stretched out by the cold fireplace, that Adelaide came down the stairs. She was dressed in a plain brown frock with a high collar. It was buttoned tight to the curve of her jaw. Her back remained straight as an aspen lodge pole.

"Still wearing her damned corset, I see," Ian muttered through clenched teeth. How did women lace themselves in so tight? And how could it be that the morning after his wedding he still had not got her out of it?

How could a man's plans go so awry?

"Adelaide—" He stumbled unsteadily toward her.

She held up a dainty hand. It halted his progress like a stone wall.

"Well, if this isn't a fine thing to find in the morning. My *husband* and Aleck . . . still senseless from too much whiskey, a no-account hound and—No, don't tell me, Ian, let me guess. These minions of Satan, Angus and Fergus did you call them? Two more *male* varmints— also part of the McTavish household. And from the looks of them, like everything else male in this territory, they are in need of a good meal."

Angus and Fergus, at hearing their names, grunted their own brand of greeting, tumbling and undulating toward Addie's skirts. She took a step back and glared at the pair.

"Don't you dare touch me," she warned, and the otters stopped, sat back on their haunches and stared. "Or I swear, you *will* be made into gloves before sundown."

The otters chirped and grunted. Aleck stirred and peeked around Darroch. Ian shuffled on unsteady feet.

"The Widow Brown sounds angry this morning," Aleck whispered in a slurred voice.

"Stop calling her that. Adelaide is my wife—not the Widow Brown," Ian snapped, wishing he hadn't been quite so loud, for the sound of his own voice set his head to pounding harder than ever.

Aleck blinked. "Are you sure 'bout that, Ian? Seems to me I remember you sleeping down here after we finished that bottle." Aleck smacked his lips and turned back over, pulling the buffalo robe more firmly about his shoulders.

Ian thought about that a minute. His wedding night had come and gone and his vows had not been consummated.

"Adelaide—"

She narrowed her eyes and silenced him with a look that could've stripped his hide right off.

"I am going to try and put together a proper breakfast,

but heed my warning, Ian. If I find more dead fish in my kitchen, I am coming right back out here and take the necessary steps to make myself a widow again!''

And then, with all the grace of a queen, she turned on her heel and strode by the otters, the hound and two stunned and mighty hung-over men.

Adelaide evidently didn't find any dead fish, because a few minutes went by and she didn't come back to do Ian to death. He went outside to heed the call of nature, but when he returned to the house the sounds of Adelaide's high temper were still intimidating enough to make the otter pups writhe in and out of Ian's legs.

As much as Ian hated to admit it, he himself could've used a little reassurance and comfort. When he thought about the sparks in his wife's eyes, he decided he wasn't likely to get any from that quarter.

"Easy, lads," he said to the otters. Angus and Fergus made little throaty grunts in response, while they continued to hide. Each time they heard the threatening din of pots and pans clang together they chirruped and gurgled.

"She is cooking, lads, nothing to get worried over." Ian stroked the sleek heads of his terrified pets.

"Are you sure about that, Ian?" Aleck said, still cocooned in his buffalo robe, with Darroch guarding his back. "What she said about becoming a widow again . . ."

"Don't be daft, man. Adelaide is a fine woman. 'Tis not as though she was planning to poison me!"

"Don't be too sure about that." Her voice brought every male head swinging round in her direction. Her cheeks were pink from either heat, exertion, temper or all three. Several tendrils of hair were curling around her jaw.

She had never looked more beautiful—or more angry.

"The thought did cross my mind and more than once,"

Adelaide said with a bit more conviction than Ian liked. "But I reckoned if you've been eating with those scamps"—she jabbed a finger in Angus's and Fergus's general direction—"and you haven't died yet, then you are probably too contrary to kill with just a little poison."

"Want to borrow my knife?" Aleck offered.

"You hold your tongue. I am none to pleased with you either, *Mr. Bowen.*"

"Aw, lass, you've gone and frightened the poor wee things." The otters stood up on their hind legs, whiskers aquiver, making little chirpy, grunty noises.

"I frightened them?" she said incredulously. "I doubt that. The little devils have found a soft life here with you, but their lives and yours are about to change."

"Change?" Ian repeated. A guttural chorus of otter language followed.

"Uh-hmmm, change. Right after breakfast."

Adelaide's dazzling smile made Ian's heart skip a beat. He dared to hope that the change she had in mind would be a pleasurable one.

"What kind of change?"

"To begin with, all of you male animals are going to help me put this disreputable excuse for a home in order!"

It was not exactly what Ian had been praying for.

Addie *had* determined to make a sort of peace with Ian when dawn broke. She had intended to approach him about making their marriage one of convenience for both of them. She had every intention of promising to be a passive, agreeable wife and helpmate—short of their marriage bed.

She had intended all and more until she walked downstairs and into the ridiculous situation with the fish, the otter, Aleck and Ian himself.

Red-eyed and none too steady on his feet, her first mad

whim had been to gently sweep that dark lock of hair back from Ian's forehead—to offer him a kind word and a cup of something to soothe his furrowed brow.

Am I a complete goose head? a voice in Addie's head asked upon the heels of that thought.

Only by remembering the conversation between Aleck and Ian the night before had she been able to cling to her anger. It took all her will and several reminders that not only her position but that of her sisters' were in jeopardy. She fought the impulse to touch him, to put that wayward strand of hair in place.

Instead she focused on the deplorable condition of *her home*—and the bruised state of her pride.

Ian had wounded her more deeply than she thought possible. More deeply than she cared to admit, by discussing her with Aleck Bowen like she was some woman of low virtue. She had been taught that men *never,* ever talked about their womenfolk that way.

"I am his wife," she reminded herself softly, trying to ignore the painful catch beneath her heart. She had deluded herself into thinking that he really had wanted to marry her—for herself alone—not for her cooking or to keep his town's virtue and peace intact, but for herself alone. When they had danced . . . when he had held her . . .

But her eavesdropping had disabused her of that fancy.

"But I am his wife and this is my home," she muttered as she cleared away the breakfast leavings, scraping bits of pancakes into a pie tin for the otter pups.

They attacked the scraps as if they had not eaten in a week, clawing and cussing, spitting like kittens. The food disappeared sometime during the fracas, though Addie could not see exactly when they took time to eat, so busy were they fighting.

She glanced around, wondering where the trout had

disappeared to. A pile of bones and a bit of fin told the tale.

"You, my fine, furry lads, are in for a surprise, and so is your master." For Addie silently vowed by all that was holy, if it took her last breath and every ounce of labor she could nag from Ian and that worthless fool Aleck, she would have order in this new home of hers!

She might not have love or the respect of the man whose name she now called her own, but she still had her pride. Bruised, battered and a bit tarnished by her own foolish lies, it was the only thing she had to cling to—the only thing that kept her from tumbling into Ian's arms.

"But, Adelaide . . . ," Ian said.

"Don't call me Adelaide," she snapped, trying to ignore the way the gray and dreary day darkened the hue of his eyes to an almost navy blue.

"But lass, it is still snowing outside," Ian said reasonably.

"I know that, and I don't care." Addie was having a tough time hanging on to her ire. How could he continue to speak to her so reasonably in that low, gravelly voice after the hours she had driven and ordered him? The very fact that he could be so understanding . . . so moderate in his temperament, only served to make her raw nerves more sensitive. A hot dry lump formed in her throat and she fought the tears forming in the only way she knew how: by becoming a hard taskmaster with her husband.

"I want all the bedding taken out and aired. The barn is big enough," Addie said, not really knowing if the barn *was* big enough but ready to defend her wishes with yet another argument.

But Ian didn't argue. "As you say . . . *Adelaide.*"

Within moments he was doing her bidding. Addie tried

not to notice the bulge and flex of his wide shoulders and powerful forearms when he shouldered the mattress and muscled it through the doorway.

It wouldn't do to notice how straight his legs were in his buckskin breeches or how long and sensitive his fingers were, or any of a dozen other things about him that made her pulse quicken.

No, it simply wouldn't do at all if she was going to protect her heart from being broken again.

The snowstorm did not abate. Fat, wet snowflakes continued to fall hard all day. Hours after the mattresses were aired and returned to the house, Ian had to dig a path to the barn to feed Gert's team. By the time he came back in he was wet, cold and annoyed to find Aleck grinning at Adelaide. His bad temper came close to exploding into violence.

The dinner his lovely Adelaide had fixed, though the best he had ever eaten, now sat hard and cold as a stone in his gut. He was bone-weary of having Aleck as a houseguest and wanting a wife that did not want him. His patience had been stretched taut as a fiddle string all day.

"Aleck, I think it has let up enough for you to make it into town." Ian tossed another log into the fire, his gaze lingering for a moment on the fresh-scrubbed pine slab that formed the mantelpiece. Adelaide had rubbed and polished every surface in his house until it gleamed and glowed from her attention—attention Ian himself craved.

"Quit joshing, Ian. You know it's falling harder than ever. I'd be stuck in a drift before I made it to the bottom of the hill."

"Good riddance," Ian grumbled under his breath.

"I am tired," Addie said suddenly. "I think I will go

up to bed.'' She rose gracefully from the rocker Ian had pulled near the fire for her comfort.

Immediately his mood lightened. He grinned at Adelaide. "You do that, lass." Her invitation was subtle, but Ian didn't mistake it.

She wanted him to join her in the bedroom!

Feeling a warm glow in his chest, he smiled at her again. He would give her a few minutes of privacy and then . . .

Addie saw the sparkle in Ian's bewitching blue eyes and knew immediately what was going through his head. He looked so handsome, the firelight flickering over the hard, chiseled planes of his face. He was a comely man . . . a virile man.

No! She could not allow herself to be lulled by him. Not now, not ever.

"I'll see to the stock one last time and be right up," Ian said with a grin.

Addie didn't bother to say anything. She simply picked up her skirts and fled to the safety and sanctuary of her bedroom.

Though he meant to give her some time, not five minutes had gone by before Ian climbed the stairs, feeling giddy and warm and itchy with randy expectations. His feelings for Adelaide were intense, and a little frightening.

Even in Ian's youth, when he pursued Fiona with all the wicked abandon of a green stripling, he had never been so on edge, so raw with lust, so hungry to know a woman's heart and needs.

"I have no control of myself. My heart is out on my cuff where Adelaide is concerned," he said with some amusement.

His amusement soon turned to bitter disappointment

when he stood outside the bedroom door and stared dumbly at the pile of quilts on the pine floor.

Ian reached out and tried to open the door, knowing it was solidly barred—again.

"Adelaide," he said in a warning voice.

"I will see you at breakfast, Ian."

"Damn, lass. Would you bar me from my own bed and shame me in front of Aleck as well?"

A long moment of silence followed. When Ian was sure Adelaide would not answer the question he heard her soft voice.

"Though you and Aleck discussed me like a loose woman, I would not do the same. If you feel the need to tell him about our personal life, then go ahead. Tell him whatever you wish about where you slept and with whom . . . but you will not sleep with me."

Ian uttered a blistering oath and kicked the pile of bedding. It tumbled in a disorderly heap halfway down the stairs. This would be the second night he had bedded down on the floor. He was willing to give Adelaide some room, but by God, his patience wasn't endless.

Chapter Twenty-one

Morning came cold and harsh upon Ian. He stretched his cramped muscles and heard the sound of his own bones cracking in protest at the movement.

"I am too old to be sleeping on the floor—alone," Ian whispered to himself as he trudged downstairs and went out into the cold to the outhouse.

His mood did not improve when he returned a while later to find Aleck laughing with Adelaide over a cup of coffee. Her initial annoyance with Aleck seemed to have disappeared, just about the same time her anger with Ian had escalated.

Something too close to jealousy and suspicion flashed through Ian's mind.

" 'Morning," Aleck said cheerfully.

" 'Morning," Ian growled. He sloshed hot coffee on his hand when he poured himself a cup, cursing under his breath. In that instant when his flesh was stinging, Ian came to a decision.

"Get ready, Aleck, we are going to town."

"Now? It ain't hardly light."

"Right now," Ian said. "Adelaide, while Aleck gets ready I wish to speak with you."

There was a hard, flinty threat in Ian's voice and his eyes. A shiver of dread crept up her spine. Addie blinked and set her full cup of coffee down with a thud. Dark liquid sloshed over the edge onto the table she had scrubbed.

"I have something to do upstairs," she said quickly and bolted from the room.

"Ian, you seemed to have lost your charm. If I didn't know better, I'd swear Addie was running from you." Aleck chuckled.

"Go saddle your horse. I be along directly to hitch up Miley's team." Ian didn't bother to wait and see if Aleck paid him any mind; he was already heading up the stairs.

It was time to set Adelaide straight about a few things.

Addie was listening to the hard, determined steps approaching, but when the knock came, sharp and loud, she jumped to her feet in fright, as if she had not expected it.

"Open the damned door, lass." Ian's voice was flat, mean and colder than a January day.

"No," she said with far more bravado than she was really feeling.

"Adelaide, I mean it."

"Go away."

"I wilna argue with you anymore, Adelaide. Now open the door."

"I said no."

There was an explosion of wood and twisted metal as the lock and hinges gave. The bedroom door crashed inward, the bolt ruined and useless, the wood splintered into fire kindling.

Ian stood there, cold lightning flashing in his eyes. "Damn it all, Adelaide. I dinna want it to be this way."

He took two long steps and pulled her against him. His embrace was so quick she couldn't fight—wasn't even sure she wanted to fight as his mouth covered hers.

The kiss wasn't gentle; it was raw, hot and possessive. The stubble of his beard scratched her face, making her even more aware of his strength. Ian's mouth moved over hers once, twice, three times, leaving no doubt what he wanted. Her fingers curled into the rough wool of his shirt.

Then he slowly set her away from him, his long fingers firm on her shoulders.

"I dinna want you to think it was a lock keeping me out, Adelaide. No door can keep me from your bed— only your own words."

Then, without another word, he turned and walked away, leaving her feeling like the sunlight had gone out of her life.

With her fingers pressed to her lips, as if she could hold the feeling of the kiss to her heart, Addie watched the buggy make laboriously slow progress down the slope. The snow had hardened into a crust, but from time to time the horses would plunge into a drift and sink to their hocks. Then, while Aleck looked on, laughing from his vantage point atop his own mount, Ian would get out and tramp down the snow in front of the team and they would begin again. She saw Ian tighten the plaid woolen scarf around his neck and shrug deeper into the shearling coat.

"Crazy man. He should've stayed here where it was warm and dry."

But was it warm? Her treatment of Ian had bordered on cruelty. She was a shrew, the kind of wife who old men complained about when they collected around the pickle barrel—the kind of woman who mothers held up to their daughters as a negative example. The kind of wife no woman ever aspired to be.

Though she tried to ignore it, her conscience stung. And it did not help that she had kept her tongue sharp and her temper high for one reason and one reason only; Addie could easily succumb to the charms of her husband.

"But I can't. Lottie and Mattie and I lied. Ian is not the kind of man to forgive such lies."

So she watched while Ian struggled down the snowy slope, becoming smaller and smaller until he disappeared altogether. And a part of her wondered . . . would he disappear from her life? And with his departure would she lose her one chance at happiness?

The smell of firesmoke and slightly scorched, too strong coffee greeted Ian the moment he opened the door to the mercantile. A flood of sensation and memory washed over him. And at the center of those memories was Adelaide.

He remembered the first moment he saw her. He remembered the look in her eyes when he told her who he was, expecting, as she did, an old man. He remembered how she felt when he pulled her into his arms and kissed her.

It had not been the kind of kiss he longed to give her, but it had been good just the same.

Ian wanted to slowly undo Adelaide's tight laces, to unbind her clothing, her hair and her soul. His blood sang through his veins when he imagined how she would look, taste and feel in his arms. He wanted to bring her pleasure, explore her body, make her his own.

"Ian? You're 'bout the last man I 'spected to see until the spring thaw." Gus was stoking a fire in the black potbellied stove. A glow of crimson showed at the top when he levered the lid into place and put the coffeepot back in the middle of it.

Slowly the cold left his bones. He shrugged out of the sheepskin coat and unwrapped the scarf from his neck. His bare cheeks, unaccustomed to the cold, felt prickly and wooden. He held his hands out toward the stove and flexed his numb joints.

"I brought you a visitor," Ian said without ever taking his gaze from the red glow around the seams of the stove.

"Addie? She wanted to come visitin'?" Gus grabbed up a piece of rag and folded it around the wire handle of the pot. Then he poured out three cups of steaming brew. "Where is she? I bet she'll like a nice hot cup."

"Not, Adelaide. Aleck Bowen."

"Now how in thunderation did you come across Aleck Bowen?" Gus's lined brow was furrowed.

"He has been holed up at my house—since the wedding."

Gus whistled low and long while he gingerly took hold of one cup and passed it on to Ian. "Sounds like it is not Paradise at the McTavish spread."

"I canna tell you how bad things have gotten, Gus." Ian hitched his buttocks up on a tall staved barrel. "Adelaide hates me."

Gus didn't say a word, just sipped his coffee as if Ian was talking about the cold weather and how his stock were faring.

"I dinna know 'twould be like this. I mean, when she picked me, I thought ..." He shook his head in bewilderment. "She is not like any widow I know."

Gus snorted. "There are widows and there are widows."

Ian's head snapped up. "And what does that mean?"

"Means Addie never did act like any regular widow.

Never did know a widow who would color up and blush like she does. Nope, Addie ain't like other widow women I ever knowed. She's something special.''

"You have the right of it there, Gus. She is special, and I am nothing but a clumsy fool. Each time I try to find the words to tell her that I am happy I was her choice, I say or do the wrong thing.''

"Ian, for a smart man you sure are dumb.''

Ian frowned. "Have a care, old friend.''

"If Addie hadn't gone and asked you to marry her, what were you going to do?''

"You know verra, verra well I was going to court her.'' Ian rubbed his fingers across the stubble beginning to grow on his chin. "That was why I went and cut the brush from my face. For all the good it has done. She hates me. She loathes the look o' me. She hates being married to me.''

"Well, maybe you still need to court her,'' Gus said softly.

Court her?

"But she is my wife. Why should I need to court her? She picked me.''

"If you can't figure it out, then I sure as Hades ain't about to waste breath trying to explain it. Addie is a rare woman, Ian. I hope you have the good sense and the grit to keep her.''

Dow plowed through the snow in bounding leaps. Ian had spent the better part of the day with Gus and Gert. The female teamster had sat him down with a cup of strong coffee and given him a few home truths. At first his manly pride had stung, being chastised for loutish behavior and finding his male charms were less than nothing. But slowly, very slowly, he had begun to get the gist of what Gus and Gert were trying to tell him.

Adelaide was a woman, and a woman needed love words and kindness to make love grow.

So, with a new determination and hat in hand, Ian had gone to see her sisters. Lottie seemed more interested in hearing tales of adventure than answering Ian's questions, but Mattie, with an odd, unfocused look in her eyes, had told Ian what he wanted to know.

Now he was headed home with a thick, well-covered bundle beating against his kidneys each time the stallion tried to leap a snowdrift. It was to be a peace offering . . . a new beginning and, he hoped, the start of a real future with Adelaide. Lovely Adelaide—his wife.

But Ian also rode with a new and nagging thought. Gus had planted the seed when he kept saying how unusual Adelaide was for a widow, and that seed had grown when Ian spent time with her sisters and not once—not even in a sort of passing way—had either of them mentioned their husbands.

There was something very odd about Adelaide and her sisters. Something that was nagging at Ian's mind, nudging the corners of his mind. He would figure it out— he knew he would. But right now he had to concentrate on getting home—home to Adelaide.

Ian turtled into the warm collar of the sheepskin coat and kept urging the horse forward. Dow was strong and used to the winters in McTavish Plain, so Ian knew he was not asking too much, but still the going was hard.

"Come on, lad. I've a woman to court and a heart to win before the spring thaw."

With a snort, Dow plunged onward toward the house that sat in the wuthering shadows of Red Bird Mountain and Adelaide.

* * *

Addie had paced the floor since midday. She told herself it was foolish to worry. After all, the way things had been between she and Ian, he might decide not to come home.

"Ever," she muttered to herself, feeling a tight constriction around her heart when she considered the possibility.

The chirping grunts of the otters drew her gaze from the door. Angus and Fergus had kept her company all day, companionship bought by the leavings she had given them at breakfast. But even if their friendship was a fleeting thing, she was grateful for it. Like great furry inchworms, they tumbled and cavorted between her feet as she walked—and waited.

Addie couldn't help but smile at the little fools while ever-faithful Darroch kept his silent vigil beside the hearth.

"You are not worried, are you?" Addie asked the dog. He never moved, but the tufts of hair above his eyes twitched as he followed her repetitious progress back and forth.

"You know Ian is strong and capable. There is no need to worry over him . . . is there?"

She opened the front door once more, chilling instantly as a blast of icy air forced her thin skirt against her legs and whipped her shawl around her neck. Addie peered out into the whiteness of the snow-covered grasslands. She knew the tall humps must be trees and the rounded mounds must be rocks, but there was nothing to tell her so but memory. Only the imposing mauve, blue and purple mountains, with a halo of misty white clouds, maintained their shape and form against the expanse of white.

"How can he find his way in such a landscape?" Addie whispered. Her voice was hollow and seemed to echo into the dreary, cold afternoon, going on and on as if there weren't another living soul in the world.

She was afraid for Ian, though having lived first as a trapper and mountain man, then as a shepherd alone in this wilderness, he was surely capable of fending for himself.

Addie missed Ian and yearned for a normal life and real marriage, if she dared even think what that would mean to her sisters and herself. Deep inside, Addie's greatest fear was that Ian could never forgive her for lying to him.

Her heart had developed a dull, steady ache that grew worse with each passing hour. Addie was torn between her own guilty conscience, loyalty for her sisters and her growing attraction her Ian.

"There has to be some way of being his wife and keeping my sisters' secret safe," she whispered. "If I have another chance, I will find a way."

But as the snow began to fall again, she wondered if that were true, or if she and Ian were doomed to a life of bitter unhappiness because she had agreed to tell one little white lie.

Ian stamped his feet and tried to cut a path through the drift. "Come, Dow, 'tis not much farther now. I can see the peaks." Ian tugged on the reins and Dow lunged forward, spraying a new cascade of snow over Ian's shoulders.

Ian had stopped more than once to hold his mittened hands over the horse's nostrils to melt the accumulation of ice formed by his warm breath. If Ian had not shaved, he would've had to do the same, for his own beard and mustache would soon freeze solid and suffocate him in this bitter cold.

"If only it hadn't started to snow again," Ian murmured

through the layers of shearling and the scarf wrapped around the lower half of his face. The flakes swirled and spun with each blast of northern air.

What would Adelaide be doing now? Would she be curled in front of the fire, her hair catching every flicker of fire, her cheeks pink?

He dared hope she might have spared a passing thought for him this day. But a nagging voice in the back of his mind warned that that was probably asking too much of her.

Ian chuckled wryly at himself and forced his numb legs up and down, taking another painful step while he focused on thoughts of Adelaide.

Up, down, he tugged the reins and urged Dow forward through the uneven snow. Up, down, he tugged the reins.

Ian's movements were mechanical now, his mind free from the aches of his cold, numb body. He could picture Adelaide, sweet, beautiful Adelaide in his home, warming herself at his fire.

Those thoughts were enough to keep him going.

Addie tugged her coat on over her nightgown and pulled on her shoes. A cold blast of wind swept down from the heights of Red Bird Mountain and swirled snow into a funnel. All day and afternoon she had kept the fire burning high in hopes that Ian would be home soon. She had intended to pull off his boots, seat him before the fire and give him warm broth and coffee . . . and her vow to see things right between them.

Now she was low on wood and hope. She would have to brave the cold . . . and the dark . . . and the possibility that Ian was not coming home tonight or any other night.

Her breath caught painfully beneath her breast the moment she allowed herself to consider that notion. Addie told herself it was the wind and the cold that made tears sting behind her eyes. But it was really the bitter sense of loss.

As if Darroch sensed her distress, he rose from his position by the hearth and came to her side.

"Ah, my faithful protector. You miss him too, don't you?" She patted his coarse head and squinted her eyes. "He has every reason not to come home to me, but he would never abandon you."

Darroch's head swung 'round. He stared motionless out into the snowy night. Darroch whined and stiffened beneath her hand.

Was something moving out there? Is that how he would act if Ian was nearby?

Addie squinted into the night. She *had* seen something . . . it was no more than a shadow, a darker shade in the snowy night, but she had definitely seen *something* . . . something moving purposefully toward the barn.

Then she heard a far-off howl that might have been the wind sweeping off the mountain except while she was praying it was only the storm, there came an answer, and another and another . . .

Only a pack of wolves could make a sound like that, a sound that chilled the blood and stopped the heart.

Dow had been more than happy to be unsaddled, rubbed down and settled in the warm, dry barn. Now Ian was anticipating the same kinds of comfort as he wrestled the bundle through the snow. His peace offering to Adelaide was heavy, more often than not dragging him to his knees in the snow.

"I hope Adelaide's sisters are right—and that she will be happy with what I have brought to her," he murmured to himself, amused by the unfamiliar, hollow sound of his own voice muffled by layers of his scarf. From time to time a gust of wind cleared the falling snow from his path. Dimly, he saw a beam of light ahead. And though it was indistinct, he saw her for a moment. Silhouetted in the doorway, Adelaide . . . his wife.

"Ah, lovely lass . . . confusing lass," Ian said. He yanked on the huge bundle and gained a little purchase through a deep drift between the house and the barn.

Then suddenly the wind died. The snow swirled and fell and blocked all view. Ian could no longer see the door or even the glow of the lantern light ahead through the grayish curtain of falling flakes.

The wind whined, screamed and drove snow into the open door. Addie heard the howls again, this time closer. She grabbed up the scattergun that Ian kept loaded and ready by the front door. She wasn't much of a shot—Lottie was the one with the deadeye—but surely at close range Addie could hit something with a scattergun.

Wouldn't she?

Darroch whined again. Then, with a sharp bark, he loped away from the open door, through the deep snow, disappearing from sight completely in the whiteness of the storm.

"Darroch!" Addie screamed, her own voice driven back by the force of the wind. "No, come back!" A sense of panic seized her with the dog's departure. She stared unblinking until her eyes burned and her lashes were thick with snowflakes.

She saw nothing and yet there was the feeling she was not alone in the storm. The short hairs on her arms and the back of her neck rose.

"Darroch, come," Addie yelled, but the wind tossed her voice back into her face. He would never be able to hear her.

She would have to go outside. She took a tentative step. Snow crunched beneath her foot and fell inside the top of her shoe. A sound . . . perhaps a bark reached her ears. Then Addie saw the dark shadow moving toward the deerhound.

"Oh, no, Darroch." She lifted the heavy gun, closed her eyes and squeezed the trigger.

Even in the wind the sound of Darroch's howling sent shivers chasing up Addie's spine. She struggled to reach him, almost falling over him when she finally found him.

He stood in the snow with his back feet planted and raised his magnificent head toward the silvery moon. The mournful sound of his howling went all the way to the marrow of Addie's bones.

"Something is not right. Darroch would not howl and take on so over a wolf."

Still clutching the scattergun, Addie stumbled and fell to her knees, snow getting under her coat.

"Darroch?"

He howled once more and touched his nose to something. Addie saw the darker spots laying on the white snowbank.

"Blood."

Addie strained to see . . . But it was not bloody fur that met her eyes. No four-legged creature had been felled by her shot.

"Ian! Oh, dear Lord, I've shot you!"

Chapter Twenty-two

"Adelaide . . ." Ian struggled to rise, but there was a fiery pinch in his hip and side that made him want to lay back in the snow.

"Ian! You are alive." Addie's weight collapsed against a fat, awkward bundle that Ian clung to.

"Adelaide?" His mind was sluggish from the cold, but that pinch was beginning to burn as if someone was sticking a branding iron to his hide. She touched his face with fingers only slightly warmer than the snow beneath him.

"I thought it was a wolf. Oh, I didn't mean it. The blood, where is the blood coming from?" Her fingers were probing, poking. "Oh, I never met to shoot you."

Ian grinned. "Ah, so you missed me?" It was not an altogether unpleasant experience to have Adelaide more or less sprawled upon him, searching his body for—whatever she was searching for. Ian's brain was muzzy. He tried to laugh, but a curtain of black folded over him. He felt himself falling, falling, falling.

"Wake up, Ian. Wake up! You can't die . . . you just can't."

A cold, wet palm whacked Ian across the face. He levered himself up and was halfway to his knees, ready to fight, when he realized it was Adelaide.

"Adelaide, by all that is holy, what are you doing to me?" Dragged down by the sodden clothes, the weight of the snow-covered bundle and an unfamiliar weakness in his side, he barely managed to gain his feet, staggering like a newborn elk calf as he did so.

"Lass, why are you clouting me? I canna have given offense so soon." His words were slurred and he was having trouble focusing.

"If we stay out here any longer we'll both freeze to death. Can you walk?"

"I can and have been doing so for quite some time, lass."

"Oh, for pity's sake, Ian. Never mind, just lean on me," Addie ordered. The added bulk of his shearling coat made it difficult, but she managed to loop her arm around his middle.

"Ah, now this is the homecoming I hoped for."

Ian blinked and looked around, making sure he had a tight grip on the strings at the top of the bag. The air looked as if someone was plucking a goose and letting the down drift softly to earth. The snow was a blue-white crust, full of shimmering diamonds and rubies.

Rubies? Rubies in the snow?

"Is that blood?" Ian felt as if wads of cotton were being stuffed inside his head.

"Yes! It's blood! It's your blood. Come inside so I can get your clothes off!" Her voice was high and raw with guilt and fear.

"There's no need to shout, Adelaide. If you want me naked, that is how you shall have me." Ian grinned and tried to kiss her, but his scarf was in the way, still wrapped around his chin and neck. This was the kind of warm welcome he had been wanting from his new bride.

"After you get me naked, what will we do?"

"I will dig the shot out of you!"

"Shot?" He blinked and tried to make sense of her words, but his mind was sluggish.

"I shot you! Do you understand? I shot you."

Ian's dark brows rose. "Adelaide, when you swore you'd make yourself a widow again, I dinna think you were serious enough to use my gun to do it."

One icy tear found its way down Addie's cheek. "Oh, I swear if you die I will never forgive you."

With Ian leaning heavily on her, still dragging the bundle, they began the torturously slow process of sloughing through the snow.

"Then I will do my best not to die, Adelaide. For I want your forgiving grace, and a few other things from you, verra, verra much."

"Oh, for pity's sake."

"Adelaide, take heart," he said when they paused to catch their breath. "You said yourself I am too ornery to die."

"Maybe I was wrong . . . Lord knows I've been wrong about many things."

They finally reached the house, and Addie managed to open the door. Ian had never felt happier or more weak in the knees. There was a hot bubble of warmth in his chest, as if he had been nipping at Gus's whiskey, only it was better, more satisfying. He knew it was because Adelaide was near and showing her concern and touching his body with her own. But there was still that annoying pinch in his side.

And why was he growing weak as a newborn lamb?

As soon as they were inside, Addie flung off her sodden coat. Without her support Ian collapsed into the rocker beside the fire. Before she managed to return to shut the door a white fan of snow lay across the floor, melting quickly in the warm house.

"Adelaide, I brought you some fine things from town . . . a wedding present of sorts." Ian swayed forward in the chair. His numb fingers were having a time trying to unwrap the scarf from his chin and neck.

"Don't try to talk, just help me get you out of this shirt." She peeled off his scarf and the heavy shearling coat. But then her progress slowed. His soft buckskin shirt was tight-fitting, molded to his broad chest and shoulders like a second hide. Down low on one side the leather was stiff and stained brown with his own drying blood.

Addie swallowed her fear. She could not allow herself to weaken before she had even seen his wounds. She had to stay strong and face what needed facing.

"Ah, lass, I seem to be stuck." Ian grinned crookedly through the neck of his shirt. The buckskin was wedged at the widest point of his shoulders. His arms jutted forward at an odd angle. A trickle of blood ran down the chair and onto the floor.

"Oh, Lord preserve us." Addie went into the kitchen and returned with a knife in her hand.

"Now, Adelaide, think before you act. I am not such a bad sort. Murder is not in you, lass."

"Shut up, Ian." She shoved a half-full bottle of whiskey into his hands. "Drink this."

When he had taken a swallow, a feat in his present position, she stuck the knife in between his hide and the shirt. The shirt fell away in one rent piece of bloody leather.

Now freed, Ian drank and drank again. "And just when Gus and I had decided you were not a proper widow . . ."

Addie stopped, frozen by Ian's words. "Not a proper widow?"

"I know, 'twas foolishness, but we began to wonder. You don't have the way of a widow woman, what with your pretty blushes and awkwardness around men.'' Ian felt light-headed. Was the whiskey going to his head?

Fear squeezed Addie's heart when she noticed how ashen Ian's face was. ''Ian, we must get you upstairs and into bed—quickly.''

''Ah, now you are behaving like a proper widow and a new bride. Eager as a vixen to get your husband upstairs into the marriage bed, eh?''

Addie tried not to blush at his bold, plainspoken words. She could not think about what he had said, not now when she was hanging on to the railing with every step just to gain a single tread. She tried not to notice the droplets of blood each of Ian's steps left behind.

''There, the last one.'' The tiny metal pellet dinged when she dropped it among a dozen others into the speckleware bowl.

The otters and hound had kept watch over their master while she dug the tiny bits of lead from his side. The trio shifted positions and made little noises of concern.

''Now all that remains is to cleanse the wounds,'' Addie whispered to herself.

Three pairs of eyes followed her hand as it moved from the basin of water to Ian's flank and back again. Darroch whined. The otters made their unique grunting chirp.

Addie had come to recognize the sound as an expression of fear—or worry.

''He will be all right. He *must* be all right.'' But she was not convinced by her own brave words.

How had she mistaken him for a wolf? And how had he been so wickedly cheerful until she had urged enough whiskey down his throat to make him pass out?

She looked at him now, with his chest exposed, the tiny black stitches small against his hard and muscular bulk. An uncontrolled shudder ran through her body as she took in the full impact of her actions. Luckily his buckskins had slowed the shot down. The scattergun blast had caught him low and on the right side, above his groin.

The bleeding had been terrible, but now her biggest worry was infection. Even now, with lost blood, unconscious and helpless as a lamb, he was big and brawny and she was slightly mesmerized by the sight of him— only the second man she had ever looked upon. And so much more handsome than Aleck Bowen.

"Stop it, Addie," she chided herself and pulled the sheet over his more manly parts.

She walked to the shuttered window and checked the latch. The storm outside still raged. Gusts of wind hammered the shutters like fists. The deep snow had cut them off, isolated them from any hope of outside help.

They were alone.

Addie sat down in the straight-back chair and took up Ian's hand. For good or ill, the two of them were bound by God's words and man's laws. And now they must cleave to each other for nurturing, for safety, for protection.

"You must be all right," she said again, as if to convince herself and Ian of that fact.

The wind howled against the shuttered window, driving a bit of fresh snow between the joins in the hand-hewn wood—wood planed and smoothed by Ian's own strong hands.

Addie pressed his hard, callused knuckles to her lips and prayed.

Weak sunlight was coming through the joints in the shutters when Addie opened her eyes. Her neck was stiff, her feet cold as blocks of ice, her back and legs leaden.

The first thing she saw was Ian.

His chest was rising and falling quickly as he took

shallow breaths. There was an unnatural, ruddy tinge to his cheeks.

She vaulted from the chair, her shawl falling to the bare floor. Even though she knew what to expect, when her palm touched his dry, hot forehead she nearly wept.

"Fever," she said hoarsely.

Ian moaned and thrashed. The bedding slipped down to expose his wounds ... the area around the stitches angry, red and swollen.

Addie tore her gaze away and headed downstairs. If she didn't get him cooled down, he could die.

"I can't lose you now, Ian. Please, not now."

Ian's larder was well stocked with wild game, both smoked and dried. Mutton from his own flocks, in addition to a half of beef that was aging, hung from the darkened rafters. A willow frame held fish, dead, lifeless eyes milky and shrunken, their tender flesh smoked and savory as anything Addie had ever tasted.

Addie grabbed several long strips of dried elk meat and ran back into the kitchen. In moments she had a hot broth cooking, the aroma filling the kitchen with familiar and comforting odors. While it was simmering she went outside and filled her shawl with fresh-fallen snow from the drift outside the larder door. After many trips she had a huge mound of snow on the kitchen table. She filled Ian's sliced-up buckskin shirt and rolled it up into an awkward bolster that she laced closed.

Then, armed with snow and broth, pitiful weapons against the fever that had Ian, Addie climbed the stairs to do what she might.

Ian's dreams were odd, tortured things—in one he would be laughing with Adelaide, in the next he would be questioning her about her husband—suspicious about her past. Ian's mouth was dry, his body wracked with chilblains.

In a distant, detached fashion he knew he was ill.

In a hot, dry fog he remembered the trip from town, putting Dow in the barn . . . pitching in enough hay to hold him for two or three days . . . checking the oak barrel for water. Then he was in the snow . . .

Adelaide shot him.

The memory ripped into his mind like a bolt of lightning, but Ian was too weak, or too fevered, to do anything about it.

Phantoms from his past did a jig with recent memory. Fiona laughed and stood with Grass Singing while Adelaide cut his shirt off.

Blood dripped from the knife and his side.

Angus and Fergus brought glistening fresh fish while Aleck smiled and had coffee with Adelaide. And Adelaide smiled at Aleck.

"No," Ian moaned. *She was his!*

Ian was sick, weak, and still his body burned with lust for a wife who didn't seem to want him. With that thought clawing at his heart, he allowed the weakness to drag him down . . . down into a deep, cottony realm where reality and fantasy merged into one.

Addie found Ian thrashing in a fevered stupor. It took all her strength, but she finally managed to wedge the rawhide-filled shirt of snow across his body. Within moments he was quieter as the bolster of snow drew the heat. Then she began the laborious process of feeding him. Each spoonful of broth that she trickled into his lips gave her hope that he would maintain his strength and fight the infection in his body. She had cleaned the wounds well and did not want to reopen them to lance the poison unless she had to.

Perhaps a poultice . . .

Two hours later, after repositioning the snow pack several times and getting most of the broth into Ian, Addie was weak with relief when she touched his forehead and found it cooler.

Angus, Fergus and Darroch had kept watch at a polite distance throughout the whole affair. Now, with the snow mostly melted, Addie wrapped the cold, sodden buckskin shirt in a spare sheet, tucked Ian up warmly and went downstairs to dump the watery snow.

She put the kettle on and collapsed into a chair. Addie longed to wrap her fingers around the solid security of a tin cup and have a moment of rest.

When Addie woke it was with a jerk. The kettle was making a dry raspy sound now that it had boiled dry. How long had she been sleeping? In a panic, with her heart beating like a runaway team of horses, she ran up the stairs to check Ian.

"Oh, Lord, no."

Ian was on the floor in a tangle of limbs and bedding. A trickle of blood had formed where some of the small stitches had torn free.

"Ian," Addie said, falling to her knees beside him. She had not a prayer of getting him back into bed alone. She touched his face. It was cold, damp to the touch—chilly as death. Her hands slid down the broad expanse of his chest, her fingers curling involuntarily into the curls of hair.

Ian shivered violently.

She stood up and shoved the mattress to the floor on the other side of the bed. Muttering oaths she had never realized she knew, she dragged it around and positioned it so she could roll Ian's big body onto it.

He moaned twice while she struggled to get him more or less in the middle of the mattress. Within moments

Ian's teeth were hitting together with sharp clicks. His mighty form was shuddering with painful spasms of cold.

"I must get you warm."

But no matter how much bedding Addie piled onto Ian's body, no matter how she stoked the fire, she could not lessen his chills.

The house was warm, warmer than a summer breeze, but Ian still shivered so hard that his knees and heels made thudding noises against the mattress on the floor. Darroch and the otters sat near his pallet. They looked from him to Addie and back again, soulful, trusting eyes, begging her to help their beloved master.

"I don't know what to do," she said, tasting the salt of her own tears while she wrung her hands and stared helplessly at her husband.

For a moment she felt paralyzed, unable to move, to respond to Ian's need. And then she thought of how he had come through the storm from McTavish Plain. She thought of how he must have suffered and been tempted to give up.

"He came back to me," she said softly. "I have to save him."

With a rough swipe at her annoying tears, she started tearing at the buttons of her dress. Somewhere in the farthest recesses of her mind she remembered a story of a couple lost in the snow. They had shared their body heat and lived to tell the tale.

The knots on her corset didn't want to come apart. She heard a ripping sound when in frustration she began to claw at the clothing, tearing it away from her body in a frenzy. Finally she was naked, standing beside Ian, looking at him while a bloom of hot emotion unfurled in her chest.

"Live or die, Ian, you'll do it in my arms." And with that Addie flung back the bedding and crawled in next to Ian. She wrapped her arms around his chilled body and held him . . . held him tight, held him against time and tide and death.

"You can't die now, Ian. Not now when I know I love you."

Chapter Twenty-three

The night wind howled and moaned around the solid stone of Ian's house, and she held him—held him against the chills and the pain and the brink of death. Ian's entire body was rigid with the effects of his infection. He spoke occasionally, garbled gibberish that made Addie's heart contract with fear that perhaps he would not live.

Addie must've slept some space of time during the night, but she wasn't sure of it. She didn't know the hour when it had happened, but some time during the long night Ian ceased to chatter with cold. His body was still. The bone-wraking chills had passed.

A sense of grateful relief filled Addie. She laid her head on his wide chest, listening to the strong beat of his heart, the deep, steady breath he dragged into his lungs.

He would live. Thank God! He would live.

She closed her eyes and let blessed sleep fold in upon her.

* * *

Addie woke in the gray moments before dawn, the lone lamp turned so low that almost no illumination reached the pallet. It took a moment or two for her to realize what had roused her from sleep.

Ian's big hands were roaming over her body. His head was hot and dry, his body giving off heat like a well-stoked stove: not a killing fever, but the warm, healthy temperature of a man who had been through much.

She was fairly certain he was not aware of what his searing hands did to her, since he appeared to be deep in sleep, so she allowed herself the guilty pleasure of his touch. For a moment she couldn't reconcile the wonderful, protected feeling of her body and the worry that had plagued her through the night.

At least I can have this memory of what a real marriage with you would be like.

Addie sighed and let the pleasure engulf her. Ian's groping became more insistent, more focused . . . more exquisite. Even though he was weak, his body was a man's body, his will a man's will.

Addie felt the nudging of his erection against her thigh. She knew what part of his body it was, having gazed upon him in stunned wonder when she had removed the shot. She had allowed her eyes to linger on him for as long as she dared. But she had no notion his flesh could grow and hardened to push and strain against her as if it had a mind of its own.

Instinctively she reached out and touched him. Velvety soft skin flinched under her fingers, and beneath that impossibly soft skin he grew harder yet.

Ian was big, well formed, and his private parts were so different from her own body that she couldn't help but be fascinated.

He was . . . beautiful.

"Adelaide." She was stunned to hear her name on his

lips, and though slurred and huskier than usual, it made her heart skip a beat.

"I'm here, Ian." Until that moment Addie had convinced herself, in some dark, stingy little corner of her heart that Ian didn't know who he touched—it could have been any woman—could have been Grass Singing. But when he called her by name something happened to that shuttered part of her being.

It was as if a great bubble had burst within her chest. All the need, desire and affection that Addie had kept laced up tight inside her corset and her soul was suddenly free—suddenly there, wanting Ian in a way she could not even begin to understand. If he had not said her name, or if he had called her by another's name, it would've been easy to stop his hands, to stop her own curiosity and desire. But while he whispered *Adelaide* over and over again in that husky voice, she was powerless to stop.

"Ian."

His rough, hot hands kneaded her breasts. She mewed like a kitten when one hand slid between her legs and paused, as if discovering some great treasure that deserved a moment of quiet reverence.

"Adelaide, my bonny Adelaide."

It was like a chant, a prayer, a benediction. Addie's bruised pride healed with each tender utterance. Her love grew with each gentle exploration.

Then Ian's movements grew slow, languorous and regular. His fingers found a rhythm, his body mimicked that rhythm . . . it was old, powerful, wild . . . it matched the pounding of Addie's pulse, hard and throbbing. It echoed the cry of her lonely heart.

"Adelaide."

He was suddenly over her, nothing more than a great looming shadow above her . . . nudging her knees apart . . .

No, they were already apart, and her pelvis was straining

toward him. Her body sung with an inner melody that
was too strong to deny.

Her fingers stroked his shoulders, feeling the hard,
corded muscles beneath his flesh. Her palms flattened
against his chest. She savored the soft abrasion of his
hair beneath her own hands while she memorized the feel
of him.

Ian.

Oh, the feeling! The wonder of his touch, his body. It
was heaven and hell and all manner of wanton hunger.
Ian's touch promised dreams long forgotten and things
forbidden. Addie had long ago given up hope of having
the things he made her long for now.

Part of his weight rested on her, part on his arms. Then
Ian nudged his body hard against hers!

And then something gave way. It was like a dam breaking or a door opening, or the last lock upon her heart
being opened. Something that had been waiting all her
life to be unleashed was set free.

Addie rejoiced for it!

He was inside her, stretching her, claiming her.

It hurt . . . it felt wonderful.

Addie writhed and moaned.

She felt hotter than Ian. She was driven by some invisible touch, some inner hunger that would have no peace
unless he gave it.

And he did!

The pace he had set now grew frantic and fast. Addie
was mortified to hear the slap of his rock-hard thighs
against her bottom as he pounded, pounded, *pounded*
himself into her!

Then it was over in a strange, shuddering climax that
made her feel light as a feather and heavy as lead. It was
over, this magical thing he had shown her. Ian collapsed
beside her.

Ian's breathing was raw and uneven. The lantern gave

off a pitiful weak glow. But slowly the room began to lighten by degrees. When pink light shot through the cracks in the shudders Addie turned to look at Ian . . . her husband.

He was still asleep.

Sorrow and heartbreak mingled with prickly relief when she realized that Ian did not know what they had done. He was still slightly fevered, lost in a deep sleep, not truly aware of the dawning day or that he had claimed the first bride of McTavish Plain as his own wife.

Ian floated in a world of unimaginable pleasure. He had dreamed that Adelaide had come to him, naked, willing and hot.

And what a dream it had been. Not only was she everything any man could want with her firm, full breasts and hips that flared in a way that made his loins ache with wanting. She had been a virgin. In his dream she had been untouched by anyone but him. Though it really made no difference in regard to how much he loved her, no man could deny there was something possessive and raw about being a woman's first lover.

In his dream he had been Adelaide's first lover.

But it was only a dream.

He seemed to know that, as his mind wrestled with fantasy to slowly come back into itself from the grip of the fever.

With a rush of aches and pains, Ian woke fully.

His mouth was so dry he couldn't get his lips apart. He tried to turn over, but his side felt as if he had been clawed by a griz. He fell back onto the mattress, trying to master the pain and drive it to the back edges of his mind.

"Ian, you're awake." Adelaide's soft voice washed over him, cool and refreshing as a spring shower.

"Water," he croaked. And it was there, her dainty hand supporting his head as he raised up to let her trickle cold water between his parched lips. It was paradise, being tended and coddled by Adelaide. He didn't know what he had done to deserve it, but he was willing to do it again, if this would be his reward.

She looked at him, and he registered the lines of worry about her mouth ... and something else. There was a kind of glow to her eyes. She had the look of a well-pleasured woman, a little tired but satisfied and thoroughly loved.

A spurt of jealousy rushed through Ian. Who had pleasured her until the effects lingered in her eyes like smoke in the sky?

Who? Who had touched his Adelaide?

Addie was stunned when Ian's fingers clamped onto the small bones of her wrist like an iron trap.

"Is Aleck back?"

His voice was more like a snarl than the burred purr she had come to love. There was a cold fury in his expression that frightened her, and at the same time it excited her.

"No. Don't be silly." She didn't try to pull away, but simply stared into his face and watched as he studied her in return.

"Then who is here? Who has come?"

Addie frowned. "Nobody has come, Ian. The storm has not let up. We are alone ... we have been alone. I only hope I can get to the barn today and see to Dow."

Ian's grip relaxed. He released her and fell back into the pillow. Fear and rage such as he had never known ebbed along with his strength. Slowly, rational thought returned.

They were alone. They had been alone.

It had not been a dream.

He closed his eyes and allowed his brain to focus on

each faint detail of memory. Adelaide *had* come to him naked and willing. Adelaide *had* pressed her soft, sleek body against him. Adelaide *had* been a virgin.

The flood of sensation caused Ian to shudder involuntarily. He was sure—well, almost sure—it had not been a dream.

"Your chills are returning." Her voice was full of fear and *affection*. Dare he hope she cared . . . a little? "Ian, you must stay covered and regain your strength."

"Where did you sleep last night?" he asked, squinting through his lashes, concentrating on cataloging all her expressions.

Ian watched Addie closely. She clasped her hands together and hesitated only a moment. But that small unguarded pause was enough to drive the last bit of doubt from Ian's mind.

"I sat in the chair and watched over you," she finally said, in a rush of words that held no ring of truth.

He had bedded his wife, but she was not going to admit it. Why would she act so . . . guilty about sharing their marriage bed? And why had she been a virgin? Questions swirled through Ian's fever-sluggish brain.

"Where did you think I slept, Ian?" She bit her bottom lip, and a flush of color rose to her lovely cheeks.

He nearly grinned and said, "In my arms." But he kept his own counsel and said nothing. There were so many mysteries within his lovely Adelaide's soul, mysteries he wanted to discover.

But he would have to go slowly . . . he would have to win her trust, gain her confidence, until the moment she came to him and willingly unburdened herself. Until then he would have to take a lesson from the fox and the possum and all the wild things that knew there was a time to feign weakness.

"I . . . feel weak as a lamb, Adelaide," he said in an attempt to divert her attention.

In a rustle of long skirts she came nearer his pallet. "Can you take some broth?"

"I can try," Ian said softly. He continued to keep his eyes squinted to small slits, watching Adelaide.

"I'll bring some up."

As soon as Ian heard Adelaide's no-nonsense steps below, he gained his feet. He was a little unsteady, but his head was beginning to clear. He looked at his side and the tiny, neat stitches while Angus and Fergus looked on.

"As gunshots go, this is'na bad, eh, lads?" he muttered to himself as he prodded the reddened flesh. "She did a fine job of sewing me up. There'll be nary a scar."

He found the chamber pot in the corner of the room and put it to use. The otters scurried from Ian's path as he scooted back beneath the covers and awaited Adelaide's return.

He still had bits and pieces of memory that were foggy, but it was all coming back—each wonderful, sensual moment of the night was coming back to him.

Ian lay back and surveyed the room from his new location. He had not slept on the floor since the ship's carpenter, John Tubman, had come from the east and set up making furniture in McTavish Plain. John also had a store of coffins in the back, but none had been used yet. McTavish Plain was full of young, hearty, robust folk and healthy babies.

Ian gently probed his side and knew with a flash of humility that he had come close to being the first to occupy one of John Tubman's coffins.

"If not for Adelaide."

From his pallet on the floor the room looked different . . . bare. Did Adelaide see it that way? Would she be pleased to see what he had brought her from town? He closed his eyes and imagined her face when she opened the bag. He had spent a deal of time listening to her sisters and

Gert and had put his heart into every item he had stuffed into that damned heavy bag Gus had given him.

"Ian?" Adelaide's voice brought his thoughts back to his pretty wife.

She was standing over him with a steaming bowl of something that smelled like heaven. And still her eyes were full of that well-loved glow that made his loins tighten and his heart swell.

Food was the last thing on Ian's mind at that moment, but he tamped down his ardor. He needed his strength and Adelaide needed time to learn to trust him.

Addie was content. It was the strangest notion that she could be so happy and satisfied to spoon broth into Ian's lips, to touch his brow and straighten his bedding, but that was what was happening.

He was going to live and she was content to care for him. At least a portion of her guilt was assuaged by her efforts, and for this small march of time she asked for no other grace from God.

"Adelaide, does the soup need a bit of salt?" Ian asked.

He was a handsome brute, laying there sprawled out like a great cat. If she hadn't been with him all through the night while he fought the fever . . . well, she knew how ill he had been, even if he now *appeared* to be quite fit.

"Salt?" she asked, gathering her thoughts.

"Mmm. Salt. Taste it."

She took a spoonful, the same spoon his lips had touched, and swallowed the rich, robust stock. "No. It seems fine."

"Ah, I must've been mistaken," he said. "I'll have some more."

Addie ladled the broth to him and felt a burst of pride when he made smacking sounds of approval. He laid his warm palm on her knee in a gesture of easy friendship. She felt a smile tugging at her lips when Ian closed his eyes, opened his mouth and waited like a hungry starling to be fed.

"You will become spoiled from this, I fear."

"I can only hope. Perhaps the broth has grown a bit too cool?"

Addie frowned and took another spoonful. The broth was warm as it trickled down her throat. "No, it seems about right to me."

Ian nearly smiled at his wife's earnest countenance. He had found a way to see that she ate a little something, and so far the little minx had not caught on to his tricks. Every now and again he would think of some reason she needed to taste the broth. Between them they finished the bowl quickly.

Ian was feeling not only stronger but considerably more randy. He longed to find a way to get his mysterious little bride to shed her frock and join him beneath the bedcovers.

"Could you take more broth, Ian?" Adelaide asked sweetly, her nose wrinkling slightly when she spoke. She was pretty in a fresh, unspoiled way that made Ian think of long summer days and nights spent in lovemaking.

"No, I canna take anymore now ... perhaps some rest." Ian sighed in a way he hoped would pluck at her heartstrings. He must have succeeded, because in an instant Adelaide was beside him, on her knees.

"Ian? Are you in pain?" She touched his forehead, his cheeks.

"No ... not pain ... exactly." He let his eyes flutter closed.

"Is your wound feverish again?"

"I canna tell, lass. Perhaps you should check for yourself." He hoped the erotic images he was visualizing didn't make him sound like an eager bridegroom.

But Adelaide evidently had no inkling that he was

playing fox to her hen. Her hands were all over his body, sliding down his chest, lingering on his flank. . . .

Whether Adelaide knew it or not, his blood did begin to burn—but not with fever, not from his puny wound.

"Water?" he said weakly, knowing if he did not find some way to get Adelaide's wonderful hand off his groin, he would explode like a stick of old dynamite.

She leaned away from him and stood up. "I'll go to the kitchen and bring you a cup of cool water."

"Ah, that would be . . . fine."

Ian raised his lids enough to watch her disappear out the door in a flurry of white petticoats. He chuckled and winked at Darroch, Angus and Fergus.

"And now, my fine lads, I think I feel another bout of chills coming on."

Addie moved about the kitchen, putting things to rights. She had been in a bit of a fog all day. One part of her was euphoric with relief that Ian was mending, and the other was caught in the web of her own guilt.

He didn't remember they had made love. He didn't know that he had taken Addie's virginity—but now that it was gone, she could come to her husband like any bride.

"Like I want to . . . like I've wanted to from the start," she whispered, hugging herself as if to keep the thrill of excitement and anticipation close to her heart.

She was in love. And now, thanks to her own foolishness of shooting Ian, she had inadvertently given them a way to be together and to keep the guilty secret of her sisters' lies. Now if she could learn to ignore the indicting voice of her own conscience, her life would be content.

* * *

Addie took the dipper of water to Ian but left him alone after he had taken a long drink. She had decided to tend Dow and see to her other chores before she lost the light. She had been expecting to do battle with Dow, but he had acted like a lamb. The black demon had whiffled her cheek and made little whickering noises as she climbed the ladder to the loft and forked down a huge pile of hay. Addie had been happy to see he was doing his business in one corner of the barn.

The horse apples were frozen solid and would be easy to shovel out—once Ian was able to get around. Until then Dow seemed to be faring well. She hoped the same was true for her flock of hens and her milking cow.

''Mattie said she'd keep that rascal Scout busy with them.'' And though Mattie had vexed her sorely with her nonsense about romance and her part in their silly scheme, Addie trusted her sister's judgment and her word.

And because of that she felt even more compelled to keep her own vow of silence, though each hour spent with Ian made it harder to do so. She wanted to confess, but the secret did not belong just to her, but to Lottie and Mattie as well.

The sun had long since disappeared behind the snow-drifts by the time Addie had carried in more wood and banked the fire in the kitchen for the night. She stomped the snow from her boots before she peeled off the snow-crusted scarf and bonnet. She didn't know if she hoped Ian was sleeping or if she hoped he would be awake, but on the slim chance he was awake she brought him some more broth.

When she walked into the bedroom and found him snoring softly her heart swelled inside her breast. Her handsome husband was sprawled out, his manly chest uncovered.

A flame of desire ignited in Addie's belly.

If only no cloud of guilt and lies lay between them.

* * *

Ian woke the moment Adelaide entered the room, but he kept his eyes closed and continued to breathe deep and noisy, a trick he had learned the winter he spent with the Salish.

Through a slitted eye he watched her move about the room with the grace and fluid motion of an angel come to earth. She paused for a moment and stood looking at him. Her expression of longing and indecision clawed at his innards. He wanted to reach out to her.

But he couldn't. . . . Adelaide was going to have to come to him.

She sighed and moved toward the straight-backed chair. The lonely, determined set of her spine nearly unmanned him. Ian had to do something to help her cross that first hurdle, something that would make her forget her shyness.

"Adelaide," he said weakly.

"Yes, Ian. I am here."

"I am so cold."

"Cold?"

"Yes, verra, verra, cold."

"Don't tell me you are chilled again." She began pulling at her buttons and laces like a madwoman. How he longed to sit up and help her . . . to free her breasts from that boned contraption that kept her cinched in.

But he couldn't. Not yet. He first had to win her trust, even if it meant a little sneaky playacting while he was waiting for her to trust him. Adelaide would have to *think* she was making all the moves. She would have to believe she was doing this for his own good until the moment Ian woke her passion. Then she wouldn't care why she had come to Ian's bed . . . only that she would remain in it forever.

Addie was careful as she slid beneath the bedding on Ian's good side. She gingerly settled herself beside him, not wanting to disturb him, only to offer him comfort and warmth in whatever way she could.

Suddenly his arm was around her. One part of her wanted to flee, but the other wanted to snuggle nearer.

"Mmm, warm." Ian nuzzled into Adelaide's neck, inhaling the wonderful womanly scent. Adelaide was as temperate and mouthwatering as a steaming apple pie— only more satisfying. She had always had an intriguing presence, a mixture of starch, fresh air, and spices.

Ian nearly chuckled at his thoughts, barely remembering to pretend he was drowsy with sleep and therefore no threat to his wife as his hand gently closed over one breast. She stiffened slightly, but she did not shrink from his touch.

He took that as a good sign and nuzzled more deeply into the hollow between her neck and shoulder. He was rewarded by a soft moan and a trail of gooseflesh at the nape of her neck.

Emboldened by her obvious reaction to his touch, Ian set about a subtle seduction. No move he made was overtly possessive, no brush of his fingers was obvious, but rather each tentative touch was designed to arouse and reassure at the same time.

He found he was enjoying this strange dance, this odd game of cat and mouse, stallion and mare. Each time his hand found sensitive flesh, he also found a trilling response within his lovely bride.

Addie could barely breathe. . . . She couldn't think. Even in half-sleep Ian knew how to play her like a musical instrument too long silent. His big, work-roughened hands skimmed over her body and left a trail of wanting in their wake.

Oh! The feeling.

She had married this man. She could find pleasure in his arms night after night; it was almost enough to assuage her guilt about the lies she and her sisters had told.

Almost, but not quite. And yet, with Ian stroking her like a contented tabby, she found it easy to push the nagging voice of her guilty conscience far to the back of her mind. She became a creature of sensation, of longing, of desire.

Soon, and Addie was not sure how it happened, her own hands were on Ian's body. A part of her lust-fogged brain made sure she stayed away from the stitches, but no other part of his body was spared her touch.

He was marvelous, a strange combination of hard and soft. His hair was coarse and thick in spots, sparse and softly curled in others.

It beckoned to her touch.

And she answered with her fingertips, her lips and her tongue.

Soon she was levered up on her elbows, tasting the flat texture of his nipples, freed from embarrassment because Ian was drowsy and only half-awake . . . half-aware.

He would never know she had taken such liberties.

But, oh, the wonder of discovery was like a rich, heady wine to her! She was a wanton! She was on an adventure of discovery of both Ian and her own sensuality.

Ian was having a tough time pretending to be sluggish and barely aware of what was happening. If he had harbored even the tiniest doubt that Adelaide was not a virgin it was gone now, for she seemed unaware of what she was doing to him—seemingly unaware that it was she who caused his loins to tighten and his shaft to swell. She touched, stroked and kissed him with innocent delight.

He was so hard, the head of his erection was throbbing—aching with need. Lord, didn't the lass know that her soft hands and sweet, warm mouth were driving him to madness?

Her hair grazed along his skin like feathery kisses and his heart hammered against his ribs. Her mews of pleasure made his breath hang in the back of his throat.

Good God! He was randy as a goat! It took all the willpower he possessed to keep from flipping her on her back and plunging deep into her.

Only his determination to win Adelaide's trust, heart and respect kept him still with his hands clenched into fists, held rigid against his thighs. Only by visualizing the prize at the end of this contest could he keep from roaring like a bull and taking her hot, long and hard.

But how long could he hold out? He was after all only a man ... and men could take only so much pleasure without giving full measure in return.

Chapter Twenty-four

A trickle of sweat meandered from the nape of Addie's neck, down her spine.

When had it gotten so hot?

She raised her head and looked at Ian. His eyes were still closed. Was his breath harsh and ragged? Every inch of his body was warm as honey in sunshine, but was he burning with fever again?

Addie brought her cheek against his. It was heaven just to lay her face against his in complete trust and affection. His beard was beginning to grow, the hair softly abrasive as she rested against his strong jaw.

He was not feverish, but warm . . . so warm, and carrying the scent of manly musk. She allowed her eyelids to close, simply savoring the beautiful feeling of being so near him. When, suddenly, he nipped her bottom lip. The surprising action was possessive, playful.

She drew back and stared at him in shock. His eyes were open and there was a question burning in the blue depths.

"Adelaide?"

She knew what he was asking, knew because the same question was also in her mind.

"Yes. Oh, yes, Ian, please."

His mouth found her own. The kiss was searing, magical. Addie drew nearer, sliding her hand beneath Ian's neck. Slowly he pulled her closer, until she was practically on top of him.

"Ah, Adelaide. Ride me—ride me hard."

"Ian . . . you're wound—"

"Will be forgotten the moment I am inside you. Adelaide, use me, take your pleasure from me."

Addie licked her lips. The thought of what Ian was saying made her heart pound. It was wicked . . . it was tempting.

"I—"

"You are my wife, Adelaide. You canna be thinking it is wrong between us. Do whatever you want."

And so, taking infinite care to position herself where she would not put pressure on his stitches, she straddled him. He grinned and slid his hand between their bodies and suddenly . . . he was inside her.

He was big, filling her in a way that was more than physical. When she saw the pure pleasure in his eyes, and the sensual grin that plucked at the corners of his mouth, something inside Addie expanded, grew and changed.

She was a woman in love, and being loved in every sense of the word. In those moments when Ian let her move as she would, when he lay there and let her take her pleasure upon his big, hard body, she knew for the first time what it truly meant to be female. She rejoiced in her womanhood.

"Ah, lass, you are a man's dream. You feel as if you were made to fit only me."

His compliments flowed over her like warm honey,

blending with the gentle burr of his voice to inflame her desire. Addie moved to a rhythm that was new and yet seemed old, practiced and necessary. Her limbs were restless, though she tried to restrain herself, to somehow maintain the tenuous control she had on herself, to keep from hurting Ian.

It was nearly impossible. She was stroked by Ian's hands and some invisible touch that went deeper . . . deep into her heart and her soul.

And then, suddenly, she had no control at all. She was a creature of lust. She was falling through space and time with only Ian there to hold her and bring her back to the world.

It was magic, satisfying, and left her both satiated and anxious to discover more pleasures with Ian.

The next several days were idyllic. Addie felt as if she and Ian were the only people in the world. The snow had stopped, leaving great sparkling drifts against the barn and the rough stones of the house on the north side. In this winter landscape Ian's stone castle was softened, tempered to a more pleasant appearance . . . or perhaps it was just Addie herself that was changed by Ian's love and acceptance.

When he was able to leave the bed, they returned the mattress to its proper position and bundled up. Darroch and the otters were cavorting and leaping with joy to have Ian and Addie outside with them. Addie had grown quite fond of the rascally otters even when they brought her presents of half-eaten fish or some other macabre treasure. They were playful as kittens and faithfully followed her wherever she went.

Today they were enthralled with the snow, flopping down on their bellies, streaking like dollops of butter skittering across a hot griddle.

Over and over they ran to the top of the incline and slid down, until Addie was so weak with laughter, Ian had to support her.

"Ah, lass, I canna tell you what the sound of your laughter does to me."

She looked up into his eyes, so blue they near rivaled the clear, cloudless sky. At night, after making love, when she was curled next to Ian, her own demons came to haunt her, and today they were not very far away. He was such a good man and she had lied to him. The guilt of her sins was weighing heavy upon her. Day by day it became harder to keep silent.

"Ian,"

"Yes, lass?"

"I have to tell you something."

"You can tell me anything, Adelaide." He looped his arm around her and held her close. Darroch decided it was time to interrupt the otters by barking and chasing them in a circle at Ian's feet, throwing up a rooster's tail of snow that sparkled and glittered in the clear day.

"This isn't easy."

"I'll ask no questions of you, lass. If you have something to say, you may say it, but if not . . . I am a patient man."

Instead of his reassurance giving her courage, it did just the opposite. She became tongue-tied, awkward and shy as the first time she laid eyes on him.

He watched her for a long minute and then with a soft exhalation of breath, said, "Come, Adelaide, 'tis time you saw what I brought you from town."

On the short walk back to the house, Ian studied his little wife's bent head. There had been a moment there when his heart had leaped for joy, thinking that Adelaide finally trusted him enough to tell him the truth about her past . . . and her marriage.

But he had been wrong. She was still wary and shy. It hurt him more than it vexed him, for if she could not trust him, Ian knew she could not fully love him.

That was a sorrow he dared not allow himself to contemplate. For he had fallen deeply in love with Adelaide, the Widow Brown. And he would not rest nor be content until she could return that love wholly.

That meant telling him the truth of her past and how or why her husband had left her untouched and virginal.

Tears threatened to choke Addie as Ian pulled things from the bag. She had not touched it, had been loath to even look at it, since stains of his blood dotted the outside. But now, with Ian looking like Father Christmas, yanking treasures from a bottomless cornucopia, she was even more miserable.

"You . . . you brought all this for . . . me?"

"A wedding present." He paused and frowned at her. "Is it all right? I had your sisters and Gert help me make the selections. They were all sure that you would, but Adelaide, if they were wrong, if you dinna like what I brought, I will make Gus take it back. Do your own choosing from any of his stock if it pleases you, lass."

She fell to her knees beside him, taking hold of his rough hand. "Oh, no, Ian, it isn't that. Everything is wonderful . . . perfect. So much more than I deserve."

He frowned and put his hands on her shoulders. "Then what, lass? You look near to tears. Have I done something?"

"No, Ian." The weight of her guilt and the goodness of this big, brawny mountain man's heart were going to be her undoing. How she wanted to tell him. "It isn't you . . . it's me."

"Your sisters said nothing makes you happier than cooking."

The mention of her sisters brought a chill to her soul. Her little sisters . . . her responsibility to protect, to shield from the cruelties of life.

"I do love to cook." She could no longer look at him . . . she couldn't face those clear blue eyes.

"Gus had a nice supply of dried apples and peaches. He said you were partial to the cinnamon sticks." Ian held up a fat bundle.

"You must have spent a fortune," Addie croaked.

"I canna count the cost, only the pleasure it brings you. You are my wife, Adelaide," Ian said simply, as if that explained everything from why the sun came up in the morning to why the moon hung in the night sky.

It was simple for him. She was his wife and as such she was his to care for, to feed, to clothe . . . to show affection and concern.

But for Addie it was not that simple, for she carried the burden of her own sin, a sin Ian surely could not understand because he was not like her. He was not devious and sneaky and a . . . *liar*.

For the next several days Addie tried to show Ian how much she cared for him by doing the things that women-folk do for their men. The dried apples, peaches and spices were made into confections that Ian joked would make him wide and fat as a bear. The ells of cloth were lovingly stroked and measured so Addie could make Ian's home more cozy by adding curtains to bare windows and small fripperies to soften hard stone.

Their days were filled with laughter, their nights with passion and wondrous discovery. Each time Ian loomed above her, hard and hot, her heart did a jig in her chest.

She was loved—and she loved.

Yet through it all was the shadow of fear that he would somehow learn his wife was not worthy of so pure a love. Addie cringed inwardly at the thought of him finding out, but she also secretly wished that Ian would discover her secret on his own. Anything to spare her from telling him and seeing the hurt and disappointment in his eyes.

One bright sunny day, when the snow sparkled with jewel-like lights so bright Addie had to squint, she decided she could not live with the cancer of her guilt any longer. Ian was outside chipping wood, taking breaks now and then from his labor to toss snowballs into the air. Darroch would leap and snap at them, sending a shower of snow over the otter pups, ready to join any game that involved jumping, running and sliding in the snow.

Ian raised his hand and waved to her. Her heart contracted. She had come to trust his love. It was time . . . perhaps things would be all right if she could just tell him the truth. Addie drew herself up and walked toward him.

Darroch stopped barking and lifted his head. He sniffed the air. His mournful howl brought chills up Addie's back. With squinted eyes Ian scanned the horizon as the hound had done. Addie followed his line of vision and saw it; a thick, dirty mark ruining the pristine sky.

"What is that?" Addie asked, feeling the tension spiraling through Ian, touching her with invisible fingers.

"Smoke. It is far away . . . near Broken Ax's village."

"What does it mean?"

"Trouble." Ian tightened his arm around Addie's shoulder as if to protect her from what he was thinking.

"Will you leave?"

He looked down at her with such intensity that she quivered. One callused finger stroked along her jaw, tipping her chin a bit up. He deposited one soft kiss on her lips.

''I canna think of much that would take me from your side. If it is bad, Aleck will come.''

Addie was touched by the bond between the two men. Ian had utter confidence that Aleck would not disappoint him.

''You've been friends a long time, haven't you?''

''I trust him to guard my back and to never lie to me, and yet, lass''—one dark brow arched—''when you smile at him I want to take an ax and cut him down to size.''

''Ian!''

He shrugged. ''I am jealous, Adelaide, jealous of any man who is blessed with your smile or has known your touch. You are mine . . . now.''

She had no answer for that. Ian was possessive and protective of her, and it was obvious he was speaking of her first husband—a man who really had not been a husband at all. When Ian looped his arm around her and turned her toward the house, she leaned into him, content to let her helpmate chart their course while her own thoughts were torn between the smoke on the horizon and her guilty lies.

One part of her wanted to stop Ian now, to tell him that no man but he had ever touched her. But she couldn't, for now his brow was furrowed with worry. She told herself that was the reason . . . that she was sparing him, but in her heart she knew the awful truth.

He put great store in truth. He would hate her.

And Ian was no fool. When he realized what Addie herself had done, it would be only a matter of minutes before he worked out the whole puzzle and tossed her sisters out of McTavish Plain in his rage and fury.

She was cursed. Cursed by the lie that kept her from truly being honest with the man she loved. It was eating her alive—eroding the foundation of her happiness with greedy, clawing fingers.

She was the eldest . . . the strong one, the one who kept

Mattie and Lottie safe and secure. She couldn't stop being that just because she had married Ian.

Aleck came the next day. Addie had been half expecting him; what she had not expected was to see him bundled up, driving Gert's big team of matched draft horses, pulling a heavy wagon with runners. It was a peculiar picture, Aleck gliding along the snow like a sled, but large enough to haul a month's supplies in the back.

"Looks like he's expecting you to ride with him, Adelaide," Ian said flatly as he stood at the front door, a steaming cup of coffee in his big hands.

"Why on earth would he think that?" Addie wasn't sure if the cool, hard look in her husband's eyes was from jealousy or some other emotion she could not identify.

Her own guilt made her overly sensitive to his moods. If he did not smile, she worried that he was growing suspicious. Sometimes she caught him looking at her with a strange, melancholy hunger in his eyes, and she wondered what offense she had committed.

"Is something wrong, Ian?" she finally asked.

"Dinna worry, lass." He kissed her forehead and rested his big arm across her shoulders, but she could not shake off the feeling of impending doom.

"Married life seems to be agreeing with you, Miss Addie," Aleck winked at Ian. "I mean, Mrs. McTavish." He jumped down from the sled and gave Addie a big hug.

"Have a care, old friend. Dinna be thinking I won't box your ears just because my wife is present."

Addie expected him to be smiling, but his expression was as somber as an undertaker's. Aleck held up his hands, swathed in knitted woolen mittens.

"Now, don't go getting all het up. You could be hospitable enough to offer me a little something before you go threatening me.''

"Come inside and have a cup of coffee, Aleck," Addie said, wondering how these two could indulge in horseplay when she was on tenterhooks, wondering why Aleck was here.

Aleck kicked the snow from his boots and shrugged out of his heavy coat as soon as he was inside the parlor. He followed Ian and Addie into the kitchen, warming his hands in front of the cook stove where Addie's cobbler was bubbling, filling the house with smells of spice.

"Ah, it is nice to get warm again. I was near half-froze."

"Have a nip of this," Ian said as he poured a half cup of coffee in a tin cup and filled it the rest of the way with whiskey.

"Ah, mother's milk," Aleck said, taking the cup with relish. He took a long, healthy sip. "That took the frost off'n my gullet. Pour a little more, Ian, so's I can thaw my innards."

"Stand awhile by Adelaide's warm stove and tell us why you came ... then you can have another nip of whiskey."

"Stingy, plain Scots' stingy," Aleck said, shaking his head, but he held his hands to the stove and spoke. "There's trouble, Ian. Big trouble at Broken Ax's camp."

"What has that to do with us?" Addie asked, feeling a chill though the kitchen was warm as hot bricks.

"It has a heap more to do with you than you might think, Addie. Grass Singing has vowed to kill you."

Chapter Twenty-five

"She has threatened to kill me?" Addie repeated dumbly. "What nonsense. You must be wrong, Aleck."

Ian's arm was around Addie's waist before she knew it. He pulled her near him, offering the silent support of his strength.

"What brought this donnybrook about?" Ian asked softly.

"Roamer and a few men from town went shooting turkeys. They met up with Broken Ax and a Lakota huntin' party. Roamer told Broken Ax about your weddin'." Aleck paused and stared at the toe of his boot.

"And . . . ?"

"One of the Lakota's was Lame Fox."

Ian stiffened, his arm flexing involuntarily. He inhaled deeply and took a step away from Addie. It felt like desertion.

"What does all this mean? Who is Lame Fox?" Addie asked, feeling like they were talking an unknown language.

"Lame Fox is a bone-mean Lakota war chief. He has wanted Grass Singing for his bride since her own husband died a while back. Broken Ax has only held him off because of Ian."

Addie's head swung 'round and she stared up at Ian. "Because of you?"

"Now, dinna look at me like that. I had nothing to do with it. 'Twas all Broken Ax's doing. There was no need for you to know about my past—you are my future." His eyes were bottomless pits of blue. Both his hands were clenched into fists at his sides.

"How convenient for you, Ian, to decide what facts you bring with you from the past to the present."

"Are you telling me, Adelaide, that you have nothing in your past you have kept from me? No little secret that you hold locked in your heart? Are you telling me, lass, that I know everything there is to know about you?"

She stood there, watching his face, and his eyes grow hard as winter ice. She had suffered inside, knowing that she did have a secret ... wanting so badly to share it with him, fearing what would happen between them ... what would happen to her sisters ... feeling unworthy of such a good man.

But this good man had secrets of his own. Dark, terrible secrets. Secrets about another woman!

"You know everything about my past you need to know, Ian. There is no other man wanting to see you dead so he may step into your place. There is no other man who is your rival."

"No, you have the right of that, Adelaide. 'Tis not one single man who is my rival but every damn single man in McTavish Plain." His eyes narrowed and his nostrils flared.

There was a moment when Addie was sure he was going to close the small space between them and shake her—hard.

But he didn't. He just gave her a look that could have frozen water and then turned away from her.

Aleck took a big gulp of coffee and nearly choked on the hot, spiked liquid.

"For pity's sake, just tell me what all this means," Addie said to Aleck, feeling more hurt by Ian's cold disregard than she thought was possible.

"Broken Ax promised Grass Singing to Lame Fox, but the night of the wedding she refused to share Lame Fox's tepee. She swore before all the Salish to kill you, and then she disappeared."

Addie looked at Ian, but he still avoided her gaze. She felt the cold chill of rejection once again when he turned to Aleck and said, "Aleck, would you help Adelaide pack?"

"I'm not going anywhere," Addie said.

Ian's jaw tightened like an iron trap when his gaze slid to Addie. "You are wrong, wife. You will go. I canna leave you out here alone. I want you in town where you can be protected."

"I am perfectly safe here," Addie said with complete confidence as she put her hands on her hips and glared up at Ian.

His frown deepened. "Not if I am gone."

"Gone?" A tendril of panic crept into Addie's mind. "Where are you going?" Was he washing his hands of her? Was their marriage such a sham that one small disagreement could wreck it all?—send him off somewhere? Would he abandon her?

"I am going to Broken Ax's camp, and then I intend to find Grass Singing."

Over the last week the sunny days had melted and the cold nights had refrozen the snow until there was a hard, thick crust of solid ice on the road from Ian's house to

McTavish Plain. The metal runners, courtesy of Roamer Tresh the blacksmith, made the wagon-sled glide effortlessly behind the big team. Like an awkward goose, the addition of the iron rails and cheerful bells on the harness had turned the wagon into a graceful swan.

Ian chose to ride Dow—Addie suspected to be spared her company—while Darroch padded faithfully at their side. Ian kept the stallion to the softer areas, where the snow lay on tufts of grass and in drifts. His journey was not as smooth as hers was in the wagon, and for that Addie took prickly satisfaction.

She could not speak to him, could not even look at him. They had not spoken all the while she was seeing the otters settled in the barn with a supply of fish. Nor had they spoken when Ian handed her up into the sled, his hand warming hers through the mittens she wore. The silence ripped at her soul, tore at her heart.

But how could she talk to him when he was going to see another woman!

Using her bonnet to shield her, she glanced back at him from time to time. The sun hung above the peaks of Red Bird Mountain behind Ian. If he saw her looking at him, he did not acknowledge it.

Aleck, to his credit, sat quietly beside Addie. She plucked at the nubbins of wool on the plaid lap robe and tried to still her turbulent thoughts.

One part of her was gleeful to find that Ian could be just as deceitful as she had been ... more so, because his sin involved a woman he had been involved with. But the other part, the part where her heart of hearts lived, was bruised and crushed.

With the devil on her shoulder, making every thought wicked and hurtful, Addie found herself speculating about how much Grass Singing had meant to Ian ... might still mean to him.

Had Ian been ready to marry Grass Singing?

Did he love her? Was that why he was so eager to get to the village?

He had told her it was to offer assistance to Broken Ax if the Lakota warrior Lame Fox sought recompense for Grass Singing's disappearance. But was that the truth?

Addie was miserable. Her own jealousy and guilt joined forces to crush down upon her. She wanted to have Aleck stop, to explain to Ian. . . . She wanted to slap his face and beat against his chest until her own pain and hurt went away. Images of Grass Singing and Ian together assaulted her, made her cringe inside with misery.

"Addie, if you keep that up, the blanket will be bald."

"What?" Addie asked, looking at Aleck. His usual cocksure grin was missing, a deep frown creasing his forehead.

"The blanket—you've just about got it sheared." He nodded in the direction of her lap. A pile of colored fuzz lay beside her hand. Her nervous fingers were still busy, pulling nap and thread.

"Oh, dear." Addie blinked to hold back the tears that suddenly stung her eyes. She held her head high and hoped Aleck would think it was the cold wind that made her tear up.

Aleck clucked his tongue, though the horses were trotting along at a brisk speed.

"Was Ian happy when he was with Grass Singing?" Addie could've bitten off the tip of her tongue.

Aleck gave her a sympathetic smile. "I was afraid the news would be a thorn in your side."

"It isn't really. . . . I mean, Ian and I got married for . . . for reasons other than affection. It would be silly for me to dwell upon such nonsense and fret over Grass Singing."

"If you say so, Addie," Aleck agreed.

She swung her head around to look at him. "What is that supposed to mean, Aleck Bowen?"

"Nothing. Ain't for me to contradict one way or 'tother.''

"You spit it out, Mr. Bowen. Say what is on your mind.''

"Have it your way then, Addie. You may not have loved Ian when you asked him to marry you, I'll give you that, but I ain't a blind man. You love the big, ornery fool now.''

She swallowed hard. Misery, jealousy and heartbreak mingled in her chest. "I never said I loved him.''

"You didn't have to say a word for me to know . . . and unless Ian is thick as an oak, he knows it too.''

Ian watched Adelaide as Dow picked his way through the snow. Her back was straight and rigid as the preacher's sermon. Every now and again she turned and looked at Aleck.

Was she smiling? How could Aleck make her smile when all Ian got from her were frowns and bitter words?

Ian thought about that a moment. Wouldn't his wife have to be jealous of Grass Singing, to react as she had? From his own experience, Ian knew that kind of jealousy only occurred when someone cared. He was jealous because Adelaide had stolen his heart.

"So if the lass is jealous of Grass Singing, it must mean she does care . . . at least a bit, eh?'' he mused with a self-satisfied chuckle. With a smile on his face, Ian allowed himself to believe that maybe, just maybe, Adelaide was also beginning to trust him a little as well. And that soon she would tell him about their first night together . . . and her past.

"But she was quick enough to condemn me for not unburdening my soul to her. It would seem the little vixen is happy to judge me by a different measure than she judges herself.''

* * *

McTavish Plain was abuzz with activity when the horses neatly turned the corner and pulled the sled down Main Street. Addie's heart was in her throat when Mattie and Lottie, looking pert and pretty as summer flowers in new woolen coats and bonnets with fur trim, appeared in front of Gus's mercantile.

"Well, if this isn't a treat for old, tired eyes." Gus walked into the street the moment the sled stopped.

"Addie!" Mattie and Lottie's voices ripped through the crisp winter air, momentarily driving away Addie's melancholy thoughts of Ian and Grass Singing and her own guilt.

These were her beloved sisters ... her little sisters. Happy smiles wreathed their faces. They were confident, wearing beautiful coats and crisp, pert bonnets. They didn't seem so young, or in need of her protection.

In a heart-lurching flash of realization, Addie acknowledged that they had grown up. Perhaps they had been grown up for a long, long time. She had told herself they were why she had left Gothenburg, why she had been willing to come to the far northern reaches of the Nebraska Territory—and why she couldn't tell Ian what they had done. Except that justification suddenly seemed hollow and cold and totally without substance.

Addie leaped from the sled. Ian, still astride Dow, stared at her with an unreadable expression in his blue eyes. They held each other's gaze for a moment longer. She fought the urge to run to him—to cling to Dow's bridle and tell him everything.

Would he forgive her?

"Addie, you look ... different." Mattie stepped in front of her and hugged her so tight she could barely breathe. "I can't quite say what it is, but there is a sort of warmth about you. Did you enjoy the presents Ian brought you?''

Addie untangled herself and looked back. Ian was riding beside Aleck. Darroch kept pace between the two horses.

"Come on, let's go get warm and you can tell us what you have been doing.''

Ian wanted to look back. He wanted to more than anything, but he didn't think he could stand to see Addie walk away, arms looped with her sisters'. A river of doubt, guilt and self-recrimination weighed on his shoulders heavier than the shearling coat.

He had fooled himself, thinking that trust and love would grow. Now he had the strangest notion that she was walking out of his life . . . leaving him forever.

"You look a long way off and a hard time gone.'' Aleck's voice brought Ian's mind back to earth.

Ian wasn't about to unburden his soul to Aleck. He stiffened his back and looked straight ahead. "Save your breath until we get to Broken Ax's village. I have a feeling you may need it.''

The ride to Broken Ax's camp was long and slow. New snow had gathered in great drifts in every shadow and nook. Treetops were bent over and boughs dragged the forest floor from the weight of the latest dusting.

"Do you really think the young men will take up the warpath?'' Ian asked. Aleck was not one to be squeamish about a good fight, but he seemed to be downright spooked by Lame Fox's threats.

"I dunno. Broken Ax was hoping the marriage would bond the two tribes. The Salish are not anxious to put on war shirts. But now Grass Singing has got them all stirred up, and those Lakotas are talking crazy about the dead grandfather's promising to wipe the white man off the face of the earth. Grass Singing made some big to-do about calling on the spirit of the Red Bird bride to save her from Lame Fox.''

''Ah, so now all the young firebrands who have been looking for an excuse have one and can turn this into a spirit war.''

''That's how I see it. The old gods and talismans have been invoked. Now it is a matter to involve old superstitions and old grudges.'' Aleck's horse leaped a small hillock of snow, then floundered in a deep drift on the other side

''And there are a deal of old grievances,'' Ian said sourly. He was happy that Dow, experienced and patient in this kind of weather, took his time and got good purchase before plunging onward.

''And if war breaks out, there is a chance the Lakota's secret will be uncovered,'' Aleck said solemnly.

''And I have no more desire to see a pack of gold hunters up here in the mountains and streams than they do. I built McTavish Plain for families . . . not gold fever.''

Aleck pulled the woolen scarf up over his chin. There were a few flecks of frost on his eyebrows. ''If the young Salish put on their war shirts and ride with the Lakota, your town may be doomed.''

''I dinna forget that.''

''This is just the kind of ballyhoo Grass Singing would like to see. She never liked your town, did she?''

''No. She dinna like the town, or the people in it.'' Ian halted and looked up at the sky. It was beginning to turn a dirty gray, the kind of sky that usually brought more snow.

''You think Addie is in real danger?''

''Not only Adelaide, but everyone in McTavish Plain.''

* * *

"Addie," Mattie said with a winsome look on her face, "is it . . . romantic?"

"Is what romantic?"

"Being married, of course. Is it wonderful to have a man around to whisper love words in your ear? Do you hold hands and read by the fire?"

"For heaven's sake, Mattie, stop mooning around like a lovesick calf. I want to hear about how Addie thought Ian was a wolf and shot him. That's about the most exciting news I've heard since we got here," Lottie said in a pout.

"I will not hush. This is my house, Charlotte, and in my house you will not order me around," Mattie said with a narrow-eyed ferocity that reminded Addie of Fergus when he was riled.

"Horsefeathers," Lottie said, and Addie had to smile. Lottie's business as McTavish Plain's only seamstress had brought her confidence and security. She had a keen, shrewd way about her now. And Mattie, though she was still a dimpled darling who spouted nonsense about poetry and romance, had developed a spine of iron. She gave orders like a military expert—a side effect, no doubt, of dealing with children all day.

They were grown women. They had carved out a life here. They no longer needed Addie to protect them, guide them and keep them from harm. Their lives, whatever the future held, were theirs alone.

Addie inhaled a painful breath and felt years of responsibility fall away. There were no more excuses to be had. Whether she told Ian the truth or not could no longer be blamed on her sisters. If she chose to deceive her husband, it was because she was shallow and deceitful, not because she was protecting her helpless sisters.

"Here, drink this. Now, tell me, Addie, what is it like having a man in the house?" Mattie said, putting a cup of steaming tea before her.

"Marriage is . . . an adjustment," Addie said softly. She hated that Ian was gone. She hated that they had parted without really saying good-bye. She hated the fact that she had foolishly clung to the image of her sisters as her responsibility.

"Pooh. You just don't want to tell me the good parts because I am still chaste," Mattie said in a pout. "Well, I am not a little girl, Adelaide, and I know what goes on between men and women. I am, after all, a school mistress."

"The way you do go on, one would wonder what you have between your ears!" Lottie said, laughing and shaking her head where the sun caught the gold and magnified it.

Addie couldn't find the energy to get in the middle of their latest row. She rose from the chair and walked to the dry sink. The small window, now framed by ruffled curtains, looked out upon a white, desolate world.

"It will be dark soon," she murmured.

Mattie's house was warm and comfortable. The scent of firewood and mint tea filled the room. But Addie longed for Ian's stone house—*their house,* with the attar of spices and hound and otter. And the woodsy, male odor of Ian himself.

What would the otters be doing now? Had they played in the snow all day? Or had they missed her? Were they wondering where she was now? And Ian . . . was he at the village? Was he warm and dry?

Had he found Grass Singing?

Her heart lurched as she finally asked herself the question she had been dreading to even think about.

"Addie?" Lottie's voice brought her back from the snow-covered hills beyond McTavish Plain.

"What?"

"Where is your mind? I thought you'd be happy to see us, anxious to have a good visit, but swan, all you can do is look out that window and sigh. You've turned as moonie as Mattie is," Lottie said critically.

"Hush, Charlotte Rosswarne. Can't you see she is pining for her husband? Can't you see she is in love?" Mattie admonished with a frown.

And that was when the first tear snaked down Addie's cheek. She couldn't deny it any longer. She was in love . . . in love with a man who was out there looking for another woman. In love with a man she had lied to.

Grass Singing hunkered down into a squat and pulled the buffalo robe tighter around her shoulders. It was cold, but she was of *the people. The people* could endure cold, and heat and hunger. They could endure all those things and more, but the people would not endure injury to their honor.

"McTavish dishonored me," she whispered bitterly. "And he will pay."

It was the custom of the people that the offending party be killed if they did not adequately atone for whatever offense they had committed.

But Grass Singing did not want to kill McTavish. She wanted the life of the fire-haired woman, for Grass Singing knew it was she who had poisoned McTavish.

"And when she is dead he will beg me to return to him."

Her cold fingers tightened on the hilt of the knife she carried. Grass Singing would wait and watch, and soon the white woman would come outside to go to the little house they used for the call of nature.

"And then she will die."

Chapter Twenty-six

Dow and Aleck's bay were tired, heads hanging, steps slowed by the drag of the snow when Ian and Aleck rode into the village just before full dark. By the time they were unsaddled and rubbed with pine needles, the horses' eyes were half-closed in exhaustion.

Broken Ax summoned them into his tepee to share his fire and talk. It was all Ian could do to observe the proprieties and customs, to sit quiet and patient while the pipe was lit, while the chants and prayers were made and feathers waved above the sacred fire's smoke.

Adelaide was much on his mind . . . Adelaide and the way they had parted. His Scots intuition warned that things would never be the same between them again.

The pinking light of dawn was beginning to filter through Mattie's frilly curtains and across Addie's face. Addie was anxious to rise—to leave McTavish Plain. Soon it would be full light, and when it was, she was going to borrow Gert's wagon sled and go back home.

She had spent the night thinking about Ian and their marriage. Though it gave her no comfort, she had come to the conclusion that she was little more than a coward and a liar. But in spite of those character flaws she prayed Ian would forgive her when she revealed all she had done.

The ticking of the small wooden table clock in Mattie's parlor sounded as loud as an ax splitting wood. Addie had wanted to go to her own house down the street. It was still furnished, still hers, but Mattie wouldn't hear of it. She had made up her spare room and ordered Addie to change out of her dress and into one of Mattie's own gowns.

Addie had obeyed as if she were the younger sister, accustomed to being told what to do. Yet in spite of Mattie's command, Addie could not sleep. It had been all she could do to remain in bed instead of pacing the room all night.

Each time she closed her eyes she saw Ian's face, hard, shuttered, his blue eyes dull with disappointment. And in her heart she knew why.

She had condemned him for not revealing his secrets, his past. But she had kept things from him. For months she had salved her conscience by telling herself it was for Mattie and Lottie's sake. Now she faced the hard, unvarnished truth.

She had lied to Ian because it suited *her* to do so. She wanted to remain in McTavish Plain every bit as much as her sisters—perhaps more.

She wasn't proud of it, but it was the way it was.

"And maybe the first honest truth I've told myself in a long time."

She had lied to herself as well as Ian. Each time she said she didn't want him . . . each time she let him think that she had come to his bed that first time as a widow . . . lies stacked upon half-truths.

"But all that is going to change." Even if Ian could

not forgive her, she was going to have it out in the open. Even if it meant she, Mattie and Lottie lost what they had built, she was going to do it.

"I have to tell Ian the truth, because I love him too much to keep lying to him or myself."

One hour and three arguments later, Addie finally made it from Mattie's house to Gert's barn and finally to Gus's store. Mattie and Lottie harped at her every step of the way, revealing to all and sundry where she was headed.

"You are a goose if you think you can travel alone," Lottie said with one delicate brow arched.

"A goose, am I?" Addie glared at her sister. "I rode with Aleck here and I saw it was no deal of trouble to drive the team pulling a wagon with runners. Evidently Gert doesn't think I am a goose, because she let me borrow it fast enough."

"Gert is as reckless as you are," Mattie said with an unladylike harrumph.

Gus inched a little closer. His movements were slow, wary, as if getting in the middle of a women's argument was terrifying. Finally he cleared his throat.

"Addie girl, Ian said he wanted you to stay here." His breath made a white cloud in front of his face. Slowly, with methodical precision, he reached out and took hold of the cheek piece of one of the big horse's rigging.

"Are you saying you are going to force me to stay?" Addie asked defiantly.

"Marriage to Ian has changed her . . . and not for the better," Lottie said with a *tsk* of her tongue.

"You're acting like you don't have good sense," Mattie said with a toss of her head.

"Let go of the horse, Gus," Addie said softly, gathering her skirts and the bulk of her long woolen coat as she climbed into the wagon.

"Ian will be mighty put out when he comes back and—" Gus began.

"The road is packed; the runners make the trip easy. Gus, I am going home before another storm hits and I am stuck here all winter. And if my sisters"—she glanced in their direction—"want to pout about it, then fine. They can pout."

Both Mattie and Lottie narrowed their eyes. They made little *O*s with their lips, but they refrained from saying anything more.

"Good, at least that much is decided," Addie said, glancing over her shoulder. Rolled up tarps, shimmering with frost and a light dusting of snow, filled the box of the wagon behind her.

"Mattie, Lottie, I love you both, but this is something I have to do . . . for me. I realize that you two are grown up and capable of caring for yourselves, now it is time you let me do the same."

"Your mind is made up?" Gus asked.

"And not about to be changed," Addie said with a nod of her head. "Now give me some room before I run this thing over all of your toes." Addie clucked her tongue, and the big team leaned forward in the traces, gaining purchase on the ice.

Gus stepped back sharply and her sisters soon followed. Addie glanced back once to see Gus with an arm looped around Mattie on one side and Lottie on the other.

Addie waved. "I'll be fine. Stop worrying," she called out, her voice carrying over the frozen landscape.

The cold wind stung Addie's cheeks. She made good time, the wagon skimming over the hard-packed snow and ice. The bells jangled merrily. Addie's heartbeat was heavy and quick with anticipation. She was going home,

to cook and clean and wait for her man. Then, when Ian
returned, she was going to tell him the truth.

"And I am going to show him how much I love him,"
she muttered aloud.

Sunrise warmed the tepee through the raised door flap.
The men had been in council all night long.

"Will the Lakota make war if Grass Singing does not
come back?" Aleck asked, drawing nearer the fire in the
middle of the tepee.

"There is no other way," Broken Ax answered, the
smoke rising toward the opening making his face look
gray and seasoned as weathered pine. "She has vowed
to ask the help of the Red Bird maiden to free her from
her Lakota husband. It is an insult Lame Fox cannot
ignore. There will be war between the tribes."

"I will do my best to find her," Ian said softly.

"And then what, McTavish? She vows she will have
no man but you in her tepee."

"I am wed to another by the white laws. There is no
future for Grass Singing with me. I will make her understand this. Where do you think she went?"

"To Red Bird Mountain . . ." Broken Ax shrugged and
shook his head. "To your woman. I know not which."

"Adelaide is safe in McTavish Plain. Grass Singing
cannot get to her there."

"Then Grass Singing will go to make a prayer to the
bride of Red Bird Mountain."

Ian stood up. He stretched his cramped back and leg
muscles. "Come on, Aleck. If we push the horses, we
can make Red Bird Mountain before sunset."

The otters tumbled and slid through the snow to greet
Addie. They chirped and grunted their happiness, running

beside the sled, bobbing in and out of the spray of snow from the horses' hooves.

"Fergus . . . Angus, you little imps. Did you really miss me? Or is it just table scraps you missed?" She climbed down from the wagon seat, touched by the otters obvious glee at her return. Whatever their motives, it was nice to have a warm homecoming.

"Let me get the horses unhitched and into the barn, and then we'll go inside and get a fire going. I might even find a little something for you two gluttons in the smokehouse." Addie crunched her way to the horses' heads. She had her hand on the lines when she felt the cold prick of steel just below her ear.

"You come me." Grass Singing's voice was hard and brittle as the crust of snow beneath Addie's high-topped shoes. There were no tracks in the snow; it was undisturbed except for the prints left by Angus and Fergus and the depressed ribbons the runners left behind them.

Addie slowly turned, not wanting to make any sudden move that might drive the knife into her flesh. "Grass Singing. You were hidden in the back of the wagon."

It was not a question. Addie realized that she had hauled the woman from McTavish Plain. The idea that she had been there all along . . .

Addie shivered at the thought.

"You come."

"I cannot leave with you," Addie said with a little laugh she hoped Grass Singing would think of as courage. "Ian will be home soon. He will be expecting me to be here . . . he will be expecting food."

"You lie. I hear in town. Ian not come home. You lie." There was a mad, wild glitter in Grass Singing's dark eyes.

"You come me. I will make prayer to the bride of Red Bird Mountain. I will make sacrifice. Red Bird bride will change everything. My love is pure—the old ones say when woman's love is pure all things are possible. I will pray. You will die and McTavish will come to me."

Addie strained against the rawhide at her hands, but with them tied behind her back any movement immediately tightened the loop around her throat. She gagged and choked, trying to release the pressure, hearing her elbows and shoulders pop. The muscles in her chest were burning, protesting against too long in this unnatural position.

Grass Singing laughed at her small moan of pain. The sound was evil and more chilling than the wind that washed over Addie as she lay, trussed like a winter turkey in the back of the wagon.

The bells on the team's harness no longer sounded cheerful as they rang. Now each tinkle and jingle echoed like a death knell. Little puffs of snow filtered over the edge of the wagon and settled on Addie's face like cold needles. Her coat was bunched up in her armpits, making her arms go numb. Her skirts had ridden high up on her thighs, leaving her legs bare to the cold. And all the while Grass Singing chanted to herself and made low, moaning sounds.

One terrible winter back in Gothenburg, a woman had gone mad when all of her children came down with lung fever. The little coffins had been lined up like shoe boxes at the cemetery. The woman had collapsed beside them, pulling her hair, keening like a wounded animal. Her eyes had been frightening, a glassy sheen of madness in them . . . just like Grass Singing's eyes.

Addie tried to shift positions, but the rawhide didn't stretch; in fact, she thought it was beginning to shrink. She was choking, strangling slowly with each passing mile.

She was going to die.

She contemplated her death with an odd detachment.

It wasn't dying that she minded, not really. But Ian would never know the truth from her lips. That made her heart ache with sorrow. He would never know how sorry she was or how very much she loved him.

Ian and Aleck had been riding for hours. Now Red Bird Mountain loomed before them, dusted white with snow. Huge, silent, the Salish holy place seemed cloaked in mystery as the clouds hung like wisps of smoke around its peaks.

"Ian, are those tracks in the snow?" Aleck asked, yanking his fur cap more snugly over his ears.

"Not like any I've seen up here before." Ian dismounted and knelt beside the tracks. Wind had partially filled the grooves, but when he stuck his fingers into the depression he found it was deep, made by something heavy . . . something like Gert's wagon sled.

Darroch snuffled the tracks, moving back and forth between the parallel lines. He ran off a yard or so, then ran back, tilted his head and loosed a howl that sent shivers up Ian's spine.

"What's wrong with that hound of yours?" Aleck asked.

Ian dropped Dow's reins and crunched through the snow to Darroch. He continued to howl, low and piteous, even after Ian laid a soothing hand on his wide head. Then Ian saw them . . . little delicate depressions . . . tiny footprints in the snow . . .

"Fergus and Angus are following these tracks and I canna think why unless . . ." Aleck paused.

With an oath he turned and sprinted through the snow as fast as he could manage. Once on Dow, he gathered his reins and kicked the horse into action. "Adelaide is in that wagon and she wouldna go to Red Bird Mountain of her own accord."

* * *

Grass Singing untied Addie's hands and shoved her out of the wagon. Luckily the snow took away some of the sting when Addie hit the ground, but she still tasted blood in her mouth. One side of Addie's face was numb from the crust of ice that had formed on it while she lay immobile in the back of the wagon.

"Cry, white woman," Grass Singing said as she kicked Addie in the stomach. "Why you not cry?"

Addie did want to cry—she wanted to wail and rage at the injustice of this—but she refused to give Grass Singing the satisfaction. Instead she thought of Ian and all she would never know of love and life because of Grass Singing.

Anger, white hot and powerful, rushed through her veins, giving her courage, giving her resolve to see this through with the dignity that any woman married to Ian McTavish should show.

"Why should I cry?" she managed to say, though the words were slurred and her thick tongue burned where she had bit it. "I am strong. That is why Ian chose me over you, Grass Singing. I can withstand this and much, much more."

She had the satisfaction of seeing the shock in Grass Singing's eyes. But her moment of triumph was short-lived. Grass Singing bent and picked up a rock sticking out of the snow. A moment later the side of Addie's head exploded in pain and the world went black and silent.

"You not die yet." Grass Singing kicked snow in Addie's face.

Addie woke to throbbing, searing pain. The cold flakes revived Addie, brought her back to the present with a chilling jolt.

She was on the ground in the snow. Pain and hot slices of agony stabbed through her head and her stomach. While she had been unconscious Grass Singing had retied her hands in front of her, and now there was a leather thong about her neck like a leading rope.

"Come," Grass Singing ordered, punctuating the command with a sharp tug on Addie's neck.

Addie awkwardly levered herself to one knee. Her vision was blurry and out of focus, but she saw the unmistakable stain of bright red blood in the hollow where her head had been. A rock with partially frozen blood and strands of her own hair lay nearby.

"Come." Grass Singing jerked hard, hard enough for the leather to tighten and cut into Addie's throat.

"Why should I go with you?" Addie snarled defiantly, gaining her feet, swaying like a willow in the wind. "Whether you kill me now or later, what difference does it make? I think this is a good place to die." Addie tilted her chin and tried not to be sick as her belly rolled and cramped with pain.

Grass Singing narrowed her dark eyes and looked at Addie in speculation. "I go pray to Red Bird bride . . . she may let you live."

"You will not let me live, Grass Singing. I know it."

At that remark Grass Singing truly looked puzzled. For a moment a myriad of emotions flitted across her face.

"If signs say you live, I let you live. Salish no lie."

Addie gathered her strength. Was Grass Singing telling her the truth? It was foolish to believe her with the knife blade glittering menacingly in Grass Singing's hand. But maybe if Addie acted as if she believed her and bided her time, there would be an opportunity to get the knife, to free herself . . . to return to Ian.

"Fine. I will go with you to make prayers to the Red Bird bride. She can decided who lives and who dies."

* * *

Ian's belly was a knotted fist of fear for Adelaide. The wagon ahead looked deserted. Was she in that wagon . . . was she dead? He urged Dow forward and dismounted along with Aleck. His eyes were riveted on the blood in the snow. Was it Adelaide's blood?

"Look here, Ian." Aleck held up rawhide thongs he found in the back of the wagon. They too had traces of blood.

"Dear Lord in heaven . . . ," Ian said under his breath. "Is she . . . in there?" he managed to ask.

Aleck shook his head and Ian released the taut breath he had been holding. Then his eyes found the rock. He bent and picked it up, watching the silken strands of russet hair flutter in the breeze.

"Lord help me. I have never laid a hand on a woman in my life, but if Grass Singing has hurt Adelaide . . ."

Gert's big horses clambered up the side of the hill, sending a spray of loose gravel and rocks down the mountain behind them. The two women rode single file up the winding, steep game trail.

Once Addie thought she saw a flash of silken fur beside the trail, but her vision was still blurred. She could not focus well and one eye was swelling shut.

Addie's head still hurt and the rawhide thong Grass Singing had tied around her neck cut in deeper each time Grass Singing jerked on it, which was often and hard. Her head pounded like Roamer Tresh beating at his anvil and her stomach was roiling, but she was determined not to be sick. Grass Singing would enjoy seeing her retch all over herself.

Addie was alert for any chance, but so far she had no

choice but to sit on the horse and go where Grass Singing led them.

The path was sheltered by the strange configuration of the rocks above and to the side, so, mercifully, the horses had good purchase on the steep grade. Addie was beyond cold, though she envied Grass Singing her thick, wooly buffalo robe.

Addie allowed her thoughts to wander to home. If she was there now she would set dried fruit to soaking and make a pie. The kitchen would soon warm the whole house and the scent of spices would bring Ian in to see what she had made for him and then he would pull her into his arms. . . .

The hard tug on the thong nearly unseated Addie. She clung to the horse's mane, gagging and coughing.

"You get down. We walk now."

Grass Singing waited until Addie had one leg halfway over the broad back of the draft horse and then she jerked. The action sent Addie sprawling backward, landing hard on the frozen stones. The breath left her in a great whoosh. For a moment all she could see was darkness.

Grass Singing's vicious laughter brought her back. Addie gulped in air and managed to stand. She glared at Grass Singing through her one good eye.

"Be very careful, Grass Singing, because if I get half a chance I am going to kill you." For the first time in her life she knew what it was to be in an icy hot rage.

The sun was hanging low in the western sky when Grass Singing finally stopped. Addie looked around, trying to clear the blurry spots from her sight, trying to muster her strength and think.

They were on a rocky outcropping, high up on Red Bird Mountain. There was a small ledge and a scooped-out depression in the wall of the rock—not quite a cave, but it afforded some shelter. Addie thought about making a run back down the mountain to the spot where the horses had been left, but Grass Singing positioned herself between Addie and the back trail. Her knife was in a scabbard on her thigh. There was no way out . . . not yet.

"Take off," Grass Singing ordered, touching her neck.

Addie stared at her, at first not understanding if she was warning her not to try and take off the leather or if she wanted Addie to remove it.

"Take off," Grass Singing said again impatiently.

Addie peeled the thong from her neck, feeling the sting as the torn flesh stuck to the leather peeled away from her throat. Tears stung the back of her eyes before she had the noose free of her neck.

"Ha, you not strong," Grass Singing sneered.

Addie tossed the leather at Grass Singing's feet. Then she lowered herself to the frozen earth and tucked up her legs. She was shivering, but at least the mountain blocked the wind and gave her a bit of protection from the dropping temperature.

Grass Singing went about gathering twigs and getting a fire going. Then she began to chant, closing her eyes and lifting her arms to the sky. This went on for a long time—exactly how long, Addie could not tell, but sometime during the long, monotonous monotone chant she slept.

Ian and Aleck were forced to leave the horses where they found Gert's team. Through Indian fights, starvation and blizzards, Ian had never known such all-consuming terror.

He was afraid for Adelaide . . . and helpless to do anything but put one mocassin-shod foot in front of the other and climb.

It was full dark. The night was more than half gone now, only a matter of hours until dawn.

But would he be too late?

Ian and Aleck inched up the mountainside, feeling their way along the rough wall of stone, hearing gravel and small stones. Darroch was somewhere nearby; they could hear his footfalls and panting from time to time.

A rock fell, and another. They froze, waiting for the inevitable plunk as the stone hit bottom.

"That one took a long time," Aleck said dryly.

"We canna stop."

"Never said we should stop. How much farther to the top?"

"I canna be sure, but we must be getting close to the holy spot where the Salish offer prayers to the old ones."

"Then let's get a move on. This place gives me the willies."

So they pushed on, seeing little, lapsing into silence as Ian said prayers of his own . . . praying for dawn and for the life of the woman he loved more than his own life.

Addie woke. She sat upright, stiff and tense, trying to figure out what sound had roused her. Grass Singing was still sitting by the fire, her long hair shimmering with blood-red light reflected from the flames. Only a few feet away from the circle of fire it was dark as pitch.

The sound came again.

The snap of a twig. No more than that, and yet Addie knew it was significant. She did not move, not wanting to alert Grass Singing, who was lost in a world of her own fashion, moaning and singing, rocking back and forth in front of the fire.

It was difficult for Addie to see, with one eye now swollen completely shut. Boulders and snow-dusted rocks lined the narrow, steep path they had taken to this ledge;

now those same giant stones were no more than darker shadows in the night.

Then Addie saw them. Glittering eyes. Two pairs of them, flashing red from the reflection of the flames. Angus and Fergus stared at Addie for a long minute. A hot tear squeezed from beneath her bulging lid. It stung the raw places on her face.

Then they were gone. She wondered if they had ever been there at all.

Grass Singing rose from her position by the fire. She stood for a moment with a feather in her hand, waving it into the smoke, inhaling deeply of the vapor. Then she turned to Addie. Half her face was dark, adding to the aura of evil that clung to her.

"It is time. Red Bird bride has heard my prayers. You must die so I will have McTavish."

Addie could see nothing behind her but a black pit. Grass Singing held the knife low, her grip firm. Murder was obviously her intent, murder without guilt, since Addie's death was sanctioned by the Salish gods.

"Tell me, Grass Singing, how will you know if your prayers have been answered?" Addie asked, stalling for time, trying to think of some way to escape.

"The gods will send a red bird to me if my prayer is answered. Only woman with pure love in her heart can hope for the red bird to help her. My love for McTavish is pure and strong. The red bird will come."

"In the night?" Addie decided to take a risk. She had nothing to lose. "You are foolish, Grass Singing. The birds roost at night. You should've started your prayers earlier. No red bird will come to you."

"You lie!"

"You have failed. The red bird will not show itself. I may die, but Ian McTavish will never love you."

Grass Singing lunged toward her.

Addie stepped backward. The ledge crumbled a bit

beneath her feet. She stopped, looking left and then right for a means of escape.

There was none.

And still Grass Singing came forward, the blade gleaming in the firelight. Out of nowhere came two writhing bundles of fur. Only their eyes were truly visible, sparkling, eerie, flashing red as blood in the night. Angus and Fergus were there, at Grass Singing's feet, twining, leaping, the sharp teeth gleaming. The Indian maiden stumbled as the otters nipped and bit at her legs. She screamed and extended her hands to break her fall. She grabbed onto Addie and they stumbled backward together.

"Adelaide!"

Ian's voice was the singing of angels in Addie's ears. She heard the deep bark of Darroch and felt the brush of his rough fur against her hand.

For a moment everything, including her heart, seemed to stop. And then she and Grass Singing were falling. Going over the edge in the darkness.

"Ian!" she yelled once.

"Dear God in heaven, no!" Ian dashed to the edge, but he could see nothing below. Darroch stood staring out into the black night, no more able to help than Ian himself.

"Mother of God, did they go over?" Aleck asked, as if he could not believe it possible.

"Yes. I have to get to her." Ian's heart was not beating. His limbs were numb. He knew nothing except that he had to reach Adelaide.

He lay down and stretched his torso over the edge. He cupped his hands around his mouth. "Adelaide! Adelaide, answer me. For the love of God, you must answer me." Ian's heart was contracting in his chest as the surge of adrenaline coursed through his veins.

The night was silent as a grave.

She was gone. His beloved Adelaide, his little virgin

widow was gone in the darkness and there was nothing he could do . . . except join her.

"No, Ian, stop." Aleck reached Ian and grabbed hold of him. They struggled, Ian trying to break free and step over the ledge, Aleck trying to prevent him.

"Let me go, man. If Adelaide is gone, I have no reason to live. Let me go." Ian twisted and fought, wanting only to drop over the precipice and join Adelaide in death.

"No. I won't let you kill yourself. Think, Ian, think. She might be alive."

The words froze Ian's blood in his veins.

"Alive?"

"Yes, she might be. We don't know how long the drop was. Now, damn it, think."

Ian took a deep breath and forced his brain to work. Aleck was right; Adelaide might be alive. He clung to that hope as he stood up and looked around the camp. There was a small length of rawhide thong. He picked it up and felt the stiff area in the loop. He looked at it closer.

Blood . . . it was caked with blood.

"She was tethered like an animal." His words came out in a strangled cry. Ian had never been one to choke up and weep. . . . He had seen many a man do so, but he himself had never done it, not through any of the tragedies of his life . . . until now.

"I know what you are thinking, but that is neither long enough nor strong enough to lower you down. Like it or not, Ian, we have to wait for sunrise."

Chapter Twenty-seven

Dawn came in a gray cloud that did little to warm the ground or Ian's broken heart. The moment he could see anything Ian was up, pacing back and forth, peering over the edge.

A copse of rough buckbrush grew just under the ledge, blocking his view of anything . . . or anyone who might've been below.

"I am climbing down," he told Aleck.

"What can I do to help?"

"You canna help. Either I will manage or I wilna."

The stone felt like frozen glass shards beneath his palms and fingertips. Ian eased his body backward, feeling for handholds and depressions to stick his feet into. He was grateful he was wearing moccasins. They were thin and flexible and gave him a bit more acuity.

It was slow going, but he forced himself to concentrate, to cling to the hope that Adelaide was alive. He had seen her and the otters go over the edge with Grass Singing. The picture was a vivid horror, seared onto his brain.

He knew he would never be able to wipe it from his mind for in that moment all his hopes for a future . . . all his love had been jerked from his grasp.

Ian was surprised when suddenly a solid ledge of rock was beneath his feet. For a moment he stood there with his arms over his head, still clinging desperately to the fingerholds he had found.

Then, with a great release of breath, Ian let go. And stood upon solid ground. He could not see the ledge above, or Aleck, though he could hear him calling out.

"There is an outcropping," Ian shouted back, turning to look around. The slender shelf of earth that supported him was no more than eighteen inches wide at its most generous spot. Snow lay in little windblown pyramids here and there. A wild berry bush had stubbornly forced its roots in a cleft in the rock, obscuring his view of anything beyond it.

Ian took a tentative step, holding his weight tense, waiting to see if the ledge would support him or flake off.

It held.

Another step, and he could see around the bush. There, in a tangled heap of arms, legs and the fur of Angus and Fergus, lay Adelaide.

"Oh, merciful God." He forgot about the ledge or the fact that he had been walking as if treading on eggshells. Ian was beside her, wiping blood and hair from her face. Her lips were blue from the cold. The otters were stretched across her chest and throat.

"Dead . . . all three dead," Ian moaned pitifully.

Fergus raised his head and slowly left the spot on Addie's chest where he had lain. He was limping and his tail was jutting at an odd angle as he nuzzled Ian's hand.

"Fergus, lad," Ian said with a rusty catch in his voice.

And then, to his utter astonishment, Angus too lifted his head. He opened one eye, the other socket was nothing but a bloody gash. He moved slowly off Adelaide's neck.

When Ian saw the blue, black and bloody stripes upon her lovely flesh he nearly roared in rage. She had been tortured, treated cruelly and brutally.

"Oh, Adelaide, what misery have I brought down upon you?"

Adelaide moaned.

Ian blinked and swallowed the lump of despair that clogged his throat. He touched her neck, trying not to make contact with the raw abrasions.

There was a pulse. It was weak, but he felt the life still pulsing through Adelaide's veins. "You canna die on me now, lass. Not if I have anythin' to say about it."

He lifted his head to heaven and with unashamed tears in his eyes, he bellowed his thanks to God.

Between Aleck above and Ian below they finally brought Adelaide up. Ian felt every jolt to her battered body when she whimpered and moaned. Finally he had her on solid ground again.

Fergus and Angus had been given water and were laying beside the fire that Aleck had revived, licking their bloody spots. Ian knew that Angus's eye was gone and Fergus's tail would never again be the same, but he also knew that their body heat had saved Adelaide's life.

"I promise you two will never be made into gloves," Ian said huskily.

"It is a wonder. I never would've believed it. Grass Singing must've gone over the edge," Aleck said softly.

"I saw no sign of her at all." Ian frowned as he looked at Adelaide, laying under his and Aleck's heavy coats. She was pale, bruised and barely alive. "Which may be God's blessing."

Addie heard Ian's voice from a long distance away. She had dreamed of him . . . prayed for him. And now it seemed God was answering her prayers by letting her imagine he was nearby.

"Ian, I know you. You couldn't hurt a woman," Aleck said.

"Never be so sure, Aleck. Look at her, for pity's sake. Treated worse than an animal."

Addie wanted to rouse from the cottony softness that held her. She wanted to open her eyes and her lips and tell Ian what she yearned for him to know. *"I love you."*

"Ah, Adelaide, darlin'." He was down on one knee beside Addie, lifting her head, trying not to touch the huge bruise and swollen area on her head while Aleck trickled water between her cut lips.

"Adelaide, lass, can you hear me?"

Her one good eye opened . . . a little. She wanted to smile, but when she tried a slice of hot pain stopped her.

It was Ian. He was real. He was here.

"Dinna talk, lass. We are going to carry you down to the wagon and get you to town. You canna die on me now, lass."

Addie was so tired. Maybe death was not so bad. She had managed to say the words she had wanted to say. They had only been a whisper, but Ian heard them. He knew she loved him even if he didn't know all.

She sighed and stared up at the blue sky, thinking how nice it would be to escape the pain and the cold and the misery of her body.

And then she saw them.

A pair of bright red birds flitted over her head. They chattered and chirped and landed on the ground between the fire and the otters. They tilted their heads and peered at her, unafraid.

And she knew.

The bride of Red Bird Mountain had heard the prayers

of a woman with a strong and pure love. They had heard her prayers and brought her back to Ian.

Addie woke to the voices of Ian and Aleck arguing as usual. It had been two days by her muddled reckoning since they made it into McTavish Plain and she had been left to the tender mercies of Lottie, Mattie and Gert. Now Addie lay on a featherbed in Gert's house, smelling the attar of a pine fire and bubbling dumplings on the boil.

"Bloody hell, I say I canna wait any longer to see her!" Ian's voice was full of male fury.

"They don't think she is strong enough yet, Ian," Aleck replied.

She smiled and once again thanked God for her safe return. So much had happened. So much could have turned out differently.

Addie was well aware of how close she had come to shaking hands with St. Peter. If the ledge had been narrower . . . if Angus and Fergus had not possessed the hearts of otter heroes . . . if Ian and Aleck had not been determined to find her body . . .

She had been on the skinny side of dead for sure.

Knowing that God had spared her made her all the more determined to tell Ian the truth and to keep her soul free from such blight in the future.

He came through the door with Lottie, Mattie and Gert in his wake. But before the trio could stop him, he turned and shut the door in their faces—and locked it.

"Ian."

"Adelaide." The expression on his face was that of a wicked mischief maker, and yet around his eyes, bluer today than the winter sky, were harsh lines of worry and concern that had never been there before.

"Lass."

"Ian," she said again.

He hooked his moccasin-covered toes around the leg of a chair to drag it closer to the bed. Then he sat down and stared into her face. "How are you today?"

"I am well, Ian."

"Truly?"

"Truly. My head hardly hurts at all and my eye is almost open ... see?" To illustrate, Addie raised her brows and opened her swollen eye as far as she could. It was still little more than a slit, but Ian was what her heart yearned to see, so her view was perfect in her opinion.

"Ah, lass, your courage breaks the heart." He took up her hands, the knuckles skinned and covered with spots that were beginning to heal, and put them to his lips. "I am so sorry—"

"No. Never apologize. You did nothing, Ian. Grass Singing was not right in her mind."

"It is good of you to try and take away my guilt," he said softly.

"Speaking of guilt, Ian, I have carried my own for long enough."

"What do you mean, lass?"

"It is time I told you the truth about myself ... and my sisters."

Ian released his grip on her hand and leaned back in the chair. It was all he could do to stop from scooping her up and showering kisses across her bruised face.

She finally trusted him. His heart swelled with pride, love and gratitude that God had given him such a woman.

"Please, let me say it all in one piece." She swallowed hard. "If you stop me, I might not ever find the courage again."

"I will sit silent as the grave, lass."

Addie tried to smile at his thin attempt at humor, but it hurt too much. So she took a deep breath and gathered her strength.

"Lottie has always wanted adventure. Mattie has always wanted a man who would spout poetry. I never wanted any man at all ... or so I told myself." Addie squeezed Ian's hand.

"I was married secretly when I was very young, little more than a girl, but my husband died with my parents in the flood that destroyed the wagon train we were traveling with."

She shut her good eye. It was so hard to face the past ... to face oneself.

"Adelaide?"

She opened her eye and looked at him. "I'm all right." She had to go on. "My *husband* died before we even had a wedding night. He was not a farmer, he was not even a man ... he was little more than a boy ... a tragic boy who never did more than kiss me."

Ian frowned and tilted his head, as if seeing her in a whole new way.

"I lied to you, Ian. So did Mattie and Lottie. They were never married to anybody. And I was not a widow ... at least not in the way you thought I was. We wanted to be part of your town, your dream, your future." She turned her head toward the frosty window wreathed in lacy curtains.

"We wanted to put down roots in McTavish Plain, and the only way we knew to have a place here was to tell a lie and keep right on lying. We were wrong, I see that now, but that is what we did."

Ian blinked.

"I ... hope you can forgive me, Ian. I never did it to hurt you or anyone. And my sisters ... I never loved anyone like I love you. And no other man ever touched me. I'm not proud of that either—I lay with you while you were fevered and I let you think ... I let you think—"

"I know all of that, Adelaide," Ian said with a crooked grin.

"You *know?*"

"Yes. I was fevered, not dead, lass. You came to me hot and willing and a virgin. A man is not likely to forget such a thing as that, even with one foot inside the pearly gates. I was honored and proud to be your first lover."

Addie felt herself blushing through her bruises. "But you never said anything."

"I wanted you to trust me. I wanted you to love me enough to believe I would do right by you . . . and I will, you know. I will do right by you and your sisters."

"Oh, Ian." Hot, stinging tears ran down her face. She sobbed, and her sore throat hurt, so she sobbed again.

"I will make you a deal, lass."

"A deal?" She could hardly see him now through the blur of tears and her half-shut eye.

"I will promise to forget everything you told me about your sisters. I will promise to take their secret to my grave on one condition."

"Name it." Addie was laughing now, sobbing and laughing and making a fool of herself. She could hear her sisters and Gert pounding on the door, demanding to come in.

"Though I wonder why I should bother to let either of them stay . . . harridans through and through, they are." He glanced toward the door.

"Ian!"

"All right, here is my bargain. They may stay and I will act as if they really are married women waiting for their husbands if you promise to stay with me until we are old, gray and toothless. If you will promise to share my bed and my life every day of my life. If you will promise to love me now and beyond death, Adelaide, my love."

"Oh, yes, Ian. Yes!" She raised up and flung her arms around his neck. She kissed him with her swollen lips and whispered "I love you" over and over again.

Finally he pulled away from her and looked into her eyes.

"Just tell me one thing, Adelaide."

"Anything."

"What is your real last name?"

"We are the Green sisters, spinster women from Gothenburg, Nebraska Territory."

"Ah . . . the Green sisters. The beautiful bogus brides of McTavish Plain."

Then he folded her into his arms and they looked at the window where a bright red bird had perched.

ABOUT THE AUTHOR

ABOUT THE AUTHOR

Linda Lea Castle is the pen name of talented, internationally renowned author Linda L. Crockett. She likes to say that some of her ancestors were standing on the North American shore when the other ancestors landed. Linda can trace her roots as far back as the Saxons on one side and the Comanche on the other and is proud of having ancestors who fought and bled for America since the Revolutionary War. Perhaps this mix of culture and ethnicity is what gives Linda her fascination with history. She is equally enchanted when penning a story of the raw West peopled with lanky cowboys, or mist-covered heaths and warrior knights seeking to uphold a code of honor. Linda loves getting mail and feedback from readers. E-mail her at *llcast@cyberport.com* or send snail mail to Linda L. Crockett-Castle, # 18 C.R. 5795, Farmington, NM 87401. You can visit her webpage at *www.geocities.com/lindacastle2000.*

If you liked *Addie and the Laird,* be sure to look for Linda Lea Castle's next release in the Bogus Brides series, *Mattie and the Blacksmith,* available wherever books are sold in April 2001.

Incurable romantic Mattie "Smith" had agreed to come to McTavish Plain with her sisters to find a husband—as long as he was the kind of man who would court her properly. Practical Roamer Tresh is not that kind of fellow at all, but his nephew Scout has other ideas about the mismatched couple—ideas with wedding bells attached. . . .

COMING IN DECEMBER FROM
ZEBRA BALLAD ROMANCES

__A SISTER'S QUEST, Shadow of the Bastille #3
by Jo Ann Ferguson   0-8217-6788-7   **$5.50US/$7.50CAN**
When Michelle D'Orage agreed to be Count Alexei Vatutin's translator at the Congress of Vienna she was excited, but then she learned the handsome Russian's true reason for hiring her. Shaken and confused, she has little choice but to trust this mysterious stranger who holds the key to her past . . . and her dreams for the future.

__REILLY'S GOLD, Irish Blessing #2
by Elizabeth Keys   0-8217-6730-5   **$5.50US/$7.50CAN**
Young Irishman Devin Reilly had just arrived in America seeking riches to bolster family business, but his fortune was about to change. After rescuing fiery Maggie Brownley he sees in her eyes that ''Reilly's Blessing'' will bind them together. Devin soon realizes that in Maggie's embrace he will find a love more precious than gold.

__THE FIRST TIME, The Mounties
by Kathryn Fox   0-8217-6731-3   **$5.50US/$7.50CAN**
Freshly graduated from medical school and eager to bury his sorrow over the tragedy in his past, Colin Fraser impulsively joins the Northwest Mounted Police. During a raid on a bootleg whiskey operation he finds Maggie, an ill bootlegger. Colin finds, while nursing the patient, the way to heal his own heart.

__HIS STOLEN BRIDE, Brothers In Arms #2
by Shelley Bradley   0-8217-6732-1   **$5.50US/$7.50CAN**
Wrongly accused of murdering his father, Drake Thornton MacDougall wants nothing more than to take revenge against his duplicitous half brother. So he strikes at the fiend the only way that he can . . . by abducting Averyl, his bride-to-be. In Averyl he finds the key to forgiving past wrongs and healing his tormented soul through pure love.

BOOK YOUR PLACE ON OUR WEBSITE
AND MAKE THE
READING CONNECTION!

We've created a customized website just for our very special readers, where you can get the inside scoop on everything that's going on with Zebra, Pinnacle and Kensington books.

When you come online, you'll have the exciting opportunity to:

- View covers of upcoming books
- Read sample chapters
- Learn about our future publishing schedule (listed by publication month *and author*)
- Find out when your favorite authors will be visiting a city near you
- Search for and order backlist books from our online catalog
- Check out author bios and background information
- Send e-mail to your favorite authors
- Meet the Kensington staff online
- Join us in weekly chats with authors, readers and other guests
- Get writing guidelines
- AND MUCH MORE!

Visit our website at
http://www.zebrabooks.com

Celebrate Romance With Two of Today's Hottest Authors

Meagan McKinney

__In the Dark	$6.99US/$8.99CAN	0-8217-6341-5
__The Fortune Hunter	$6.50US/$8.00CAN	0-8217-6037-8
__Gentle from the Night	$5.99US/$7.50CAN	0-8217-5803-9
__A Man to Slay Dragons	$5.99US/$6.99CAN	0-8217-5345-2
__My Wicked Enchantress	$5.99US/$7.50CAN	0-8217-5661-3
__No Choice But Surrender	$5.99US/$7.50CAN	0-8217-5859-4

Meryl Sawyer

__Thunder Island	$6.99US/$8.99CAN	0-8217-6378-4
__Half Moon Bay	$6.50US/$8.00CAN	0-8217-6144-7
__The Hideaway	$5.99US/$7.50CAN	0-8217-5780-6
__Tempting Fate	$6.50US/$8.00CAN	0-8217-5858-6
__Unforgettable	$6.50US/$8.00CAN	0-8217-5564-1

Call toll free **1-888-345-BOOK** to order by phone, use this coupon to order by mail, or order online at **www.kensingtonbooks.com**.

Name _____

Address _____

City _____ State _____Zip _____

Please send me the books I have checked above.

I am enclosing	$_____
Plus postage and handling*	$_____
Sales tax (in New York and Tennessee only)	$_____
Total amount enclosed	$_____

*Add $2.50 for the first book and $.50 for each additional book.

Send check or money order (no cash or CODs) to:

Kensington Publishing Corp., Dept. C.O., 850 Third Avenue, New York, NY 10022

Prices and numbers subject to change without notice.

All orders subject to availability.

Visit our website at **www.kensingtonbooks.com**.